D0271621

The Neighbour

BY LISA GARDNER

The Neighbour

LISA GARDNER

First published in Great Britain in 2009 by Orion Books,
an imprint of The Orion Publishing Group Ltd
Orion House, 5 Upper Saint Martin's Lane
London WC2H 9EA

An Hachette UK Company

3 5 7 9 10 8 6 4

A CIP catalogue record for this book is
available from the British Library.

ISBN (Hardback) 978 1 4091 0102 4
ISBN (Export Trade Paperback) 978 1 4091 0103 1

Printed in Great Britain by Clays Ltd St Ives plc

The Orion Publishing Group's policy is to use papers that are natural,
renewable and recyclable products and made from wood grown in sustainable
forests. The logging and manufacturing processes are expected to
conform to the environmental regulations of the country of origin.

www.orionbooks.co.uk

The Neighbour

| CHAPTER ONE |

I've always wondered what people felt in the final few hours of their lives. Did they know something terrible was about to occur? Sense immi-nent tragedy, hold their loved ones close? Or is it one of those things that simply happens? The mother of four, tucking her kids into bed, worrying about the morning car pool, the laundry she still hasn't done, and the funny noise the furnace is making again, only to catch an eerie creak coming from down the hall. Or the teenage girl, dreaming about her Saturday shopping date with her BFF, only to open her eyes and discover she's no longer alone in her room. Or the father, bolting awake, thinking, What the fuck? *right before the hammer catches him between the eyes.*

In the last six hours of the world as I know it, I feed Ree dinner. Kraft Macaroni & Cheese, topped with pieces of turkey dog. I slice up an ap-ple. She eats the crisp white flesh, leaving behind curving half-smiles of red peel. I tell her the skin holds all the nutrients. She rolls her eyes—four going on fourteen. We already fight over clothing—she likes short skirts, her father and I prefer long dresses, she wants a bikini, we insist she wear a one-piece. I figure it's only a matter of weeks before she demands the keys to the car.

Afterward Ree wants to go "treasure hunting" in the attic. I tell her it's bath time. Shower, actually. We share the old claw-foot tub in the upstairs bath, as we've been doing since she was a baby. Ree lathers up two Barbies and one princess rubber duckie. I lather up her. By the time we're done, we both smell like lavender and the entire black-and-white checkered bathroom is smothered with steam.

I like the post-shower ritual. We wrap up in giant towels, then make a beeline down the chilly hallway to the Big Bed in Jason's and my room, where we lie down, side by side, arms cocooned, but toes sticking out, lightly touching. Our orange tabby cat, Mr. Smith, jumps on the bed, and peers down at us with his big golden eyes, long tail twitching.

"What was your favorite part of today?" I ask my daughter.

Ree crinkles her nose. "I don't remember."

Mr. Smith moves away from us, finding a nice comfy spot by the headboard, and begins to groom. He knows what's coming next.

"My favorite part was coming home from school and getting a big hug." I'm a teacher. It's Wednesday. Wednesday I get home around four, Jason departs at five. Ree is used to the drill by now. Daddy is daytime, Mommy is nighttime. We didn't want strangers raising our child and we've gotten our wish.

"Can I watch a movie?" Ree asks. Is always asking. She'd live with the DVD player if we let her.

"No movie," I answer lightly. "Tell me about school."

"A short movie," she counters. Then offers, triumphantly, "Veggie Tales!"

"No movie," I repeat, untucking an arm long enough to tickle her under the chin. It's nearly eight o'clock and I know she's tired and willful. I'd like to avoid a full tantrum this close to bedtime. "Now tell me about school. What'd you have for snack?"

She frees her own arms and tickles me under my chin. "Carrots!"

"Oh yeah?" More tickling, behind her ear. "Who brought them?"

"Heidi!"

She's trying for my armpits. I deftly block the move. "Art or music?"

"Music!"

"Singing or instrument?"

"Guitar!"

She's got the towel off and pounces on me, tickling anyplace she can find with fast, poky fingers, a last burst of energy before the end-of-the-day collapse. I manage to fend her off, rolling laughing off the edge of *the bed. I land with a thump on the hardwood floor, which makes her giggle harder and Mr. Smith yowl in protest. He scampers out of the room, impatient now for the completion of our evening ritual.*

I find a long T-shirt for me, and an Ariel nightgown for her. We brush our teeth together, side by side in front of the oval mirror. Ree likes the synchronized spit. Two stories, one song, and half a Broadway show later, I finally have her tucked into bed with Lil' Bunny clutched in her hands and Mr. Smith curled up next to her feet.

Eight-thirty. Our little house is officially my own. I take up roost at the kitchen counter. Sip tea, grade papers, keep my back to the computer so I won't be tempted. The cat clock Jason got Ree one Christmas meows on the hour. The sound echoes through the two-story 1950s bungalow, making the space feel emptier than it really is.

My feet are cold. It's March in New England, the days still chilly. I should put on socks but I don't feel like getting up.

Nine-fifteen, I make my rounds. Bolt lock on the back door, check the wooden posts jammed into each window frame. Finally, the double bolt on the steel front door. We live in South Boston, in a modest, middle-class neighborhood with tree-lined streets and family-friendly parks. Lots of kids, lots of white picket fences.

I check the locks and reinforce the windows anyway. Both Jason and I have our reasons.

Then I'm standing at the computer again, hands itching by my side. Telling myself it's time to go to bed. Warning myself not to take a seat. Thinking I'm probably going to do it anyway. Just for a minute. Check a few e-mails. What can it hurt?

At the last moment, I find willpower I didn't know I possessed. I turn off the computer instead. Another family policy: The computer must be turned off before going to bed.

A computer is a portal, you know, an entry point into your home. Or maybe you don't know.

Soon enough, you'll understand.

Ten o'clock, I leave the kitchen light on for Jason. He hasn't called, so apparently it's a busy night. That's okay, I tell myself. Busy is busy. It seems we go longer in silence all the time. These things happen. Especially when you have a small child.

I think of February vacation again. The family getaway that was either the best or the worst thing that happened to us, given your point of view. I want to understand it. Make some sense of my husband, of myself. There are things that once done can't be undone, things that once said can't be unsaid.

I can't fix any of it tonight. In fact, I haven't been able to fix any of it for weeks, which has been starting to fill me with more and more dread. Once, I honestly believed love alone could heal all wounds. Now I know better.

At the top of the stairs, I pause outside Ree's door for my final goodnight check. I carefully crack open the door and peer in. Mr. Smith's golden eyes gaze back at me. He doesn't get up, and I can't blame him: It's a cozy scene, Ree curled in a ball under the pink-and-green flowered covers, sucking her thumb, a tousle of dark curls peeking up from above the sheets. She looks small again, like the baby I swear I had only yesterday, yet somehow it's four years later and she dresses herself and feeds herself and keeps us informed of all the opinions she has on life.

I think I love her.

I think love is not an adequate word to express the emotion I feel in my chest.

I close the door very quietly, and I ease into my own bedroom, slipping beneath the blue-and-green wedding quilt.

The door is cracked for Ree. The hallway light on for Jason.

The evening ritual is complete. All is as it should be.

I lie on my side, pillow between my knees, hand splayed on my hip. I am staring at everything and nothing at all. I am thinking that I am tired, and that I've screwed up and that I wish Jason was home and yet I am grateful that he is gone, and that I've got to figure out something except I have no idea what.

I love my child. I love my husband.

I am an idiot.

And I remember something, something I have not thought about for months now. The fragment is not so much a memory as it is a scent: rose petals, crushed, decaying, simmering outside my bedroom window in the Georgia heat. While Mama's voice floats down the darkened hall, "I know something you don't know...."

"Shhh, shhh, shhh," I whisper now. My hand curves around my

stomach and I think too much of things I have spent most of my life try-ing to forget.

"Shhh, shhh, shhh," I try again.

And then, a sound from the base of the stairs ...

In the last moments of the world as I know it, I wish I could tell you I heard an owl hoot out in the darkness. Or saw a black cat leap over the fence. Or felt the hairs tingle on the nape of my neck.

I wish I could tell you I saw the danger, that I put up one helluva fight. After all, I, of all people, should understand just how easily love can turn to hate, desire to obsession. I, of all people, should have seen it coming.

But I didn't. I honestly didn't.

And God help me, when his face materialized in the shadow of my doorway, my first thought was that he was just as handsome now as when we first met, and that I still wished I could trace the line of his jaw, run my fingers through the waves of his hair....

Then I thought, looking at what was down at his side, that I mustn't scream. I must protect my daughter, my precious daughter still sleeping down the hall.

He stepped into the room. Raised both of his arms.

I swear to you I didn't make a sound.

| CHAPTER TWO |

Sergeant Detective D.D. Warren loved a good all-you-can-eat buffet. It was never about the pasta—filler food to be sure, and just plain bad strategy if there was a carving roast to be had. No, over the years she had developed a finely honed strategy: stage one, the salad bar. Not that she was a huge fan of iceberg lettuce, but as a thirty-something single workaholic, she never bothered with perishables in her own fridge. So yeah, first pass generally involved some veggies, or God knows, given her eating habits, she'd probably develop scurvy.

Stage two: thinly sliced meat. Turkey was okay. Honey-baked ham, a step up. Rare roast beef, the gold medal standard. She liked it cherry red in the middle and bleeding profusely. If her meat didn't jump a little when she poked it with her fork, someone in the kitchen had committed a crime against beef.

Though of course she would still eat it. At an all-you-can-eat buffet, one couldn't have very high standards.

So a little salad, then on to some thinly sliced rare roast beef. Now the unthinking schmuck inevitably dished up potatoes to accompany her meat. Never! Better to chase it with cracker-crusted broiled haddock, maybe three or four clams casino, and of course chilled shrimp. Then one had to consider the sautéed vegetables, or perhaps some of that green bean casserole with the crunchy fried onions on top. Now, that was a meal.

Dessert, of course, was a very important part of the buffet process. Cheesecake fell into the same category as potatoes and pasta—a rookie mistake, don't do it! Better to start with puddings or fruit crisps. And, as the saying went, there was always room for Jell-O. Or for that matter, chocolate mousse. And crème brûlée. Topped with raspberries, dynamite.

Yeah, she could go with some crème brûlée.

Which made it kind of sad that it was only seven in the morning, and the closest thing to food she had in her North End loft was a bag of flour.

D.D. rolled over in bed, felt her stomach rumble, and tried to pretend that was the only part of her that was hungry.

Outside the bank of windows, the morning looked gray. Another cold and frosty morning in March. Normally she'd be up and heading for HQ by now, but yesterday, she'd wrapped up an intensive two-month investigation into a drive-by shooting that had taken out an up-and-coming drug dealer, as well as a mother walking her two young children. The shooting had occurred a mere three blocks from Boston PD's Roxbury headquarters, adding yet more insult to injury.

The press had gone nuts. The locals had staged daily pickets, demanding safer streets.

And the superintendent had promptly formed a massive taskforce, headed, of course, by D.D., because somehow, a pretty blonde white chick wouldn't get nearly the same flack as yet another stuffed suit.

D.D. hadn't minded. Hell, she lived for this. Flashing cameras, hysterical citizens, red-faced politicians. Bring it on. She took the public flogging, then retreated behind closed doors to whip her team into a proper investigative frenzy. Some asshole thought he could massacre an entire family on her watch? No fucking way.

They'd made a list of likely suspects and started to squeeze. And sure enough, six weeks later, they busted down the doors of a condemned warehouse near the waterfront, and dragged their man from the dark recesses into the harsh sunlight, cameras rolling.

She and her team would get to be heroes for twenty-four hours or so, then the next idiot would come along and the whole pattern would repeat. The way of the world. Shit, wipe, flush. Shit again.

She sighed, tossed from side to side, ran her hand across her five-hundred-thread-count sheets, and sighed again. She should get out of bed. Shower. Invest some quality time in doing laundry and cleaning the disaster that currently passed as her living space.

She thought of the buffet again. And sex. Really hot, pounding, punishing sex. She wanted her hands palming a rock-hard ass. She wanted arms like steel bands around her hips. She wanted whisker burn between her thighs while her fingernails ripped these same cool white sheets to shreds.

Goddammit. She threw back the covers and stalked out of the bedroom, wearing only a T-shirt, panties, and a fine sheen of sexual frustration.

She'd clean her condo. Go for a run. Eat a dozen doughnuts.

She made it to the kitchen, yanked the canister of espresso beans out of the freezer, found the grinder, and got to work.

She was thirty-eight for God's sake. A dedicated investigator and hard-core workaholic. Feeling a little bit lonely, no hunky husband or two-point-two rugrats running around? Too late to change the rules now.

She poured the fresh-ground coffee into the tiny gold filter, and flipped the switch. The Italian machine roared to life, the scent of fresh espresso filling the air and calming her a little. She fetched the milk and prepared to foam.

She'd purchased the North End loft three months ago. Way too nice for a cop, but that was the joy of the imploding Boston condo market. The developers built them, the market didn't come. So working stiffs like D.D. suddenly got a chance at the good life. She liked the place. Open, airy, minimalist. When she was home, it was enough to make her think she should be home more. Not that she was, but she thought about it.

She finished preparing her latte, and padded over to the bank of windows overlooking the busy side street. Still restless, still wired. She liked her view from here. Busy street, filled with busy people, scurrying below. Lots of little lives with little urgencies, none of whom could see her, worry about her, want anything from her. See, she was off duty, and still, life went on. Not a bad lesson for a woman like her.

She blew back a small batch of foam, took several sips, and felt some of her tension unknot a little more.

She never should've gone to the wedding. That's what this was about. A woman her age should boycott all weddings and baby showers.

Damn that Bobby Dodge. He'd actually choked up when saying his vows. And Annabelle had cried, looking impossibly lovely in her strapless white gown. Then, the dog, Bella, walking down the aisle with two gold bands fastened to her collar with a giant bow.

How the hell were you not supposed to get a little emotional about something like that? Especially when the music started and everyone was dancing to Etta James's "At Last" except you, of course, because you'd been working so damn much you never got around to finding a date?

D.D. sipped more latte, gazed down at busy little lives, and scowled.

Bobby Dodge had gotten married. That's what this was about. He'd gone and found someone better than her, and now he was married and she was...

Goddammit, she needed to get laid.

She'd just gotten her running shoes laced up when her cell phone rang. She checked the number, frowned, placed the phone to her ear.

"Sergeant Warren," she announced crisply.

"Morning, Sergeant. Detective Brian Miller, District C-6. Sorry to bother you."

D.D. shrugged, waited. Then when the detective didn't immediately continue, "How can I help you this morning, Detective Miller?"

"Well, I got a situation...." Again, Miller's voice trailed off, and again, D.D. waited.

District C-6 was the BPD field division that covered the South Boston area. As a sergeant with the homicide unit, D.D. didn't work with the C-6 detectives very often. South Boston wasn't really known for its murders. Larceny, burglary, robbery, yes. Homicide, not so much.

"Dispatch took a call at five A.M.," Miller finally spoke up. "A husband, reporting that he'd come home and discovered his wife was missing."

D.D. arched a brow, sat back in the chair. "He came *home* at five A.M.?"

"He reported her missing at five A.M. Husband's name is Jason Jones. Ring any bells?"

"Should it?"

"He's a reporter for the *Boston Daily*. Covers the South Boston beat, writes some larger city features. Apparently, he works most nights, covering city council meetings, board meetings, whatever. Wednesday it's the water precinct, then he got a call to cover a residential fire. Anyhow, he wrapped up around two A.M., and returned home, where his four-year-old daughter was sleeping in her room but his wife was MIA."

"Okay."

"First responders did the standard drill," Miller continued. "Checked 'round the house. Car's on the street, woman's purse and keys on the kitchen counter. No sign of forced entry, but in the upstairs bedroom a bedside lamp is broken and a blue-and-green quilt is missing."

"Okay."

"Given the circumstances, a mom leaving a kid alone, etc., etc., the first responders called their supervisor, who contacted my boss in the district office. Needless to say, we've spent the past few hours combing the neighborhood, checking with local businesses, tracking down friends and families, etc., etc. To make a long story short, I haven't a clue."

"Got a body?"

"No, ma'am."

"Blood spatter? Footprints, collateral damage?"

"Just a busted-up lamp."

"First responders check the *whole* house? Attic, basement, crawl space?"

"We're trying."

"Trying?"

"Husband...he's not refusing, but he's not exactly cooperating."

"Ah crap." And suddenly D.D. got it. Why a district detective was calling a homicide sergeant about a missing female. And why the homicide sergeant wouldn't be going for her run. "Mrs. Jones—she's young, white, and beautiful, isn't she?"

"Twenty-three-year-old blond schoolteacher. Has the kind of smile that lights up a TV screen."

"Please tell me you haven't talked about this over the radio."

"Why do you think I called you on your cell phone?"

"What's the address? Give me ten minutes, Detective Miller. I'll be right there."

D.D. left her running shoes in the family room, her running shorts in the hall, and her running shirt in the bedroom. Jeans, white button-down top, a killer pair of boots, and she was ready to go. Clipped her pager to her waist, hung her creds around her neck, slipped her cell phone into her back pocket.

Last pause for her favorite caramel-colored leather jacket, hanging on a hook by the door.

Then Sergeant Warren hit the road, on the job and loving it.

South Boston had a long and colorful history, even by Boston standards. With the bustling financial district on one side, and the bright blue ocean on the other, it functioned as a quaint harbor town with all the perks of big-city living. The area was originally settled by the lower end of the socioeconomic scale. Struggling immigrants, mostly Irish, cramming thirty people to a room in vermin-ridden tenement housing, where a slop bucket served as latrine and a straw pile became a flea-infested mattress. Life was hard, with disease, pests, and poverty being everyone's closest neighbor.

Fast-forward a hundred and fifty years, and "Southie" was less of a place and more of an attitude. It gave birth to Whitey Bulger, one of Boston's most notorious crime lords, who spent the seventies turning the local housing projects into his personal playground, addicting one half of the population while employing the other half. And still, the area soldiered on, neighbor looking after neighbor, each generation of tough, wiseass kids producing the next generation of tough, wiseass kids. Outsiders didn't get it, and by Southie standards, that was just fine.

Unfortunately, all attitudes sooner or later got adjusted. One year, a major harbor event brought droves of city dwellers into the area. They arrived expecting squalid neighborhoods and decrepit streets. They discovered waterfront views, an abundance of green parks, and outstanding Catholic schools. Here was a neighborhood, ten minutes from downtown Boston, where your toughest choice on a Saturday morning was whether to go right and head to the park, or go left and hang out on the beach.

Needless to say, the yuppies found real estate agents, and the next thing you knew, old housing projects became million-dollar waterfront condos, and fourth-generation triple-deckers were sold to developers for five times the money anyone thought they'd ever bring.

The community became both more and less. Different economics and ethnicities. Same great parks and tree-lined streets. Added some coffee bars. Kept the Irish pubs. More upwardly mobile professionals. Still a lot of families and kids. Good place to live, if you'd bought in before the prices went nuts.

D.D. followed her GPS navigator to the address provided by Detective Miller. She found herself close to the water at a quaint little brown-and-cream painted bungalow with a postage-stamp lawn and a nude maple tree. She had two thoughts at once: Someone had built a bungalow in Boston? And two, Detective Miller was good. He was five and a half hours into a call out, and thus far, no ribbons of crime-scene tape, no parking lot of police cruisers, and better yet, no long lines of media vans. House appeared quiet, street appeared quiet. The proverbial calm before the storm.

D.D. drove around the block three times before finally parking several streets down. If Miller had managed this long without advertising, she wasn't gonna give the game away.

Walking back, hands fisted in her front pockets, shoulders hunched for warmth, she discovered Miller standing in the front yard, waiting for her. He was smaller than she expected, with thinning brown hair and a 1970s mustache. He looked like the kind of cop who would make an excellent undercover officer—so nondescript no one would notice him, let alone realize he was eavesdropping on important conversations. He also had the pale complexion of a man who spent most of his time under fluorescent lights. Desk jockey, D.D. thought, and immediately reserved judgment.

Miller crossed the lawn and fell in step beside her. He kept walking, so she did, too. Sometimes, policing involved a bit of acting. Today, apparently, they were playing the role of a couple out for a morning stroll. Miller's rumpled brown suit was a bit formal for the part, but D.D., in her slim-fitted jeans and leather jacket, looked dynamite.

"Sandra Jones works over at the middle school," Miller started out, speaking low and rushed as they ate up the first block, heading toward the water. "Teaches sixth grade social studies. We've got two uniforms over there now, but no one has heard from her since she left the school yesterday at three-thirty. We've canvassed the local businesses, taverns, convenience stores; nothing. Dinner dishes are in the sink. A stack of graded papers next to her purse on the kitchen counter. According to the husband, Sandra didn't usually start work until after putting their daughter to bed at eight P.M. So we're working on the assumption that she was at home with her daughter until sometime after eight-thirty, nine P.M. Cell phone shows no activity after six; we're pulling the records for the landline now."

"What about family? Grandparents, aunts, uncles, cousins?" D.D. asked. The sun had finally burned through the gray cloud cover, but the temperature remained raw, with the wind blowing off the water and slicing viciously through her leather coat.

"No local family. Just an estranged father in Georgia. The husband refused to specify, just said it was old news and had nothing to do with this."

"How nice of the husband to do our thinking for us. You call the father?"

"Would if I had a name."

"The husband won't give you the name?" D.D. was incredulous.

Miller shook his head, jamming his hands in his pants pockets while his breath came out in faint clouds of steam. "Oh, wait till you meet this guy. Ever watch that show? The medical drama?"

"*ER?*"

"No, the one with more sex."

"*Grey's Anatomy?*"

"Yeah, that's the one. What's the name of that doctor? McDuff, McDevon...?"

"*McDreamy?*"

"That's the one. Mr. Jones could be his twin. That rumpled thing going on with the hair, the five o'clock shadow...Hell, minute this story breaks, this guy is gonna get more fan mail than Scott Peterson. I say we have about twenty more hours, and then either we find Sandy Jones or we're totally, completely screwed."

D.D. sighed heavily. They hit the waterfront, made a right, and kept moving. "Men are stupid," she muttered impatiently. "I mean, for heaven's sake. It's like once a week now some good-looking, got-everything-going-for-him guy tries to solve his marital difficulties by killing off his wife and claiming she disappeared. And every week the media descends—"

"We got a pool going. Five to one odds on Nancy Grace. Four to one on Greta Van Susteren."

D.D. shot him a look. "And every week," she continued, "the police assemble a taskforce, volunteers comb the woods, the Coast Guard sweeps the harbor, and you know what?"

Miller appeared hopeful.

"The wife's body is found, and the husband ends up serving twenty to life in maximum security. Wouldn't you think that by now at least one of these guys would settle for an old-fashioned divorce?"

Miller didn't have anything to say.

D.D. sighed, ran a hand through her hair, sighed again. "All right, gut reaction. Do you think the wife's dead?"

"Yep." Miller said it matter-of-factly. When she waited, he offered up, "Broken lamp, missing quilt. I'd say someone wrapped up the body and carted it off. Quilt would contain the blood, which accounts for the lack of physical evidence."

"All right. You think the husband did it?"

Miller pulled out a folded yellow sheet of legal pad paper from inside his brown sports jacket, and handed it to her. "You'll like this. While the husband has been, shall we say, reluctant, to answer our questions, he did provide his own timeline for the evening, including the names and phone numbers of people who could corroborate his whereabouts."

"He provided a list of *alibis*?" D.D. unfolded the sheet, noting the first name listed, *Larry Wade, Fire Marshall,* then *James McConnagal, Massachusetts State Police,* then three more names, this time from the BPD. She kept reading, her eyes growing wider, then her hands starting to shake with barely suppressed rage. "Who the hell is this guy again?"

"Reporter, *Boston Daily.* House burned last night. He claims he was there, covering that story, along with half of Boston's finest."

"No shit. You call any of these guys yet?"

"Nah, I already know what I'm gonna get."

"They saw him, but they didn't see him," D.D. filled in. "It's a fire, everyone's working. Maybe he asked each one of them for a quote, so they noticed him at that moment, then when he slips away…"

"Yep. As alibis go, this guy scores straight out of the gate. He's got half a dozen of our own people to say where he was last night, even if some of the time he wasn't there at all. Meaning," Miller wagged his finger at her, "don't let Mr. Jones's good looks fool you. McDreamy is also McSmarty. That's so unfair."

D.D. handed the paper back. "He lawyer up?" They hit the corner, and by mutual consent turned around and headed back. They were walking into the wind now, the force of the breeze flattening their coats against their chests while carrying the sting of the water into their faces.

"Not yet. He just won't answer our questions."

"Did you invite him down to the station house?"

"He asked to see our arrest warrant."

D.D. arched a brow, registering that bit of news. McDreamy *was* McSmarty. At least, he knew more about his constitutional rights than the average bear. Interesting. She tucked her chin down, turning her face away from the wind. "No sign of forced entry?"

"No, and get this, both the front and back doors are made of steel."

"Really?"

"Yep. With key in and key out bolt locks. Oh, and we found wooden dowels jammed into most of the window frames."

"No shit. What'd the husband say?"

"One of those questions he declined to answer."

"Is there a home security system? Maybe a camera?"

"No and no. Not even a nanny cam. I asked."

They were approaching the house now, the adorable fifties bungalow that apparently was reinforced tighter than Fort Knox.

"Key in and key out locks," D.D. murmured. "No cameras. Makes me wonder if the setup is about keeping someone out, or keeping someone in."

"Think the wife was abused?"

"Wouldn't be the first time. You said there was a kid?"

"Four-year-old girl. Clarissa Jane Jones. They call her Ree."

"Talk to her yet?"

Miller hesitated. "Kid's spent the morning curled up on her father's lap, looking pretty traumatized. Given that I don't see any hope of this guy letting us speak to her alone, I haven't pushed. Figured I'd approach them both when we had a little more ammunition."

D.D. nodded. Interviewing kids was messy business. Some detectives had a knack for it, some didn't. She was guessing, based on Miller's reluctance, that he didn't feel too good about it. Which would be why D.D. made the big bucks.

"Is the husband confined?" she asked. They climbed the bungalow's front steps, approaching a bright green welcome mat, where the blue scripted word was surrounded by a sea of bright green and yellow flowers. It looked to D.D. like the kind of welcome mat a little girl and her mother might pick out.

"Father and daughter are sitting in the family room. I left an officer in charge. Best I can do at the moment."

"At the moment," she agreed, pausing in front of the doormat. "You've searched the home?"

"Ninety percent of it."

"Cars?"

"Yep."

"Outbuildings?"

"Yep."

"Checked with local establishments, neighbors, friends, relatives, and coworkers?"

"Efforts are ongoing."

"All without sign of Sandra Jones."

Miller glanced at his watch. "Approximately six hours from the husband's first call, there remains no sign of twenty-three-year-old white female Sandra Jones."

"But you do have a potential crime scene in the master bedroom, a potential witness in Sandra's four-year-old daughter, and a potential suspect in Sandra's journalist husband. That about sums it up?"

"That about sums it up." Miller gestured to the front door, revealing his first hint of impatience. "How do you wanna play it: house, husband, or kid?"

D.D. put a hand on the doorknob. She had an immediate gut reaction, but paused to think it through. These first few hours, when you had a call out, but not yet a crime, were always a critical time in an investigation. They had suspicions, but not yet probable cause; a person of interest, but not yet a prime suspect. From a legal perspective, they had just enough rope to hang themselves.

D.D. sighed, realized she wasn't going home any time soon, and made her choice.

| CHAPTER THREE |

I've always been good at spotting cops. Other guys, they can bluff with a pair of deuces in poker. Me, I'm not that lucky. But I can spot cops.

I noticed the first plainclothes officer over breakfast. I'd just poured myself a bowl of Rice Crispies, and was leaning against the dull Formica counter to take a bite. I glanced out the tiny window above the kitchen sink, and there he was, framed neatly in Battenberg lace: white male subject; approximately five ten, five eleven; dark hair; dark eyes, striding south down the far sidewalk. He wore plain-front chinos, tweedish-looking sports jacket, and button-up blue collar shirt. Shoes were buffed dark brown with thick black rubber soles. His right hand held a small spiralbound notebook.

Cop.

I took a bite of cereal, chewed, swallowed, and repeated.

Second guy appeared approximately a minute and a half after the first. Bigger—six one, six two, with short-cropped blond hair and the kind of meaty jaw scrawny guys like me automatically want to punch. He wore similar tan pants, different sports jacket, and a white-collared shirt. Officer Number Two was working the right side of the street, my side of the street.

Thirty seconds later, he banged on my front door.

I took a bite of cereal, chewed, swallowed, and repeated.

My alarm goes off at 6:05 A.M. every morning, Monday through Friday. I get up, shower, shave, and change into a pair of old jeans and an old T-shirt. I'm a tighty-whities kind of guy. I also prefer knee-high white athletic socks with three navy blue bands around the top. Always have, always will.

Six thirty-five A.M., I eat a bowl of Rice Crispies, then rinse my bowl and spoon and leave them to dry on the faded green dish towel spread flat next to the stainless steel sink. Six fifty A.M., I walk to work at the local garage, where I will pull on a pair of oil-stained blue coveralls and take my place beneath the hood of a car. I'm good with my hands, meaning I'll always have a job. But I'll always be the guy under the hood, never the guy out front with the customers. I'll never have that kind of job.

I work until six P.M., with an hour off at lunch. It's a long day, but OT is the closest to real money I'll ever get, and again, I'm good with my hands and I don't talk much, meaning bosses don't mind having me around. After work, I walk home. Probably heat up ravioli for dinner. Watch *Seinfeld* on TV. Go to bed by ten.

I don't go out. I don't visit bars, I never catch a movie with friends. I sleep, I eat, I work. Every single day pretty much the same as the day before. It's not really living. More like existing.

The shrinks have a term for it: *pretend normal.*

It's the only way I know how to live.

I take another bite of cereal, chew, swallow, and repeat.

More knocking on the front door.

Lights are out. My landlord, Mrs. H., is in Florida visiting her grandkids, and it doesn't make sense to waste electricity on just me.

I set down the bowl of soggy cereal and the cop chooses that moment to turn on his heel and walk back down the front steps. I move to the other side of the kitchen, where I can monitor his progress as he moves on to my neighbor's and bangs on the door.

Canvassing. The cops are canvassing the street. And they came from the north. So something happened, probably on this street, immediately to the north.

It comes to me, what I didn't really want to think about, but what has been floating around in the back of my mind since the instant the alarm went off and I went to the bathroom and stared at my own reflection above the sink. The noise I heard right after I snapped off the TV last night. What I probably know that I don't want to know, but now can't get out of my head.

I give up on breakfast and sit down hard in a kitchen chair instead.

Six forty-two A.M. Today is not going to be pretend normal after all.

Today is going to be the real thing.

I have a hard time breathing. My heart races, I can feel my palms start to sweat. And I think so many things at once, my head begins to hurt and I hear someone groan and it confuses me until I realize it is myself.

Her smile, her sweet, sweet smile. The way she looks at me, as if I'm ten feet tall, as if I can hold the world in the palm of my hand.

And then, the tears streaming down her cheeks. "No, no, no. Please, Aidan, stop. No…"

The cops will come for me. Sooner or later. Two of them, three of them, an entire SWAT team, converging upon my doorstep. That's why guys like me exist. Because every community has gotta have a villain, and no amount of pretend normal is ever gonna change that.

Gotta think. Gotta plan. Gotta get the fuck out of here.

To where? For how long? I don't have that kind of cash.…

I try to get my breathing under control. Find some sort of comfort. Tell myself it's gonna be all right. I'm keeping with the program. No drinking, no smoking, no Internet. I'm attending my meetings, keeping my nose clean.

Live normal, be normal, right?

None of that helps me. I fall back on old habits, on the one realization I know to be true.

I'm a damn good liar, especially when it involves the police.

D.D. started her tour in the kitchen. If she turned her head to the left and peered through the doorway, she could just make out the silhouette of a man sitting on a dark green love seat, the back of the couch covered in a rainbow-hued afghan. Jason Jones sat very still, and tucked beneath his chin was another curly-topped head, also not moving: his daughter, Ree, who appeared to have fallen sleep.

D.D. made it a point not to stare too long. She didn't want to call attention to herself this early in the game. Miller's instinct had been correct: They were dealing with an intelligent person of interest, who seemed to know how to navigate the legal system. Meaning they needed to get their ducks in a row, quickly, if they were going to proceed with any kind of meaningful questioning of the husband or the four-year-old potential witness.

So, she focused on the kitchen.

The kitchen, like the rest of the house, retained a semblance of period charm, while definitely showing its age. Peeling black-and-white checked linoleum. Appliances that some would call retro, but D.D. considered ancient. The room was very tiny. A curved counter-top bar offered enough space for two to perch on a pair of red vinyl bar stools. A small parlor table sat in front of the windows, but held a computer versus providing any additional seating.

That struck D.D. as interesting. A family of three that only had seating for two. Did that say something about the family dynamics right there?

The kitchen was neat, countertops wiped down, clutter confined to appliances lined up in a row against the checkered tile backsplash, but not too neat—dirty dishes were stacked in the sink, while the drying rack held clean dishes still waiting to be returned to appropriate cupboards. An old diner's clock with a fork and spoon serving as the hands was mounted cheerfully above the stove, while pale yellow curtains patterned with brighter yellow sunny-side up eggs adorned the tops of the windows. Old, but homey. Clearly, someone had made an effort.

D.D. spotted a red checkered dish towel hanging up on a hook and leaned forward to give it an experimental sniff. Miller looked at her funny, but she just shrugged.

Early in her career, she'd worked a domestic abuse case—the Daleys, that was their name—where the domineering husband, Pat, had forced his wife, Joyce, to scrub the house with military precision every single day. D.D. still remembered the overwhelming scent of ammonia that had made her eyes water as she went from room to room, until, of course, she came to the back room and the scent of ammonia was replaced with the cloying scent of drying blood. Apparently, good old Joyce hadn't made the bed properly that morning. So Pat had punched her in the kidneys. Joyce had started peeing blood and, deciding that she was dying, she'd retrieved the shotgun from the back of her husband's truck, and ensured that he joined her in the hereafter.

Joyce had survived the damage to her kidneys. The husband, Pat, who lost most of his face to the shotgun blast, hadn't.

So far, the kitchen struck D.D. as an average kitchen. No manic compulsions—or orders—to clean and sterilize. Just a place where a mother had served dinner, with mac-n-cheese–encrusted dishes still awaiting attendance in the sink.

D.D. turned her attention to the black leather purse perched on the kitchen counter. Miller silently handed her a pair of latex gloves. She nodded her thanks, and started sifting through the purse's contents.

She started with Sandra Jones's cell phone. The husband had no expectation of privacy on his wife's cell, so they were in the clear to study the phone to their heart's content. She reviewed text messages and the phone log. Only one phone number jumped out at her, and that was labeled HOME. A mom calling in to check on her daughter, no doubt. Second most often called number was labeled JASON'S CELL, a wife calling in to check on her husband, D.D. would assume.

D.D. couldn't listen to the voice messages without the password, but didn't sweat it. Miller would follow up with the cell phone company and have them freeze the messages as well as pull their own log. A provider retained copies of even deleted messages in its own database, handy information for inquiring minds that wanted to know. Miller would also have the provider trace Sandra's final few phone calls, tracking the cell towers the calls pinged off, to help establish her final movements.

The rest of the purse yielded three different tubes of lipstick—muted shades of pink—two pens, a nail file, a granola bar, a black hair-scrunchy, a pair of reading glasses, and a wallet with forty-two dollars cash, a valid MA driver's license, two credit cards, and three grocery store and one bookstore member cards. Finally, D.D. pulled out a small spiral notebook filled with various lists: groceries to buy, errands to run, times for appointments. D.D. left the notebook out as a priority item, and Miller nodded.

Sitting next to the purse was a large set of car keys. D.D. held them up questioningly.

"Automatic starter belongs to gray Volvo station wagon parked in the driveway. Two keys are house keys. Four keys we don't know, but we're guessing at least one is her classroom. I'll get an officer on it."

"You checked the back of the station wagon?" she asked sharply.

Miller gave her a look, clearly wanting a little credit. "Yes, ma'am. No surprises there."

D.D. didn't bother with an apology. She just set down the keys and picked up a stack of school papers, marked neatly in red ink. Sandra Jones had given her class a one-paragraph writing assignment, each student needing to answer "If I were starting my own village, the first rule for all the colonists would be... and why."

Some kids managed only a sentence or two. A couple nearly filled the page. Each paper had at least one or two comments, then a letter grade circled at the top. The writing was feminine, with some of the kids earning smiley faces. D.D. decided that was the kind of detail a forger wouldn't think to include. So for now, she was satisfied that Sandra Jones had sat at this counter, grading these papers, an activity that according to her husband wouldn't happen until little Ree was tucked into bed.

So at approximately nine o'clock at night, Sandra Jones had been alive and well in her own kitchen. And then...

D.D.'s gaze went to the computer, a relatively new-looking Dell desktop sitting on top of the little red parlor table. She sighed.

"Turned on?" she asked with barely disguised longing.

"Haven't wanted to tempt myself," Miller answered.

The computer was tricky. They definitely wanted it, but definitely needed the husband's permission, as he had a right to privacy. Something to negotiate, assuming they found some ammunition to negotiate with.

D.D. turned to the tiny, narrow staircase ascending from the back side of the kitchen.

"Evidence techs already up there?" she asked.

"Yep."

"Where'd they park the van?"

"Five blocks over, by a pub. I'm feeling coy."

"I like it. Have they processed the stairs?"

"First thing I had them do," Miller assured her. Then added: "Look, Sergeant, we've been here since six A.M. At one point, I had ten officers swarming the house, checking basements, bedrooms, closets, and shrubbery. Only thing we have to show for it is one broken lamp and one missing quilt in the master bedroom. So I sent the evidence techs upstairs to do what they gotta do, and the rest of the guys out into the broader universe to either bring me back Sandra Jones or some evidence of whatever the hell happened to her. We know the basics. They're just not getting us anywhere."

D.D. sighed again, grabbed the handrail, and headed up the chocolate-painted stairs.

Upstairs was as cozy as the downstairs. D.D. had to fight the urge to duck, as a pair of old light fixtures brushed the top of her hair. The hallway boasted hardwood floors, colored the same dark chocolate as the stairs. Over the years, dust had become trapped in the tight corners of the floorboards, with a couple tumbleweeds of fine hair and dander drifting across her footsteps. Pet, D.D. guessed, though no one had mentioned one yet.

She paused long enough to look back the way she came, a parade of footsteps mixing and mingling in an indistinct blur against the dusty floor. Good thing the floor had already been processed, she thought. Then frowned, as another thought struck her and made her immediately, acutely concerned.

She almost opened her mouth to say something, then at the last minute thought better of it. Better to wait. Get all the ducks in a row. Quickly.

They passed a cramped bathroom that had been decorated in the same fifties motif as the kitchen. Across from it was a modest bedroom with a single-sized bed covered in a pink comforter, tucked under the heavily slanted eaves of the room. The ceiling and eaves had been painted a bright blue, and dotted with various clouds, birds, and butterflies. Definitely a little girl's room, and just cute enough that D.D. felt a pang for little Clarissa Jane Jones, who had gone to bed nestled inside such a pretty sanctuary, only to wake up to a nightmarish parade of dark-suited officials traipsing through her home.

D.D. didn't linger in the bedroom, but continued down the hall, to the master bedroom.

Two evidence techs were in front of the windows. They'd just pulled the shades and were now shooting the room with blue light. D.D. and Miller stayed respectfully in the hallway, as the first white-garbed figure scanned the walls, ceiling, and floor for signs of bodily fluids. As spots emerged, the second figure marked them with a placard, for further analysis. The process took about ten minutes. They didn't do the bed. No doubt the sheets and blankets had already been rolled up to be processed at the lab.

The first figure snapped up the blinds, turned on the surviving bedside lamp, then greeted D.D. with a cheery, "Hiya, Sergeant."

"How goes the battle, Marge?"

"Winning as always."

D.D. stepped forward to shake Marge's hand, then the hand of the second evidence tech, Nick Crawford. They all went way back, spending too much time at these kinds of scenes.

"What do you think?" D.D. asked them.

Marge shrugged. "Some hits. We'll test them, of course, but nothing glaring. I mean, every bedroom in the United States has bodily fluids somewhere."

D.D. nodded. When processing a room for bodily fluids there were two red flags: one, an obvious display such as spatter lighting up across a wall or a giant puddle illuminating the floor; two, the total lack of bodily fluids, which indicated someone had used chemicals for one helluva cleanup job. Like Marge said, every bedroom had something.

"What about the broken lamp?" D.D. asked.

"We recovered it from the floor," Nick spoke up, "with all the shards in the immediate vicinity. At first glance, the lamp toppled and shattered against the floor, versus being used as a weapon. Visual inspection, at least, didn't reveal any sign of blood on the lamp's base."

D.D. nodded. "Bedding?"

"Blue-and-green top quilt is missing, but the rest of the bedding appears intact."

"You process the bathroom?" D.D. asked.

"Yep."

"Toothbrushes?"

"Two were still damp when we got here. One a pink Barbie electric toothbrush belonging to the child. The second a Braun Oral-B electric toothbrush, which according to the husband belonged to his wife."

"Pajamas?"

"Per the husband, wife wore a long purple T-shirt, sporting the graphic of a crowned baby chick on the front. Currently unaccounted for."

"Other clothing? Suitcase?"

"Husband's initial inventory revealed nothing missing."

"Jewelry?"

"Biggest items are her watch and wedding ring, both gone. Also her favorite pair of gold hoops, which according to the husband she wore habitually. All we found in the jewelry box were some necklaces, and a couple of homemade bracelets apparently gifted by the child. Husband thought that looked about right."

D.D. turned to Miller. "No activity on her credit card, I assume?"

Miller went back to his I'm-not-an-idiot stare. She figured that was answer enough.

"So," she mused out loud, "by all accounts, Sandra Jones came home from work yesterday afternoon, fixed dinner for her child, put her child to bed, then proceeded with her nightly chore of grading papers. At some point, she brushed her teeth, put on her nightshirt, and at least made it to the bedroom, where..."

"Some kind of struggle broke a lamp?" Marge offered up with a shrug. "Maybe someone was already here, ambushed her. That would explain the lack of blood spatter."

"The subject manually subdued her," Miller supplied. "Asphyxiation."

"Test the pillow cases," D.D. said. "Could have suffocated her in her sleep."

"Suffocated, strangled. Something quiet and not too messy," Nick agreed.

"Then wrapped the body in the comforter and dragged it out of the house," Miller concluded.

D.D. shook her head. "No, no dragging. This is where things get complicated."

"What do you mean, no dragging?" Miller asked in confusion.

"Look at the dusty hallway. I can see our footprints, which is a problem, because if someone dragged a corpse wrapped in a giant quilt, what I should be seeing is a long, clean smear from this bedroom to the top of the stairs. No clean streak. Meaning, the body wasn't dragged."

Miller frowned. "Okay, so the subject carried her out."

"One man carried the burritoed body of an adult female through that narrow hallway?" D.D. arched a brow skeptically. "First off, that would have to be one strong man. Secondly, no way he could've made the corner of that staircase. We'd see evidence everywhere."

"Two men?" Margie ventured.

"Twice as much noise, twice as much chance of being caught."

"Then what the hell happened with the comforter?" Miller demanded.

"I don't know," D.D. said. "Unless…Unless she wasn't killed in this room. Maybe she made it back downstairs. Maybe she was sitting on the sofa watching TV, then the doorbell rang. Or maybe the husband came home…." She thought about it, trying out various scenarios in her mind. "He killed her elsewhere, then came up here for the comforter, knocking over the lamp as he tugged it off the bed. Quieter that way. Less chance of waking the kid."

"Meaning we still haven't found the primary crime scene," Miller muttered, but he was frowning as he said it. Because according to him, they'd done the basics, and the basics should've turned up signs of blood.

They all looked at one another.

"I vote for the basement," D.D. said. "When bad things happen, it always seems to be in the basement. Shall we?"

———

The four of them traipsed downstairs, passing by the front room, where a uniformed officer stood in the doorway, still keeping tabs on Jason Jones and his sleeping child. Jones looked up as they crossed the foyer. D.D. had a brief glimpse of shuttered brown eyes, then Miller opened the door, revealing a flight of treacherous wooden stairs leading down to a musty cellar dimly lit by four bare bulbs. They took it slow and careful. Honest to God, officers fell down stairs and hurt their backs more often than the public ever knew. It was embarrassing for everyone concerned. You gonna get hurt on the job, you should at least have a good story to tell.

At the bottom, D.D. made out a basement that looked an awful lot like a basement. Stone foundation. Cracked cement floor. An ivory-colored washer and dryer sat in front of them, old coffee table stacked with a plastic laundry basket and laundry detergent in front of that. Then came the ubiquitous collection of damaged lawn chairs, old moving boxes, and outgrown baby furniture. Directly beside the stairs was a set of plastic shelves that appeared to hold the overflow from the kitchen pantry. D.D. noted boxes of cereal, macaroni and cheese, crackers, dry pasta, cans of soup, the usual kitchen detritus.

The cellar was dusty, but not messy. Items were neatly stacked against the wall, the center floor clear for laundry duties, perhaps some indoor bike riding, to judge by the purple tricycle parked next to the bulkhead stairs.

D.D. crossed to the bulkhead, investigating the collection of cobwebs in the right-hand corner, the thick coating of dust on the dark handle. Doors obviously hadn't been opened for a bit, and now that she was down here, she was already changing her mind. If you killed someone in the basement, would you really traipse all the way back upstairs? Why not stick the body beneath the pile of boxes, or grab an old sheet to bundle it out of the bulkhead in the dead of night?

She poked through the collection of discarded crib parts, baby strollers, and bouncy seats. Moved on to the collection of boxes next to the wall, the decaying lawn furniture.

Behind her Nick and Marge were surveying the floor with spotlights while Miller remained off to the side, hands in his pockets. Having already walked through the basement once, he was merely waiting for the group to arrive at the same conclusion he'd formed hours before.

After a matter of minutes, D.D. was already getting there. The cellar reminded her of the kitchen, not too dirty, not too clean. Just about right for a family of three.

Just for kicks she checked the washer and the dryer. Then, her heart stopped in her throat.

"Oh crap," she said, washer lid still open, one blue-and-green quilt staring her in the face.

Miller came hustling over, evidence techs on his heels. "Is that . . . ? You've got to be kidding me. When I get my hands on the two yokels who first searched this space—"

"Hey, isn't that the quilt?" Nick said, rather stupidly.

Marge was already hunched over, pulling out the comforter from the top-loading machine while being careful not to drag it on the floor.

"He washed it?" D.D. was thinking out loud. "The husband washed the quilt, but didn't have time to dry it before calling the police? Or the wife had it in the wash all along and we've been chasing our tails for the past few hours?"

Marge was carefully spreading the quilt out, handing Nick one end, while holding the other. The comforter bore the deep wrinkles of a wet item that had been left in a washing machine for a bit. It smelled vaguely of detergent—fresh, clean. They fluffed it once, and a wet purple ball fell splat on the floor.

D.D. still had on latex gloves, so she did the honors. "Sandra Jones's nightshirt, I presume," she said, unrolling the sodden purple T-shirt, which did have a crowned chick on the front.

They studied both items for a bit, looking for faded pink stains, like the kind left behind by blood, or maybe jagged tears that might indicate a struggle. Signs of something.

D.D. had that uncomfortable feeling again. As if she was seeing something obvious but not quite getting it.

Who took the time to wash a quilt and nightshirt, but left a broken lamp in plain sight? What kind of woman disappeared, but left behind her child, her wallet, her car?

And what kind of husband came home to discover his wife missing, but waited three hours before calling the police?

"Attic, crawl space?" D.D. asked Miller out loud. Nick and Margie were folding up the quilt to take back to the lab. If the subject hadn't used bleach, the comforter might still yield some evidence. They took the purple nightshirt from D.D., put it in a second bag for processing.

"No crawl space. Attic is small and mostly filled with Christmas decorations," Miller reported.

"Closets, refrigerators, freezers, outbuildings, barbecue pits?"

"Nope, nope, nope, nope, and nope."

"Of course, there is that big, blue harbor."

"Yep."

D.D. sighed heavily. Tried one last theory: "Husband's vehicle?"

"Pickup truck. He walked out with us to peer in the back. He refused, however, to open the doors of the front cab."

"Cautious son of a bitch."

"Cold," Miller corrected. "Wife's been missing for hours now, and he hasn't even picked up the phone to call any family or friends."

That decided the matter for her. "All right," D.D. said. "Let's go meet Mr. Jones."

| CHAPTER FOUR |

When I was a little girl, I believed in God. My father would take me to church every Sunday. I would sit in Sunday school and listen to stories of His work. Afterward, we would gather in the churchyard for a potluck of fried chicken, broccoli casserole, and peach cobbler.

Then we would return home, where my mother would chase my father around the house with a meat cleaver, screaming, "I know what you're up to, mister! Like those church hussies sit next to you just to share a hymnal!"

Round and round they would go, my parents racing around the house, myself curled up small in the front coat closet, where I could hear every word they said without having to see what would happen if my father ever lost his footing, missed a corner, tripped on a stair.

When I was a little girl, I believed in God. Every morning when I woke up and my father was still alive, I considered it a sign of His work. It wasn't until I grew older that I started to truly understand Sunday mornings in my parents' house. My father's survival had nothing to do with God's will, I came to see. It was a sign of my mama's will. She never killed my father, because she didn't want him to die.

No, my mama's goal was to torture my father. To make every living moment of his life feel like an eternity in hell.

My father lived, because in my mama's mind, death would've been too good for him.

"Did you find Mr. Smith?"

"Excuse me?"

"Did you find Mr. Smith? My cat. Mommy went to look for him this morning, but she hasn't come back yet."

D.D. blinked her eyes several times rapidly. She had just opened the door at the top of the basement steps, to find herself confronted by a very solemn, curly-headed four-year-old. Apparently, Clarissa Jones was now awake and running the investigation.

"I see."

"Ree?" A male baritone broke through the silence. Ree obediently turned around, and D.D. glanced up to find Jason Jones standing in the foyer, studying both of them.

"I want Mr. Smith," Ree said plaintively.

Jason held out his hand and his daughter crossed to him. He didn't utter a word to D.D., simply vanished back into the family room, his daughter at his side.

D.D. and Miller followed suit, Miller giving a faint nod of his head to excuse the uniformed officer who'd been standing guard.

The family room was small. A tiny love seat, two wooden chairs, a hope chest covered in lace doilies, which served double duty as a coffee table. A modest TV was propped on a fake-oak microwave stand in the corner. The rest of the room was occupied by a child-sized craft table, and a row of bins that housed everything from a hundred crayons to two dozen Barbies. To judge by the toys, four-year-old Ree liked the color pink.

D.D. took her time. She surveyed the room, pausing at the grainy photos framed on the mantel, the picture of a newborn baby girl, that same baby girl in an annual procession of first food, first steps, first tricycle. No other family members in the photos. No obvious signs of grandmas, grandpas, aunts, uncles. Just Jason, Sandra, and Ree.

She noted a small shot of a toddler clutching a very tolerant orange cat, and supposed that must be the infamous Mr. Smith.

She worked her way to the toy cubbies, glancing at the table-top and noting a half-finished coloring project featuring Cinderella with two mice. Normal things, D.D. thought. Normal toys, normal items, normal furniture for a normal family in a normal South Boston home.

Except this family wasn't normal, or she wouldn't be here.

She passed by the cubbies one more time, trying to get a bead on the father without turning to look at him. Most men would be agitated by now. A missing wife. Law enforcement officers encroaching on his home, intruding into his private sanctuary, picking up and handling personal photos of his family while his four-year-old daughter was present.

She felt nothing from him. Nothing at all.

It was almost as if he weren't in the room.

She turned at last. Jason Jones was sitting on the love seat, his arm around his complacent daughter, his gaze fixed upon the empty TV screen. Up close and personal, he was everything Miller had advertised. Thick rumpled hair, masculine five o'clock shadow, nicely toned chest accentuated by a simple navy blue cotton shirt. He was sex and fatherhood and mysterious boy-next-door all rolled into one. He was an anchorwoman's wet dream, and Miller was right—if they didn't find Sandra Jones before the first news van found them, they were screwed.

D.D. picked up one of the wooden chairs, placed it in front of the sofa, and took a seat. Miller, for his part, had faded into the backdrop. Better for approaching the kid. Two cops could pressure a reluctant husband. For an anxious child, however, it would be too much.

Jason Jones's gaze finally flickered to her, resting upon her face, and in spite of herself, she nearly shivered.

His eyes were empty, like staring into pools of starless night. She had only seen such a gaze twice before. Once when interviewing a psychopath who'd resolved an unhappy business relationship by executing his partner and the man's entire family with a crossbow. Secondly when interviewing a twenty-seven-year-old Portuguese woman who had been held as a sex slave for fifteen years by a wealthy couple in their elite Boston brownstone. The woman had died two years later. She'd walked into oncoming traffic on Storrow Drive. Never hesitated, witnesses said. Just stepped off the curb straight into the path of a Toyota Highlander.

"I want my cat," Ree said. She had straightened on the sofa, pushing slightly away from her father. He didn't try to pull her back.

"When did you last see Mr. Smith?" D.D. asked her.

"Last night. When I went to bed. Mr. Smith always sleeps with me. He likes my room best."

D.D. smiled. "I like your room, too. All the flowers and the pretty butterflies. Did you help decorate it?"

"No. I can't draw. My mommy and daddy did it. I'm four and three-quarters, you know." Ree puffed out her chest. "I'm a big girl now, so I got a big girl's room for my fourth birthday."

"You're four? No way, I would've said you're five, six, easy. What have they been feeding you, 'cause you're awfully tall for four."

Ree giggled. Her father said nothing.

"I like macaroni and cheese. That's my favorite food in the whole world. Mommy lets me eat it if I have turkey franks, too. Need protein, she says. If I have enough protein, I can have Oreos for dessert."

"Is that what you ate last night?"

"I had mac-n-cheese and apples. No Oreos. Daddy didn't have time to make it to the grocery store."

She gave her father a look, and for the first time Jason Jones fired to life. He ruffled his daughter's hair, while his gaze filled with a mixture of love and protectiveness. Then he turned away from her and, as if a switch had been thrown, resumed his dead man's stare.

"Who fed you dinner last night, Ree?"

"Mommy feeds me dinner, Daddy feeds me lunch. I have PB and J for lunch, but no cookies. Can't have cookies all the time." Ree sounded faintly mournful.

"Does Mr. Smith like Oreos?"

Ree rolled her eyes. "Mr. Smith likes *everything*! That's why he's so fat. He eats and eats and eats. Mommy and Daddy say no people food for Mr. Smith, but he does not like that."

"Did Mr. Smith help you eat dinner last night?"

"He tried to jump on the counter. Mommy told him to scat."

"I see. And after dinner?"

"Bath time."

"Mr. Smith takes a bath?" D.D. tried to sound incredulous.

Ree giggled again. "No, Mr. Smith is a cat. Cats don't take baths. They *groom* themselves."

"Ooh. That makes much more sense. So who took a bath?"

"Mommy and me."

"Does your mom hog all the hot water? Use up all the soap?"

"No. But she won't let me have the soap. Once I poured the whole bottle into the tub. You should've seen the bubbles!"

"That must've been most impressive."

"I like bubbles."

"So do I. And after the bath?"

"Well, we took a shower."

"My apologies. After your shower…"

"Went to bed. I get to pick two stories. I like Fancy Nancy and Pinkalicious books. I also get to pick a song. Mommy likes to sing 'Twinkle, Twinkle Little Star,' but I'm too old for that, so I made her sing 'Puff the Magic Dragon.' "

"Your mother sang 'Puff the Magic Dragon'?" D.D. didn't have to fake her surprise this time.

"I like dragons," Ree said.

"Umm, I see. And Mr. Smith, what did he think of this?"

"Mr. Smith doesn't sing."

"But does he like songs?"

Ree shrugged. "He likes stories. He always curls up with me during story time."

"Then your mother turns out the light?"

"I get a nightlight. I know I'm four and three-quarters, but I like having a nightlight. Maybe…I don't know. Maybe when I'm five…or maybe thirty, then I won't have a nightlight."

"Okay, so you're in bed. Mr. Smith is with you—"

"He sleeps at my feet."

"Okay, he's at your feet. Nightlight is glowing. Your mom turns off the light, closes the door, and then..."

Ree stared at her.

Jason Jones was staring at her now, too, his gaze faintly hostile.

"Anything happen in the middle of the night, Ree?" D.D. asked quietly.

Ree stared at her.

"Other noises. People talking. Your door opening? When did Mr. Smith leave you?"

Ree shook her head. She wasn't looking at D.D. anymore. After another second, she curled back into her father's side, her skinny arms wrapping tightly around his waist. Jason put both arms around her shoulders and regarded D.D. flatly.

"Done," he said.

"Mr. Jones—"

"Done," he repeated.

D.D. took a deep breath, counted to ten, and debated her options. "Perhaps there is a family member or neighbor who could watch Clarissa for a bit, Mr. Jones."

"No."

"No, there is no one who can watch her, or no, you won't do it?"

"We look after our daughter, Detective..."

"Sergeant. Sergeant D.D. Warren."

He didn't blink at the mention of her title. "We look after our daughter, Sergeant Warren. No point in having a child if you're simply going to let others raise her."

"Mr. Jones, surely you understand that if we're going to help find...Mr. Smith...we're going to need more information, and more cooperation, from you."

He didn't say anything, just held his daughter close.

"We require the keys to your truck."

He said nothing.

"Mr. Jones," D.D. urged impatiently. "The sooner we establish where Mr. Smith *isn't,* the sooner we can establish where she is."

"*He,*" came Ree's muffled voice from against her father's chest. "Mr. Smith is a *boy.*"

D.D. didn't respond, simply continued to study Jason Jones.

"Mr. Smith is not in the cab of my pickup truck," Jason said quietly.

"How do you know that?"

"Because he was already gone when I came home. And just to be safe, I checked the vehicle myself."

"With all due respect, sir, that would be our job."

"Mr. Smith is not in my truck," Jason repeated quietly. "And until you get a search warrant, you'll get to take my word for it."

"There are judges who would grant us a warrant based on your lack of cooperation alone."

"Then I guess you'll be back shortly, won't you?"

"I want access to your computer," D.D. said.

"Talk to the same judge."

"Mr. Jones. Your ... *cat* has been missing for seven hours now. No sign of her—"

"Him," Ree's muffled voice.

"*Him*, in the neighborhood or at the usual ... cat haunts. The matter is growing serious. I would think you'd want to help."

"I love my cat," Jones said quietly.

"Then give us access to your computer. Cooperate with us, so we can resolve this matter safely and expediently."

"I can't."

"Can't?" D.D. pounced. "Or won't?"

"Can't."

"And why can't you, Mr. Jones?"

He looked at her. "Because I love my daughter more."

Thirty minutes later, D.D. walked with Detective Miller back to her car. They had printed Jason Jones and Clarissa Jones as a matter of protocol; in order to determine if there were any strange fingerprints in the house, they had to start by identifying the prints of the known occupants. Jones had volunteered his hands, then assisted with Ree's, who thought the whole thing was a grand adventure. Most likely, Jason had realized that one act of cooperation cost him very little— after all, there was nothing suspicious about his prints being in his own home.

Jason Jones had washed his hands. Jason Jones had washed Ree's hands. Then he'd basically kicked the police officers out. His daughter needed to rest, he announced, and that had been that. He escorted each and every one of them to the door. No *What are you doing to find my wife?* No *Please, please please I'll do whatever I can to help.* No *Let's organize a search party and tackle the entire neighborhood until we find my beautiful, beloved spouse.*

Not Mr. Jones. His daughter needed a nap. And that was that.

"Cold?" D.D. muttered now. "Arctic is more like it. Clearly, Mr. Jones has never heard of global warming."

Miller let her rant.

"Kid knows something. Notice the way she shut down the moment we got past bedtime? She heard something, saw something, I don't know. But we need a forensic interviewer, someone who specializes in children. Quick, too. More time that girl spends around dear old Dad, harder it's going to be for her to recall any inconvenient truths."

Miller nodded his head.

" 'Course, we're also gonna need doting Dad's permission to interview his child, and somehow, I don't think he's gonna grant us access. Fascinating, don't you think? I mean, his wife vanished in the middle of the night, leaving their daughter all alone in the house, and far from cooperating with us, or asking us any logical questions about what we're doing to find his wife, Jason Jones sits on that sofa as mute as a mime. Where's his shock, his disbelief, his panicked need for information? He should be calling friends and relatives. He should be digging out recent photos of his wife for us to canvass the neighborhood. He should, at the very least, be arranging for someone to watch his daughter so he can personally assist with our efforts. This guy—it's like a switch has been thrown. He's not even home."

"Denial," Miller offered up, trudging along beside her.

"We're gonna have to do this the hard way," D.D. declared. "Get a search warrant for Jason Jones's truck, get an affidavit permitting us to seize the computer, as well as requesting printouts of the wife's cell phone records. Hell, we should probably just have the entire house frozen as a crime scene. That'd give Jason Jones something to think about."

"Tough on the kid."

"Yeah, well, that's the kicker." If the house was declared a crime scene, Jason and his daughter would be forced to evacuate. Pack a bag, move into a motel under escort from a police cruiser kind of thing. D.D. wondered what little Ree would think, giving up her garden oasis for a cheap hotel room with brown carpets and the stale scent of a decade's worth of cigarettes. It didn't make D.D. feel too good about things, but then she had another thought.

She stopped walking, pivoting toward Miller so abruptly, he nearly ran into her.

"If we move Jason and Ree out of the house, we'll have to assign officers to cover them twenty-four/seven. Meaning there'll be fewer officers actively searching for Sandra Jones, meaning our investigation will slow down during a time when it's critical to ramp up. You know that. I know that. But Jason doesn't know that."

Miller frowned at her, stroked his mustache.

"Judge Banyan," D.D. said, resuming walking at a much brisker pace. "We can prepare the affidavits now, and get 'em to her chamber right after lunch. We'll get warrants for the computer, the truck, and dammit, we'll have the house declared a crime scene. We'll knock Mr. Arctic right out on his ass."

"Wait, I thought you just said—"

"And we'll hope," D.D. interjected forcefully, "that when Jason Jones is given a choice between vacating his own home, or letting a certified forensic specialist talk to his child, he'll opt for the interview."

D.D. glanced at her watch. It was just after twelve now, and on cue, her stomach rumbled for lunch. She remembered her early-morning fantasy of an all-you-can-eat buffet, and felt just plain pissy.

"We'll need more manpower to execute the warrants," she added.

"All right."

"And we're gonna have to think of a way to broaden our search without alerting the media yet."

"All right."

They were at her car. D.D. paused long enough to look Miller in the eye and sigh heavily.

"This case sucks," she declared.

"I know," Miller said affably. "Aren't you glad I called?"

| CHAPTER FIVE |

At 11:59, Jason finally got the last law enforcement officer out of the house. The sergeant retreated, then the lead detective, the evidence technicians, and the uniformed officers. Only a plainclothes detective remained behind, sitting obtrusively in a brown Ford Taurus parked in front. Jason could watch him from the kitchen window, the officer sitting with his gaze straight ahead, alternately yawning and taking sips of Dunkin' Donuts coffee.

After another minute, Jason moved away from the window, realized that his house was all his again, and nearly staggered under the weight of what to do next.

Ree was staring at him, her big brown eyes so much like her mother's.

"Lunch," Jason said out loud, slightly startled by the hoarse sound of his own voice. "Let's have lunch."

"Daddy, did you buy Oreo cookies?"

"No."

She exhaled heavily, turning toward the kitchen anyway. "Maybe you should call Mommy. Maybe, if she's near a grocery store looking for Mr. Smith, she can bring home some cookies."

"Maybe," Jason said, and managed to get the refrigerator door open even though his hand had started to shake violently.

He made it through lunch on autopilot. Found the bread, pulled out whole wheat slices. Mixed the natural peanut butter, spread the jelly. Counted out four carrots, picked out some green grapes. Arranged it all on a flowered daisy plate with the sandwich cut on the requisite diagonal.

Ree prattled about Mr. Smith's great escape, how no doubt he would be meeting up with Peter Rabbit and maybe they'd both come home with Alice in Wonderland. Ree was at the age where she easily blended fact and fantasy. Santa was real, the Easter Bunny was best friends with the Tooth Fairy, and there was no reason Clifford the Big Red Dog couldn't have a play date with Mr. Smith.

She was a precocious child. All energy and high hopes and huge demands. She could throw a forty-five-minute temper tantrum over not having the right shade of pink socks to wear. And she had once spent an entire Saturday morning refusing to come out of her room because she was furious that Sandra had bought new curtains for the kitchen without consulting her first.

Yet, neither Sandra nor Jason would have it any other way.

He looked at her, Sandra looked at her, and they saw the childhood neither one of them had ever had. They saw innocence and faith and trust. They relished their daughter's easy hugs. They lived for her infectious laugh. And they both, early on, had agreed that Ree would always come first. They would do anything for her.

Anything.

Jason glanced at the unmarked police car sitting outside his house, felt his hand curl into an automatic fist, and checked the reflex.

"She's pretty."

"Mr. Smith is a boy," he said automatically.

"Not Mr. Smith. The police lady. I like her hair."

Jason turned back toward his daughter. Ree's face was smudged with peanut butter in one corner, jelly in another. And she was looking at him again with her big brown eyes.

"You know you can tell me anything," he said softly.

Ree set her sandwich down. "I know, Daddy," she said, but she wasn't looking at him anymore. She ate two green grapes halfheartedly, then rearranged the others on her plate, around the white petals of the daisy. "Do you think Mr. Smith is okay?"

"Cats have nine lives."

"Mommys don't."

He didn't know what to say. He tried to open his mouth, tried to summon some kind of vague reassuring phrase, but nothing would come out. He was mostly aware that his hands were shaking convulsively again, and he had gone cold somewhere deep down inside, where he would probably never be warm again.

"I'm tired, Daddy," Ree said. "I want to take a nap."

"Okay," he said.

They headed upstairs.

Jason watched Ree brush her teeth. He wondered if this is what Sandy had done.

He read Ree two stories, sitting on the edge of Ree's bed. He wondered if this is what Sandy had done.

He sang one song, tucked the covers around his daughter's shoulders, and kissed her on the cheek. He wondered if this is what Sandy had done.

He made it all the way to the doorway, then Ree spoke up, forcing him to turn around. He had his arms crossed over his chest, his fingers fisted beneath his elbows, where Ree couldn't see the tremors in his hands.

"Will you stay, Daddy? Until I fall asleep?"

"Okay."

"Mommy sang me 'Puff the Magic Dragon.' I remember her singing 'Puff the Magic Dragon.'"

"Okay."

Ree shifted restlessly beneath the covers. "Do you think she's found Mr. Smith yet? Do you think she'll come home?"

"I hope so."

She finally lay still. "Daddy," she whispered. "Daddy, I have a secret."

He took a deep breath, forced his voice to sound light. "Really? Because remember the Daddy Clause."

"The Daddy Clause?"

"Sure, the Daddy Clause. Whatever the secret, you're allowed to tell one daddy. Then he'll help keep the secret, too."

"You're my daddy."

"Yep, and I assure you, I'm really good at keeping secrets."

She smiled at him. Then, her mother's daughter, she rolled over and went to sleep without saying another word.

He waited five more minutes, then eased out of the room, and just barely made it down the stairs.

He kept the picture in the kitchen utility drawer, next to the pen flashlight, green screwdriver, leftover birthday candles, and half a dozen wine charms they never used. Sandra used to tease him about the tiny photo in its cheap gilded frame.

"For God's sake, it's like hiding away a picture of your old high school sweetheart. Stick the frame on the mantel, Jason. She's like family to you. I don't mind."

But the woman in the photo was not family. She was old—eighty, ninety, he couldn't remember anymore. She sat in a rocking chair, birdlike frame nearly lost in a pile of voluminous hand-me-down clothes: man's dark blue flannel shirt, belted around brown corduroy pants, nearly covered by an old Army jacket. The woman was smiling the large, gleeful smile of the elderly, like she had a secret, too, and hers was better than his.

He had loved her smile. He had loved her laugh.

She was not family, but she was the only person who, for a very long time, had made him feel safe.

He clutched her photo now. He held it to his breast like a talisman, and then his legs gave out and he sank to the kitchen floor. He started to shake again. First his hands, then his arms, then his chest, the bone-deep tremors traveling down to his thighs, his knees, his ankles, each tiny little toe.

He didn't cry. He didn't make a sound of protest.

But he shook so hard it felt as if his body should break apart, his flesh flying from his bones, his bones splintering into a thousand pieces.

"Goddammit, Sandy," he said, resting his shaking head upon his shaking knees.

Then he realized, quite belatedly, that he'd better do something about the computer.

The phone rang ten minutes later. Jason didn't feel like talking to anyone, then thought, a little foolishly, that it might be Sandy, calling from ... somewhere ... so he picked up.

It wasn't his wife. It was a male voice, and the man said, "Are you home alone?"

"Who is this?"

"Is your child there?"

Jason hung up.

The phone rang again. Caller ID reported the same number. This time Jason let the machine get it. The same male voice boomed, "I'll take that as a yes. Back yard, five minutes. You'll want to talk to me." Then the man hung up.

"Fuck you," Jason told the empty kitchen. It was a foolish thing to say, but it made him feel better.

He went upstairs, checked on Ree. She was tucked almost all the way under the covers, sleeping soundly. He looked automatically for the familiar copper pile of Mr. Smith curled up at his daughter's feet. The spot was empty, and Jason felt the familiar pang again.

"Goddammit, Sandy," he muttered tiredly, then found his coat and stepped into his back yard.

The caller was younger than he expected. Twenty-two, twenty-three. The thin lanky build of a young man who hadn't filled out yet and probably wouldn't until his early thirties. The kid had scaled the wooden fence around Jason's yard.

Now he leapt down and sprang forward a few steps, moving like a golden retriever puppy with floppy blond hair and long, rangy limbs. The kid stopped the instant he spotted Jason, then wiped his hands on his jeans. It was cold out, and he wore only a white T-shirt with faded black print and no coat. If the March chill bothered him, he didn't show it.

"Umm, cop out front. Sure you know. Didn't want to be seen," the kid said, as if that explained everything. Jason noticed he wore a green elastic band around his left wrist and was snapping it absently, like a nervous habit.

"Who are you?"

"Neighbor," the kid said. "Live five houses down. Name's Aidan Brewster. We've never met." *Snap, snap, snap.*

Jason said nothing.

"I, uh, keep to myself," the kid offered, again as if that explained everything.

Jason said nothing.

"Your wife has gone missing," the kid stated. *Snap, snap.*

"Who told you?"

Kid shrugged. "Didn't have to be told. Cops are canvassing the neighborhood, looking for a missing female. A detective has set up camp outside your house, so obviously this is ground zero. You're here. Your kid is here. Ergo, your wife is missing." The kid started to snap the elastic again, caught himself this time, and both hands fell to his sides.

"What do you want?" Jason asked.

"Did you kill her?"

Jason looked at the boy. "Why do you think she's dead?"

Kid shrugged. "That's the way these things work. Report starts with a missing white female, mother of one, two, three kids. Media kicks in, search teams are organized, neighborhoods are canvassed. And then, approximately one week to three months later, the corpse is recovered from a lake, the woods, the oversized freezer in the garage. Don't suppose you have any large blue plastic barrels, do you?"

Jason shook his head.

"Chain saws? Barbecue pits?"

"I have a child. Even if I had such items, the presence of a small child would curtail my activities."

Kid shrugged. "Didn't seem to stop the others from getting the job done."

"Get out of my yard."

"Not yet. I need to know: Did you kill your wife?"

"What makes you think I would tell you?"

Kid shrugged. "Dunno. We've never met, but I thought I'd ask. It matters to me."

Jason stared at the kid for a minute. He found himself saying, "I didn't kill her."

"Okay. Neither did I."

"You know my wife?"

"Blonde hair, big brown eyes, kind of a quirky smile?"

Jason stared at the kid again. "Yes."

"Nah, I've never met her, but I've seen her out in your yard." The kid resumed snapping the green elastic band.

"Why are you here?" Jason asked.

"Because I didn't kill your wife," the kid repeated. He glanced at his watch. "But in about one to four hours, the police are gonna assume that I did."

"Why would they assume that?"

"I got a prior."

"You killed someone before?"

"Nah, but that won't matter. I have a prior, and like I said, that's how these things work. A woman has gone missing. The detectives will start with the people close to her, making you the first 'person of interest.' Next, however, they'll check out all the neighbors. That's when I'll pop up, the second 'person of interest.' Now, am I more interesting than you? I don't have the answer to that, so I figured I'd better stop by."

Jason frowned. "You want to know if I harmed my wife, because then you're off the hook?"

"It's a logical question to ask," the kid said neutrally. "Now, you claim you didn't kill her. And I know I didn't kill her, which leads us to the next problem."

"Which is?"

"No one is gonna believe either of us. And the more we claim our innocence, the more they're gonna come down on us like a ton of bricks. Wasting valuable time and resources trying to get us to admit guilt, versus finding out exactly what did happen to your wife."

Jason couldn't argue with that. It's why he'd kept his mouth shut all morning long. Because he was the husband, and the husband started the process automatically suspect. Meaning every time he spoke, the police would not be listening for proof of his innocence, but rather for any gaffe indicating his guilt. "You seem to know a lot about how the system works," he told the kid.

"Am I wrong?"

"Probably not."

"Okay, so going with the old adage that the enemy of your enemy is your friend, the cops are our mutual enemies, and we're now friends."

"I don't even know who you are."

"Aidan Brewster. Neighbor, auto mechanic, innocent party. What more do you need to know?"

Jason frowned. He should be quicker than this, seeing the obvious flaw in such a statement. But he could feel the stress and the fatigue catching up with him now. He had not slept in nearly thirty hours, first watching Ree, then going off to work, then returning to the scene at home. His heart had literally stopped beating in the space of time it had taken him to discover the empty master bedroom and walk the twelve feet to Ree's room, his hand curling around the doorknob, twisting, pushing, so deeply unsure of what he might find inside. Then, when he'd spotted his daughter's sprawled shape, sound asleep under the covers, he had staggered backward, only to realize in the next instant that Ree's presence raised more questions than it answered. All of a sudden, after five years of almost leading a normal life, of almost feeling like a real person, it was over, done, finished, in the blink of an eye.

He had returned to the abyss, in a space he knew better than anyone, even better than convicted felon Aidan Brewster.

"So," the kid was saying now, snapping, "did you ever hit your wife?"

Jason stared at him.

"Might as well answer," his neighbor said. "If the police didn't get to drill you this morning, they'll get to it soon enough."

"I didn't hit my wife," Jason said softly, mostly because he needed to hear himself say the words, to remind himself that that much, at least, was true. Forget February vacation. Forget it ever happened.

"Marital difficulties?"

"We worked alternate schedules. We never saw each other enough to fight."

"Ah, so extramarital activities, then. You, her, both?"

"Not me," Jason said.

"But she had a little something, something going on?"

Jason shrugged. "Isn't the husband always the last to know?"

"Think she ran off with him?"

"She never would have left Ree."

"So she was having an affair, and she knew you'd never let her take her daughter with her."

Jason blinked his eyes, feeling his exhaustion again. "Wait a minute..."

"Come on, pull it together, man, or you'll be rotting in jail by the end of the day," the kid said impatiently.

"I wouldn't harm my daughter, and I would've granted my wife a divorce."

"Really? Given up this house, prime real estate in Southie?"

"Money is not an issue for us."

"You're loaded, then? Even more moola to have to surrender."

"Money is not an issue for us."

"That's crap. Money is an issue for everyone. Now you do sound guilty."

"My wife is the mother of my daughter," Jason found himself saying testily. "If we did separate, I would want her to have the resources necessary to take care of my child."

"Wife, child, wife, child. You're depersonalizing them. Claiming to love them so much you'd never harm 'em, but on the other hand, you can't even bring yourself to call them by name."

"Stop it. I don't want to talk anymore."

"Did you kill your wife?"

"Get out. Leave me alone."

"You're right. I'm outta here. I've only spoken with you eight minutes, and I already think you're guilty as hell. But hey, that means I got nothing to worry about. So see ya."

Kid headed for the fence. He already had his hands curled around the wooden slats, preparing to lift himself up and over, when it came to Jason, the piece he'd been missing since the very beginning.

"You asked if my child was home," he called out across the yard. "You asked about my child."

The kid was up now, one leg slung over the fence. Jason started to run toward him.

"*Son of a bitch!* Your prior. Tell me what you did, tell me exactly what you did!"

Kid paused at the top of the fence. He no longer looked like a golden retriever puppy. Something about his eyes had changed, his expression growing secretive, growing hard. "Don't need to; you already figured it out."

"Background check, my ass! You're a convicted sex offender, aren't you? Your name is in the fucking sex offender database. They'll be at your door by two."

"Yep. But they'll still be arresting you by three. I didn't kill your wife. She's too old for my tastes—"

"*Fucking prick!*"

"And I know something you don't know. I heard a car last night. Best I can figure, I saw the vehicle that took your wife away."

| CHAPTER SIX |

*I fell in love the first time when I was eight years old. The man didn't ac-
tually exist, but was a character on TV: Sonny Crockett, the cop played
by Don Johnson on* Miami Vice. *My mama didn't hold with such non-
sense, so I'd simply wait until she'd pass out cold from the afternoon
"ice tea," then pop open a Dr Pepper and watch the reruns to my heart's
content.*

*Sonny Crockett was strong, world-weary. The kind of tough guy
who'd seen it all and still went out of his way to save the girl. I wanted a
Sonny Crockett. I wanted somebody to save me.*

*When I turned thirteen I developed breasts. Suddenly, there were a
lot of boys interested in saving me. And for a while, I thought that might
work. I dated indiscriminately, with a slight preference for older boys
with body art and really bad attitudes. They wanted sex. I wanted somebody to load me up in the front seat of his Mustang and drive a hundred
miles an hour in the middle of the night with no headlights. I wanted
to scream my name with the wind tattooing my face and whipping
my hair. I wanted to feel wild and reckless. I wanted to feel like anyone
but me.*

I developed a reputation for really great blow jobs and for being even crazier than my mad-as-a-hatter mother. Every small town has a mother like mine, you know. And every small town has a girl like me.

I got pregnant for the first time when I was fourteen. I didn't tell anyone. I drank a lot of rum and Coke and prayed real hard for God to take the baby away. When that didn't get it done, I stole money from my father's wallet and went to a clinic where they do those kinds of things for you.

I didn't cry. I considered my abortion an act of public service. One less life for my mama to ruin.

I'm telling you, every small town has a girl like me.

Then I turned fifteen and my mother died and my father and I were finally free and I...

I dreamed for so long of somebody to save me. I wanted Sonny Crockett, the world-weary soul who still sees the true heart within the battered exterior. I wanted a man who would hold me close and make me feel safe and never let me go.

I never found Sonny Crockett. Instead, the day before my eighteenth birthday, at a local bar, I met my husband. I sat on Jason's bar stool, downed his Coke, and then, when he started to protest, ran my hands up the hard denim lines of his thighs. He told me to fuck off. And I knew at that moment that I would never let him go.

Of course, no one can save you.

But knowing now all the things I know about Jason, I understand why he felt he had to try.

By 2:02 P.M., D.D. was feeling pretty good about the investigation. They had a game plan, and were executing it well considering they were looking for an adult female who could not yet legally be declared missing but needed to be found ASAP.

At 2:06, she received the first piece of bad news. Judge Banyan had denied their petition to seize the Jones family's computer and refused to declare the house a crime scene. She cited the lack of physical evidence of foul play as the overriding factor in her consideration, plus not enough time had passed. Missing ten hours was nothing for an adult. Maybe Sandra Jones had ended up at a friend's house. Maybe she'd suffered some kind of injury and was at a local hospital, unable to provide her name. Maybe she'd gone sleepwalking and was still roaming the back streets of the city in a daze. In other words, a lot of maybes.

However, the judge continued, if Sandra Jones was still gone after twenty-four hours, Banyan would be willing to reconsider things. In the meantime, she did grant them access to Jason Jones's truck.

One for three, D.D. thought, resigned. Discovering the quilt and nightshirt in the washing machine had complicated things. A missing quilt and broken lamp had seemed ominous. A quilt and a nightshirt in the washing machine...

D.D. still wasn't sure what the hell a quilt and nightshirt in the washing machine meant. That a husband had been trying to cover his tracks, or that the wife had liked to do laundry? Assumptions were dangerous.

At 2:15 Detective Miller reported in. D.D. gave him the bad news from Judge Banyan. Miller provided an update from Sandra Jones's middle school. According to the principal, Sandy Jones had taught social studies at the school for the past two years—first as a student teacher for the seventh grade class, then taking over sixth grade social studies in September. Thus far, kids seemed to like her, parents seemed to like her, fellow teachers seemed to like her. Sandra didn't socialize a lot with her peers, but then again, she had a small child at home and a husband who worked nights, so that kind of thing was to be expected. Principal had met the husband once and thought he'd seemed nice enough. Principal had met the daughter, Ree, many times, and thought she was adorable.

The principal couldn't think of any reason for Sandra not to show up for work, and yes, it was out of character for her not to at least phone in. He was concerned and wanted to do anything he could to assist the investigation.

P.S., the principal was a fifty-year-old happily married man, who according to the secretary was already engaged in a torrid affair with the drama teacher. Everyone knew about it, no one much cared, and there wasn't enough Viagra in the world for one fifty-year-old to juggle both the red-headed drama coach and a twenty-three-year-old new conquest. Odds were, the principal only had a working relationship with Sandra Jones.

Miller had also run preliminary financial reports on the Joneses. They had a staggering hundred and fifty thousand sitting in savings, with another two million stashed in various mutual funds with an investment bank. Monthly income was modest, same with monthly expenses. It looked to him like they had paid cash for the house, and did their best to live off their paychecks.

Miller would guess the high net worth came from a lump sum deposit, such as an inheritance or insurance settlement. He had detectives working on tracing the money now.

In other news, the Joneses had been married in 2004 in a civil ceremony in Massachusetts. Their daughter, Clarissa, had been born two months later. There were no outstanding tickets or warrants for either Sandra Jones or Jason Jones. Neither had there been any indication of domestic violence or public disturbance.

According to the neighbors, the Joneses were a quiet couple who kept to themselves. Did not party, did not entertain. If you saw them on the street, they would smile and wave, but were not the kind to stop and make polite chitchat. Except for Ree. Everyone agreed Clarissa Jones was precocious and would talk your ear off. Apparently, she was also hell on wheels on a tricycle. If you saw her coming it was up to you to get off the sidewalk.

"Parents yell at her a lot?" D.D. asked.

"Parents doted on her. And I'm reading verbatim here, three different accounts from three different neighbors: Parents 'doted' on daughter."

"Huh. 'Course, parents are also described as quiet and reserved, meaning, how well did any of the neighbors know them?"

"True."

"Life insurance policies?"

"Still inquiring."

"Two million dollars in the bank," D.D. mused. "Plus cash, plus prime Boston real estate . . . what are we talking about, nearly three-point-five million in assets? People have killed for less."

"Figure the standard divorce would run the husband nearly two mil. That's a lot of money for a starter marriage."

"Speaking of which, what year were they married again?"

"Two thousand and four."

"Which would make Sandra Jones, what, eighteen years old? And already pregnant?"

"Given that Clarissa was born two months later, yep."

"And Jason Jones is, what, thirty, thirty-one?"

"That would be my guess. Still working on rounding up a birth certificate for him."

"Let's consider that for a second. You got a young, beautiful pregnant girl, an older—richer?—man..."

"Don't know who had the money yet. Could've been Jason or Sandra."

"Somehow, I'm willing to bet the money was his."

"Somehow, I'm thinking you're right."

"So Jason snags himself a pregnant teenage bride. Has an 'adorable' little girl, and four/five years after that..."

"Is living a quiet life in South Boston, in a house reinforced tighter than Fort Knox, in a neighborhood where no one really knows him."

D.D. and Miller both fell silent for a bit.

"You know what struck me most when we walked through the house?" D.D. said abruptly. "It was how... 'just right' everything felt. Not too dirty, not too clean. Not too cluttered, not too organized. Everything was absolutely, positively *balanced*. Like the principal said, Sandra Jones socialized enough for people to like her, without socializing so much that her fellow teachers might actually know her. Jason and Sandra smiled at their neighbors, but never actually entertained them. They wave, but don't talk. They get out, but never invite anyone in. Everything is carefully modulated. It's a balancing act. Except nature isn't balanced."

"You think their life is manufactured?"

She shrugged. "I think real life is messy, and these guys aren't messy enough."

Miller hesitated. "We haven't checked in with Jason's employer yet...."

D.D. winced. Which would be the *Boston Daily*, a major media outlet. "Yeah, I understand."

"I'm thinking of having one of my gals call in. Claim she's doing a background check for security clearance, something like that. Somehow, it's less suspicious if you have a female make the call."

"Good idea."

"And we'll follow up with the daughter's preschool. See what the teachers and staff have to say. Don't little girls travel in packs, have little friends, attend sleepovers? Seems to me there's gotta be some parents somewhere who know more about the family."

"Works for me."

"Finally, I got a copy of the marriage certificate faxed over. Now that I have Sandra's maiden name, I'll start tracking down the father, get more info out of Georgia."

"All right. I'm assuming there's still no sign of Sandra nor activity on her credit card?"

"Nope. Local establishments haven't seen her. Local hospitals and walk-in clinics have no unidentified women. Morgue has no unidentified females. Credit card was last used two days ago at the grocery store. ATM card has no hits. Closest thing we have to activity is half a dozen calls on her cell phone. One call from the husband at two-sixteen A.M.—probably when he figured out his wife's phone was ringing right behind him on the kitchen counter. Then a couple of calls from the school principal this morning trying to track her down, as well as three other calls from students. That's been it."

"She received calls from her sixth grade students?"

"Placed from their own cell phones, of course. Welcome to the brave new world of grown-up twelve-year-olds."

"I'm so glad I don't even have a plant."

Miller grunted. "I have three boys—seven, nine, and eleven. I plan on working overtime for the next ten years."

She couldn't blame him. "So you'll track financials, cell phones, and grown-up twelve-year-olds. I'll go to work on searching the truck and lining up a forensic interviewer."

"Think he'll let us talk to the daughter? We don't have anything to threaten him with anymore."

"I think if Sandra Jones hasn't magically been found by tomorrow morning, he won't have a choice."

———

D.D. had just risen from her chair when her desk phone rang. She picked it up.

"Jason Jones is holding on line one," the receptionist said.

D.D. sat back down. "Sergeant D.D. Warren," she announced into the phone.

"I'm ready to talk," Jason said.

"Excuse me?"

"My daughter is napping. I can talk now."

"You mean you would like to meet with us? I'll be happy to send two officers to pick you up."

"By the time the officers get here, my daughter will be awake and I will no longer be available. If you want to ask me questions, it needs to be now, by phone. It's the best I can do."

D.D. highly doubted that. It wasn't the best he could do, it was the most convenient. Again, the man's wife had been missing for twelve hours, and this was his idea of cooperation?

"We have arranged for a specialist to interview Ree," she said.

"No."

"The woman is a trained professional, specializing in questioning children. She will handle the conversation delicately and with the least amount of stress on your daughter."

"My daughter doesn't know anything."

"Then the conversation will be short."

He didn't answer right away. She could feel his turmoil in the long pause.

"Did your wife run off?" she asked abruptly, trying to keep him off balance. "Meet a new guy, head for the border?"

"She never would've left Ree."

"Meaning she could've met a new guy."

"I don't know, Sergeant. I work most nights. I don't really know what my wife does."

"Doesn't sound like a happy marriage."

"Depends on your point of view. Are you married, Sergeant?"

"Why?"

"Because if you were, you'd understand that marriage is about phases. My wife and I are raising a small child while juggling two careers. This isn't the honeymoon phase. This is work."

D.D. grunted, let the silence drag out again. She thought it was interesting that he used the present tense, *are* raising a child together, but couldn't decide if that was calculated or not. He used the present tense, but not the actual names of his wife and child. Interesting person, Jason Jones.

"You having an affair, Jason? Because we're asking enough questions at this point, it's gonna come out."

"I haven't cheated on my wife."

"But she cheated on you."

"I have no evidence of that."

"But you suspected it."

"Sergeant, I could've caught her in bed with the man, and I still wouldn't have killed her."

"Not that kind of guy?"

"Not that kind of marriage."

D.D.'s turn to blink. She turned this around in her head, still couldn't sort it out. "What kind of marriage is it?"

"Respectful. Sandra was very young when we married. If she needed to work some things out, I could give her space for that."

"Mighty understanding of you."

He didn't say anything.

Then D.D. got it: "Did you make her sign a prenup? Some kind of clause, if she cheated on you, then you wouldn't owe her anything in the divorce?"

"There's no prenup."

"Really? No prenup? With all that money sitting in the bank?"

"The money came from an inheritance. I never expected to have it, ergo I can't mind too much if I lose it."

"Oh please, two million dollars—"

"Four. You need to run better reports."

"Four million dollars—"

"Yet we live on twenty-five hundred a month. Sergeant, you're not asking the right question yet."

"And what would that be?"

"Even if I had motive to harm my wife, why would I harm Mr. Smith?"

"Excuse me?"

"Did you ever read about Ted Bundy? He murdered and mutilated over thirty women, yet he wouldn't steal an uninsured car because he thought it was cruel. Now, a husband who murders his wife rather than settle for a divorce is clearly psychopathic. His needs come first. His wife is little more than an animated object. She interferes with his needs. He feels justified in disposing of her."

D.D. didn't say anything. She was still trying to figure out if she'd just heard a confession.

"But the cat, Sergeant. Mr. Smith. Even if I had objectified my wife to a point where I decided I would be better off without her, what had the cat ever done to me? Maybe I could justify taking my daughter's mother from her. But harming my daughter's pet, that would be just plain cruel."

"Then what happened to your wife, Mr. Jones?"

"I have no idea."

"Has she ever disappeared before?"

"Never."

"Has she ever not shown up for something, without bothering to call?"

"Sandra is very conscientious. Ask the middle school where she works. She says what she's going to do, she does what she says."

"Does she have a history of going to bars, drinking heavily, doing drugs? By your own admission, she's still very young."

"No. We don't drink. We don't do drugs."

"She sleepwalk, use any prescription medication?"

"No."

"Hang out socially?"

"We lead a very quiet life, Sergeant. Our first priority is our daughter."

"In other words, you're just regular, everyday folks."

"Regular as clockwork."

"Who happen to live in a house with reinforced windows and steel doors?"

"We live in an urban environment. Home security is nothing to be taken lightly."

"Didn't realize Southie was that rough."

"Didn't realize the police had issues with citizens who favor locks."

D.D. decided to declare that interaction a draw. She paused again, trying to find her bearings in a conversation that should be taking place in person and not by phone.

"When you first arrived home, Mr. Jones, were the doors locked?"

"Yes."

"Anything out of the ordinary catch your eye? In the kitchen, hallway, entryway, anything at all as you entered your house?"

"I didn't notice a thing."

"When you first realized your wife was not home, Mr. Jones, what did you do?"

"I called her cell. Which turned out to be in her purse on the kitchen counter."

"Then what did you do?"

"I walked outside, to see if she had stepped out back for something, was maybe stargazing. I don't know. She wasn't inside, so I checked outside."

"Then what?"

"Then I checked her car."

"And then?"

"Then . . . what?"

"What you described takes about three minutes. According to the first responders, you didn't dial nine-one-one for another three hours. Who did you call, Mr. Jones? What did you do?"

"I called no one. I did nothing."

"For three hours?"

"I waited, Sergeant. I sat on the sofa and I waited for my world to right itself again. Then, when that didn't magically happen, I called the police."

"I don't believe you," D.D. said flatly.

"I know. But maybe that also proves my innocence. Wouldn't a guilty man manufacture a better alibi?"

She sighed heavily. "So what do you think happened to your wife, Mr. Jones?"

She heard him pause now, also considering.

He said finally, "Well, there is a registered sex offender who lives down the street."

| CHAPTER SEVEN |

On October 22, 1989, a boy named Jacob Wetterling was kidnapped by a masked man at gunpoint, and never seen again. Now, in 1989, I was only three years old, so you can trust me when I say I didn't do it. But thanks to the abduction of Jacob Wetterling nearly twenty years ago, my adult life was changed forever. Because Jacob's parents formed the Jacob Wetterling Institute, which got the Jacob Wetterling Crimes Against Children and Sexually Violent Offender Registration Act signed into law in 1994; basically, Jacob's parents helped create the very first sex offender database.

I know what you're thinking. I'm an animal, right? That's the conventional wisdom these days. Sex offenders are monsters. We should not only be denied all contact with children, but we should be ostracized, banned, and otherwise forced to live in squalid conditions under a Florida bridge. Look at what happened to Megan Kanka, kidnapped from her own bedroom by the sex offender living right next door. Or Jessica Lunsford, snatched from her unlocked home by the sex offender living with his sister in the trailer just across the street.

What can I tell you? According to my parole officer, there are nearly six hundred thousand registered sex offenders in the United

States. A few of them are bound to behave badly. And when they do, we all get punished, even a guy like me.

I get up, I go to work, I attend my meetings, I keep my nose clean. I'm a regular success story. Yet, here it is, five P.M., I'm wrapping up at work, but mostly I'm waiting to get arrested by the police.

By five-fifteen, when half a dozen squad cars still haven't careened down the streets with lights flashing, I give it up and begin the walk home. I retrace the day in my mind, trying to control my growing anxiety. After spotting the canvassing officers this morning, I did the sensible thing and went to work. After all, the police will find me soon enough, and when they do, how I've spent the hours since Mrs. Jones went missing is going to be a key topic of discussion. As it stands, I was half an hour late from lunch, given my talk with Mr. Jones. This anomaly will stand out, but nothing I can do about it now. I had to talk to the guy. After all, my only hope is that they arrest him instead of me.

Now, approaching my front steps, still not seeing signs of men in blue—or, more likely, SWAT team members in flak vests—I realize it's Thursday night and if I don't hustle, I'm gonna be late for my meeting. I can't afford another deviation from my schedule, so I hustle, bursting into my bedroom for the five-minute shower-and-change, then I'm back out the door, hailing a cab for the local mental health institute; it's not like eight registered sex offenders can hold their weekly support group meetings at the neighborhood library.

I arrive at the front doors at 5:59 P.M. This is important. The signed contract states you cannot be even one minute late for meetings, and our group leader is a stickler on this point. Mrs. Brenda Jane is a licensed clinical social worker with the looks of a six-foot blonde cover girl and the personality of a prison guard. She doesn't just run our meetings, she controls every facet of our life from what we do or do not drink to who we do or do not date. Half of us hate her. The other half are extremely grateful.

Meetings are approximately two hours long, once a week. One of the first things you learn as a registered sex offender is how to do a lot of paperwork. I have an entire three-ring binder filled with such documents as my signed "Sex Offender Program Contract," my customized "Safety Plan for Future Well-Being," as well as half a dozen

"Program Rules for Group Sessions," "Program Rules for Dating/ Relationships," and "Program Rules for Offenses Within the Family Unit." Tonight is no exception. Each of us begins by filling out the weekly status report.

Question one: *What feelings have you experienced this week?*

My first thought is guilt. My second thought is that I can't write that down. There is no confidentiality when it comes to statements made in support group. Yet one more piece of paper we all had to read and sign. Whatever I say tonight, or any night, can be used against me in a court of law. Adding to the daily paradox that is any sex offender's life. On the one hand, I need to work on improving my skills in the honesty department. On the other hand, I can be punished for doing so at any time.

I write down the second answer that comes to me: *fear.* Police can't deny me that, can they? A woman has gone missing. I'm the registered sex offender living on her block. Damn right I'm afraid.

Question two: *What five interventions did you use this week to avoid unhealthy situations?*

This question is easy. First day in group, you receive a list of approximately one hundred and forty "interventions" or ideas on how to break the abuse cycle. Most of us laugh at the list first time through. One hundred and forty ways not to re-offend? Including such winners as call the police, take a cold shower, or my personal favorite, jump in the ocean in the middle of winter.

I go with the usual: Wasn't alone with children, stayed out of bars, didn't drive aimlessly, didn't place high expectations on myself, and snapped a rubber band.

Sometimes I include "avoided self-pity" as one of my five, but even I know I didn't achieve that this week. The "didn't place high expectations" makes a nice substitute. I haven't had expectations in years.

Question three: *What five interventions did you use this week to promote a healthy lifestyle?*

Another rote answer: Worked full time, exercised, avoided drugs and alcohol, got plenty of rest, and stayed on an even keel. Well, maybe I didn't stay on an even keel today, per se, but that is only one day out of seven, and the form is technically a weekly status report.

Question four: *Describe all inappropriate or uncaring urges, fantasies, or sexual thoughts you had this week.*

I write: *I fantasized about having sex with a bound-and-gagged adult female.*

Question five: *Explain why you think each fantasy occurred.*

I write: *Because I'm a twenty-three-year-old celibate male who is horny as hell.*

I think about it, then erase "horny as hell" and replace it with "in his sexual prime." Mrs. Brenda Jane, the group leader, has rules about proper language for the meetings. Nobody in our group has cocks, pricks, or dicks. We have penises. Period.

For question six, I get to describe my emotional state before masturbation, during masturbation, and after masturbation. Most guys describe feeling angry or anxious. So much pressure out there and it builds and builds and builds until they have to do something about it. Some guys report crying afterward. Feeling guilty, ashamed, intensely alone, all for whacking their willy.

I don't have anything like that to describe. I'm an auto mechanic and my masturbation these days has that same clinical feel. I'm not blowing off steam; I'm simply making sure all the parts remain in proper working order.

Question seven: *What mutual sexual activity did you experience this week?*

I have nothing to report.

Question eight: *What age-appropriate relationships (nonsexual) have you had or attempted this week?*

I have nothing to report.

Question nine: *For all child contact, please list child's name and age, child's relationship to you, kind of contact, and name of chaperone present.*

I have nothing to report.

And so it goes. Another weekly report, another support group meeting.

You know what we really do in these meetings? We rationalize. The father who slept with one daughter pretends he's better than the priest who slept with fifteen altar boys. The guy who fondled pretends he's better than the guy who penetrated. The predators who entice their victims with promises of candy, affection, or extra privileges argue they are better than the monsters who resort to violence, and the monsters who resort to violence argue they inflict less damage than the enticers who make their victims feel like they are an equal party to the crime. The state has lumped us all together, and like any organized group of people, we are desperate to differentiate.

You know why these meetings work? Because no one can spot a liar like another liar. And face it, in this room, we're all pros.

We spend the first thirty minutes of the meeting running through the weekly status reports, then, for the first time in months, I finally have something to say.

"I think I'm going to be arrested."

That halts conversation. Mrs. Brenda Jane clears her throat, adjusts her clipboard on her lap. "Aidan, it sounds like you have something to discuss."

"Yeah. A woman has gone missing on my street. I figure if they don't find her soon, they're gonna blame me." The words come out angry. I'm a little surprised by that. Up until now, I have considered myself resigned to my fate. But maybe I do have some expectations after all. I find myself snapping the rubber band on my wrist, a sure sign of agitation. I force myself to stop.

"You kill her?" Wendell asks. Wendell is an enormously fat white guy with neatly trimmed black facial hair. He's well educated, quite, wealthy, and has a voice that comes straight from a helium balloon. Wendell is also the reigning master of the rationalization game. He's just a poor, picked-on exhibitionist, all show, no touch. For him to be grouped with the likes of us proves just how inhumane the criminal justice system really is.

I don't know if Wendell is all show and no touch. In theory, as part of the intake process for the sex offender treatment program, he supplied a full autobiography of all crimes he ever committed, then was polygraphed against this history, at a cost of $150. (Which we pay ourselves, I might add, and must keep paying until we pass the polygraph test.)

Personally, I think Wendell is a freaking psychopath. Poor,

picked-on exhibitionist, my ass. Wendell always targeted a specific victim group. For example, he liked to visit old folks' homes and flash three hundred pounds of white ass before the bedridden patients who barely had the strength to shield their eyes. Then he'd motor over to the teen health clinic, where he could wag his dingdong in front of the overwhelmed fourteen-year-old who'd just learned she was eight weeks pregnant. Mostly, however, he liked to operate outside rape crisis clinics, where he could spring a massive mountain of flesh upon already traumatized women.

His final victim went home and hanged herself. But as Wendell will tell you, he's not as bad as the rest of us.

"I didn't touch her," I answer now, ignoring Wendell's knowing grin. "I didn't even know her. But it doesn't matter. The police will check the database and my name will come up. They'll arrest me just on principle, and it's not like I can make bail. They get me, I'm done." I'm snapping the band again. I can see Mrs. Brenda Jane watching me, and once again force myself to stop.

I can already tell what she's thinking: *And how does this make you feel, Aidan Brewster?*

Trapped, I want to scream. *Very, very trapped.*

"A woman disappeared? In Southie? When did this happen?" Another group member, Gary Provost, speaks up. Gary is a thirty-seven-year-old alcoholic investment manager, who was caught inappropriately touching his friend's eleven-year-old daughter. His wife left him, taking with her their two sons. His extended family is still not speaking to him. Yet of all of us, he probably has the most hope. For one thing, he still looks like a respected professional, versus a convicted pervert. For another, he seems genuinely remorseful and very dedicated to his recently achieved sobriety. Gary's a serious one. Quiet but intelligent. Of everyone in the room, I almost like him.

"The woman disappeared last night."

"I haven't heard anything on the news."

"Dunno." I shrug.

"How old is she?" Wendell asks, cutting to the heart of the matter.

I shrug again. "She's a mom, so mid-twenties, something like that."

"That'll cut you some slack," Jim offers, "that she's an adult and all. Plus, you don't have a history of violence."

Jim smiles as he says this. Jim is the only Level III sex offender in our group, meaning of all of us, he's the one the state fears the most. An exhibitionist such as Wendell might have the highest rate of recidivism, but a hard-core pedophile such as Jim is the true monster under the bed. By Jim's own admission, he's attracted solely to eight-year-old boys and has probably had inappropriate relationships with thirty-five kids in a span of nearly forty years. He started when he was a fourteen-year-old babysitter. Now, at the age of fifty-five, his own flagging testosterone is finally slowing him down. Plus, the docs got him on a heavy regimen of antidepressants, the side effects of which repress the libido.

As we get to discuss in our weekly meetings, however, it's very difficult to change sexuality. You can try to teach someone to desire adults, but it's difficult to "remove" an object from someone's sexual orientation, or, in other words, teach that same person not to desire kids.

Jim has a tendency to dress in Mister Rogers sweaters and suck on hard butterscotches. From that alone, I'm guessing he still fantasizes mostly about prepubescent boys.

"I don't know if that will matter," I say now. "A registered offender is a registered offender. I think they'll arrest first, ask questions later."

"No," Gary the investment manager interjects. "They'll visit your parole officer first. That's how it works."

My parole officer. I blink in surprise. I have totally forgotten about her. I've been on parole two years now, and while I am required to check in each month, my own behavior has been so constant I've stopped noticing the meetings. Just another bout of paperwork and dutifully signed forms. Guy like me, the whole thing is over and done in about eight minutes. I copy my pay stubs, hand over a letter from my treatment counselor, prove I've paid my weekly fees for counseling, etc., and we're good to go for another thirty days.

"What d'you think your PO will say?" Wendell asks now, eyes narrowing.

"Not much to report."

"You went to work today?" Mrs. Brenda Jane inquires.

"Yes."

"No drinking, no drugs, no Internet?"

"I work. I walk. I'm keeping my nose clean."

"Then you should be fine. Of course, you have the right to a lawyer, so if you start to feel uncomfortable, you should ask for one."

"I think the husband did it," I hear myself say. No good reason. Just that whole rationalization thing again. *See, I'm not the monster. He is.*

My group goes to bat for me, nodding their heads. "Yep, yep," several reply. "Ain't it always the husband?"

Wendell still has that smirk on his face. "It's not like she's fourteen—" he starts.

"Wendell," Mrs. Brenda Jane interrupts.

He feigns innocence. "I'm just saying it's not like she's a beautiful jail-bait blonde."

"Mr. Harrington—"

Wendell puts up a meaty hand, finally acknowledging defeat. But then, at the last minute, he turns back to me and finally has something useful to say.

"Hey, kid, you're still working at the neighborhood chop shop, right? Hope for your sake the missing woman didn't get her car serviced there."

In that instant, I can picture Sandra Jones perfectly, standing in front of the industrial gray counter, long blonde hair tucked behind her ears, smiling as she hands over her keys to Vito: "Sure, we can pick it up at five...."

I realize for the second time in my life that I will not be going home again.

| CHAPTER EIGHT |

What makes a family?

It is a question I have pondered most of my life. I grew up in the typical Southern clan. I had a stay-at-home mom, famous for her meticulously groomed appearance and award-winning rose garden. I had the highly respected father who'd founded his own law firm and worked hard to provide for his two "lovely ladies." I had two dozen cousins, a passel of aunts and uncles. Enough relatives that the annual family reunions, hosted at my parents' sprawling home with its acres of green lawn and its wraparound front porch, were less a summer barbecue, and more a three-ring circus.

I spent the first fifteen years of my life smiling obediently as fat aunts pinched my cheeks and told me how much I resembled my mother. I turned in my homework on time so teachers could pat my head and tell me how I made my father proud. I went to church, I babysat my neighbors' children, I worked after school at the local store, and I smiled and smiled and smiled until my cheeks hurt.

Then I went home, collected the empty gin bottles off the hardwood floors, and pretended I didn't hear my mama's drunken taunt from down the hall, "I know something you don't know. I know something you don't know. ..."

When I was two years old, my mama made me eat a lightbulb so she could take me to the doctor and tell him what a naughty girl I was. When I was four, she made me put my thumb in a doorjamb and hold it there while she slammed the door shut, so she could show the doctor how reckless I was. When I was six, she fed me bleach so the doctors could understand just how terrible it was to be my mother.

My mama hurt me, time and time again, and no one ever stopped her. Did that make us family?

My father suspected, but never asked, even as his drunken wife chased him around the house with knives. Did that make us family?

I knew my mama was actively hurting me and hoping to hurt my father, but I never told. Did that make us family?

My father loved her. Even at a young age, I got that. No matter what Mama did, Papa stood beside her. That was marriage, he told me. And she wasn't always like this, he would add. As if once my mama had been sane, and having been sane once, maybe she could be sane again.

So we would go about our routine, starting each evening with my mother laying out a properly prepared dinner, and ending each meal with her hurling fried chicken, or heaven help us, a leaded crystal glass, at one or both of our heads. Eventually, my father would lead her back to the bedroom, tucking her in with another gin-laced sweet tea.

"You know how she is," he'd tell me quietly, half excuse, half apology. We would spend the rest of the night reading together in the front parlor, both of us pretending not to hear Mama's drunken warble floating down the hall: "I know something you don't know. I know something you don't know...."

When my mother died, I stopped asking so many questions. I thought the war was finally over. My father and I were free. Now came the happily ever after.

One week after the funeral, I tore up my mother's prized rosebushes. I ran them through the wood chipper, and my father cried harder over those damn flowers than he'd ever cried over me.

I started to understand a few things then, about the true nature of families.

Looking back now, I think it was inevitable that I wound up pregnant, married to a stranger, and living in a state where everyone dropped their R's. I had never been alone one single day in my life. So of course, the instant I was on my own, I immediately re-created the one thing I knew: a family.

Going into labor scared the bejesus out of me. Nine months later, I still wasn't ready. The ink was barely dry on my marriage certificate. We were still settling into our new home, a teeny tiny little bungalow that would've fit inside my parents' front parlor. I couldn't be a mom yet. I hadn't set up the crib. I hadn't even finished reading the parenting book.

I didn't know what I was doing. I was not qualified for this.

I remember thinking, struggling my way to the car, that I could smell my mother's prized roses. I threw up in the grass. Jason patted me on the back, and in his calm, controlled voice, told me I was doing just fine.

He loaded up my hospital bag, then helped me into the passenger's seat.

"Breathe," he said over and over again. "Breathe, Sandy. Just breathe."

At the hospital, my courteous new husband held the bucket while I vomited. He supported my weight as I moaned and panted in the birthing shower. He lent me his arm, which I bloodied with my fingernails as I fought to push the world's biggest bowling ball out of my uterus.

The nurses watched him with open admiration and I remember thinking vividly that my mama was right—the world was filled with bitches and I would kill them all. If only I could stand up. If only I could get the pain to stop.

And then . . . success.

My daughter, Clarissa Jane Jones, slid into the world, announcing her arrival with a throaty cry of protest. I remember the hot, sticky feel of her wrinkled little body being plopped down upon my chest. I remember the sensation of her little button mouth, rooting, rooting, rooting, until at last she latched onto my breast. I remember the indescribable feeling of my body feeding hers, while the tears streamed down my face.

I caught Jason watching us. He stood apart, his hands in his pockets, his face as impossible to read as ever. And it hit me then:

I had married my husband to escape from my father. Did that make us family?

My husband had married me because he wanted my child. Did that make us family?

Clarissa became our daughter because she was born into this mess. Did that make us family?

Maybe you simply have to start somewhere.

I held out my hand. Jason crossed to me. And slowly, very slowly, he reached out a finger and brushed Clarissa's cheek.

"I will keep you safe," he murmured. "I promise nothing bad will ever happen to you. I promise, I promise, I promise."

Then he was clutching my hand and I could feel the true force of his emotions, the dark tide of all the things he would never tell me, but that I understood, one survivor to another, lurked beneath the surface.

He kissed me. He kissed me with Clarissa nestled between us, a hard kiss, a powerful kiss.

"I will always keep you safe," he whispered again, his cheek against my cheek, his tears mingling with my tears. "I promise you, Sandy. I will never hurt you."

And I believed him.

At 5:59, as Aidan Brewster was checking in for his weekly support group meeting, Jason Jones was putting in a movie for his daughter, and beginning to panic.

He'd called in sick to work. Didn't know what else to do. Night was falling. Still no word from Sandy. Still no sign of the police. Ree had woken from her nap in the same quiet mood as before. They had played Candy Land and Chutes and Ladders and Go Fish.

Then they had sat at her teeny art table, him with his chin on his knees, and colored oversized pictures of Cinderella from Ree's favorite coloring book. Mr. Smith did not magically appear on the front stoop and Ree stopped asking about either her cat or her mom. Instead, she regarded Jason with serious brown eyes that were beginning to haunt him.

After dinner—meatballs, angel hair pasta, and sliced cucumbers— he put in a movie. Ree had perked up in anticipation of the rare treat, and was now seated on the green love seat, holding Lil' Bunny. Jason claimed he needed to do laundry and beat a hasty retreat to the basement.

There, he started pacing, and once he started, he couldn't stop.

When he had first come home and realized Sandra was not in the house, he had been confused, perhaps even anxious. He'd gone through the normal steps: checked the basement, checked the attic, checked the old shed out back. Then he'd called her cell, only to hear it ring in her purse. That had led him to rifling the contents halfheartedly, looking through her little spiral notebook to see if she'd magically recorded a middle-of-the-night meeting. When at two-thirty A.M. he confirmed his wife hadn't planned to go missing, he'd walked around the neighborhood, calling her name in a low whisper, much like how one might call a cat.

She wasn't in her car. She wasn't in his car. And she still wasn't at home.

He'd sat down on the love seat to consider the matter.

The house had been locked when he'd come home, including the doorknob and two dead bolts. That had implied Sandy had done her usual bedtime routine. He'd checked the kitchen counter and discovered the graded papers, meaning Sandy had done her usual post-Ree routine.

So where had the evening gone wrong?

His wife was not perfect. Jason knew that as well as anyone. Sandy was young, she'd led a wild and reckless youth. Now, at the relatively tender age of nearly twenty-three, she was trying to raise a toddler while adjusting to a new job and living in an unfamiliar state. She'd been more distant since the school year began, first overly quiet, then since December, almost overly friendly, in a forced sort of way. He'd started thinking about going away for February vacation precisely because her mood had grown so tangled, so...different.

He was sure she got homesick, especially in the winter, though she never said. He was sure there were times she wished she could go out, feel at least a little bit young, though she never said.

He himself had wondered about how long she would remain married to him, though again, she never said.

He missed her now. That thought pained him. He had grown accustomed to coming home and finding her curled up in their bed, her sleeping position an uncanny mimic of their daughter's. He liked her Southern drawl, and her addiction to Dr Pepper, and the way she smiled with one dimple appearing in her left cheek.

When she was quiet, there was a softness to her that soothed him. When she was giggling with Ree, there was a spark to her that electrified him.

He liked watching her read to their daughter. He liked listening to her hum as she puttered in the kitchen. He liked the way her hair fell around her face in a curly gold curtain, and how when she caught him watching her, it made her blush.

He didn't know if she loved him. He had never figured that out. But for a while she had needed him, and for him, that had been enough.

She's left me; that had been his first thought at three in the morning as he sat in the empty shadows of the family room. He had tried to make amends in February, and it had been a disaster. So Sandy had finally left him.

But then, half a beat later, he dismissed that conclusion: While Sandy may have been ambivalent about marriage, she was not ambivalent about Ree. Meaning if Sandy had left the house willingly, she would've taken Ree, and at the very least, grabbed her own purse. The absence of such steps led to a different conclusion: Sandy had not left willingly. Something bad had happened, here, inside Jason's own home, while his daughter had slept upstairs. And he had no idea what.

Jason was a reserved man. He acknowledged that. He preferred logic to emotion, fact to supposition. It was one of the reasons he made a good reporter. He was excellent at sifting through vast pools of data and coming up with the perfect nugget of information that brought everything together. He did not get bogged down with outrage or shock or grief. He did not suffer any preconceived notions about Boston's citizens or humanity in general.

Jason believed at all times that the worst could happen. That was a fact of life. And so, he armed himself with many other facts, perhaps believing, rather foolishly, that if he knew enough, this time he could be secure. His family would not suffer. His daughter would grow up safe and sound.

Except here he was, confronted by several great big unknowns, and he could feel his control already beginning to unravel.

The police had been gone for nearly six hours now, just the lone officer sitting in the car outside the house, switched out once, around five o'clock. Jason had thought having the police in his home all morning had been long and painful. He now realized their absence was far worse. What were the detectives doing? What was Sergeant D. D. Warren thinking? Had she taken the bait regarding his sex offender neighbor, or was he still considered the prize catch?

Did they have a warrant yet for the computer? Could they kick him out of the house, force him down to the station? Exactly what kind of evidence did they need?

Worse yet, if they arrested him, what would happen to Ree?

Jason walked around the coffee table again and again, hard tight circles that made him dizzy and still he couldn't stop. He didn't have local family, didn't have close friends. Would the police contact Sandy's father, ship Ree to Georgia, or invite Max up here?

And if Max came up here, exactly how much might Max say or do?

Jason needed a strategy, some kind of contingency plan.

Because the longer Sandy remained missing, the worse this was going to get. The police would keep digging, asking harder questions. And inevitably, the word would leak out, the media would descend. Jason's own peers would turn on him like cannibals, beaming his image all over the free world. Jason Jones, husband of the missing woman and person of interest in an ongoing investigation.

Sooner or later, someone was going to recognize that image. Someone was going to start to connect dots.

Especially if the police got their hands on his computer.

Jason careened around the table too fast, catching his knee on the corner of the washing machine. The pain lanced up his thigh and finally forced him to stop. For an instant, the world spun, so he clung to the top of the washer, breathless with pain.

When he could finally focus again, the first thing he noticed was the spider, the tiny little brown garden spider hanging right in front of him by a thread.

Jason jumped back, clipping the edge of the beat-up table with his shin and nearly yelping from the pain. But that was okay. He could take the pain. He didn't mind the pain, just so long as he didn't see that spider again.

And for a moment, it was too much. For a moment, one tiny little cellar spider had him spinning back to a place where it was always dark except for the eyes that glowed from the dozens of terrariums edging the room. A place where screams started in the basement and worked their way up through the walls. A place that smelled routinely of death and decay and no amount of ammonia was ever going to make a difference.

A place little boys and big girls went to die.

Jason placed a fist in his mouth. He bit his own knuckle until he tasted blood and he used that pain to ground himself again.

"I will not lose control," he murmured. "I will not lose control, I will not lose control, I will not lose control."

The phone rang upstairs. He gratefully left the basement and went to answer it.

The caller was Phil Stewart, the principal from Sandy's school, and he sounded uncharacteristically flummoxed.

"Is Sandra there?" Phil started.

"She's not available," Jason said automatically. "May I take a message?"

There was a long pause. "Jason?"

"Yes."

"Is she home? I mean, have the police located her yet?"

So the police had interviewed people where Sandra worked. Of course they had. That was a logical next step. After checking here, they might as well check there. Of course. Jason needed something intelligent to say. A statement of fact, a party line that summed up the current state of affairs without delving into personal territory.

He couldn't think of a single damn word.

"Jason?"

Jason cleared his throat, glanced at the clock. It was 7:05 P.M., meaning Sandy had now been gone for what, eighteen, twenty hours? Day one nearly done, day two nearly beginning. "Umm... she's...she's...she's not home, Phil."

"She's still missing," the principal stated.

"Yes."

"Do you have any ideas? Do the police have a lead? What's going on, Jason?"

"I went to work last night," Jason said simply. "When I came home, she was gone."

"Oh my God," Phil expelled as a long sigh. "Do you have any idea what happened?"

"No."

"Do you think she's coming home? I mean, maybe she just needed to take a break or something." This was delving into personal territory, and Jason could practically hear Phil's blush over the phone lines.

"Maybe," Jason said quietly.

"Well." Phil seemed to pull himself together. "Sounds like I should arrange a sub for tomorrow."

"I would think so."

"Will the search begin in the morning? I imagine much of the staff would like to assist. Probably some parents of the students, as well. Of course you'll need help distributing flyers, canvassing neighborhoods, that sort of thing. Who will be leading the charge?"

Jason faltered again, feeling the edge of panic. He caught it this time, stiffened his backbone, forced himself to sound firm. "I will get that information to you."

"We'll need to think of what to tell the children," Phil stated, "preferably before they catch it on the news. Perhaps a public statement for the parents, as well. Nothing like this has happened around here before. We need to start preparing the kids."

"I will get that information to you," Jason repeated.

"How is Clarissa holding up?" Phil asked abruptly.

"About as well as can be expected."

"If you need any help on that front, just let us know. I'm sure some of the teachers would be happy to assist. These things can all be managed, of course. All it takes is a plan."

"Absolutely," Jason assured him. "All it takes is a plan."

| CHAPTER NINE |

At 5:59 P.M. Sergeant D.D. Warren was a happy camper. She had a warrant to search Jason Jones's truck. She had an appointment with a registered sex offender's parole officer. And better yet, it was trash night in the neighborhood.

She drove around South Boston with Detective Miller, getting the lay of the land while they plotted next steps.

"According to Detective Rober," Miller was reporting, "Jones kept a low profile for the afternoon. No guests, no errands, no activities. He seems to be hanging out at home with his daughter, doing his thing."

"Has he been out to the truck?" D.D. wanted to know.

"Nope, hasn't even cracked open the front door."

"Huh," D.D. said. "Working on the computer? Your guy should be able to see him sitting there in the kitchen window."

"I asked that question, and the answer is uncertain. Afternoon sun made the view into the kitchen window unclear. But in the officer's professional assessment, Jones spent most of the day entertaining his kid."

"Interesting," D.D. said, and meant it. What a spouse did after a loved one went missing was always a source of fodder for the inquisitive detective. Did the spouse go about business as usual? Suddenly invite over a new female friend for "comfort"? Or run around purchasing accelerants and/or unusual power tools?

In Jason's case, his behavior seemed to be mostly defined by what he didn't do. No relatives or friends coming over to help him cope, maybe assist with childcare. No trips to the local office supply store to blow up photos of his missing wife. No quick visits to his neighbor's house for standard inquiries: *Hey, have you happened to see my wife? Or maybe hear anything unusual last night? Oh, and by the way, catch any sign of an orange cat?*

Jason Jones's wife disappeared and he did nothing at all.

It's almost as if he didn't expect her to be found. D.D. found that fascinating.

"Okay," she said now, "given that Jason is holding tight, I think our first stop should be with Aidan Brewster's PO. We got Suspicious Husband under our thumb. Now it's time to learn more about Felonious Neighbor."

"Works for me," Detective Miller said. "You know, tomorrow morning happens to be trash day for the neighborhood." He nodded his head toward the collection of trash cans starting to proliferate on the curb. Trash in a house was private property and required a warrant. Trash on the curb, on the other hand... "Say two or three A.M., I have an officer swing by and pick up Jones's garbage? Give us something to sort through in the morning."

"Ah, Detective, you read my mind."

"I try," he said modestly.

D.D. winked at him, and they swung back into the city.

Colleen Pickler agreed to meet with them in the nondescript space that passed for her office. The floor was light gray linoleum, the walls were covered in battleship gray paint, and her filing cabinets sported a dull gray finish. In contrast, Colleen was a six-foot athletically built Amazon, sporting a head of shocking red hair and wearing a deep red blazer over a kaleidoscope T-shirt of oranges, yellows, and reds. When she first stood up from her desk, it looked like a torch had suddenly been lit in the middle of a fog bank.

She crossed the room in three easy strides, shook their hands vigorously, then gestured them into the two low-slung blue chairs across from the desk.

"Forgive the office," she announced cheerfully. "I work mostly with sex offenders, and the state seems to feel that any color other than gray might overstimulate them. Clearly," she gestured to her top, "I disagree."

"You work mostly with sex offenders?" D.D. asked in surprise.

"Sure. Nicest group of parolees there is. The heroin pushers and petty burglars bolt first time they smell fresh air. Can't track 'em down, can't get 'em to complete a single piece of paperwork, can't get 'em to make a meeting. The average sex offender, on the other hand, is eager to please."

Miller was staring up at Pickler as if he were having a religious experience. "Really?" he said, stroking his thin brown mustache, checking the motion, then smoothing it again.

"Sure. Most of these guys are scared out of their minds. Prison was the worst thing that ever happened to them and they're desperate not to go back. They're very compliant, even anxious for approval. Hell, the really hard-core pedophiles will check in almost daily. I'm the only adult relationship they have, and they want to make sure I'm happy."

D.D. arched her brows and took a seat. "So they're just a bunch of regular Joes."

Pickler shrugged. "As much as anyone is. 'Course, you wouldn't be here if you didn't think someone was behaving badly. Who is it?"

D.D. checked her notes. "Brewster. Aidan Brewster."

"Aidan Brewster?" Pickler parroted. "No way!"

"Yes way."

Pickler's turn to arch a brow. But then she turned to the first gray metal filing cabinet and got busy. "B . . . B . . . Brewster. Aidan. Here we go. But I can tell you now, he's a good kid."

"For a registered sex offender," D.D. filled in dryly.

"Ah please. Now see, this is where the system is its own worst enemy. First, the system has managed to vilify an entire class of perpetrators. Second, the system has created a class of perpetrators too big for its own good. On the one hand, you rape thirty kids, you're a registered sex offender. On the other hand, a nineteen-year-old has consensual sex with a fourteen-year-old, and he's also a registered sex offender. It's like saying a serial killer is the same as the guy who gave his wife a black eye. Sure, they're both pieces of garbage, but they're not the *same* pieces of garbage."

"So what kind of sex offender is Aidan Brewster?" D.D. asked.

"The nineteen-year-old who had consensual sex with his younger stepsister's fourteen-year-old friend."

"He's on probation for that?"

"He served two years in jail for that. If she'd been a year younger, he would've gotten twenty. That'll teach a boy to keep his pants zipped."

"Fourteen is too young to give consent," Miller spoke up, having finally taken a seat. "Nineteen-year-old boy should know better."

Pickler didn't argue. "A lesson that Brewster will get to spend the rest of his life learning. You know, being a sex offender is a one-way ticket. Brewster could be clean the next thirty years; he'll still be a registered sex offender. Meaning every time he applies for a job, or looks for an apartment, or crosses state lines, he'll pop up in the system. That's a lot of baggage for a twenty-three-year-old."

"How's he taking it?" D.D. asked.

"As well as can be expected. He's entered a treatment program for sex offenders and is attending his weekly meetings. He has an apartment, a job, the semblance of a life."

"Apartment," D.D. stated.

Pickler rattled off an address that matched what D.D.'s team had already found in the system. "Does the landlord know?" D.D. inquired.

"I told her," Pickler reported. "It's not standard protocol for his level of offender, but I always think it's better to be safe than sorry. If the landlord found out later and booted Aidan unexpectedly, that could create stress and strain. Perhaps set him adrift. As Aidan's PO, I feel my job is to help him avoid unnecessary turmoil."

"How'd the landlord take it?"

"She needed to hear the whole story, and wanted my number on speed dial. Then she seemed to be okay with it. You'd be surprised how many people are. They just want to know up front."

"What about the neighbors?" D.D. pressed.

"Didn't notify the neighbors or the local PDs," Pickler supplied briskly. "Brewster shows up in SORD, of course, and I considered that adequate given his risk assessment and current level of programming."

"Meaning...?" Miller quizzed.

"Meaning Brewster's been doing just fine. He's lived in the same place and held the same job and attended the same weekly support group for nearly two years now. As parolees go, I'd take more just like Aidan Brewster."

"A regular success story," Miller quipped.

Pickler shrugged. "As much as one expects to see. Look, I've been at this eighteen years now. Sixty percent of my parolees will figure things out, maybe not the first time they're paroled, but eventually. The other forty percent..." She shrugged again. "Some will return to prison. Some will drink themselves to death. A few will commit suicide. Technically speaking, they don't re-offend, but I'm not sure I'd call it success. Then there are the Aidan Brewsters of the world. From a PO's perspective, he's a good guy, and that's the best I can tell you."

"Employment?" D.D. asked with a frown.

"Local garage. Vito's. Kid's really good with his hands. That's helped him mainstream more easily than some of these guys."

D.D. wrote that down. "You say he's been there two years?"

"Their top mechanic," Pickler specified. "His boss, Vito, can't say enough nice things about him. Employment-wise, kid's doing aces, which matters, given his current expenses."

"What expenses?" Miller wanted to know.

"Programming. Sex offenders are responsible for treatment costs. So in Brewster's case, that means he's forking over sixty bucks a week for his group counseling. Then there's the cost of his maintenance polygraph, two-fifty a pop every ten months, to make sure he's on track. If he had an ankle bracelet he'd have to pay for that, too, but he got lucky and hit the streets the year before the GPS became SOP. Plus, he's got Boston rent due, transportation costs, etc., etc. Not a cheap life for someone who's starting the game with limited employment options."

"You mean because he can't be around kids," D.D. said.

"Exactly. So even at a local garage, Brewster can only work on the cars, never at the front counter. After all, you never know when a woman might walk in with two-point-two kids."

"But he's a good employee."

"The best." Colleen shot them a grin. "Vito can work Brewster to the bone, and the kid'll never complain because they both know he can't just quit and get a job elsewhere. People think sex offenders can't find employment. In fact, there are certain 'savvy' employers out there who are more than happy to have them on board."

Miller was frowning now. "Poor little Aidan Brewster? Couldn't keep his hands off a fourteen-year-old, so now we should all feel sorry for him?"

"I'm not saying that," Colleen replied evenly. "The law is the law. I'm just saying that for most of the judicial system, you do your crime, you serve your time. Brewster went to jail, but he's still serving time, and will be for the rest of his life. Ironically enough, he would've been slightly better off had he killed the girl instead of sleeping with her. And as a member of the judicial system, I'm not comfortable with that analysis."

D.D., however, was already pondering something else. She turned to Miller. "Do you know where the Joneses got their cars serviced?"

He shook his head, jotted down a note. "I'll get on it."

"Who are the Joneses?" Colleen asked.

"Jason and Sandra Jones. They live on the same block as Aidan Brewster. Except sometime in the middle of last night, Sandra Jones disappeared."

"Ahh," Colleen said with a sigh. She sat back in her chair, hooked her hands behind her fireball hair. "You think Aidan had something to do with it?"

"Have to consider him."

"How old is Sandra Jones?"

"Twenty-three. A sixth grade teacher at the middle school. Has a four-year-old daughter."

"So, you're thinking Aidan abducted the mom from her house in the middle of the night, with the husband there?"

"Husband was at work—he's a local reporter."

Colleen narrowed her eyes. "You think Brewster was after the kid? Because Aidan's taken four or five polygraphs where he's had to volunteer his entire sexual history. Pedophilia has never come up."

"I don't know what I think," D.D. said. "Except, by all accounts, Sandra Jones is a very beautiful woman, and let's face it, twenty-three isn't that old. In fact, what does that make her? The same age as Brewster?"

Colleen nodded. "Same age."

"So, we have a beautiful young mom and a registered sex offender living just houses away. Any chance that Aidan is good-looking?"

"Sure. Shaggy blond hair. Blue eyes. Kind of surfer dude, but in a sweet sort of way."

Miller rolled his eyes.

D.D., however, kept spinning the theory out. "So Sandy's husband works most nights. Meaning she's alone a lot, isolated with the kid. Maybe some evening she's out in the yard with her daughter, and Aidan comes by, strikes up a conversation. Maybe the conversation leads to a relationship, which leads to..."

"She runs away with him?" Colleen suggested.

"Or they get into a fight. She finds out about his history, gets mad. After all, he's been around her kid, and according to all reports, Sandra Jones would do anything for her kid."

"So he kills her," Colleen said matter-of-factly.

"Like you said, these guys are desperate not to go back to prison."

"So Aidan Brewster seduces the lonely housewife down the street, then murders her to cover his tracks."

D.D.'s turn to shrug. "Stranger things have happened."

Colleen sighed. Picked up a pencil, bounced the eraser end on her desk half a dozen times. "All right. For the record, I think you're off base. Aidan already entered a high-risk relationship once before and he got nailed for it big-time. Given that, I think if he saw a woman like Sandra Jones out in her yard, he'd turn around and run the other way. No need to tempt fate, right? But the fact remains, Sandra Jones is missing and Aidan Brewster is the unlucky SOB that lives down the street. Protocol is protocol, so we'd better check him out."

"Glad to hear it."

Colleen bounced the pencil twice more. "Timeline?"

"Sooner versus later. We're trying to get as much done under the radar as we can. We figure by seven A.M. tomorrow, Sandra Jones will be missing more than twenty-four hours, meaning she'll be upgraded to an official missing persons case and the media..."

"Will swarm you like bees on honey."

"You got it."

Colleen grunted. "You said she's pretty, a young mom, a local teacher."

"Yep."

"You're screwed."

"Totally."

"All right. You convinced me. I'll pay Brewster a call this evening. Do a little walk-through of his home, ask about his recent activities. See if I can sniff out anything that warrants further investigation."

"We'd like to help you pay that call."

Colleen stopped bouncing the pencil. "No dice," she said firmly.

"You're not an agent of the court," D.D. countered. "You walk through his house and see blood, violence, disarray, you can't seize it as evidence."

"I can give you a call."

"Which will alert Brewster that we're coming."

"Then I'll sit on the sofa with him as we both wait. Look, I'm Aidan's PO, meaning I've spent two years building a relationship with him. I ask him questions, I have two years' worth of history pressuring him to answer. You ask him questions, and he'll shut down. You'll get nowhere."

D.D. thinned her lips, feeling stubborn and resigned all at once.

"He's a good kid," Colleen argued softly. "For what it's worth, I really doubt he did it."

"You been through this before?" Miller spoke up evenly. "Have one of your sex offenders re-offend?"

Colleen nodded. "Three times."

"You see it coming?"

Pickler sighed again. "No," she admitted quietly. "All three times... never had a clue. Guys were doing okay. They dealt with the pressure. Until one morning... they snapped. Then there was no going back."

| CHAPTER TEN |

I have always been fascinated by secrets. I grew up living a lie, so of course I see subterfuge everyplace I look. That child in my classroom who always wears long sleeves, even on warm days—totally being beaten by his stepdad. That elderly woman who works at the dry cleaner with her pinched face and bony shoulders—totally being abused by her big brute of a son who hangs out around back.

People lie. It's as instinctive as breathing. We lie because we can't help ourselves.

My husband lies. He looks me in the eye as he does it. As liars go, Jason is a class act.

I think I had known him six weeks before I figured out that beneath his restrained facade there lurked a deep ocean of bad voodoo. I noticed it in small things first. The way a drawl would sometimes creep into his voice, particularly at night when he was tired and not paying as much attention. Or the times he would say he got out of bed to watch TV, except when I turned on the TV in the morning, it would go straight to the Home & Garden channel, which I had watched last, and which Jason has no use for whatsoever.

Sometimes, I tried to tease the truth out of him: "Hey, you just said 'coke.' I thought only a true Southerner asked for a coke instead of a soda."

"Must be hanging out with you too much," he'd say, but I'd see a hint of wariness crease the corners of his eyes.

Or sometimes I tried to get straight to the point. "Tell me what happened to your family. Where are your parents, your siblings?"

He'd try to hedge. "Why does it matter? I have you now, and Clarissa. That's the only family that matters."

One night, when Ree was five months old, and sleeping well, I was feeling edgy and restless, the way a nineteen-year-old girl does when she's sitting across from a dark, handsome man and she's looking at his hands and thinking about how gently they can cradle a newborn baby. Then thinking, much more importantly, how they might feel on her naked breasts, I found myself approaching the matter much more directly.

"Truth or dare," I said.

He finally looked up from the paperback he was reading. "What?"

"Truth or dare. You know, like the game. Surely when you were a teenager you played Truth or Dare."

Jason stared at me, his dark eyes as fathomless as always. "I'm not a teenager."

"I am."

That seemed to finally get his attention. He closed the book, set it down. "What do you want, Sandra?"

"Truth or dare. Just pick. It's not so hard. Truth or dare." I sidled closer to him. I had bathed after putting Ree down for the night. Then I smoothed an orange-scented lotion all over my body. It was a subtle scent, light, clean, but I knew he caught it, because his nostrils flared, just a fraction, then he leaned away.

"Sandra..."

"Play with me, Jason. I'm your wife. It's not too much to ask."

He was going to do it. I could tell by the way he steeled his spine, squared his shoulders. He had been putting me off for months. Surely he realized at a certain point he'd have to acknowledge me somehow. It couldn't all be about Ree.

"Dare," he said at last.

"Kiss me," I ordered. "For one minute."

He hesitated. I thought he'd renege, and I braced myself for the rejection. But then he sighed, ever so softly. He leaned forward, puckered up, and touched his mouth to mine.

He was going to be chaste about it. I knew him well enough by then to anticipate. And I knew that if I tried to be aggressive or demanding, he would shut down. Jason never yelled. Jason never raised his hand in rage. He simply disappeared, someplace deep inside him where nothing I said or did seemed to reach him, until I could be standing right beside him, and I would still be alone.

My husband respected me. He treated me kindly. He showered me with compassion. He did his best to anticipate my every need.

Except when it came to sex. We had been together nearly a year now, and he had yet to lay a single hand on me. It was driving me crazy.

I didn't open my mouth. I didn't grab his shoulders, bury my fingers in his thick dark hair. I didn't do anything that I longed to do. Instead, I fisted my hands at my sides, and ever so slowly, I kissed him back.

He gave me gentleness, so I returned his sweetness, my breath whispering across his closed lips. He gave me compassion, so I showered it upon the corner of his mouth, the full expanse of his bottom lip. He gave me respect, so I never once pushed the boundaries he had set. But I daresay I gave him the best damn kiss two closed-mouth people had ever shared.

When the minute was up, he drew back. But he was breathing harder now, and I could see something lurking in his eyes. Something dark, intense. It made me want to leap onto his lap, flatten him into the sofa, and fuck his brains out.

Instead, I whispered, "Truth or dare. Your turn. Ask me. Truth or dare."

I could see the conflict. He wanted to say dare. He wanted me to touch him again. Or maybe take off my nice silky shirt. Or trail my hands across his hard chest.

"Truth," he said huskily.

"Ask."

"Why are you doing this?"

"Because I can't help myself."

"Sandy." He closed his eyes, and for a moment, I could feel his pain.

"Truth or dare," I demanded.

"Truth," he nearly groaned.

"What is the worst thing you've ever done?"

"What do you mean?"

"What is the worst thing you've ever done? Come on. Have you lied? Stolen? Seduced your best friend's baby sister? Killed anyone? Tell me, Jason. I want to know who you are. We're married, for God's sake. Surely you owe me that much."

He looked at me funny. "Sandra…"

"No. No whining, no negotiating. Just answer the question. Have you ever killed anyone?"

"Yes."

"What?" I asked, genuinely surprised.

"Yes, I've killed someone," Jason said. "But that's not the worst thing I've ever done."

Then my husband got off the sofa, took his paperback, and left me alone in the room.

Jason didn't think he'd fallen asleep, but he must have, because shortly after one A.M., a sound roused him from the love seat. He jerked upright, registering a distant banging. The noise seemed to be coming from outside the house. He stood, crossing to the front windows, where he parted the curtains one inch and peered out.

Two uniformed officers had taken the lids off his trash cans. They were now in the process of moving the white kitchen bags from the refuse containers to the trunk of their police cruiser.

Shit, he thought, and nearly opened the front door to yell at them to stop. Then caught himself.

Rookie mistake. He'd taken his trash out from long habit, and in doing so, had effectively turned it over to the police. He searched through his mind, trying to anticipate how much such a mistake might cost him. He couldn't think of anything, so he finally relaxed, shoulders coming down, expelling all his pent-up breath in one giant sigh.

All right. So the police had seized his garbage. Now what?

Sergeant D.D. Warren, and her sidekick, Detective Miller, had returned to the house shortly after eight-thirty P.M. to execute the search warrant on his truck. He'd met them at the door, skimmed the warrant as was his right, then dutifully handed over the keys.

Then he'd pointedly shut and locked the front door, spending the rest of the time tucked inside with Ree. Let them stew on that, he thought. He didn't give a rat's ass about his truck. He just needed something to keep them occupied so they didn't focus solely on his computer.

Speaking of which...He glanced at the clock. It was 1:52 A.M. Now or never, he decided, and headed quietly upstairs.

It pained him to wake Ree. She looked at him with bleary eyes, still groggy and disoriented from sleep, let alone the emotional toll of missing her mother and her cat. He had her sit up in bed, slipping her arms into her winter coat, producing boots for her bare feet. She didn't protest, just leaned her head against his shoulder as he carried her downstairs, her blankie and Lil' Bunny clutched in both hands.

He stopped by the door to grab a dark green duffel bag, tucking it over his shoulder. He positioned Ree and her blanket to shield the bag from prying eyes. Then he opened the door and carried both the bag and his daughter out to Sandy's Volvo station wagon.

He could feel the eyes of the patrolman upon his back. No doubt the officer was now picking up a notebook and writing urgent notes: *1:56 A.M., subject appears in front yard carrying sleeping child. 1:57 A.M., subject approaches wife's car...*

Jason latched Ree into her booster seat, sliding the duffel bag unobtrusively onto the floor by her feet. Then he closed the back passenger door and headed straight for the unmarked police car.

He tapped on the driver's-side window. The cop lowered the glass a notch. "I have to go to work," Jason stated briskly. "Wrap up a few things before I take time off. You want the address or are you gonna stay here?"

He saw the officer debate his options. Watch the subject or watch the house? What were the officer's orders?

"Late to be out with a child," the officer observed, obviously stalling for time.

"Got kids, Officer? This won't be the first time I've had to drag my daughter to the office. Good news is, she can sleep through anything."

Minute Jason said those words, he wished he could call them back. 'Course, it was too late, as he observed in the officer's responding smirk. "Good to know," the officer said, and proceeded to make a very long entry into his logbook.

Jason gave up, returning to the station wagon and firing it to life. As he drove down the street, he didn't see the officer pulling out behind him. But then, around six blocks later, a police cruiser suddenly nosed out from a side street. His next handler, he supposed, and gave a silent salute to Boston's finest.

The offices of the *Boston Daily* were like any other news media, which was to say it was a crazy, hectic bull pen of activity during the day, and still warranted a few dedicated souls even late at night. Stories were written, copy was edited, and pages were laid out even in the odd hours of the morning, perhaps even more so, because it was only after midnight that the place grew quiet enough for anyone to think.

Jason entered the building with a dozing child cradled against his chest, the duffel bag slung over his shoulder and now effectively covered by Ree's giant fleecy bear blanket. He looked like a man carrying a heavy load, but then, one glance at the fairly large four-year-old collapsed like dead weight in his arms, and no one thought to question it. He swiped his reporter's ID across the various door pads, and made his way into the inner sanctum.

Most of the reporters worked both at home and in the office, so guys like Jason shared space with more than one person, in a system called "hoteling." Basically, there were desks and computers everywhere. You found an available space and used it. Tonight was no exception.

Jason took refuge in a corner cubicle, kicking the dark green duffel bag under the desk, while sliding Ree onto the floor and making a little nest for her with her blankie and her bunny. She was awake now, staring at him somberly.

"It's okay," he whispered to her. "Daddy's just gotta do a little work, then we'll go home."

"Where's Mommy?" Ree asked. "I want Mommy."

"Go to sleep, honey. We'll be home shortly." Ree obediently closed her eyes, drifting back into slumber.

Jason watched her for a moment longer. The smudge of her dark lashes against her pale cheeks. The purple stain of exhaustion rimming her closed eyelids. She looked small to him. Delicate. An impossible burden that was also the most important purpose of his life.

He was not surprised by how well she was holding up. Kids did not externalize their bone-deep terrors. A kid could scream for ten minutes over a small bump received on the playground. The same child would clam up tight when confronted by an armed stranger. Kids understood instinctively that they were small and vulnerable. Thus, in crisis the majority of children simply shut down, focusing on becoming even smaller, because maybe if they disappeared completely, the bad man would leave them alone.

Or maybe, if a four-year-old girl slept enough, when she woke up, her mommy and her cat would have returned and life would magically be back to normal.

Jason turned his attention to the desk. The newsroom was quiet at this hour, the neighboring workspaces unoccupied. He decided this was as good as it was going to get, and slowly unzipped the dark green duffel bag to reveal the desktop computer from the kitchen table.

Technically speaking, Jason owned three computers: his laptop, which he used for work; the family desktop, which sat in the kitchen and was shared by all; and finally, an older desktop, once the primary family computer, but relegated to the basement last year when he'd upgraded to a newer Dell. Jason was not worried about his laptop. He used it solely for reporting, understanding the risks inherent in a portable computer that could be lost or stolen at any time. He was slightly more concerned about the old computer in the basement. True, he'd used an official Department of Defense program to overwrite the hard drive with meaningless strings of ones and zeros, but not even the DoD trusted such specs anymore. For the really classified stuff, they incinerated the hard drives, turning the internal workings to powder. He didn't have an incinerator handy, so he'd done the basics. Ninety-five percent of the time, that should get the job done.

Unfortunately, the family computer, the relatively new 500-gigabyte Dell desktop used by him in the early hours of the morning while Sandra slept, scared the crap out of him. He could not afford for the police to seize this computer; hence he had sicced them on his truck. Now, glancing at his watch, he estimated he had approximately three hours to run damage control.

He began by inserting a memory stick into the E drive. Then, he started moving files after files. Program files, Internet files, document files, jpeg files, pdf files. There were lots of them, more than could be transferred in three hours, so he was strategic in his focus.

While those files started to copy, he logged on to the Internet and did some basic research. He started with registered sex offender Aidan Brewster. Always good to know the neighbors, right? He found some basics and lots of jargon, such as "sealed files." But he was a reporter, not one who stalled out every time he hit a shut door. He jotted down some phone numbers, did a little more digging, and got some happy results.

First mission accomplished, he then opened up AOL and logged in as his wife. He had figured out her password years ago; she'd gone with LilBun1, the name of Ree's favorite plush toy. But if he hadn't cracked the code with good guesses, he would've used a computer forensic program such as AccessData's Forensic Toolkit or Technology Pathways' ProDiscover to do the same. These were the kinds of things he did. This was the kind of husband he was.

Had Sandy figured that out? Was that why she had left?

He didn't know, so he started scrolling through her e-mail, looking for clues regarding his wife's final hours.

Her account registered sixty-four e-mails, the majority of which offered penile implants or urgent requests to transfer funds from third world countries. According to Sandra's e-mail folder, she was either obsessed with male genitalia or about to become rich assisting some faraway colonel with a financial transfer.

He worked his way through the spam, then through the phishing, then finally hit six e-mails that seemed actually intended for his wife. One was from the preschool Ree attended reminding parents to save the date for an upcoming fundraiser. Another was from the school principal, reminding teachers of an upcoming workshop. The final four were replies from an original mass e-mail from one teacher asking other teachers if they'd be interested in forming a group to walk together after school.

Jason frowned at this. Last time he'd checked, several months ago, she'd had at least twenty-five personal e-mails, ranging from notes from students to information from various mom e-mail loops.

He checked his wife's old e-mail folder. All he found was the spam he'd just deleted. He tried the sent e-mail folder. Also empty. And then, with a growing feeling of dread, he began to search in earnest. Her address book: cleared. Favorite places: cleared. AOL buddies: cleared. Browser history of most recent Internet searches: cleared.

Holy crap, he thought, and for a moment, he couldn't breathe. He was the deer caught in the headlights, feeling the panic in him grow and grow until it threatened to spiral out of control.

Date and time, he thought frantically. Nail down date and time. It all boiled down to date and time.

He clicked back on her old e-mail folder, scrolling to the oldest dated spam with a hand that was starting to tremble again. Sixty-four clicks and there it was: Oldest e-mail sent had been delivered Tuesday at 4:42 in the afternoon, over twenty-four hours before Sandra had disappeared.

Jason sat back, hands clutched against his knotted stomach while he sought to make sense of this.

Someone had systematically purged Sandra's AOL account. If it had happened Wednesday night, the same night as her disappearance, one logical conclusion would be that whoever had taken Sandra had also cleared the account, possibly as a way of covering his tracks.

But the purging had come first, by nearly twenty-four hours. What did that imply?

Occam's razor, right? The simplest explanation is generally the correct explanation. Meaning Sandra herself had probably purged her account. Most likely because she had been doing something online she now felt a need to hide. An Internet flirtation? A genuine physical relationship? Something she didn't want him or anyone else to find.

That explanation was less ominous than the image of a shadowy man, first attacking Sandra, then sitting smugly at the kitchen table and covering his computer tracks while Ree presumably slept overhead.

And yet that explanation hurt him more. It implied premeditation. It implied that Sandra knew she was leaving, and had wanted to ensure that he wouldn't be able to find her.

Jason lifted a weary hand. He shielded his eyes, and for a moment, the flood of emotion that choked his throat surprised him.

He had not married Sandra for love. He was not a man who had that kind of expectation out of life. And yet, for a while … For a while, it had been very nice to feel like part of a family. It had been nice to feel normal.

He had screwed up in February. The hotel room, the dinner, the champagne … He never should've done what he'd done in February.

Jason cleared his throat, rubbed his eyes. He pushed his own exhaustion away, and gazing down at his sleeping child, forced himself back to the matters at hand.

Sandra was not as technologically gifted as he was. He assumed that if she had been the one to purge the account, she'd done it through purging the cache file, meaning the information was all still on the hard drive, just the directory identifying the location of each data point had been removed. And, by utilizing any number of simple forensic programs, he could restore most of the deleted information.

Time was the issue. It would take at least an hour to run such a program, and then hours more to comb through the re-created data until he found what he was looking for. He didn't have hours. Jason glanced at his watch. He had thirty minutes. *Crap.*

He rubbed his face again with tired hands, and took a deep breath. All right, time for plan B.

His memory stick had reached capacity. He disengaged it, returned to the system menu, and perused the contents menu. He had removed both too much and too little. He selected half a dozen more files to delete, glancing at his watch again and feeling the urgency.

Originally, he had hoped to capture what he could, then run an official purge program. Now, however, he couldn't bring himself to trash the hard drive, not when it might contain clues regarding Sandra's final hours. Which created an interesting dilemma. The computer potentially held the power both to find his wife and to put him in jail forever.

He thought about it. Then he knew what to do.

He would return the old family computer from the basement to the kitchen table, uploading it with all the current software programs from the new computer. He could transfer over basic files from his memory stick, enough garbage to give the old computer the appearance of an active one.

A good evidence tech would figure it out, eventually. That there were date gaps in the computer's memory. Perhaps even Sergeant D.D. and Detective Miller would catch the switch. He didn't think so, however. Most people noticed a person's monitor, and maybe a person's keyboard, but they didn't notice the computer itself, the functional tower that was generally propped under a desk or kitchen table. If anything, perhaps they'd noted that he owned a Dell, in which case his brand loyalty was about to be rewarded.

So the old computer would become his current computer, buying him some precious time.

Which left him with the issue of what to do with his current computer. Couldn't put it in his house, which was probably destined to be searched a few more times. Equally risky to stash it in his vehicle, for the same reason. Which left him one option. To leave the computer right here, set up just as it was, a computer on a desk, in a room full of computers on desks. He would even connect it to the network, making it a fully functional, completely indistinguishable *Boston Daily* computer. Hide in plain sight, as it were.

Even if the police thought to search the *Boston Daily* offices, he sincerely doubted they could obtain a warrant to seize computers from a major news outlet. Why, the breach in confidentiality alone... Besides, in the modern world of "hoteling," Jason didn't have an official work space. Meaning there wasn't a single computer or office space the police could definitively list in a warrant as being his. Technically speaking, all the computers were used by him, and no judge in this day and age was going to let the police carry away every single computer belonging to the *Boston Daily*. That just wasn't going to happen.

At least he hoped not.

Jason pushed away from the desk. He crumpled up the duffel bag and stuffed it in the back of a metal filing cabinet. Then he picked up his sleeping daughter and, very gently, carried her back out to the car.

Five forty-five A.M. Sun would be coming up soon, he thought. He wondered if Sandra could see it.

| CHAPTER ELEVEN |

I'm working on a letter. In order to graduate from my treatment program, I need to write a letter to the victim, in which I take responsibility for my actions and express my remorse. This letter is never sent; wouldn't be fair to the victim, we're told. Dredging up bad business and all that. But we have to write it.

So far, I have two words: *Dear Rachel.*

Rachel is an alias, of course—no confidentiality in group therapy, remember? So basically, after six weeks of work, I have two words, one of which is a lie.

Tonight, however, I think I can make some progress on my Dear Rachel letter. Tonight, I'm learning what it feels like to be a victim.

I wanted to run. Thought about it. Tried it out in my head. Couldn't see how it could be done. Running away involves some serious logistics in this post–9/11 world where Big Brother is always watching. Can't catch a plane or train without a license, and I don't have a car. What am I supposed to do, walk my way across Massachusetts state lines?

Truth is, I don't have the cash or the wheels for a hard-core disappearing act. I've been paying for polygraphs and support group, not to mention the hundred a week I send straight to Jerry. He calls it restitution. I call it insurance that he doesn't track me to South Boston and break every goddamn bone in my miserable body.

So the bank account is a little low on exit funds.

What can I do? After support group, I headed home.

Colleen knocked on my door just thirty minutes later.

"Can I come in?" my parole officer asks, very polite, very firm. Her red hair is spiked tonight, but it doesn't distract from the serious look on her face.

"Sure," I say, and hold the door wide open. Colleen has visited once before, in the very beginning when she was confirming my address. It's been two years now, but not much has changed. I'm not exactly big on interior decorating.

She walks down the cramped hallway to the back of the house, where my thrifty landlord, Mrs. Houlihan, has converted a sitting room and screened-in porch into a five-hundred-square-foot one-bedroom apartment. I pay eight hundred bucks a month for use of this magnificent space. In return, Mrs. H. can make the property tax payments on the home she's owned for fifty-odd years, and doesn't want to lose just because some yuppies finally discovered the neighborhood and sent property values sky high.

Truth is, I kind of like Mrs. H., even if she did hang lace over every damn window, as well as place crocheted doilies on all pieces of upholstered furniture (which she pins into place, as I know because I get pricked by the pins at least every other day). For starters, Mrs. H. knows I'm a registered sex offender, and she still lets me stay, even though her own kids yelled at her for it (I heard them from my apartment; it's not like the house is that big). For another, I catch her in my room all the time.

"Forgot something," she barks at me, playing to her age. Mrs. H. is eighty years old and built like a garden gnome. There is nothing fragile, absentminded, or remotely forgetful about her. She's checking up on me, of course, and we both know it. But we don't talk about it, and I like that, too.

Just for her, I half tuck my porn magazines underneath my mattress, where she's sure to find them. I figure it makes her feel better to know that her "young man" renter is catching up on adult titty magazines. Otherwise, she might worry about me, and I don't want that.

Maybe I could've used a mother growing up. Maybe that would've helped me. I don't know.

Now, I lead Colleen into my little slice of paradise. She peruses the tiny kitchenette, the sparse sitting area with a pink floral love seat graciously supplied by Mrs. H. Colleen spends about sixty seconds in the main room, then moves on to the bedroom. I watch her crinkle her nose as she enters the room, and it reminds me that it's been a while since I washed the sheets.

Well shit, I think. Can't do anything about that now. Fresh laundering of bedding will be interpreted as a sign of guilt for sure.

Colleen wanders back into the family room, takes a seat on the pink sofa. A doily scratches her behind the neck. She straightens for a minute, stares at the crocheted Kleenex, then shrugs and leans back.

"Whatch'ya been up to, Aidan?"

"Work, walking, support group." I shrug, remain standing. I can't help myself. I'm too antsy to sit. I snap the green rubber band on my wrist. Colleen watches me do it, but doesn't say anything.

"How's the job?"

"Can't complain."

"Got any new friends, new hobbies?"

"Nope."

"Catch any movies lately?"

"Nope."

"Check any books out at the library?"

"Nope."

She cocks her head to the side. "How about attending any neighborhood barbecues?"

"In March?"

She grins at me. "Sounds like your life is quieter than a church mouse's."

"Oh, it is," I assure her. "It really, really is."

She finally cuts to the chase, leaning forward, away from the doily, and planting her elbows on her knees. "I heard there was some excitement in the neighborhood."

"I saw the cops," I tell her. "Going door to door this morning."

"You talk to them, Aidan?"

I shake my head. "Had to get to work. Vito tans my hide if I'm late. 'Sides," I throw in defensively, "I don't know nothin' 'bout nothin'."

She smiles, and I can almost hear her thinking, *Oh, if only I had a nickel for every time I've heard that one.*

I start pacing, quick, agitated steps. "I'm writing a letter," I say abruptly, because she's staring at me with that knowing PO sort of way, and you just have to say something when an authority figure stares at you that way.

"Yeah?"

"To Rachel," I say. She won't know who Rachel is, since it's an alias and all, but that doesn't stop her from nodding understandingly. "Gotta put into words how it feels to be helpless. Been tough to do, you know. Nobody likes to feel helpless. But I think I'm getting pretty good at it now. Think I'm gonna get a lot of quality time to know just what helpless feels like."

"Talk to me, Aidan."

"I didn't do it! Okay? I didn't do it. But this woman is gone, and I live five houses away, and I'm in the friggin' sex offenders database, and that's just it. Game over. Got pervert, will make arrest. Not like anyone's gonna believe anything I say."

"Did you know the woman, Aidan?"

"Not really. Just saw her around and all. But they got a kid. Saw that, too. And I'm following the rules. Don't need no more trouble, not me. They have kids, I stay away."

"I understand she's very pretty."

"Got a kid," I say firmly, almost like a mantra, which hell, maybe it is.

"You're nice-looking." Colleen tilts her head as she says this, almost as if she's appraising me, but I'm not fooled. "Living a quiet life, not getting out much. I can imagine how frustrating that must be for you."

"Trust me, I whack off every day. Just ask my support counselor. She makes us tell her all about it."

Colleen doesn't flinch at my vulgarity. "What's her name?" she asks abruptly.

"Whose name?"

"The woman."

"Jones, I think. Something Jones."

She's watching me shrewdly, trying to figure out how much I know, or how much she can trick me into giving away. For example, will I confess that I met with the husband of the missing woman, even though the child was at home? I figure this is a detail I should keep to myself. Rule of thumb once you're a felon—volunteer nothing, make the law enforcement officer do all the work.

"I believe it's Sandra Jones," she muses at last. "She teaches over at the middle school. Husband works nights. Tough gig, that. Her working days, the hubby working nights. I imagine she might have been feeling frustrated, too."

I snap the elastic at my wrist. She hasn't asked a question, so I'll be damned if I answer.

"Kid's pretty cute."

I don't say a word.

"Precocious, I understand. Loves to ride her trike all over the neighborhood. Maybe you've seen her a time or two?"

"See child, cross street," I report. *Snap, snap, snap.*

"What were you doing last night, Aidan?"

"Already told you: nothin'."

"Got an alibi for the nothing you were doing?"

"Sure, call Jerry Seinfeld. I hang out with him every night, seven P.M."

"And after that?"

"Went to bed. Mechanics have an early start."

"You went to bed alone?"

"Believe I already answered that, too."

Now she arches a brow. "Really, Aidan, don't dazzle me with your charm. Keep up this attitude, police are gonna toss you behind bars for sure."

"I didn't do anything!"

"Then convince me of it. Talk to me. Tell me all about this nothing you've been doing, because you're right, Aidan—you're a registered sex offender living five houses from where a woman has gone missing, and so far you're looking pretty good for this."

I lick my lips. Snap my band. Lick my lips. Snap my band.

I want to tell her about the car, but I don't. Volunteering the car tidbit will bring the police to my house for sure. Better to wait, use the information as barter once they've hauled in my sorry ass for questioning and have me locked up in a holding cell. Better to talk when I can trade the information for freedom. Never give somethin' for nothin', another rule of thumb for the convicted felon.

"If I *had* done something," I say at last, "then I damn well woulda put together a better story, don't you think?"

"The lack of alibi is your alibi," Colleen states drolly.

"Yeah, something like that."

She rises off the sofa, and I have one second where I honestly feel relieved. I'm gonna survive after all.

Then she asks: "Can we walk outside?"

And I feel my good mood disappear just like that. "Why?"

"Nice night. I want to get some fresh air."

I can't think of a thing to say, so we walk outside, her, six feet high in some crazy platform boots, me, all hunched up in jeans and a white T-shirt. I've stopped snapping the rubber band at least. My wrist has gone numb and turned bright red. I look like a suicide victim. It's something to consider.

She walks around the house, to the back yard. I can see her, intently checking the grounds. Any bloody power tools lying around? Perhaps some fresh-turned earth?

I want to say *Fuck you.* Of course, I say nothing at all. I keep my head down. I don't want to look up. I don't want to give anything away.

Later, she will tell me she's doing this for my own good. She is looking out for me, trying to protect me. She only wants to help me.

And I can suddenly picture myself, sitting down on my stupid pink floral sofa, writing full force:

Dear Rachel:

I am sorry for what I did. Sorry for all the times I told you I only wanted to talk, when we both knew I just wanted to get you naked.
Sorry for all the times I got you in bed, then said I only wanted what was best for you.

I'm sorry I fucked you, then told you it was all your fault. You wanted it. You needed it. I did it for you.

And I'm sorry that I still think about you every single goddamn day.
How much I want you. How much I need you. How you did it just for me.

Then, just as I'm really on a roll, writing away in my head,
Colleen's voice suddenly cuts through the gloom.

"Hey, Aidan," she calls out. "Is that your cat?"

| CHAPTER TWELVE |

The meeting started at six A.M. sharp. They began with the board. They had Person of Interest A: Mr. Jason Jones, relation—spouse. They had Person of Interest B: Aidan Brewster, relation—registered sex offender living on same block. From there, they outlined means, motives, and opportunity.

Means was left blank, as they lacked information on what exactly had happened to Sandra Jones. Killed, kidnapped? Ran away? Never good to make assumptions at such an early stage in an investigation, so they moved on.

Motives. Jones stood to gain millions of dollars he might otherwise lose in divorce, plus custody of his daughter. Brewster was a known sexual predator, perhaps acting out long-festering impulses.

Opportunity. Jones had an alibi for the night and time in question, but the alibi was hardly airtight. Brewster—no alibi, but could they connect Brewster to Sandra Jones? At this time, they had no phone messages, e-mails, or text messages linking the two. But geography remained in their favor. Suspect and victim lived only five houses apart. A jury could reasonably assume that Brewster and the victim had known each other in some capacity. Plus, there was the matter of the garage where Brewster worked. Perhaps Sandra Jones had serviced her car there—they planned on asking first thing this morning.

They moved on to background. Jones was a freelance reporter and "devoted" father, who'd married a very young pregnant bride and transplanted her to South Boston from Atlanta, Georgia. He had millions of dollars in assets from sources unknown. He was deemed "uncooperative" by both Detective Miller and Sergeant Warren, which was not in his favor. He also appeared to have a fetish for bolt locks and steel doors.

Brewster, on the other hand, was a registered sex offender, having engaged in sexual relations with a fourteen-year-old. Worked the same job for the past two years, lived at the same address. His PO liked him and had called in at nine P.M. to report she'd found nothing suspicious at his apartment. So a plus in his favor.

Victim herself was not considered high-risk. A devoted mom and new schoolteacher, she had no history of drugs, alcohol, or sexual wantonness. Principal of the middle school described her as punctual, reliable, and conscientious. Husband claimed she'd never willingly leave her daughter. On the flip side, victim was young, living in a relatively strange city, and seemed to lack a support network of close friends and/or relatives. So they had early-twenties, socially isolated beautiful mom who spent most nights alone with her small child.

Crime scene: no sign of forced entry. No blood spatter or overt signs of violence. They had one broken lamp in the master bedroom, but no evidence it had been used as a weapon or destroyed as part of a larger struggle. They had a blue-and-green quilt that used to be on the master bed, but someone had stuffed it in the washing machine along with a purple nightshirt. They had the wife's purse, cell phone, car keys, and vehicle all accounted for at the scene. No missing clothes, jewelry, or luggage. Husband's truck was searched, but came up clean. Crime lab was currently searching the family's trash. BRIC—Boston Regional Intelligence Center—would really like to search family's computer.

At the last minute, D.D. added: *1 missing orange cat.*

She stepped back from the white board. They all studied it.

When no one had anything new to add, she capped her pen and turned to the deputy superintendent of homicide.

"Sandra Jones has now been missing over twenty-four hours," D.D. concluded. "She has not turned up at any local hospital or morgue. Nor has there been any activity on her credit cards or bank accounts during this time period. We have searched her house, her yard, the two vehicles, and her neighborhood. As of this time, we do not have a single lead on her whereabouts."

"Cell phone?" the deputy superintendent barked.

"We are working with her cellular provider to procure a complete log of all deleted voice messages and text messages, as well as a list of all incoming and outgoing calls. In the past twenty-four hours, the activity on her cell phone has mostly been limited to her teaching position, with various staff members and students trying to track her down."

"E-mail?" Clemente prodded.

"We tried unsuccessfully yesterday to get a warrant to seize the family computer. The judge argued Sandra Jones had not been missing for a sufficient length of time. We will resubmit our affidavit this morning, now that we have passed the twenty-four-hour benchmark for missing persons."

"Strategy?"

D.D. took a deep breath, eyed Detective Miller. They'd been at this since five this morning, having regrouped after only a few hours of desperately needed sleep. Passing the twenty-four-hour mark was both the best and worst thing to have happened for them. On the one hand, they could officially open a case file for Sandra Jones. On the other hand, the odds of finding said female had just dropped in half. Before, they'd had a window of opportunity. Now, they had an hourly race against time, as each additional minute Sandra Jones remained missing spelled only further doom and gloom.

They needed to find her. Within the next twelve hours, or chances were, they'd be digging up a body.

"We believe we have two logical courses of action," D.D. reported. "One, we believe the child, Clarissa Jones, may have information on what happened in her home that night. We need to force Jason Jones to consent to a forensic interview so that we can determine what details Clarissa may have to offer."

"How you gonna do that?"

"We're going to tell him he either allows us to interview Clarissa, or we will declare the house a crime scene and have him and Clarissa booted from the premises. We believe that in the interest of maintaining a stable environment for his child, he'll consent to the interview."

Clemente looked at her. "Not if he believes his daughter may offer details that incriminate him."

D.D. shrugged. "Either way, we'll have information we didn't have before."

Clemente considered this. "Agreed. Second course of action?"

She took another deep breath. "Given the current lack of leads, we need to make a public appeal for help. It's been twenty-four hours. We don't know what happened to Sandra Jones. Our best bet is to get the public involved. To accomplish this mission, we'd like to form an official taskforce to handle the multitude of inquiries that would come our way. We would also need to partner with other law enforcement agencies to identify local search team leaders, as well as other avenues of investigation. Finally, we would hold a press conference by nine A.M. this morning, where we would post pictures of Sandra Jones along with a hotline number for caller information. Of course, a case of this nature could potentially leap straight to national attention, but then again, maybe that will be useful to our efforts."

Clemente stared at her doubtfully.

D.D. relaxed her formal pose enough to shrug. "Hell, Chuck, media's gonna catch wind of this sooner or later. Might as well make it on our terms."

Clemente sighed, picked up the manila file folder in front him, tapped it a few times on the table. "Cable shows are gonna love this one."

"We'll need a dedicated public affairs officer," D.D. commented.

"Ninety-five percent of 'tips and inquiries' are gonna be from lonely men with tinfoil hats and tales of alien abductions."

"It's been a while since we've gotten to hear from them," D.D.

said, straight-faced. "Maybe we can assign a second officer just to update their addresses."

Clemente snorted. "Like I got the budget and they're ever moving out of their mothers' basements." He clutched the file in two hands. "Press is gonna ask you about the husband. What do you plan on saying?"

"We are pursuing all leads at this time."

"They'll ask if he's cooperating with the investigation."

"Meaning I'm gonna call him at eight-thirty A.M. and suggest he let us interview his daughter, just so I can answer yes to that question and save him some grief."

"And the registered sex offender?"

D.D. hesitated. "We're pursuing all leads at this time."

Clemente nodded sagely. "That's my girl. I don't want to hear any deviation from that party line. Last thing we need leaked is that we have two equally viable persons of interest. Next thing you know, they'll point the finger at each other, providing instant reasonable doubt to the defense attorney of choice."

D.D. nodded, without feeling the need to volunteer that Jason Jones was already going down that path. That was the problem with profiling two suspects, and why they had written everything on an erasable white board instead of in an official police report. Because once an arrest was made, all police reports became subject to disclosure to the defense attorney, who could then take suspect B and dangle him in front of the jury as the real mastermind. *Ta-da,* one dose of reasonable doubt, delivered by the earnest detective's own thorough investigation. Sometimes you were the windshield. Sometimes you were the bug.

"Nine A.M. press conference, you say?" Clemente glanced at his watch, stood from the table. "Better get cracking."

He tapped the file one last time, like a judge adjourning the trial. Then, he was out the door, while D.D. and Miller, finally officially empowered to assemble a taskforce and pressure a suspect, scrambled to get to work.

———

The phone rang shortly after 8 A.M. Jason turned his head slightly, eyed it ringing across the room on the little table by the window. He should get up, answer it. He couldn't find the energy to move.

Ree sat on the carpet in front of him, half-eaten bowl of Cheerios sitting in front of her, her eyes glued to the TV. She was watching *Dragon Tales*, which had followed *Clifford the Big Red Dog*, which had followed *Curious George*. She had never been allowed to watch as much TV as she had watched in the past twenty-four hours. Last night, the promise of a movie had excited her. This morning, she simply appeared as glassy-eyed as he.

She had not come skipping down the hall at six-thirty A.M. to pounce on top of his prone form and shriek with four-year-old glee, *"Wake up! Wake up, wake up, wake up! Daaaaa-dddeeeee. Wake. Up!"*

Instead, he had appeared in her room at seven, to find her lying wide-eyed in bed, staring up at her ceiling as if memorizing the pattern of birds and butterflies floating across the painted eaves. He had opened her blinds to another chilly March day. Got out her fleecy pink bathrobe.

She climbed out of bed without a word, took the bathrobe, found her slippers, and followed him downstairs. The cereal sounded uncommonly loud pouring from the box. The milk made a positive racket, sloshing into the daisy-patterned bowl. He hadn't been sure they'd be able to survive the sound of the silverware, but somehow, they had made it through.

She had carried her bowl into the family room and snapped on the TV without even asking. As if she'd known he wouldn't deny her this. And he hadn't. He couldn't find the heart to say, *Sit at the counter, young lady. TV will rot your brain, child. Come on, let's have a real meal.*

Somehow, brain rot seemed a minor inconvenience compared to what they were facing this morning—the second day without Sandra. The second day without Ree's mom, and his wife, a woman who thirty-six hours ago had intentionally purged her own Internet account. A woman who had possibly left them.

Phone rang again. This time, Ree turned to stare at him. Her gaze was slightly accusing. Like, as the adult, he should know better.

So he finally slung himself off the sofa and crossed to the phone. It was Sergeant Warren, of course. "Good morning, Mr. Jones."

"Not really," he replied.

"I trust you had a productive night at work."

"Did what I had to do." He shrugged.

"How is your daughter this morning?"

"Have you found my wife, Sergeant?"

"Well, no—"

"Then let's cut to the chase."

He heard her take a deep breath. "Well, as it has been more than twenty-four hours, you should know that your wife's status has been upgraded to an official missing person."

"How lucky for her," he murmured.

"In a way, it is. Now we can open an active case file, and bring more resources to bear. Including which, we will be holding a press conference at nine A.M. to announce your wife's disappearance."

He stiffened. Felt her words hit him between the eyes, a sharp, stinging blow. He opened his mouth to protest, then caught himself. He clutched the bridge of his nose and pretended the stinging in his eyes was something other than tears. "All right," he said quietly. He needed to start making phone calls, he realized. Get a lawyer. Start planning for Ree. He tucked the cordless phone more tightly between his shoulder and ear and headed into the kitchen, away from his child's acute hearing.

He opened the refrigerator door, found himself staring at Sandra's precious Dr Pepper, and closed the door again.

"Of course," Sergeant Warren was saying, "it would be excellent if you were available to make your own appeal to the public. Personalize the case and all that. We could hold the conference in your front yard. You and Ree could both be present," she concluded pleasantly.

"No thank you."

"No thank you?" She sounded stunned, but they both knew she was faking it.

"My primary concern is for my daughter. I don't think involving her in a media circus is to her benefit. I also think having reporters traipse across our yard and intrude in our private lives would be very traumatizing for her. Therefore, I think it's best if I stay home, preparing her for what will come next."

"And what do you think will come next?" Sergeant Warren asked, clearly baiting him.

"You will broadcast my wife's photo on the TV and the newspaper. Copies will be made. It will be distributed and stapled up all over the city. Search parties will be organized. People from Sandy's school will volunteer. The neighbors will stop by with offers of casseroles and hopes for the inside scoop. You will request clothing for canine teams. You will request hair for DNA tests, should you discover human remains. You will request a family photo, because the media will like that better than a lone shot of Sandy. Then the media vans will park outside my house with klieg lights that will power on every morning at four A.M. And you will have to assign uniforms simply to hold the hordes at the perimeter of my property line, where they will stand eighteen out of every twenty-four hours, screaming questions they hope I will magically appear to answer. If I serve as my own spokesman, everything I say can and will be used against me in a court of law. On the other hand, if I hire an attorney to serve as a spokesperson, I will look like I'm hiding something.

"A memorial will start to form on my front yard. People dropping off flowers, notes, teddy bears, all intended for Sandy. Then there will be the candlelight vigils, where good-intentioned souls will pray for Sandra's safe return. More likely than not, a few psychics will also volunteer their services. Then there will be the young ladies who will start sending me condolence notes because they find the allure of a single father to be strangely seductive, particularly if I may or may not have harmed my wife. Of course, I will decline their offers of free babysitting."

There was a long pause. "You seem to know the process very well," D. D. said.

"I'm a member of the media. Of course I know this process well."

We're dancing, he thought idly. It made him picture Sergeant D.D. Warren, whirling around him in some hot pink flamenco dress, while he stood there in solid black, trying to look strong and stoic, when really, he just didn't know the moves.

"Of course, now that the investigation is ramping up," the detective was saying, "it's important that we get as much information to the taskforce team as fast as possible. You understand that with every hour that passes, the odds of successfully finding your wife diminish significantly."

"I understand that not finding her yesterday means that most likely we won't find her at all."

"Got anything you want to add to that?" Sergeant Warren asked it quietly.

"No ma'am," he said, then immediately wished he hadn't. He caught the Southern drawl that crept into the words, as it always did when he used phrases from home.

Sergeant Warren was quiet for a bit. He wondered if that meant she caught the Southern-fried inflection, as well.

"I'm going to be honest," she said abruptly.

He doubted that very much, but didn't feel the need to say so.

"It's extremely important that we interview Ree. The clock is ticking, Jason, and it's possible that your daughter is the only witness to what happened to your wife."

"I know."

"Then of course you'll agree to a ten A.M. appointment with a forensic interviewer. Her name is Marianne Jackson and she is excellent."

"All right."

Now there was dead silence. "You agree?"

"Yes."

He heard a long sigh, then, almost as if the sergeant couldn't help herself: "Jason, we asked you this yesterday, and you refused. Why the change of heart?"

"Because I'm worried about her."

"Your wife?"

"No. My daughter. I don't think she's doing very well. Perhaps talking to a professional will help her. I'm not really a monster, Sergeant. And I do have my daughter's best interests at heart."

"Then ten A.M. it is. At our offices. Neutral territory is better."

"Daddy?"

"You don't have to convince me," he said into the phone, then turned to find Ree standing in the entryway, staring at him with that unerring instinct children had when they knew you were talking about them.

"We're going to talk to a nice lady this morning," he said, holding the receiver away from his mouth. "Don't worry, sweetheart, it'll be okay."

"There's a sound at the door, Daddy."

"What?"

"There's a sound. At the door. Can't you hear it?"

Then he did. The sound of shuffling, scratching, as if someone were trying to get in.

"I have to go," he told the detective. Then, without waiting for D.D.'s response, he slammed down the receiver. "Into the family room. Now, sweetheart. I mean it."

He motioned Ree down onto the floor by the love seat, while placing his body between hers and the massive steel weight of the front door. He heard more scratching, and flattened himself against the wall next to the window, trying not to look alarmed when every nerve in his body was jangling with panic. First thing he noticed when he peered outside was that the unmarked police car remained at the curb; the watch officer appeared to be sitting placidly, still sipping his morning coffee. Next thing Jason noticed was that he didn't see any sign of a human being outside the window at all.

But he heard the sound again. Shuffling, scratching, and then...

"Meow."

Ree sprang to her feet.

"Meow..."

Ree raced to the door. She moved faster than he could imagine, grabbing at the doorknob with frantic little fingers, and tugging, tugging, tugging while he belatedly worked the locks. Together they got it undone.

Ree threw open the door, and Mr. Smith came sailing into the house. *"Mrrrow!"*

"Mr. Smith, Mr. Smith, Mr. Smith!" Ree flung her arms around the copper-orange beast, squeezing so hard, Mr. Smith howled in protest.

Then, just as quickly, she let him go, threw herself to the floor and burst into tears. "But I want Mommy!" she wailed plaintively. "I want *Mama!*"

Jason lowered himself to the floor. He pulled his daughter onto his lap. He stroked her dark curly hair and held her while she wept.

| CHAPTER THIRTEEN |

I cheated on Jason for the first time when Ree was eleven months old. I couldn't take it anymore. The sleepless nights, the exhausting ritual of feeding, tending, diapering, feeding, tending, diapering. I'd already registered for online college courses and it seemed any minute I wasn't tending a baby, I was writing a paper, researching a subject, trying to recall high school math.

I felt both incredibly drained and unbelievably tense. Edgy, like my skin was on too tight, or my scalp was squeezing my brain. I found myself noticing everything from the silky feel of Ree's pink baby blanket to the needle-sharp pain of hot shower spray stinging my breasts.

Worse, I could feel the darkness growing inside my head. Until I could smell the cloying scent of decaying roses in every corner of my own home, and I dreaded falling asleep because I knew I'd only bolt awake to the sound of my mother's voice warbling down the hall, "I know something you don't know. I know something you don't know. . . ."

One day, I caught myself at the kitchen sink, scrubbing my hands with a wire-bristled brush. I was trying to erase my own fingerprints, trying to scour the DNA right out of my skin. And it occurred to me that's what the darkness was—my mother, my own mother, taking root inside my head.

There are some people that just killing once will never be enough.

I told Jason I needed to get away. Twenty-four hours. Maybe a hotel where I could crash for a bit, order room service, catch my breath. I produced a brochure for a downtown spa by the Four Seasons and its menu of treatments. Everything was ridiculously expensive, but I knew Jason wouldn't deny me, and he didn't.

He took a Friday and Saturday off, to be with Clarissa.

"Don't rush home," he told me. "Take your time. Relax. I understand, Sandy. I do."

So I went off to a four-hundred-a-night hotel room, where I used my spa money to hit Newbury Street and buy one micro mini suede skirt, black Kate Spade stiletto heels, and a silver sequined halter top that did not permit one to wear a bra. Then I hit the Armani Bar, and worked my way from there.

Remember, I was still only nineteen years old. I recalled all the tricks, and believe me, I know a lot of tricks. Girl like me, in a halter top and stiletto heels. I started the night popular and stayed that way until two in the morning, tossing back shots of Grey Goose in between lap dancing dirty old men and fresh-faced boys from BU.

My skin itched. I could feel it starting to catch fire, the more I drank, the more I danced, the more I wiggled my hips with some stranger's hands palming my ass, pressing his groin into my strategically spread legs. I wanted to drink all night. I wanted to dance all night.

I wanted to fuck until I couldn't remember my own name, until I screamed with rage and need. I wanted to fuck until my own head exploded and the darkness finally went away.

I took my time making my final choice for the evening. Not one of the old guys. They were good for buying drinks, but would probably drop dead of a heart attack trying to keep up with a girl like me. I went with one of the young college studs. All hard muscle and raging testosterone and silly, I-can't-believe-she's-really-leaving-with-me grin.

I let him take me back to his dorm, where I showed him things you could do while hanging from the underside of a bunk bed. When I was done with him, I fucked his roommate, too. Bachelor number one was too far gone to complain, and his roommate, a geeky nerd with no muscle tone at all, was extremely grateful and useful in his own way.

I left shortly after dawn. I hung my hot pink thong on the doorknob as a little souvenir, then walked to the T stop and caught the subway back to my hotel. Doorman 'bout had a fit when he saw me. Probably thought I was a hooker—or, excuse me, a high-class call girl, which now that I think about it, would've been a decent line of work for me. But I already had my room key, so he had no choice but to let me in.

I went up to my room, brushed my teeth, showered, brushed my teeth again, and fell onto the bed. I slept for five hours without moving a muscle. I slept like the dead. And when I woke up, I felt sane for the first time in months.

So I did the sensible thing. I balled up the skirt, the heels, the halter top, and threw them away. I showered yet again, scrubbing at my hands, which smelled of semen and sweat and lime-twisted vodka. Then I smoothed orange-scented lotion over my bruised ribs, my whisker-burned thighs, my bite-marked shoulder. And I dressed back into my gray cords and lavender turtleneck and headed home to my husband.

I'll be good, I told myself, all the way back to Southie. I'll be good from now on.

But I already knew that I'd do it again.

The truth is, it's not so hard to live a lie.

I greeted my husband with a kiss on the cheek. Jason returned the peck and inquired politely about my weekend.

"I feel much better now," I told him honestly.

"I'm glad," he said, and I understood, just by looking into his dark eyes, that he knew exactly what I had done. But I didn't say another word, and neither did he. That is all part of how you live a lie—you don't acknowledge it. You let it remain like an elephant, standing in the middle of the room.

I went upstairs. Unpacked my bag. Picked up my daughter and rocked with her tucked against my chest. And I discovered, whore or no whore, adulteress or not an adulteress, my daughter felt exactly the same, smelled exactly the same, loved me exactly the same, as I sat there, reading her Runaway Bunny and kissing her softly on top of the head.

I spent the next week dressing and undressing only when I was alone, as a form of courtesy. Jason spent the next week hunched over the computer until the odd hours of the morning, obviously avoiding me.

Sometime around the seventh or eighth night, once the bite marks had healed and I was still waking up to an empty bed, I decided this had gone on long enough. I loved Jason. I really did. And I believed he loved me. He really did. He was just never going to have sex with me. The irony of all ironies. The one man who finally showed me respect, compassion, and understanding was the one man who didn't want my body at all. But love is still love, right? And according to The Beatles, isn't that all we'll ever need?

I put on my bathrobe and crept downstairs to ask my husband to come back to bed. I found him, as usual, hunched over the family computer.

I noticed that his cheeks were flushed, his eyes overbright. He had, spread out in front of him, all kinds of financial papers, including an on-line application for a credit card.

"Get the fuck out of here," he told me sharply, and given his tone of voice, I did exactly as he asked.

Four hours later, we sat side by side at the kitchen bar, both eating bowls of cereal, Ree cooing away in the automatic swing, and neither of us saying a word.

He chewed. I chewed. Then he reached over and, very slowly, took my hand. We were okay again, just like that. Until the next time I had to disappear into a hotel room, I supposed. Until the next time he needed to disappear into the computer.

I wonder if the darkness grew inside his head. I wonder if he ever smelled decaying roses and cursed the color of his eyes or the feel of his own skin. But I didn't ask him. I would never ask him.

First rule of lying, remember? You never acknowledge it.

And it occurred to me, over a bowl of soggy cereal, that I could live like this. Compartmentalized. There, but separate. Together, but alone. Loving, but isolated. This is how I had been living most of my life, after all. In a household where my mother might appear in the middle of the night to do unspeakable things with a hairbrush. Then hours later, we'd sit across from one another sharing a platter of buttermilk biscuits for breakfast.

My mother had prepared me well for this life.

I glanced over at my husband, crunching away on Cheerios. I wondered who had prepared him.

The Boston Police Department's press conference started at 9:03 A.M. And Jason knew the second it ended, because his cell phone rang.

He hadn't watched the briefing. Once he'd wiped his daughter's tears and fed one very demanding Mr. Smith, he'd loaded both his daughter and the cat into Sandy's Volvo. Mr. Smith had sprawled out in a sunny spot and gone immediately to sleep, the rare cat who actually liked car rides. Ree, in turn, sat in her booster seat, clutching Lil' Bunny to her chest while she stared at Mr. Smith as if she were willing him to stay put.

Jason drove. Mostly because he needed to move. He felt as if he were on the open plains of Kansas, watching a twister touch down and helpless to get out of its path. He could only watch the sky darken, feel the first whip of hurricane-force winds against his face.

The cops had held a press conference. The media machine was now slowly but surely roaring to life. There was nothing he could do about it. There was nothing anyone could do.

His phone rang again. He eyed his screen, feeling his sense of fatalism swell.

Using the rearview mirror, he glanced at his daughter again, the serious look on her face as she tried to find happiness in watching her cat sleep when what she wanted most in the world was to hug her mother.

He flipped the phone open and held it to his ear.

"Hello, Greg."

"Holy shit," the senior news editor of the *Boston Daily* exploded in his ear. "Why didn't you tell us, Jason? Hell, we're like family. We woulda understood."

"It's been a trying time," Jason said automatically, feeling the words come out by rote as they had before, so long ago. *Wanna be on the front page?* All it will cost you is your life. Or maybe your child's. Or maybe your wife's.

"What's the deal here, Jason? And I'm not talking editor to reporter. You know I wouldn't do that to you." Another lie. There would be many lies in the days to come. "I'm talking as a member of your journalistic family, the guy who's seen the photos of your family and knows how much you love them. Are you doin' all right?"

"I'm taking it one day at a time," Jason recited evenly.

"Any word? Gotta say, the police were pretty damn vague."

"We are hoping the public can provide clues," Jason filled in dutifully.

"And your daughter? Clarissa? How's she holding up? Need any help, buddy?"

"Thank you for your offer. We are taking it one day at a time."

"Jason... Jason, my man."

"I won't be able to work tonight, Greg."

"Of course not! Holy crap, of course we understand. You need to take a week off, maybe a leave of absence. You name it, we're there for you, man." *Just don't forget about us, right, buddy? Front-page scoop, the inside skinny straight from the husband's mouth to our front page, right, buddy?*

"Thank you for your understanding."

"We're there for you, Jason. You name it, you got it. We believe in you, man. Why, the thought of you doing anything to harm Sandra..."

"Thank you for your understanding." Jason hung up the phone.

"Who's that?" Ree demanded from the back seat.

"Daddy's former boss," Jason said, and meant it.

The BPD's headquarters was a glass-and-granite monstrosity that had been plopped down in the middle of the housing projects of Roxbury. The hope had been that the overwhelming police presence would help jumpstart the gentrification process of this particular inner-city. Mostly, it made both workers and visitors to the building fear for their lives.

Jason eyed his parking options with much trepidation. He did not expect to come out to find his Volvo intact. And honestly, he worried for the cat. Mr. Smith had obviously spent the past thirty-six hours using up at least one of his nine lives. Who knew how many the cat had left?

"We shouldn't be here, Daddy," Ree said when she climbed out of the back of the car, clutching her bunny. The parking lot featured a lot of broken asphalt, framed by concrete barriers. Interior decorating by way of Beirut.

Jason thought about it, then reached inside the car for his notebook and Ree's red Crayola marker. He tore out two sheets of paper and wrote in big block letters: *QUARANTINED: Rabid Cat. Warning. Do Not Touch.*

He placed one sheet of paper on the front of the car and one on the back. Then he looked in at Mr. Smith, who opened one lazy golden eye, yawned, and went back to sleep.

"Be a good rabid cat," Jason murmured, then took Ree firmly by the hand and headed for the crosswalk.

As they neared the giant glass building, his footsteps slowed. He couldn't help himself. He looked down at Ree's hand, tucked securely in his own, and it seemed like the past five years had been both too fast and too slow. He wanted to call it all back. He wanted to pull every single moment and hold them close because the tornado was coming. The twister was coming, and he couldn't get out of the way.

He remembered the very first time his daughter had grabbed his finger, only one hour old, her impossibly tiny hand wrapping with determination around his ridiculously large index finger. He remembered those same fingers a year later, receiving their first burn when she grabbed the candle on her birthday cupcake before he or Sandy could warn her that it was hot. And he remembered one afternoon, when he'd thought she was napping, he'd gone online and read too many sad stories about sad children, and he had started to cry, hunched over at the kitchen table. Suddenly, there had been Ree, her little two-year-old hands upon his face, wiping away his tears.

"No sad, Daddy," she'd whispered to him calmly. "No sad."

And the sight of his tears on his daughter's little fingers had almost made him weep all over again.

He wanted to speak to her now. He wanted to tell her he loved her. He wanted to tell her to trust him, he would keep her safe. He would figure this out. Somehow, he would make the world be right again.

He wanted to thank her for four beautiful years, for being the best little girl in the world. For being the sun on his face and the glow in his smile and the love of his life.

They hit the glass doors, her fingers twitching nervously in his hand as the police headquarters loomed.

Jason looked down at his daughter.

In the end he told her none of those things. Instead, he gave her the best advice he could.

"Be brave," he said, and opened the door.

| CHAPTER FOURTEEN |

After consulting with Marianne Jackson, the forensic interviewer, D.D. had commandeered a room from white-collar crimes. The space was nicer than anything the homicide unit had to offer, and hopefully less likely to scare the kid. Marianne brought with her two child-sized folding chairs, a bright, flower-shaped rug, and a basket crammed with a collection of trucks, dolls, and art supplies. In ten minutes or less, the child specialist had the place looking like a cool kids' hangout, versus the fraud squad's interrogation room of choice. D.D. was impressed.

She'd been happy with the morning's press conference. She had intentionally kept it brief. Less was more at this point. Fewer innuendos to come back to haunt them later, should they decide the registered sex offender was their suspect of choice, versus the husband, or heaven help them, an unknown subject yet to be identified. Besides, their biggest goal was to increase the number of eyes and ears actively seeking Sandra Jones. Find the wife alive, save them all a headache. Thirty-seven hours into the investigation, D.D. still had hope. Not a lot of it. But some hope.

Now she busily arranged her notepad and two pens on the table of the observation room. Miller was already present, sitting in the chair closest to the door, where he seemed to be lost in thought, given his rhythmic stroking of his mustache. She thought he should shave the mustache. A mustache like that practically cried out for a powder blue leisure suit and she really did not want to see Detective Brian Miller in a powder blue leisure suit. She didn't say anything, though. Men could be very touchy when it came to facial hair.

D.D. fiddled with her pens again, clicking and unclicking the ballpoints into place. The speakers were already turned on, allowing them to hear what was said in the interrogation room. In turn, Marianne was fitted with a tiny earpiece so she could receive any follow-up questions or additional inquiries they made into a cordless mic. Marianne had already warned them to be tight and focused. The rule of thumb for interviewing children was five minutes per year of child, meaning they had roughly twenty minutes to learn everything there was to know from four-year-old potential witness Clarissa Jones.

They had formulated their strategy in advance: key questions to determine Clarissa's credibility and capability as a witness, followed by ever more specific questions regarding Sandra Jones's last known moments on Wednesday night. It was a lot of ground to cover in the time they had, but Marianne had emphasized the need to be thorough—follow-up interviews with a child witness were risky. Next thing you know, a defense attorney was arguing the half a dozen interviews you required for specificity were actually a half a dozen times you badgered, cajoled, and otherwise corrupted your young, impressionable subject. Marianne gave them two shots at talking to the child, max, and for better or worse, D.D. had already used up one, questioning Clarissa at her house on Thursday morning. So this was it.

The downstairs sergeant notified them that Jason and his daughter had arrived. Marianne headed down immediately to hustle them upstairs before Ree became too overwhelmed by the full police headquarters experience. Some kids were enthralled by men and women in uniform. A lot, however, were just plain intimidated. Talking to a stranger was tough enough without Ree starting the process scared witless.

D.D. and Miller heard footsteps in the hall. Both turned expectantly toward the door and, despite her best intentions, D.D. felt nervous. Questioning a kid was twenty times worse than facing the news media or a new deputy superintendent, any day of the week. She didn't care about reporters or, most of the time, a new supervisor. On the other hand, she always felt bad for the kids.

First time she'd ever interrogated a child, the eleven-year-old girl had asked them if they wanted to see her menu; then she'd proceeded to pull from her back pocket a tiny scrap of paper, folded into an impossibly small square. It was a menu of sex acts, prepared by the girl's stepfather: *Hand Job quarter, Oral Sex fifty cents, Fucking one dollar.* The girl had taken twenty bucks from her stepdad's wallet. This was his way of letting her repay the loan. Except last time she'd performed a "service," he had refused to pay, and *that* had made her mad enough to come to the police. Oh, the sad stories that had been told in this room...

The footsteps stopped outside the door. D.D. heard Marianne talking.

"Clarissa, have you ever been in a magic room before?"

No answer, so D.D. assumed that Ree was shaking her head.

"Well, I'm going to take you into a special room now. It has a pretty rug, two chairs, maybe some toys you'd like to check out. But it's also a very special room with special rules. I'll tell you all about it, okay, but first, you gotta say goodbye to your daddy. He's going to wait for you in this room right here, so he'll be close by if you need him, but this magic room, it's just for you and me."

Still no answer.

"Say, what's the name of this fellow right here? Oh, I'm sorry, this gal. Lil' Bunny? I should've guessed she was a girl, look at that pink dress. Well, Lil' Bunny, do you like big pink flowers, because you look to me like the kind of rabbit that might enjoy a really *large* pink flower. I'm talking huge. Kind of flower you have to see to believe. Really? Well, come on, I'll show you. And I'll explain to you a little bit about magic."

The door opened. Jason Jones entered the room. Clarissa's father walked stiffly, as if he was moving on autopilot. The shuttered expression was back on his face, that one where D.D. couldn't decide if he was a complete psychopath or the most stoic man she'd ever met. He closed the heavy door behind him, then looked at D.D. and Miller a bit warily. D.D. twisted around the permission slip she'd already printed out, and slid it across the table toward him, producing a black ink pen.

"This forms shows you've given consent for a certified forensic interviewer to question your child on behalf of the BPD."

Jason gave her a look as if he was surprised his permission really mattered. But he signed the form without a word, returning it to her before taking up position on the wall farthest from the observation window. He leaned back with his arms crossed over his chest. His gaze went to the window, through which they could now see Marianne and Ree entering the interrogation room. Ree was clutching a tattered-looking brown bunny for dear life, its long floppy ears obscuring her hands.

Marianne closed the door. She moved to the middle of the room, but rather than taking a seat in one of the little red folding chairs, she sat cross-legged on the edge of the pink rug. She ran her hand over it a few times, as if inviting the girl to take a seat.

D.D. picked up the mic, and stated for Marianne's sake, "Consent form has been signed. You may begin."

Marianne nodded slightly, her fingers brushing over the receiver nestled inside her ear. "What do you think?" she stated out loud to Clarissa Jones, gesturing to the pink rug. "Is this a pretty flower? It looks like a sunflower to me, except I don't think sunflowers come in pink."

"It's a daisy," Ree said in a small voice. "My mommy grows them."

"A daisy? Of course! You know a lot about flowers."

Ree remained standing, clutching her well-worn rabbit. Her fingers had found one of its ears and were rubbing it rhythmically. The unconscious movement pained D.D. She used to do that as a kid. Had a stuffed dog. Wore its ears right off its threadbare head.

"So, as I told you downstairs, my name is Marianne Jackson," the specialist was saying brightly. "My job is to talk to children. That's what I do. I talk to little boys and little girls. And just so you know, Ree, it's not as easy as you think."

For the first time, Ree responded, her forehead crinkling into a tiny frown. "Why not?"

"For one thing, there are special rules for talking to boys and girls. Did you know that?"

Ree edged closer, shook her head. Her toe touched the pink flower. She seemed to study the rug.

"Well, as I mentioned outside, this is a magic room, and there are four rules for talking in a magic room." Marianne held up four fingers, ticking off. "One, we only talk about what really happened. Not what might have happened, but what really happened."

Ree frowned again, moved a tiny bit closer.

"Do you understand the difference between the truth and a lie, Clarissa?" Marianne reached into the toy basket, came up with a stuffed dog. "If I say this is a cat, is that a truth or a lie?"

"A lie," Ree said automatically. "That's a dog."

"Very good! So that's rule number one. We only talk about the truth, okay?"

Ree nodded. She seemed to get tired of standing, taking a seat just beyond the flower rug, her bunny now on her lap.

"The second rule," Marianne was saying, "is that if I ask you a question and you don't know the answer, you just say you don't know. Does that make sense?"

Ree nodded.

"How old am I, Clarissa?"

"Ninety-five," Ree said.

Marianne smiled, a bit ruefully. "Now, Clarissa, do you *know* how old I am? Have you asked or has anyone told you?"

Ree shook her head.

"So really, you don't know how old I am. And what are you supposed to say if you don't know something?"

"I don't know," Ree filled in obediently.

"Good girl. Where do I live?"

Ree opened her mouth, then seemed to catch herself. "I don't know!" she exclaimed, a trace of triumph this time.

Marianne grinned. "I can tell you're very good in school. Are you an excellent student?"

"I'm very pre-pre-cushush," Ree said proudly. "Everyone says so."

"Precocious? I fully agree and I'm very proud of you. Okay, rule number three. If you don't remember something, it's okay to say you don't remember. So how old were you when you first walked?"

"I've been walking since I was born," Ree started, then caught herself as she remembered rule number three. She let go of her stuffed bunny and clapped her hands gleefully. "I DON'T REMEMBER!" she shrieked with delight. "I. Don't. Remember."

"You are the best pupil I've ever had," Marianne said, still sitting cross-legged on the rug. She held up her four fingers. "All right, star student—last rule. Do you know what rule four is?"

"I DON'T KNOW!" Ree shouted happily.

"You are so good. So, rule four, if you don't understand something I say or ask, it's okay to say you don't understand. *Capisce?*"

"*Capisce!*" Ree yelled right back. "That means 'I understand' in Italian! I know Italian. Mrs. Suzie's been teaching us Italian."

For a moment, Marianne blinked her eyes. Apparently, even in a forensic interviewer's world, there was precocious, and then there was precocious. Frankly, D.D. was having a hard time keeping a straight face. She slid a glance in Jason's direction, but he had the same blank look on his face. *Light switch,* she thought again. He was in the room, but shut off.

That made her think of a thing or two, and she found herself scrawling a quick question on her notepad.

In the interrogation room, Marianne Jackson seemed to recover herself. "All right, then. You know the rules. So, tell me, Clarissa—"

"Ree. Everyone calls me Ree."

"Why do they call you Ree?"

" 'Cause when I was a baby, I couldn't say Clarissa. I said Ree. And Mommy and Daddy liked that, so they call me Ree, too. Unless I'm in trouble. Then Mommy says, '*Clarissa Jane Jones,*' and I have until the count of three or I get the timeout stair."

"The timeout stair?"

"Yeah. I gotta sit on the bottom step of the staircase for four minutes. I don't like the timeout stair."

"What about the little gal you're holding? Lil' Bunny. She ever get into trouble?"

Clarissa looked at Marianne. "Lil' Bunny is a toy. Toys can't get in trouble. Only people can."

"Very good, Clarissa. You are a smart cookie."

The child beamed.

"I like Lil' Bunny," Marianne continued conversationally. "I had Winnie the Pooh when I was your age. He had a music box inside that when you wound it up, played 'Twinkle, Twinkle, Little Star.' "

"I like Pooh, too," Ree said earnestly. She had moved closer now, onto the rug, peering around Marianne to the wicker basket. "Where is your Pooh bear? Is he in the basket?"

"Actually, he's at home, on my bookshelf. He was a special toy for me, and I don't think we ever outgrow our special toys." But Marianne moved the basket onto the rug, closer to Ree, who was clearly engaged now and very curious about the rest of the contents of the magic room.

D.D. sneaked a second glance at Jason Jones. Still no response. Happy, sad, worried, anxious. Nada. She made a second note on her pad.

"Ree, do you know why you are here today?"

Some of the spark went out of the child. She hunched a little, her hands rubbing her rabbit as she sat back. "Daddy said you are a nice lady. He said if I spoke to you, it would be all right."

Now D.D. could feel Jason tense. He didn't move, didn't speak, but the veins suddenly stood out on his neck.

"What would be all right, sweetheart?"

"Will you bring my mommy back?" Ree asked in a muffled voice. "Mr. Smith came back. Just this morning. He scratched on the door and we let him in and I love him, but... Will you bring my mommy back? I miss my mommy."

Marianne didn't speak right away. She seemed to be studying the child sympathetically while letting the silence stretch on. Through the observation window, D.D. contemplated the pink rug, the folding chairs, the basket of toys, anything but the pained look on the little girl's face. Beside her, Miller shifted uncomfortably in his chair. But Jason Jones still didn't move a muscle or say a word.

"Tell me about your family," Marianne said. D.D. recognized the interview technique. Back away from the sensitive topic. Define the child's broader world. Then circle back to the wound. "Who's in your family?"

"There is me and Mommy and Daddy," Ree began. She was rubbing Lil' Bunny's ear again. "And Mr. Smith, of course. Two girls and two boys."

D.D. made more notes, the family genealogy as seen through the eyes of the four-year-old child.

"What about other relatives?" Marianne was asking. "Aunts, uncles, cousins, grandparents, or anyone else?"

Ree shook her head.

D.D. wrote down, *Extended Family???* The child apparently didn't know about her own grandfather, perhaps confirming Jason's assertion that Sandra and her father were estranged, or perhaps confirming that Jason Jones had done an excellent job of isolating his much younger wife.

"What about babysitters? Does anyone else help take care of you, Ree?"

Ree regarded Marianne blankly. "Mommy and Daddy take care of me."

"Of course. But what if they're working, or maybe they need to go somewhere?"

"Daddy works, Mommy watches me," Ree said. "Then Daddy comes home, and Mommy goes to work, but Daddy has to sleep, so I go to school. Then Daddy picks me up and we have Daddy-Daughter time."

"I see. Where do you go to school, Ree?"

"I go to preschool. In the brick building with the big kids. I'm in the Little Flowers room. Next year, though, when I am five, I will go to the big classroom with the kinnygardeners."

"Who are your teachers?"

"Miss Emily and Mrs. Suzie."

"Best friends?"

"I play with Mimi and Olivia. We like to play fairies. I'm a Garden Fairy."

"So you have best friends. What about your mommy and daddy, who are their best friends?"

It was another routine question, generally used in CSAs, or Child Sexual Assaults, when the person of interest might not be a relative, but a suspected neighbor or friend of the family. It was important that the child define her own world, so later, should the interviewer bring up a name, it did not appear as if the interviewer were leading the witness.

Ree, however, shook her head. "Daddy says I'm his best friend. 'Sides, he works a lot, so I don't think he gets to have friends. Daddies are very busy."

This time Miller looked at Jason. Ree's father, however, remained immobile against the wall, staring resolutely through the window as if he were watching a TV show and not a trained specialist interviewing his only child. After another moment, Miller turned back around.

"I like Mrs. Lizbet," Ree was volunteering. "But she and Mommy don't play together. They're teachers."

"What do you mean?" Marianne asked.

"Mrs. Lizbet teaches seventh grade. Last year, she helped teach Mommy how to be a teacher. Now Mommy teaches sixth grade. But we still get to see Mrs. Lizbet at the basketball games."

"Oh really?"

"Yes, I like basketball. Mommy takes me to watch. Daddy works, you know. So it's Mommy-Daughter night, every night. Yeah!" For a moment, Ree seemed to forget why she was in the room. Then, in the next instant, D.D. could see the realization crash down onto the child, the little girl's eyes widening, then her whole body collapsing back into itself, until she was hunched once more over her stuffed rabbit, rubbing the poor bunny's ears.

Behind D.D., Jason Jones finally flinched.

"When did you last see your mommy?" Marianne asked softly.

A muffled reply: "She put me to bed."

"Do you know the days of the week, Ree?"

"Sunday, Monday, Tuesday, Wednesday," Ree sang in a little voice. "Thursday, Friday, Saturday, Sunday."

"Very good. So do you know what day it was when your mommy put you to bed?"

Ree looked blank. Then she began to sing again, "Sunday, Monday, Tuesday, Wednesday..."

Marianne nodded her head and moved on; it was obvious the child knew a song about the days of the week, but not the days themselves. Fortunately, there were other tricks for establishing date and time when dealing with a young witness. Marianne would start asking about shows on TV, songs on the radio, that sort of thing. Children may not know a lot from an adult's perspective, but they had a tendency to *observe* a lot, making it possible to fill in the necessary information, often with more credible results than a witness simply saying, "Wednesday night at eight P.M."

"So tell me about your night with your mother, Ree. Who was home?"

"Me and Mommy."

"What about Mr. Smith, or Lil' Bunny or your daddy or anyone else?"

The anyone else was another standard interview technique. When presenting a child with a list of options, the last item always had to be "anyone else" or "something else" or "somewhere else"; otherwise, you were leading the witness.

"Mr. Smith," Ree said. "And Lil' Bunny. But not Daddy. I see Daddy during the day, Mommy at night."

"Anyone else?"

Ree frowned at her. "Nighttime is Mommy and me time. We have ladies' night."

D.D. made a note.

"So what did you do for ladies' night?" Marianne asked.

"Puzzles. I like puzzles."

"What kind of puzzles?"

"Um, we did the butterfly puzzle, then the princess puzzle that takes up the *whole rug*. Except it got hard, 'cause Mr. Smith kept walking on the puzzle and I got mad, so Mommy said, maybe we should *move on*."

"Do you like music, Ree?"

The girl blinked. "I like music."

"Did you and your mommy listen to music while doing the

puzzles, or maybe have the TV on, or the radio on, or something else?"

Ree shook her head. "I like to rock out to Tom Petty," she said matter-of-factly, "but puzzles are quiet time." She made a face, perhaps like her mother, embarking on a lecture with one wagging finger: " 'Children need quiet time. That's what makes brains grow!' "

"I see." Marianne sounded suitably impressed. "So you and your mother had quiet time with puzzles. Then what did you do?"

"Dinner."

"Dinner? Oh, I like dinner. What is your favorite dinner?"

"Mac-n-cheese. And gummy worms. I love gummy worms, but you can't have them for dinner, just for dessert."

"True," Marianne said sympathetically. "My mother never let me eat gummy worms for dinner. What did you and your mommy eat for dinner?"

"Mac-n-cheese," Ree supplied without hesitation, "with little bits of turkey dog and some apples. I don't really like turkey dogs, but Mommy says I need protein to grow muscle, so if I want mac-n-cheese, I have to eat turkey dogs." The girl sounded mournful.

D.D. jotted down the menu, impressed not only by Ree's level of detail, but the consistency with her first statement given Thursday morning. A consistent witness always made a detective happy. And the level of detail meant they could corroborate Ree's account of the first half of the evening, making it harder for a jury to discount what the child might say about events in the second half of the night. All in all, four-year-old Clarissa Jones was a better witness than eighty percent of the adults D.D. encountered.

"What did you do after dinner?" Marianne asked.

"Bath time!" Ree sang.

"Bath time?"

"Yep. Me and Mommy shower together. Do you need to know who was in the shower?" Ree apparently recognized the pattern by now.

"Okay."

"Well, not Mr. Smith, 'cause he hates water, and not Lil' Bunny, because she takes a bath in the washing machine. But Princess Duckie and Mariposa Barbie and Island Princess Barbie all needed baths, so they came in with us. Mommy says I can only wash three things, otherwise I use up all the hot water."

"I see. What did your mommy do?"

"She washes her hair, then she washes my hair, then she yells at me I'm using too much soap."

Marianne blinked her eyes again.

"I like bubbles," Ree explained. "But Mommy says soap costs money and I use too much, so she puts soap in this little cup for me, but it's never enough. Barbies have a lot of hair."

"Ree, if I tell you I have blue hair, is that the truth or is that a lie?"

Ree grinned, recognizing the game again. She held up her first finger. "That's a lie, and in the magic room, we only tell the truth."

"Very good, Ree. Excellent. So you and your mommy are in the shower, and you have used a lot of soap. How do you feel in the shower, Ree?"

Ree frowned at Marianne, then something seemed to click. She held up four fingers. "I don't understand," she said proudly.

Marianne smiled. "Excellent again. I will try to explain. When you and your mommy shower . . . do you like it or do you not like it? How do you feel?"

"I like showers," Ree said earnestly. "I just don't like having my hair washed."

D.D. could sense Marianne's hesitation again. On the one hand, a mother and her four-year-old girl showering together was hardly inappropriate. On the other hand, Marianne Jackson wouldn't have a job if all parents were appropriate. Something had gone wrong in this family. Their job was to help Ree find a way to tell them what.

"Why don't you like your hair being washed?" Marianne asked.

" 'Cause my hair snarls. My hair's not really short, you know. Nope, when it's wet, it goes halfway down my back! It takes forever for Mommy to get all the shampoo out, and then she has to condition it or it gets all snarly and I don't much like my hair at all. I wish I had straight hair like my best friend, Mimi." Ree sighed heavily.

Marianne smiled, moved on. "So what did you do after your shower?"

"We got dry," the girl reported, "then we go to the Big Bed, where Mommy wants me to talk about my day, but mostly I tickle her."

"Where is the Big Bed?"

"Mommy and Daddy's room. That's where we go after bath time. And Mr. Smith hops up, but I like to wrestle and he does not like that."

"You like to wrestle?"

"Yeah," Ree said proudly. "I'm strong! I rolled Mommy onto the floor and that made me laugh." She held up her arms, apparently in imitation of flexing. "It made Mommy laugh, too. I like my mommy's laugh." Her voice trailed off wistfully. "Do you think my mommy's mad because I pushed her off the bed? She didn't sound mad, but maybe...Once, at school, Olivia tore the picture I drew and I told her it was okay, but it wasn't really okay and I got madder and madder and madder. I was mad all day! Do you think that's what happened? Did my mommy get mad all day?"

"I don't know, sweetheart," Marianne said honestly. "After you and your mommy wrestled, then what happened?"

The girl shrugged. She looked tired now, wrung out. D.D. glanced at her watch. The interview had been going on for forty-four minutes, well beyond their twenty-minute target time.

"Bedtime," Ree mumbled. "We got on PJs—"

"What did you wear, Ree?"

"My green Ariel nightgown."

"And your mother?"

"She wears a purple shirt. It's very long, almost to her knees."

D.D. made a note, another detail that could be corroborated, given the presence of the purple nightshirt in the washing machine.

"So after pajamas?"

"Brush teeth, go potty, climb into bed. Two stories. A song. Mommy sang 'Puff the Magic Dragon.' I'm tired," the girl declared abruptly, a trace petulant. "I want to be done now. Are we done?"

"We're almost done, honey. You've been doing a really good job. Just a few more questions, okay, and then you can ask me anything you want. Would you like that? To ask me a question?"

Ree regarded Marianne for a bit. Then, with a sudden, impatient exhalation, she nodded. The girl had the stuffed bunny on her lap again. She was rubbing both ears.

"After your mother tucked you in, what did she do?"

"I don't understand."

"Did she turn out the light, close the door, something else? How do you sleep at night, Ree? Can you describe your room for me?"

"I have a nightlight," the girl said softly. "I'm not five yet. I think when you are four, you can have a nightlight. Maybe, when I ride the school bus . . . But I'm not on the school bus yet, so I have a nightlight. But the door is closed. Mommy always closes the door. She says I am a light sleeper."

"So the door is closed, you have a nightlight. What else is in your room?"

"Lil' Bunny, of course. And Mr. Smith. He always sleeps on my bed 'cause I go to bed first and cats really like to sleep."

"Is there anything else that helps you sleep? Music, a sound machine, a humidifier, anything else?"

Ree shook her head. "Nope."

"What is the name of my cat, Ree?"

Ree grinned at her. "I don't know."

"Very good. If I told you those chairs were blue, would I be telling the truth or would I be telling a lie?"

"Nooo! The chairs are red!"

"That's right. And we only tell the truth in the magic room, don't we?"

Ree nodded, but D.D. could read the tension in the child's body again. Marianne was circling around. Circling, circling, circling.

"Did you stay in bed, Ree? Or did you maybe get up to check on your mommy or go potty or do anything else?"

The girl shook her head, but she did not look at Marianne anymore.

"What does your mom do after you go to bed, Ree?" Marianne asked softly.

"She has to do her schoolwork. Grade papers." The girl's gaze slid up. "At least, I think so."

"Do you ever hear noises downstairs, maybe the TV, or the radio, or the sound of your mother's footsteps, or something else?"

"I heard the tea kettle," Ree whispered.

"You heard the tea kettle?"

"It whistled. On the stove. Mommy likes tea. Sometimes we have tea parties and she makes me real apple tea. I like apple tea." The girl was still talking, but her voice had changed. She sounded subdued, a shadow of her former self.

D.D. eyed Jason Jones, still standing against the far wall. He had not moved, but there was a starkness to his expression now. Oh yeah, they were homing in.

"Ree, after the tea kettle, what did you hear?"

"Footsteps."

"Footsteps?"

"Yeah. But they didn't sound right. They were loud. Angry. Angry feet on the stairs. Uh-oh," the girl singsonged. "Uh-oh, Daddy's mad."

Behind D.D., Jason flinched for the second time. She saw him close his eyes, swallow, but he still didn't say a word.

In the interrogation room, Marianne was equally quiet. She let the silence draw out until abruptly, Ree began speaking again, her body rocking back and forth, her hands rubbing, rubbing her stuffed toy's ears:

"Something crashed. Broke. I heard it, but I didn't get out of bed. I didn't want to get out of bed. Mr. Smith did. He jumped off the bed. He stood by the door but I didn't want to get out of bed. I held Lil' Bunny. I told her to be very quiet. We must be quiet."

The girl paused for an instant, then spoke suddenly in a soft, higher-pitched voice: *"Please don't do this."* She sounded mournful. *"Please don't do this. I won't tell. You can believe me. I'll never tell. I love you. I still love you..."*

Ree's gaze went up. D.D. swore to God the child looked right through the one-way mirror to her father's face. "Mommy said, 'I still love you.' Mommy said, 'Don't do this.' Then everything went crash, and I didn't listen anymore. I covered Lil Bunny's ears, and I swear I didn't listen anymore, and I never, ever, ever got out of bed. Please, you can believe me. I didn't get out of bed."

"Am I done?" the child asked ten seconds later, when Marianne still hadn't said anything. "Where's my daddy? I don't want to be in the magic room anymore. I want to go home."

"You're all done," Marianne said kindly, touching the child softly on the arm. "You've been a very brave little girl, Ree. Thank you for talking to me."

Ree merely nodded. She appeared glassy-eyed, her fifty minutes of talking having left her spent. When she tried to rise to her feet, she staggered a step. Marianne steadied her.

In the observation room, Jason Jones had already pushed away from the wall. Miller made it to the door just ahead of him, opening up the room to the brilliant fluorescent wash of hallway light.

"Miss Marianne?" Ree's voice came from the interrogation room.

"Yes, honey."

"You said I could ask you a question . . ."

"That's right. I did. Would you like to ask me a question? Ask me anything." Marianne had risen, too. Now D.D. saw the interviewer pause, squat down in front of the child, so she would be at eye level. The interviewer had already unclipped her tiny mic, the receiver dangling down low, in her hands.

"When you were four years old, did your mommy go away?"

Marianne brushed back a lock of curly brown hair from the girl's cheek, her voice sounding tinny, far away. "No, honey, when I was four years old, my mommy didn't go away."

Ree nodded. "You were lucky when you were four years old."

Ree left the interrogation room. She spotted her father waiting for her just outside the door, and hurled herself into his arms.

D.D. watched them embrace for a long time, a four-year-old's rail-thin arms wrapped tautly around her father's solid presence. She heard Jason murmur something low and soothing to his child. She saw him lightly stroke Ree's trembling back.

She thought she understood just how much Clarissa Jones loved both of her parents. And she wondered, as she often wondered in her line of work, why for more parents, their child's unconditional love couldn't be enough.

They debriefed ten minutes later, after Marianne had escorted Jason and Ree out of the building. Miller had his opinion. Marianne and D.D. had theirs.

"Someone entered the home Wednesday night," Miller started out. "Obviously had a confrontation with Sandra, and little Ree believes that someone is her father. 'Course, that could be an assumption on her part. She heard footsteps, assumed they had to be from her dad, returning home from work."

D.D. was already shaking her head. "She didn't tell us everything."

"No," Marianne agreed.

Miller glared at the two of them.

"Ree totally got out of bed Wednesday night," D.D. supplied. "As is exhibited by the fact she went out of her way to tell us she didn't."

"She got out of bed," Marianne seconded, "and saw something she's not ready to talk about yet."

"Her father," Miller stated, sounding dubious. "But at the end, the way she hugged him..."

"He's still her father," Marianne supplied softly. "And she's vulnerable and terribly frightened by everything going on in her world."

"Why'd he let her come in, then?" Miller challenged. "If she came into the bedroom Wednesday night and saw her father fighting with her mom, he wouldn't want her to testify."

"Maybe he didn't see her appear in the doorway," D.D. suggested with a shrug.

"Or he trusted her not to tell," Marianne added. "From a very early age, children get a feel for family secrets. They watch their parents lie to neighbors, officials, other loved ones—I fell down the stairs, of course everything is fine—and they internalize those lies until it becomes as second nature to them as breathing. It's very difficult to get children to disclose against their own parents. It's like asking them to dive into a very deep pool and never take a breath."

D.D. sighed, eyed her notes. "Not enough for a warrant," she concluded, already moving on to next steps.

"No," Miller agreed. "We need a smoking gun. Or, at the very least, Sandra Jones's dead body."

"Well, start pushing," Marianne informed them both. "Because I can tell you now, that child knows more. But she's also working very hard at not knowing what she knows. Another few days, a week, you'll never get the story out of her, particularly if she continues to spend all her time with dear old dad."

Marianne started picking up the toys in the interrogation room. Miller and D.D. turned away, just as the buzzer sounded at the pager clipped to D.D.'s waist. She eyed the display screen, frowning. Some detective from the state police trying to summon her. Figures. Throw a little party with the media, and all of a sudden everyone wants in on the action. She did the sensible thing and ignored it, as she and Miller headed back up to homicide.

"I want to know where Jason Jones comes from," D.D. stated, working her way up the stairs. "Guy as cool and collected as that. Working as a small-time reporter, sitting on four million, and according to his own child doesn't even have a best friend. What the hell makes this guy tick?"

Miller shrugged.

"Let's get two detectives digging into some deep background," D.D. continued. "Cradle to grave, I want to know everything about Jason Jones, Sandra Jones, and their respective families. I can tell you now, something there is gonna click."

"I want his computer," Miller murmured.

"Hey, at least we have his garbage. Any news?"

"Got a crew on it now. Give them a couple of hours, they'll have a report."

"Miller?" she asked with a troubled look on her face.

"What?"

"I know Ree saw something that night. You know Ree saw something that night. What if the perpetrator knows it, too?"

"You mean Jason Jones?"

"Or Aidan Brewster. Or the unidentified subject 367."

Miller didn't answer right away, but started to look concerned, as well. Marianne Jackson had been right: Ree was very, very vulnerable right now.

"Guess we'd better hurry up," Miller said grimly.

"Yeah, guess so."

| CHAPTER FIFTEEN |

I dreamed of Rachel last night. She was saying, "No, no, no," and I was finding all the right spots to change her "no, no, no" to "yes, yes, yes."

"It's not my fault," I was saying in my dream, "you have such perfect breasts. God wouldn't have given you such perfect breasts if He'd really meant for me to leave you alone."

Then I was pinching her nipples between my fingers and she was leaning back and breathing heavy and I knew I was winning. Of course I was winning. I was bigger, stronger, smarter. So I rubbed and stroked and cajoled until that magic moment when I was sinking deep inside her and maybe she was crying a little but what did it matter? She was also gasping and writhing and I made it good for her. I swear I made it good.

In my dream world I could feel it all building. Her legs wrapping around my waist. Her breasts rubbing against my chest. And I wanted. Oh God, I wanted. And then...

Then I woke up. Alone. Hard as a rock. Mad as hell.

I rolled out of bed still breathing hard. Made it to the shower, cranked it on as hot as it would go. Barreled into the steam and finished my business, because when you're a twenty-three-year-old registered pervert, this is as good as it gets.

Except it's not. In my mind I can still touch and taste the girl I want. The girl I have always wanted. The girl I can never have.

So I whack off, and I hate every minute of it. Touching Rachel was purity. This is an aberration. Pure transactional lust, nothing more, nothing less.

But I get it over with, clean up, towel off.

I get dressed without turning on a light or looking into a mirror and I know before I ever leave the house that it's gonna be a bad day. A real shitkicker. My quiet little existence is over. I'm just waiting to see who delivers the death blow.

Colleen ended our little session last night by recommending that I continue with my usual routine. Sure, the police will pay me a visit. Can't blame them for asking. And of course it's my constitutional right to ask for counsel the moment I feel the need. But hey, I'm doing well. I'm a regular freaking success story. Don't give up ground too easily, that's what she tells me.

What she means is, running will be worse than staying. Something I'd already figured out for myself, thank you very much.

So hey, I walk to work. Seven-thirty A.M., I'm garbed in blue coveralls, my head under the hood of an old Chevy, pulling spark plugs. Look at me, Joe Schmoe, fighting the good fight. Yes sirree, Bob.

I'm tending, fixing, tightening, pretending that my grease-covered hands aren't shaking a hundred miles per hour, or that my body isn't still hard as a rock, or that I haven't worked myself into such an agitated state that for the first time in my life, I'm honestly praying no female walks through the door because I can't be held responsible for what I'll do. I'm fucked up. I'm just plain fucked up, and it's not even nine A.M.

Vito's got the radio on in the shop area. Local station. Plays a mix of eighties and nineties music. Lotta Britney Spears and Justin Timberlake. Nine-fifteen, the news comes on, and for the first time I hear the official announcement that a woman has gone missing in

South Boston. Young wife, beloved sixth grade teacher, vanished in the middle of the night, leaving behind a young child. Some female detective is laying it on thick.

I finish the Chevy, move on to a big Suburban that needs new rear brakes. The other guys are muttering now, making conversation.

"In Southie? No way."

"It's drugs, gotta be drugs. It's always drugs."

"Nah. It's the husband. Twelve to one he's got a little project on the side, and doesn't feel like paying alimony. Prick."

"Hope they get him this time. Who was that last year, two of his wives disappeared, but they still couldn't build a case...?"

On and on they go. I don't say a word. Just attack the lug nuts with the impact wrench, then wrestle off the two rear tires. The old Suburban has drum brakes. What a bitch.

Only vaguely do I become aware of the whispering, of the pointing. My face reddens automatically, I find myself sputtering to speak. Then realize no one is pointing at me. They're pointing at the front office, where Vito is currently standing with two cops.

I want to crawl inside the huge Suburban. I want to disappear into a pile of metal and plastic and chrome. Instead, I work my way around the vehicle, taking off the front tires now, like I'm gonna inspect the front disk brakes as well, even though nothing's written on the order sheet.

"You're a success story," I mutter to myself, "a regular freaking success story." But I'm not even buying it anymore.

I finish the Suburban. Cops are gone. I eye the clock, decide it's close enough to the mid-morning break. I go to fetch my lunch pail and discover Vito standing in front of my locker, arms crossed over his chest.

"My office. Now," he orders.

I don't fight Vito. I unpeel my blue coveralls, 'cause I can tell from the look on his face I won't be needing them anymore. He doesn't say a word, just stares at me the entire time, making sure buddy boy doesn't get out of his line of sight. Nothing bad is gonna happen on Vito's watch.

When I'm cleaned up, lunch box in hand, sweatshirt slung over my arm, Vito finally grunts and leads the way to his office. Vito knows what I've done. He's one of those employers who doesn't mind hiring sex offenders. He's got work that doesn't involve mixing with the public, and being a big, burly guy, he probably believes he can keep a kid like me in line. To be fair, he has moments where he's actually kind. Hell, maybe employing a felon is his idea of public service. He's taking in untouchables and turning them into productive members of society and all that. I don't know.

I just find myself thinking that Vito has never made me feel as low as he does now, his arms crossed over his chest, his expression a mix of disappointment and disgust. We arrive in his cramped office. He sits behind his dust-covered desk. I stand because there isn't another chair. He gets out the checkbook and starts writing.

"Police were here," he says crisply.

I nod, then realize he's not looking up, and force myself to say out loud: "I saw."

"Woman's gone missing. Sure you heard it on the news." He skewers me with a glance.

"I heard it."

"Police wanted to know if she got her car serviced here. Wanted to know if either she, or her cute four-year-old kid, had ever met you."

I don't say a word.

"How ya doin, Aidan?" Vito barks abruptly.

"Good," I whisper.

"Been attending your meetings, sticking with your program?"

"Yes."

"Drinking? Even a sip? Tell me the truth, meat, 'cause I'll know if you're lying. This is my town. All of Southie is my business. You hurt anyone in my town, you hurt me."

"I'm clean."

"Really? Police don't think so."

I wring my hands. I don't want to. The gesture shames me. Here I am, twenty-three years old and reduced to hunch-shouldered groveling in front of a man who can take me out with one swat of his platter-sized hand. He sits. I stand. He wields the power. I pray for pity.

At that moment, I hate my life. Then I hate Rachel, because if she hadn't been so pretty, so ripe, so *there*, maybe this never would've happened. Maybe I could've found myself in love with one of those slutty cheerleaders on the football field, or even the slightly buck-toothed girl who worked in the local deli. I don't know. Someone more appropriate. Someone polite society would've thought was okay for a nineteen-year-old boy to fuck. And then I wouldn't be in this mess. Instead, I would've gotten a chance to become a real man.

"I didn't do it," I hear myself say.

Vito just grunts, stares at me with his beady little eyes. His arrogance finally pisses me off. I've passed half a dozen lie detector tests with no one being the wiser. Like hell I'm gonna break for some thick-necked grease monkey.

I meet his gaze. I hold steady. And I can tell he can tell I'm angry, but that mostly it amuses him, and that sets me off all over again. My hands fist at my sides and I think for a second if something doesn't give soon, I'm gonna plant my fist into his face. Or maybe not his face. Maybe the wall. Except maybe not the wall. Maybe the glass window. That will shatter my hand, and wake me up with a symphony of broken bones and sliced-up flesh. And that's what I need: a good wake-up call to get me out of this nightmare.

Vito squints his eyes at me, then grunts and tears out the check.

"Final week's pay," he announces. "Take it. You're done."

I keep my hands fisted at my sides.

"I didn't do it," I say again.

Vito merely shakes his head. "Doesn't matter. You work here, the woman had her car serviced here. This is a business, meat, not a freakshow. I don't have time for the morning wash of your dirty laundry."

He places the check on the desk, and with one finger pushes it toward me. "Take it, don't take it. Either way, you're done."

So of course I take it. I leave, hearing Vito roar at the other mechanics to get back to work, then hearing each of them start to whisper.

It's not over, I realize then. Vito's gonna tell them the truth, three manly men hearing for the first time they worked day in, day out with a pervert. And now a woman is missing and they're gonna start doing some math in their heads, the kind where two plus two suddenly equals five.

They're gonna come for me. Soon. Very soon.

I try doing some math of my own in my frantic, pulse-pounding head.

Running equals being arrested by the police, locked away for life.

Staying equals being beaten by the goon squad, probably castrated for life.

I vote for running, then realize it doesn't matter, 'cause even with Vito's measly check, I still don't have the cash. Then I feel the agitation build, build, build again, until I'm nearly running down the street, crashing by some chick with floral-scented perfume, and I'm running faster with her perfume in my nose and a dozen unholy fantasies in my head and I'm not gonna make it. I'm not gonna make it.

The system's biggest success story is about to break. Yes sirree, Bob. The kid's gonna blow.

| CHAPTER SIXTEEN |

You know what people want more than anything else in the world? More than love, more than money, more than peace on earth? People want to feel normal. They want to feel like their emotions, their lives, their experiences, are just like everyone else's.

It's what drives us all. The Type-A workaholic corporate lawyer who hits the bars at eleven P.M. to bolt back Cosmos and pick up a nameless fuck, only to rise at six A.M., rinse all evidence of the night away, and garb herself in a sensible Brooks Brothers suit. The respected soccer mom, famous for her homemade brownies and Martha Stewart décor, who is secretly popping her son's Ritalin just so she can keep up. Or, of course, the highly esteemed community leader, who is secretly banging his male secretary, but still appears in front of the eleven o'clock news to tell the rest of us how we need to take more responsibility for our lives.

We don't want to feel freakish or different or isolated. We want to feel normal. We want to be just like everyone else, or at the very least, just like what some TV commercial for Viagra or Botox or debt consolidation tells us our lives should be. In our mission for normalcy, we will ignore what we must ignore. We will cover up what we must cover up. And we will disregard anything we need to disregard, just so we can hold on to our illusion of perfectly regulated bliss.

And maybe, in wanting so badly to be normal, in our own way, normal Jason and I became.

So I took off for a night or two every six to nine months. Working moms need a break, right? How kind and considerate of my husband to allow me occasional "spa" breaks. So he stayed up late, hunched over the computer, typing furiously. Writers often have long and irregular hours, right? How kind and understanding of me to never complain of my husband's demanding job.

We gave each other space. We disregarded what we needed to disregard. And in the process, we stood side by side and watched Ree careen down the sidewalk on her first tricycle. We cheered her first jump into a swimming pool. We laughed the first time she tiptoed into the freezing Atlantic Ocean and came screaming full speed back up the beach. We celebrated our daughter. We worshipped every giggle, laugh, burp, and chattering word that tumbled from her mouth. We adored her innocence, her free spirit, her spunk. And maybe in loving her, we learned also to love each other.

At least that's how it felt to me.

One night, toward the end of summer, when Ree was due to start preschool in September and I would start my first gig as a student teacher, Jason and I stayed up late. He had a George Winston CD playing. Something soft and melodic. Ree and I were constantly torturing him with rock-n-roll, but he always gravitated toward classical music. He would close his eyes, and enter some Zen state where I was certain he was sound asleep, only to realize he was humming softly under his breath.

Tonight, we sat on the little love seat. His left arm was thrown across the back, his fingers touching the nape of my neck and rubbing gently. He did this more and more. Light, little touches, caressing me almost absently. In the beginning, I had startled at the contact. I had learned since to sit still, not say a word. The longer I relaxed, the longer he touched me, and I enjoyed my husband's touch. Heaven help me, I liked the feel of his calloused fingertips grazing the back of my shoulders, sifting through my hair. Sometimes, he rubbed my scalp and I arched and shifted under his hand like a kitten.

Once I had tried to reciprocate, to scratch his back. The second my fingers went to lift his shirt, however, he got up and left the room. I never tried again.

A husband stroking his wife's neck while they cuddled on the love seat, on the other hand... Welcome to our little slice of normalcy.

"Do you believe in heaven?" I asked him casually. We'd watched some Harrison Ford movie that night, where the vengeful ghost of the husband's first wife had wreaked havoc on the household.

"Maybe."

"I don't."

His fingers tugged gently on my earlobe, firm, erotic pressure. I nestled closer to him, trying not to startle him, but having a harder and harder time sitting still. Who knew ears could be such an erogenous zone? But mine were, mine were.

"Why not?" he asked me, fingers moving from my earlobe, down the side of my neck, then back up again. A husband touching his wife. A wife snuggling with her husband. Normal. All perfectly normal.

So normal that some nights when I woke up alone in my marriage bed, my heart shattered into a thousand pieces. Yet I got up the next morning and did it all over again. Sometimes, I even heard my mother's voice in my mind, "I know something you don't know. I know something you don't know...."

She was right, in the end. At the ripe old age of twenty-one, I was finally seeing all of life's great truths: You can be in love and still feel incredibly lonely. You can have everything you ever wanted, only to realize that you wanted all the wrong things. You can have a husband as smart and sexy and compassionate as mine, and yet not really have him at all. And you can look at your own beautiful, precious daughter some days, and be genuinely jealous of how much he loves her, instead of you.

"Just don't," I said now. "Nobody wants to die, that's all. So they make up pretty stories of an eternal afterlife, to take away the fear. If you think about it, however, it doesn't make any sense. Without sadness, there can be no happiness, which means a state of eternal bliss really wouldn't be that blissful. In fact, at a certain point, it would be mostly annoying. Nothing to strive for, nothing to look forward to, nothing to do." I slid him a look. "You wouldn't last a minute."

He smiled, a lazy look on his dark features. He hadn't shaved today. I liked the days he skipped the razor, his unkempt beard a nice compli-

ment to his deep brown eyes and perpetually rumpled hair. I'd always appreciated the bad boy look.

I wished I could feel his beard, trace the line of his jaw until I could find his pulse point at the base of his throat. I wished I could know if his heart was beating as hard as mine.

"I saw a ghost once," he said.

"You did? Where?" I didn't believe him and he could tell.

He smiled again, unconcerned. "An old house near where I used to live. Everyone said it was haunted."

"So you just stopped by to check it out? Test out your male prowess?"

"I was visiting the owner. Unfortunately, she had died the night before. I found her body on the sofa, with her brother sitting beside her, which was interesting since he had died fifty years earlier."

I was still dubious. "What did you do?"

"I said thank you."

"Why?"

"Because once upon a time, her brother saved my life."

I scowled, agitated by the coyness of his reply, and worse, the ten thousand nerve endings he had now stroked to life.

"Is it always going to be like this between us?" I asked abruptly.

"Like what?" But his hand was retreating, his face shuttering up.

"Half answers. Semi-truths. I ask a simple question, you dole out one tidbit of information while hoarding the rest."

"I don't know," he said quietly. "Will it always be like this between us?"

"We're married!" I said impatiently. "It's been three years, for God's sake. We should be able to trust each other. Tell each other our deepest darkest secrets, or at least the basics of where we come from. Isn't marriage supposed to be a conversation that lasts a lifetime? Aren't we supposed to take care of each other, trust one another to keep each other safe?"

"Says who?"

I startled, shook my head. "What do you mean, says who?"

"I mean, says who? Who makes up these rules, sets these expectations? A husband and wife should keep each other safe. A parent should take care of a child. A neighbor should look after a neighbor. Who sets these rules and what have they done for you lately?"

His voice was gentle, but I knew what he meant and the starkness of his words made me flinch.

He said softly, "Tell me about your mother, Sandy."

"Stop it."

"You claim to want to know all my secrets, but you keep your own."

"My mother died when I was fifteen. End of story."

"Heart attack," he stated, repeating my previous assertions.

"It happens." I turned away.

After a moment, Jason's fingertips brushed my cheek, whispering across my lowered eyelashes.

"It will always be like this between us," he said quietly. "But it won't be this way for Ree."

"There are things you lose you can't get back," I whispered.

"I know."

"Even if you want them. Even if you search and pray and start completely over. It doesn't matter. There are things you lose you can't get back again. Things that once you know, you can never unknow."

"I understand."

I got off the sofa. Agitated now. I swear I could smell roses and I hated that smell. Why wouldn't it leave me alone? I had fled my parents' house, I had fled my parents' town. The damn roses ought to leave me alone.

"She was mentally ill," I blurted out. "A raging alcoholic. She did… crazy, crazy things and we covered for her. That's what my father and I did. We let her torture us every single day and we never said a word. Life in a small town, right? Gotta keep up appearances."

"She beat you."

I laughed but it wasn't a pleasant sound. "She fed me rat poison so she could watch the doctors pump my stomach. I was a tool for her. A beautiful little doll she could break every time she wanted attention."

"Münchhausen."

"Probably. I've never sought an expert opinion."

"Why not?"

"She's dead. What's the point?"

He gave me a look, but I refused to take the bait.

"Your father?" he asked at last.

"Successful lawyer with a reputation to uphold. Can't really be admitting that his wife bashes gin bottles over his head every other night. Wouldn't be good for business."

"He put up with it?"

"Isn't that how these things work?"

"Sadly, yes. Tell me again, Sandy, how did she die?"

I thinned my lips, refused him.

"Carbon monoxide poisoning," he said at last, a statement, not a question. "Found in her car in the garage. Suicide, I would guess. Or maybe she drank too much and passed out behind the wheel? What I don't understand is why the authorities let it go. Especially given that it was a small town, and someone, somewhere, had to know how she treated you."

I stared at him. I couldn't help myself. I stared and I stared and I stared. "You knew?"

"Of course. I wouldn't have married you otherwise."

"You investigated me?"

"It's a prudent thing to do, before asking a girl to become your wife." He touched my hand. This time, I jerked away. "You think I married you for Ree. You have always believed I married you for Ree. But I didn't. Or at least, not for her alone. I married you because of your mother, Sandy. Because you and I are alike that way. We know monsters are real, and they don't all live under the bed."

"It wasn't my fault," I heard myself say.

He was silent.

"She was mentally unstable. Suicide was probably only a matter of time. Last way to screw with us and all that." I was babbling. Couldn't shut up. Couldn't stop myself. "I was getting a little too big to keep dragging to the emergency room, so she upped and killed herself instead. After planning the biggest funeral the town had ever seen, of course. Oh, the roses she demanded for the event. The mounds and mounds of fucking roses..."

My hands fisted at my sides. I stared at my husband. Dared him to call me a freak, an ungrateful daughter, a white trash piece of shit. Look at me, I wanted to cry. My mother lived and I hated her. She died and I hated her more. I am *not* normal.

"I understand," he said.

"Afterward, I thought I would be happy. I thought, finally, my father and I could live in peace."

Jason was studying me intently now. "When you first met me, you said you wanted to get away, never look back. You weren't kidding, were you? All these years later, you've never called your father, never told him where we live, never let him know about Ree."

"No."

"You hate him that much?"

"All that and more."

"You think he loved your mother more than you," Jason stated. "He didn't protect you. Instead, he covered for her. And you've never forgiven him for it."

I didn't answer right away. Because at that moment, I was picturing my father again, his charming smile, the crinkle lines that appeared at the corners of his bright blue eyes, the way he could make you feel as if you were the center of the universe just by touching your shoulder. And I was so filled with rage, I could barely speak.

I know something you don't know. I know something you don't know....

She had been right. She had been so fucking right.

"You said we're different," I whispered hoarsely. "You said we know better, that the monsters aren't all under the bed."

Jason nodded.

"Promise me, then: If you ever see my father, if he should ever show up at our front door, you'll kill him first, and ask questions later. He'll never touch Ree. Promise me that, Jason."

My husband looked me in the eye. He said, "Consider it done."

Ree fell asleep in her booster seat before Jason even pulled out of the parking lot. Mr. Smith was curled up in the passenger's seat now, licking his paw, rubbing his cheek, licking his paw, rubbing his cheek. Jason drove aimlessly toward the interstate, not sure what to do.

He was tired. Exhausted. What he wanted most in the world was to curl up in the sanctuary of his own home, and let the world disappear.

He would sleep like the dead, and when he woke up again, Sandra would be standing beside the bed, smiling down at him.

"Wake up, sleepyhead," she would say, and he'd take her in his arms, and hold her as he should've been holding her the past five years. He would hug his wife, and he and Ree could be happy again. They would be a family.

He couldn't go home. News vans would be there, staked out across the street. Lights would flash, reporters shouting out questions Ree was too young to understand. They would scare her, and after the morning she'd had, he couldn't bear for her to be traumatized again.

The police believed he was guilty. He had seen it in their eyes, the minute the interview had concluded. His own daughter had implicated him, but he didn't blame her. Ree had done what they'd asked of her; she had told the truth the best she understood it to be. He'd spent four years preaching to his daughter not to lie. He couldn't be angry at her now for following the values he and Sandra had so carefully instilled in her.

He was proud of Ree, and that saddened him, because the more he turned the matter around in his mind, the more he arrived at the same inescapable conclusion: He would be arrested. Any day now, he supposed. The police were putting it all together now, building their case, buttoning it up tight. They'd taken his trash. They'd interrogated his child. Next would come a fresh sweep of his house, followed by a search warrant for his computer.

They would dig deeper into his background, trying to contact associates and friends; that would stall them for a bit. He never socialized with his associates and he never bothered to make friends. Plus, he checked his "firewalls" from time to time; they were holding tight. But nothing was impenetrable, especially once the right expert was brought to bear, and the Boston police had those kinds of resources. It wasn't like he was dealing with backwoods yokels here.

Of course, they would have to tend to the registered sex offender. That would demand additional time and resources. Maybe the guy would confess, but having met the pervert in question, Jason didn't see that happening. Aidan had seemed pretty cool, the kind of customer who'd been around. He'd make the police sweat for it.

So the police still had plenty of legwork to do, particularly with two viable suspects. Maybe that bought him more like three days, or five. Except that with every passing hour, the chances of Sandy being discovered alive dramatically decreased. Yesterday, there'd been a chance at a happy ending. Or maybe this morning.

If it became nightfall and Sandy still hadn't appeared...

The instant they discovered Sandy's body, that would be that. They'd come for him at his home. They would take Ree away from him. She would become a ward of the state. His daughter. The little girl he loved more than his very own life would be stuck in foster care.

He could hear Ree again, in the interrogation room, her singsong voice, reciting: "*'Please don't do this. I won't tell. You can believe me. I'll never tell. I love you. I still love you....'*"

His hands trembled lightly on the steering wheel. He caught the tremor, forced himself to steady. Now was not the time. Had to keep thinking. Had to keep moving. He had the media in front of him, the police behind him, and his daughter to consider. Push it away, lock it up tight. That's what he did best.

Keep thinking, keep moving. Figure out what happened to Sandy, quick, before the police took his daughter from him.

Then, in the next second, he thought of what his daughter had said again, all of what she'd said, and it came to him, his first glimmer of hope. Grieving husband, he reminded himself. Grieving husband.

He headed for Sandy's middle school.

| CHAPTER SEVENTEEN |

When Jason was fourteen years old, he had heard his parents talking late one night, when they thought he was asleep.

"Have you noticed his eyes?" his mother was saying. "Whether he's playing with Janie, or saying thank you for a bowl of ice cream, or asking permission to turn on the TV, his eyes are exactly the same. Flat. Empty. Like he doesn't feel a thing. I'm worried, Stephen. I mean, I'm really, really worried about him."

You should be, Jason had thought at the time. *You really, really should be.*

Now, adult Jason pulled into the middle school parking lot, found a space, and killed the engine. Ree stirred in the back, blinking awake with that internal monitor kids had that registered vehicles stopping. She'd need a moment or two, so he flipped down the Volvo's sun visor and contemplated his expression in the vanity mirror.

His sunken eyes were rimmed with dark shadows. He'd forgotten about shaving, and his thick beard was rapidly overtaking his gaunt face. He looked weary, worn around the edges. But he also looked rough, perhaps even dangerous, the kind of man who might have a hot temper and secretly beat his wife and kid.

He tried various positions with his lips, screwing up his features this way and that. Grieving husband, he reminded himself. Grieving husband.

His mother was right—he could rearrange his entire face, and his eyes still gave him away. He looked like a man with a thousand-yard stare.

He'd keep his head down, he decided. Bowed with grief. It was the best he could do.

In the back, Ree finally yawned, stretching out her arms and legs. She looked at him, then looked at Mr. Smith, then at the scene outside her window.

She recognized the building and perked up immediately. "Is Mommy here? Are we picking up Mommy?"

He winced, choosing his words carefully. "Do you remember how the police sent out officers to help us find Mr. Smith?"

"Uh-huh."

"Well, we're going to do the same thing for Mommy. The police are sending officers to look for her, but also, our friends want to help. So we're going to talk to Mommy's friends and see if they can help us find her. Just like we did with Mr. Smith."

"Mr. Smith came home," Ree said.

"Exactly. And with any luck, Mommy will come home, too."

Ree nodded, seemed content. It was the first real discussion they'd had regarding Sandy's disappearance, and it went about as well as he could expect. Of course, children cycled in and out of strong emotions. At the moment, Ree was still exhausted from the morning's ordeal and eager to be pacified. Later, when the grief and rage returned...

He got out of the car, unloaded Ree. They left Mr. Smith behind with the same *Rabid Cat* signs posted on the front and back windows. Jason didn't trust middle school students any more than the gangs of Roxbury.

They hit the front admin office, Jason with his head bowed, Ree clutching Lil' Bunny.

"Mr. Jones!" Adele, the school secretary, greeted them immediately. The rush of sympathy in her voice, the pitying look she bestowed upon Ree hit him in the solar plexus, and for a moment, he stood there, honestly stunned, blinking at the rush of moisture in his eyes. He didn't have to pretend anything, because at that precise moment, for the first time, Sandy's disappearance became real. She was gone, and he was the grieving husband, alone with his bewildered kid.

His knees wobbled. He almost went down, in the middle of his wife's school, looking at the linoleum she trod upon five days a week, the walls she gazed at five days a week, the front desk she passed by five days a week.

No one had offered him any sympathy. Up until this point, it had all been about gamesmanship with the police, his own employer, the pervert down the street. Now, here was Adele, coming around the counter to give him a quick pat on the back while wrapping his daughter in a great big hug. And he decided at that moment, in his typical way, that he hated Adele the school secretary. Her sympathy burned. He'd take gamesmanship any day of the week.

"I'm sure Phil would love to speak with you." Adele was chattering away, referring to the school principal. "He's in a meeting at the moment—why, the phone has been ringing off the hook since this morning's announcement. We've hired a grief counselor, of course, and you know all of the staff wants to help. We're having a special meeting at four to discuss organizing search efforts for tomorrow. Phil thought we could stage everything out of the gymnasium, get other locals coming in to assist—"

Adele broke off abruptly, seeming to realize she might be saying too much in front of the child. She had the good grace to blush, then gave Ree another bolstering hug.

"Would you like to wait?" the secretary asked him kindly. "I can get you some coffee or water. Maybe some crayons for Ree?"

"Actually, I was wondering if I could swing by Mrs. Lizbet's classroom first. Just for a minute, if you don't mind…"

"Of course, of course. Second period lunch break will be starting in about three minutes. I'm sure she'd be willing to take time for you."

Jason managed a quick smile of gratitude, then held out his hand for Ree. She went with him down the hall. Sure enough, a bell rang and the space began to fill with students, pouring out from various classrooms. The sudden commotion distracted Ree, saving him from all the questions he was sure she now had.

They took a right turn down past a row of blue-painted lockers, then a left down a bright orange row. Elizabeth Reyes, aka Mrs. Lizbet, taught seventh grade social studies, her classroom at the very end of the hall. Early fifties, gracefully thin, with long silver-streaked hair generally wound into a thick knot, she was still erasing the chalkboard when he and Ree walked in.

"Mrs. Lizbet!" Ree cried, and ran over immediately for a hug.

Mrs. Lizbet returned the embrace, kneeling down so she and Ree would be at eye level. "Ree-Ree! How are you, sweetheart?"

"Good," Ree replied shyly, because even at the age of four, she already understood that was the only answer one gave in polite society.

"Hey, who is this?"

"Lil' Bunny."

"Hi, Lil' Bunny. Nice dress!"

Ree giggled and leaned into Mrs. Lizbet again, wrapping her arms around the woman's waist. It wasn't like Ree to be so affectionate with other adults, and Jason could see in his daughter's eyes her longing for her mother, for the familiar comfort of a female embrace. Mrs. Lizbet met his gaze above Ree's head, and he tried not to flinch at her steady appraisal. She was granting him neutral status, it appeared, a step above the police's immediate distrust, a step below Adele's sympathetic rush.

"Sweetheart," Mrs. Lizbet said now, pulling back from Ree, "do you remember Jenna Hill, from the basketball team? Well, I happen to know this is Jenna's lunch period, and she's been dying for someone to practice with. What do you think? Can you shoot some hoops?"

Ree's eyes lit up. She nodded her head vigorously.

Mrs. Lizbet held out her hand. "All right, come with me, child. I'll take you to Jenna and you can practice together. Your father and I need just a minute, then we'll join you there."

It was a gracious way of buying time for frank conversation, and Jason was impressed.

His daughter followed Mrs. Lizbet toward the door, balking only at the last moment. He watched the emotions play out over her face. Her need to be with him, her only anchor in a rapidly disintegrating world, warring with her desire to play with Jenna, a bona fide basketball player, which ranked up there with rock star in a four-year-old's universe.

Then Ree squared her little shoulders and headed with Mrs. Lizbet down the hall. Jason was left alone in the classroom, already missing Ree ten times more than she could ever miss him, and wondering why he had to be so miswired that hatred fortified him, while love cut him to the bone.

Elizabeth Reyes had served as Sandy's instructor last year and her mentor this year. Over that time frame, Jason supposed that he had met her at least a dozen times. Him bringing Ree to join Sandy for the occasional lunch. Drop-offs or pickups after school. He would wave, Elizabeth would wave. So many meetings and yet he was certain she would agree that neither of them knew the other well.

Upon returning to the classroom, she closed the door behind her. He watched her glance at the clock, then smooth her skirt nervously. The woman had survived twenty years teaching seventh-graders, however. She stiffened her spine and got on with it.

"So," she said briskly, moving to the front of the classroom, where he imagined she felt most comfortable. "Phil announced this morning that Sandy has been missing since Wednesday night. He said the police aren't sure what happened. No one has any leads."

"I was covering a fire Wednesday night," Jason supplied. "When I returned home around two, Ree was sleeping in her room, but the rest of the house was empty. Sandy's purse and cell phone were in the kitchen. Her car was still in the driveway. But there was no sign of my wife."

"My God." Elizabeth staggered back a step, then braced herself against the side of her desk, her hands trembling noticeably. "When Phil announced it this morning, it was hard to take seriously. I mean, Sandy, of all people. I figured it was some kind of mistake. A miscommunication, maybe even a fight between the two of you." She eyed him boldly. "You're a young couple. Sometimes young couples need time to cool off."

"She wouldn't have left Ree," he said simply.

The woman sagged again. "No," she murmured. "Quite right. She would never have left Ree." She sighed again, seemed to pull herself together. "Phil arranged for grief counselors for the kids and staff. There are protocols for these kinds of things, you know. We held a small assembly, got the news out. Better for the kids to hear it from us than from the rumor mill."

"What did he say?"

"Just that Mrs. Jones was missing, that everyone was working really hard to find her, and if the kids had any questions, they should feel free to talk to their teachers. The police are doing everything in their power, and he hoped to have good news shortly, etc., etc."

"I understand they are organizing a search party for tomorrow, meeting in the gymnasium."

She gave him a look. "Are you going to help?"

"I'm not sure the police would welcome my efforts. I'm the husband, you know, the default person of interest."

Elizabeth continued to regard him evenly, which he took as a hint.

Grieving husband, grieving husband. He spread his hands, looked down at them.

"I don't know what happened," he murmured. "I went to work as a husband and father, and I returned to a nightmare. Did someone abduct my wife? There is no sign of breaking and entering. Did she run off with some other guy? I can't imagine her leaving Ree. Did she just need some time away to think? I hope and I pray, Elizabeth. I hope and I pray."

"Then I will do the same."

He took a shaky breath, into it now, needing to complete his mission. "We *are* a young couple," he stated. "It's not easy, juggling two jobs and a small child. I would understand if Sandy was unhappy. I could see that maybe she would be drawn to someone else."

Elizabeth didn't say anything, merely continued to regard him coolly.

"It doesn't matter to me," he said hastily. "If she needs time to breathe, hell, even if she's found someone else...I can deal with that, Elizabeth. I will have to deal with that. I just want her back. If not for me, then at least for Ree."

"You think she met someone," Elizabeth said bluntly. "And you think she told me about it."

He went with the helpless shrug. "Women talk."

"Not your wife," she informed him sharply. "And not with me."

"Then with whom? Last I knew, you were her closest friend."

Elizabeth sighed again, breaking off eye contact to glance instead at the clock. He found himself clenching his stomach, as if steeling for a blow. She would only look away for one reason—because she had something to say.

"Look, I respected Sandy a great deal," Elizabeth began. "She's an excellent teacher. Patient with the children, but also...steady. You don't see a lot of that in young teachers these days. Especially the females. They bring their personal dramas to work, and maybe that gives them a certain cachet with the students, but it doesn't buy them brownie points with the staff. Sandy was different. She was always composed, always reliable. I can't picture her sitting around and gossiping with anyone, including me. Besides, when would she have the time?"

Jason nodded, dealing with that stumbling block himself. The simplest explanation for Sandy's disappearance, of course, was another man. She'd run off with a lover, or she'd taken a lover who'd suffered a change of heart.

"Don't do this. I still love you. Please..."

But Jason didn't know how such a thing could've happened. So his wife took a "spa" break every six to nine months? He understood he did not meet all of her needs as a husband. But it was only a couple of nights a year. Surely, even a woman as attractive as Sandy couldn't forge a relationship out of two nights a year.

"After school?" he murmured.

Elizabeth shook her head. "Sandy lingered only for staff meetings. Then she was out the door to pick up Ree, with whom I presume she spent most of her nights."

Jason nodded. Aside from Sandy's spa breaks, her afternoons and evenings were dominated by caring for Ree. And as he could attest from the past forty-eight hours, a four-year-old made an excellent chaperone.

"Lunch?" he tried.

"It would only work if the other man was a fellow teacher, and they found a broom closet," Elizabeth said dubiously.

"What about the male teachers?"

"I never noticed her fraternizing with anyone in particular, male or female. When Sandy was here, she was about her students."

"Free period, open period, what do they call it these days?"

"Every teacher has one free period," she explained for him. "Most of us spend it grading papers, or preparing ourselves for later classes, though there's nothing that says Sandy couldn't have left the grounds. Though, now that I think about it…"

She hesitated, eyed him again.

"Starting in September, Sandy took on a special project. She was working with one of the eighth-graders, Ethan Hastings, on a teaching module."

"A teaching module?"

"For his computer science class, Ethan was supposed to design a beginner's guide to the Internet, which would be tested out on the sixth grade social studies class. Hence, Sandy's involvement. The project ended months ago, but I still see the two of them huddled together in the computer lab. I had the impression from Sandy that Ethan is now working on something bigger and she was continuing to help him out."

"Sandy…and a student?" Jason couldn't wrap his brain around it. It was inconceivable.

Elizabeth arched a brow. "No," she said firmly. "One, because young and pretty or not, I would never assume such a lack of professionalism from Sandy Jones. And two, well, if you saw Ethan Hastings, you'd understand point two. What I'm trying to tell you is that Sandy had only one free period each day, and hers was occupied."

Jason nodded slowly, looking down at the floor, scuffing his toe. There was something here, though. He had to believe there was something here, if only because it was better than his other options.

"What about Thursday nights?" he asked abruptly. "When Sandy and Ree came to see the basketball games?"

"What about them?"

"Did she sit in the same place? Maybe beside the same guy? Perhaps she met someone during those nights, a fellow parent."

Elizabeth shrugged. "I don't know, Jason. I never noticed. But then, I haven't made it to many of the games this season." She gestured to her silvered hair. "I'm a grandma now, can you believe it? My daughter had her first child in November. I've spent most of my Thursday nights rocking my grandson, not sitting courtside. Though I can tell you who would know about Thursday nights. The basketball team picked up a new statistician for the season: Ethan Hastings."

| CHAPTER EIGHTEEN |

Sergeant D.D. Warren didn't give a flying fig what Colleen Pickler had said about sex offenders being model parolees, full of repentance and eager to please their court-appointed babysitters. D.D. had served eight years in uniform, and as a first responder to too many scenes of hysterical mothers and glassy-eyed children, she was firmly of the opinion that when it came to sex offenders, hell was not big enough.

Homicides in her world came and went. The CSAs, on the other hand, always left their mark. She could still recall the time she was called out to a preschool after a five-year-old boy disclosed to his teacher that he had been assaulted in the bathroom. The alleged perpetrator—the kid's classmate, another five-year-old boy. Upon further investigation, D.D. and her partner had determined that the suspect lived with not one, but two registered sex offenders. The first being his father, the second being his older brother. D.D. and her partner had dutifully reported the incident to DCF, naive enough to believe that would make a difference.

No. DCF had determined it was not in the boy's best interest to break up the family. Instead, the kid was kicked out of the preschool for inappropriate contact with another classmate and absolutely nothing else happened until six months later when D.D. encountered the same kid yet again. This time, he was a witness to a triple homicide, perpetrated by his older brother.

D.D. still dreamed of the kid's empty gray eyes sometimes. The learned hopelessness as he flatly recounted his sixteen-year-old brother pulling into the mini-mart, how he followed his older brother into the store, thinking he was gonna get a Twinkie. Instead, his brother had pulled a gun, and then, when the nineteen-year-old store clerk hesitated, the brother had opened fire on the clerk, as well as two other kids, who happened to be in the wrong place at the wrong time.

D.D. had taken the boy's testimony. Then she'd sent him home to his sex offender father. Nothing else the system would allow her to do.

That had been twelve years ago. Every now and then, D.D. was tempted to run the boy's name, see what had happened to him. But she didn't really need to. A kid like that, who by the age of five had been a repeated victim of sexual assault, a perpetrator of sexual assault, and then a witness to a triple homicide... Well, it's not like he was gonna grow up to be President, now, was he?

There were other stories, of course. The time she'd arrived at a dilapidated triple-decker to discover the wife standing over her husband's dead body, still holding the butcher knife, just in case after being stabbed two dozen times, he managed to get back up. Turned out, the wife had discovered her husband's secret file on the computer, where he stored home videos he'd been shooting every night of himself having sex with their two daughters.

Interestingly enough, the daughters had disclosed for the first time when they were seven and nine, but when the police followed up, they'd found no evidence of abuse. The girls tried again when they were twelve and fourteen, but by then, given their penchant for micro minis and tube tops, not even their own mother had found them credible.

The video, on the other hand, had done the trick. So the mother had filleted the husband, then promptly sunk deep into depression after her court-appointed attorney got her off. As for the two girls, victims of incest from the time they were four and six, with full video footage of the repeated attacks so broadly disseminated on the Internet it could never be called back...Once again, it wasn't like either girl was gonna grow up to be President, now, was she?

D.D. and Miller pulled up to the address Colleen Pickler had provided for Aidan Brewster. D.D. was already practicing deep breathing exercises and trying to keep her fingers from forming an automatic fist. The PO had advised them to play nice.

"Most sex offenders are inherently spineless, with low self-esteem—that's why they prey on children, or, as a nineteen-year-old, feel most comfortable with a fourteen-year-old girlfriend," she'd counseled. "You come down on Aidan like a ton of bricks, and he won't be able to take it. He'll shut down and you'll be left spinning your wheels on the road to nowhere. Become his friend first. Then screw him over."

The whole friend thing was never gonna work for D.D., so by tacit agreement, Miller would be taking the lead. He got out of the car first, and she followed him up the walk to the modest, 1950s home. Miller knocked. No answer.

They'd expected as much. They'd already learned from the two uniformed officers that Sandra Jones had her car serviced at the same garage where Aidan Brewster worked. Colleen Pickler had called them just an hour later to say she'd been informed by the garage owner, Vito Marcello, that he'd terminated Aidan Brewster's employment.

Mutual feeling was that Aidan was feeling spooked. Better to grab him now, before the guy bolted into the wind.

Miller knocked again, then pressed his shield against the side window.

"Aidan Brewster," he called out. "Boston PD. Open up, buddy. We just want to talk."

D.D. raised a brow, and huffed impatiently. Breaking down the door would feel so much better, in her opinion, even if judges frowned on that sort of thing.

Just when she was thinking she might get her wish, there came the sound of a bolt lock drawing back. Then the creak of the front door cracking open.

"I want police protection," Aidan Brewster stated. He stood with his body hidden behind the door, a wild look in his eyes. "Guys in the shop are gonna kill me. I just know it."

Miller didn't step forward. Like D.D., he moved just slightly, onto the balls of his feet, his right hand hovering inside his jacket, close to his holstered weapon. "Why don't you step out from behind the door," Miller said calmly, "where we can talk face to face?"

"I'm looking at your face," the sex offender said in bewilderment. "And I'm trying to talk. I'm telling you, Vito ratted me out—told the guys I was a registered pervert. And they're mad, you know. Guys like them aren't supposed to hang out with pussies like me. I'm dead for sure."

"Did someone say something explicit?" D.D. spoke up, her voice striving for the same measured calm of Miller's tone, even as she stood one step behind the detective, her fingers dancing across the butt of her Glock .40.

"Say it?" The kid sounded even more agitated. "It's not something you have to say. I heard them whispering. I know what's going down. Everyone thinks I killed that woman, thanks to your lackeys." The kid finally came out from behind the door, to reveal disheveled clothing and two empty hands. He stabbed a finger at Miller. "It's your fault I'm in this mess," he told the older detective. "You gotta help me out. You *owe* me that much."

"Why don't we talk about it?" Miller finally stepped forward, pushing open the door with his foot, then gently pressing Aidan back into the hallway. The kid seemed oblivious to the anxiety he'd raised in the cops. Instead, he was already turning around and heading to the back of the house, where they understood he had a one-bedroom apartment.

The space was small. Kitchenette, floral love seat, ancient TV. D.D. figured that the landlord, a Mrs. April Houlihan, was responsible for the décor, because she couldn't imagine a twenty-something male being quite so into crocheted doilies. Aidan didn't take a seat, but stood next to the kitchen counter. He wore a green elastic band around his left wrist, and was snapping it compulsively.

"Who are these guys, and what did they say to you?" she asked now, watching the skin on his wrist turn red and wondering why the stinging sensation didn't make him flinch.

"I'm not saying anything more," Aidan declared in a rush. "More I tell you, the more I'm dead. Just…assign me protection. A police cruiser, a local motel. Something. You gotta do *something*."

D.D. decided Colleen Pickler had been right—Aidan Brewster was a first-class whiner.

As the bad cop, she felt entitled to say, "If at some point you'd like to file a formal complaint against one of your coworkers, we'd be happy to look into the matter. Until then, however, there's nothing we can do."

She thought Aidan's eyes might roll back in his head from sheer panic. Miller shot her a warning glance.

"Why don't we start from the beginning," Good Cop said in a soothing manner, taking out the mini-recorder, turning it on. "We'll have a chat, get the matter resolved here and now. A little cooperation from you, Aidan, and maybe we can reciprocate by getting the word out that you're in the clear on this. 'Kay?"

" 'Kay," the kid whispered. *Snap, snap, snap* with the elastic.

"So." Miller pushed the mini-recorder closer to Aidan, got down to business. He held the kid's attention, so D.D. seized the opportunity to roam the apartment. Without a warrant, she was restricted to only things in plain sight, but it never hurt to recon. She hit the bedroom, wrinkling her nose at the smell.

"Have you ever met Sandra Jones?" Miller was asking in the front room.

D.D. spied rumpled bedding, a pile of dirty clothes—mostly blue jeans and white T-shirts—a trash can that held used Kleenex. A corner of a magazine peeked out from underneath the mattress. Porn, she guessed, because what else would you hide under the mattress?

"Yeah, I mean, I met her. But I didn't *know* her, know her," Aidan was saying. "I saw her sometimes on the street, playing with her kid. But I always crossed to the other side of the street. Swear it! And yeah, okay, I remember her coming into the garage, now that you mention it. But I don't work the counter. I'm in the back and only the back. Vito knows the terms of my parole."

"What color is her hair?" Miller asked.

Kid shrugged. "Blonde."

"Eyes?"

"Dunno."

"She's young. Close to your age."

"Now, see, I don't even know that much."

D.D. wanted to gag. She used the tip of her pen to ease out a bit more of the magazine. *Penthouse*, it looked to her. No big deal. She let it go, but already wondered what else Aidan Brewster might have under his mattress.

"Talk to me about Wednesday night," Miller was saying. "Did you go out, meet with your friends? Do anything in particular?"

D.D. eased over to what appeared to be a closet. She saw more clothes poking out, some white socks, dirty underwear. Door was open four inches. She decided to make it six. She saw a chain dangling down from the ceiling, and used it to click on the overhead light.

"I don't have friends," Aidan protested. "I don't go to bars, I don't hang out with buddies. I watch TV, mostly reruns. I like *Seinfeld,* maybe a little *Law & Order.*"

"Tell me what you saw Wednesday night."

"Seinfield was master of his domain," Aidan said dryly. "And McCoy prosecuted some cult leader guy who thought he was God."

D.D. saw more piles of clothes. She frowned, withdrew, then paused. She glanced again at the piles of dirty laundry on the bedroom floor, then the pile of clothing in the closet. How many pairs of blue jeans and white T-shirts could one guy own?

Plain sight, plain sight, plain sight.

She kicked her foot into the closet pile, pressing down. And sure enough, hit something hard. Metal, she thought. Rectangular. Decent-sized. Computer? Lockbox? House safe? A computer would violate the terms of the kid's parole. Interesting.

She drew back again, chewing her lower lip, debating her options.

"Don't be yanking my chain," Miller was saying now. "Because I can look up what aired Wednesday night. You get this wrong, we're gonna be calling you down to the station, and this time, we won't be friends."

"I didn't do anything!" Aidan exploded.

"Woman vanishing on your block is entirely coincidental?"

"She's a grown woman. Come on, you've seen my record. What the hell would I want with a mom?"

"Ah, but she's a young, pretty mom. Same age as yourself. Lonely, too. Husband that works nights. Maybe she just wanted to talk. Maybe it started out with you two as friends. Did she learn what you had done, Aidan? Find out about your first love and freak out?"

"I never spoke to her! Ask anyone. If that woman was outside, she was with her kid. And I stay clear of kids!"

"You lost your job, Aidan. Must make you mad."

"Hell yeah!"

"Everyone thinks you're good for this. Got a garage full of guys who want to make an example of you. I don't blame you for being agitated."

"Hell yeah!"

"Wrist hurt?" Miller asked abruptly.

"What?"

"Wrist hurt? You've been snapping away for ten minutes now. Tell me about the elastic, Aidan. Is that part of your program? Snap the elastic every time you're thinking impure thoughts involving little kids? My, my, you're having an impure day."

"Hey, knock it off! You don't know nothin' about nothin'. I'm not into kids. I was never into kids."

"So a twenty-three-year-old mom isn't out of the question?"

"Stop it! You're putting words into my mouth. I fell in love with the wrong girl, okay? That's all I did wrong. I fell in love with the wrong girl, and now my life's shit. Nothing more, nothing less."

D.D. came out of the bedroom. Her sudden reappearance startled Aidan, and she could tell that for the first time he realized she'd left the room and where she must have gone. His gaze dropped immediately to the floor. She liked it when liars were predictable.

"Hey, Aidan. How 'bout giving me a tour of your room?"

He gave her a bitter smile. "Looks to me like you already got one."

"Yeah, but I'm curious about something. How 'bout we look together?"

"No."

"No?" She feigned surprise. "Now, Aidan, you were doing such a nice job of cooperating. Like Miller said, sooner we clear you on this, sooner we can pass the word along in the community. I'm sure Vito'd love to hear his favorite mechanic can return to work."

Aidan didn't reply. He'd stopped snapping the band. His gaze was zipping around the room instead, around and around and around. He was looking for the out. Not physically. But the lie, the excuse. The magic words that would make his problem go away.

He couldn't come up with any, and she watched his shoulders hunch as if steeling for the blow.

"I want you to go now," he said.

"Aidan—" Miller began.

"You're not going to help me," the kid interjected bluntly. "We all know you won't, so cut the bullshit. I'm a pervert to you, too. And it doesn't really matter that I've served my time or that I've stuck with the program and the terms of my parole. Once a pervert, always a pervert, isn't that how it goes? I didn't touch the woman. I told Vito that, I told the husband that—"

"You told the husband that?" D.D. interjected.

"Yeah." Aidan raised his head belligerently. "I had a little chat with the husband. He seemed mighty interested that a registered sex offender lived down the street. In fact," now the kid's gaze was calculating, "I bet he told you all about me."

D.D. didn't answer.

"It's pretty convenient for him, don't you think? Why, you being *here*, questioning me, means you can't be *there*, questioning him. Yeah, I'd say my presence is the best thing that ever happened to Mr. Jones. Wonder how long before he tells the press about me, hmmm? That'll get them good and excited.

"So, come to think about it, it's not just in *my* best interest to be cleared of these ugly accusations, it's in *your* best interest as well, isn't it? 'Cause as long as you're looking at me, you can never move against him. And I bet he knows that. Cool cat, Mr. Jones. I bet he knows an awful lot of things."

D.D. didn't say a word. She kept her features smooth, composed. Just her hand fisted behind her back.

"Show me your closet, Aidan."

"No thank you."

"Help me now, or be arrested by me later."

The trapped look was gone. Now the kid was downright cocky. "I'll take my chances."

"You know, Aidan, I'm not partial to my predators. You, Mr. Jones, hell, the Boogey Man in the closet. I'll arrest you all, let the court sort it out. That works for me."

"Can't. Multiple suspects would lead to reasonable doubt."

"Yeah, but it can take months to go to trial. Months of you sitting in jail, unable to make bail, while word travels round that a known sex offender lives in cell eleven."

He blanched. Sex offenders didn't do well in prison. Inmates had their own code of ethics, and according to the jailhouse value system, shanking a pervert was a great way to move up in the world. Build a rep and add a teardrop to your cheek, while making the world a better place.

Aidan had been right the first time—his life was shit, and so were his options.

But the kid surprised her. Showed some of the backbone he'd been missing earlier.

"I didn't hurt the woman," he said stiffly. "But I did see something."

That caught D.D.'s attention. Miller jolted as well. Seemed a little late for such a disclosure, which made them both automatically suspicious.

"I heard a noise Wednesday night. Something woke me up. I had to pee. So I got out of bed. I was looking out the window—"

"Which window?" D.D. interrupted.

"Kitchen window. Above the sink." Aidan gestured, and she crossed to the kitchenette. Most houses in Southie were stacked side by side. The house next to Aidan's, however, was set way back, allowing him a decent enough view of the street.

"Saw a car go by, moving slow, as if it had just pulled out of a driveway. Wouldn't normally think much of such a thing, but one A.M. is a crazy time for someone to be coming or going on this block."

D.D. didn't say anything, though, in fact, Aidan's neighbor Jason Jones routinely came and went in the small hours of the morning.

"Car looked peculiar," Aidan offered. "Lots of antennas sticking up from the top. Like a limo, one of those car service vehicles."

"What color?" Miller asked.

Kid shrugged. "Dark."

"License plate?"

"At one A.M.? Hell, I don't have X-ray vision."

"Where did the car come from?"

"Same direction as Sandy Jones's house."

"You know her name," D.D. spoke up sharply.

Aidan shot her a look. "Everyone knows her name. You announced it on the freaking news."

"You playing us, Aidan? Seems convenient, suddenly offering an eyewitness account."

"I was saving it up. Can't give something for nothing, right? Well, you want to arrest me, so consider this the consolation prize. I didn't hurt the woman, but maybe, you find that car, you'll find the guy who did. I think I've already mentioned that would be in our mutual best interests."

D.D. had to hand it to the kid. She did want to deck him, and he'd totally shut her down from searching his closet.

She glanced at Miller, saw the same assessment in his eyes. Interview was done. Real or not, a vague description of a mystery vehicle was as good as they were gonna get.

"We'll be in touch with your PO," she informed Aidan.

Kid nodded.

"Of course you'll let us know if you have any change of address."

"Of course you'll provide police protection once I'm beaten to a pulp," he countered.

"Then we agree."

She and Miller headed for the door. Aidan followed in their wake, pointedly locking the door behind them.

"Well, that was a barrel of laughs," Miller said as they headed down the walk.

"He totally has something stashed in his closet. A computer, safe, something."

"So many search warrants, so little probable cause." Miller sighed.

"No shit."

They hit the car, D.D. turning around for a last look at the house. She took in the long narrow lot, the trees in the back that offered some privacy between the modest little home and its sprawling neighbor. "Wait a sec," she called out. "Gotta check something."

She jogged around the house, leaving Miller to stare after her in confusion. It only took her a minute or two. She'd always been a champ tree climber as a girl, and the old oak offered the perfect ladder of limbs. She went up, looked out, then scrambled back down and around before anyone could be the wiser.

"Get this," she called out, huffing it back to the car. She opened the door, slid in as Miller started the engine. "From the tree in the back yard—perfect view into Sandy and Jason's bedroom."

"Lying sack of shit," Miller muttered.

"Yeah. But is he our lying sack of shit?"

"I'm not getting warm fuzzies."

D.D. nodded thoughtfully as Miller pulled away from the curb. They'd no sooner hit the bridge, when Miller's radio fired to life. He took the call, then hit the switch for his lights and swung into a crazy U-turn that had them roaring back into South Boston.

D.D. grabbed the dash. "What the hell—"

"You're gonna love this," Miller reported excitedly. "Report of an incident—at Sandra Jones's middle school."

| CHAPTER NINETEEN |

Jason and Elizabeth Reyes had just exited her classroom when something hard hit Jason from behind. Jason stumbled, almost caught himself, then got nailed a second time behind his left knee.

He went down flat on his face, feeling the breath swoosh out of his chest. Then a small, furious form was upon him, pummeling the back of his neck, the side of his face, the top of his head. Jason's hands were trapped beneath his stomach, hard knots against his kidneys. He struggled to get his arms beneath him, to heave himself up and over, while a sharp-cornered textbook connected with the side of his face.

"You killed her, you killed her, you killed her! You bastard, you big stupid son of a bitch. She warned me about you. She warned me!"

"Ethan! For heaven's sake, Ethan Hastings, stop it!"

Ethan Hastings was not interested in Mrs. Lizbet's command. From what Jason could tell in his shocked state, the computer nerd had a schoolbook and knew how to use it. The corner of the primer had cut his eye; Jason could feel the blood trickling down his temple even as the kid walloped him again.

Running footsteps now. Other people drawn by the commotion.

"Ethan, Ethan," a male voice was shouting down the hall. "You get off him. Right now!"

Get up, get up, get up, get up, Jason was thinking. *For heaven's sake, get your hands beneath you and GET UP.*

"I loved her. I loved her, I loved her. How dare you? How dare you?"

The third blow caught Jason beneath the ear and he saw stars. His vision blurred. He could tell his eyes wanted to roll up inside his head. His chest was too tight, he couldn't draw a breath, making his lungs burn. He was going to pass out. He couldn't afford to pass out.

"I fucking hate you!"

Then as quickly as it had started, it was done. Footsteps arrived, strong male arms grabbing the eighth-grader's furious body and dragging him, kicking, off of Jason's back. Jason seized the opportunity to flip over, struggling like a beached whale to draw breath. His chest hurt. His head, his back, behind his knee, where apparently he'd been slugged with the complete set of *Encyclopedia Britannica.* Holy crap.

Mrs. Lizbet was looking down at him, worry creasing her brow. "Are you okay? Don't move. We'll call an ambulance."

No, he tried to say, but the word didn't come out. He finally managed to inhale, his chest expanding with a grateful rush. He managed the word better on the exhale, low and pitiful as it sounded: "No."

"Don't be stupid—"

"No!" He rolled back over onto his hands and knees, his head hanging down, his skull still ringing. Leg hurt. Face hurt. Chest was better. See, real progress.

He got himself to his feet and became aware of approximately eight dozen wide-eyed teenagers and half a dozen very concerned adults standing around him. Ethan Hastings was being pinned in place by a man who appeared to be the gym teacher. The kid, all hundred and thirty pounds of him, was still struggling furiously, his carrot-topped, freckle-covered face staring at Jason with unadulterated hatred.

Jason put a hand to his face and wiped away the first streak of blood. Then the second. Kid had cut him pretty good, next to his left eye, but it was nothing that wouldn't heal.

"What in the world…" The principal finally arrived at the scene. Phil Stewart took one look at Jason's bruised and bleeding face, then Ethan's rage-filled features, and started snapping commands. "You," finger at Ethan, "in my office. And the rest of you," finger at gawking kids, "back to class."

The principal had spoken. Kids dispersed as swiftly as they had gathered, and Jason found himself following Ethan Hastings down the hallway, Mrs. Lizbet's concerned hand on his elbow. He was trying to understand what had just happened to him, and doing a lousy job of it.

"Ree?" he asked in a low voice.

"Still in the gym. I'll have Jenna walk her to the home ec class. They spend half their time baking cookies. That should keep her busy."

"Thank you." They came to the nurse's office. Elizabeth steered him inside, where he met the shocked gaze of a matronly woman wearing cat-patterned surgical scrubs.

"Playing dodgeball at your age?" she asked.

"You know, for a small guy, a computer geek can be awfully quick."

The nurse stared at Elizabeth. "There was an altercation," the social studies teacher explained. "Unfortunately, Mr. Jones was attacked by a student."

The nurse's gaze widened more. For some reason, this affronted Jason's masculinity and he felt compelled to add, "He had a textbook!"

That seemed to break the spell and the nurse got busy, fussing over his cut eye, giving him ice for the rapidly growing knot on his head. "You need to take two aspirin," she informed him, "then sleep for eight hours."

He wanted to laugh. Eight hours? He needed to sleep for eight days. But it wasn't going to happen. Wasn't going to happen.

He staggered his way out of the nurse's office, back to admin, where he was sure the adventures were just beginning.

Jason found Phil Stewart sitting behind a massive oak desk, the kind of furniture meant to inspire awe in students and adults alike. A small flat-screen monitor occupied the left-hand corner of the desk, accompanied by a complicated-looking phone. The rest of the desk contained nothing but a desk blotter, and Phil's clasped hands.

Ethan Hastings was sitting in a chair in the proverbial corner. He looked up when Jason entered, and for a moment, it appeared as if he might launch a fresh attack.

Jason decided to remain standing.

"I have called Ethan's parents," the principal announced crisply. "As well as the police. An assault by a student is a very serious matter. I have already informed Ethan's parents that he will be suspended for the next five days, while an expulsion hearing is scheduled in front of the superintendent. Naturally, Mr. Jones may pursue criminal charges with the police."

Ethan blanched, then fisted his hands mutinously and stared down at the carpet.

"I don't think that will be necessary," Jason said.

"Have you looked in a mirror?" Phil asked dryly.

Jason shrugged. "I understand how high emotions might be running at a time like this. For Ethan and for myself."

If he was hoping for a relationship with the red-headed boy, it wasn't happening. Ethan shot him another threatening look, then the office door opened and Adele stuck her head in.

"Police are here."

"Send them in."

The door opened wider, and Jason had the unpleasant shock of seeing Sergeant D.D. Warren and her sidekick, Detective Miller, enter. Wouldn't uniformed officers normally respond to this kind of petty incident? Unless, of course, the detectives heard about it on the radio and connected their own dots.

Jason glanced ruefully at Ethan Hastings, understanding now that the pummeling had been nothing compared to the damage the boy was about to inflict.

"Sergeant D.D. Warren," the female detective introduced herself, then Miller. They shook Phil's hand, nodded at Ethan, then regarded Jason with the kind of flinty stares most cops reserved for gangbangers or serial killers.

Grieving husband, he reminded himself, but didn't really feel like playing anymore today.

"Heard you had an incident," Warren stated.

Phil gestured to Ethan, whose head was ducked between his bony shoulders. "Ethan?" he asked quietly.

"It's his fault," the boy exploded, head coming up, finger stabbing at Jason. "Mrs. Sandra warned me about him. She *warned* me."

D.D. gave Jason a look, still cool, but with an element of smug. "What did Mrs. Sandra say, Ethan?"

"She married young," the boy said earnestly. "She was eighteen. That's not that much older than me, you know."

The adults didn't say anything.

"But she didn't love him anymore." The boy sneered, staring boldly at Jason. "She told me she didn't love you anymore."

Did the words hurt? Jason didn't know. He was in his zone, and when he was in his zone, nothing could hurt him. That was the point of the zone. The whole reason he had developed it when he had been too young and too weak to do anything else to stop the pain.

"Sandy told me she was working with you on a project," Jason said softly. "She said you are an excellent student, Ethan, and she enjoyed working with you very much."

Ethan flushed, ducked his head again.

"How long have you loved her?" Jason pressed, aware of D.D. stiffening beside him as Phil Stewart's eyes widened in shock.

"No—" the principal started.

"You don't deserve her!" Ethan burst out. "You work all the time. You leave her alone. I would treat her better. I'd spend every second of every day with her if I could. I'm helping her with her teaching module, you know. I go to the basketball games, just for her. Because that's what you're supposed to do if you love someone. You're supposed to stay with them, talk to them. You're supposed to *be* with them."

"How often were you with Mrs. Sandra?" Sergeant Warren asked now.

"Every day. Free period. I was teaching her all about navigating the Internet, how to explain it to the sixth-graders. I'm very good with computers, you know."

Crap, Jason thought. *Holy crap.*

"Ethan, did you and Mrs. Sandra ever go out together?" Warren asked.

"I saw her every Thursday at the basketball games. Thursday nights are my favorite night of the whole week."

"Did you go to her house or maybe someplace else?"

Principal Stewart looked like he was going to have a heart attack.

But Ethan shook his head. "No," he said mournfully, then spun his overexcited gaze back to Jason. "She said I couldn't come over. She said it would be too *dangerous.*"

"What else did Mrs. Jones say about her husband?" Warren asked.

The boy shrugged. "Just things. Stuff. But she didn't have to say everything. I could see it for myself. She was so lonely. Sad. One day, she even started to cry. She wanted away from him, I could tell. But she was scared. I mean, look at him. I'd be scared, too."

Everyone dutifully turned to Jason, his shadowed eyes, his heavily bearded face. He looked back down at the floor. *Grieving husband, grieving husband.*

"Ethan, it sounds like you and Mrs. Sandra talked a lot. Did you maybe e-mail her, or call her on her cell phone, or contact her some other way?" the sergeant asked.

"Yeah. Sure. I guess. But she told me not to call or write too often. She didn't want her husband to get suspicious." Another furious glare.

"So you and Mrs. Sandra would meet outside of school," Principal Stewart asked now, looking gravely concerned.

But Ethan shook his head. "I already told you, we met during her free period. And Thursday nights. At the basketball games."

"What else would you do during the basketball games?" Warren asked.

"What do you mean?"

The sergeant shrugged. "Did you go for walks together, maybe around the school, or sit and talk in a classroom, or anything else?"

The boy frowned at her. "Of course not. She had her daughter with her. She couldn't just wander off and leave Ree all alone. Mrs. Sandra is a very good mom!"

Warren slid Jason a glance. "I work Thursday nights," he supplied quietly. "So yes, she would have Ree with her."

The sergeant nodded slightly and he could see her debating the same questions he was debating. Ethan Hastings clearly thought he had a relationship of some type with Sandy. Just how far had this relationship progressed? A genuine physical relationship between teacher and student? Or just wishful thinking on the part of one socially awkward kid?

In retrospect, Sandy's bright blonde hair and youthful features appeared not so dissimilar to other young, pretty blonde teachers recently arrested for their inappropriate relationships with teenage students. And Ethan probably hadn't missed the mark—no doubt Sandra felt lonely, neglected, overextended by the demands of juggling work and motherhood. Obviously Ethan was an adoring audience, quick to shower her with praise and attention.

But he was still a boy. Jason would like to believe that if his wife had betrayed him, it wasn't with a thirteen-year-old boy. Then again, the other husbands had probably thought the same.

There was a discreet knock on the office door again. It cracked open enough for Adele to appear. "Ethan Hastings's parents are here," she said.

Principal Stewart nodded and the door opened wide enough to reveal two very shocked and distressed parents.

"Ethan," the mom cried, pushing her way past the standing adults to her son. Ethan flung his arms around his mother's waist, instantly converting from budding Don Juan to frightened little boy. They had the same hair, Jason thought idly. The mother's short, reddish blonde bob blending in with her son's disheveled carrot top. They were two peas in a pod. A perfect fit.

He forced himself back into the zone, that magic place where nothing could hurt.

"I don't understand," the father started, then noticed the bandage on Jason's face. "He assaulted you? My *son* assaulted a grown man?"

"He has a promising right hook," Jason offered, and then, when the man blanched, "Don't worry, I'm not going to press charges."

Sergeant Warren regarded him with fresh interest.

"Ethan was upset," Jason continued. "I can understand that. I'm not having a very good week myself."

The father appeared even more confused, but Jason didn't feel like explaining anymore. He'd hit the wall. That was it. He was going home.

He didn't bother with goodbyes, just exited the office while behind him Principal Stewart started explaining the "alleged incident" and the discipline ramification to two parents who probably never imagined their computer-nerd son so much as swatting a fly.

Sergeant Warren caught up with him in the school entryway. Jason wasn't surprised. He was tired and ragged, so of course she was going to press her advantage.

"Leaving so soon?" she called behind him.

"I need to get my daughter."

"You finally found someone worthy of babysitting?"

He turned, keeping his face composed, refusing to rise to the bait. "She is with the home ec class. I understand they're baking cookies."

"She misses her mother, doesn't she?"

He didn't say anything.

"Gotta be tough. Being only four years old, and the last one who saw her mother alive."

He didn't say anything.

D.D. crossed her arms, moved closer to him now. She had an aggressive walk, with her long, denim-clad legs. An alpha, sizing up game. "How's your cat?"

"Very cat-like."

"Mr. Smith's reappearance must've made your daughter very happy."

"Actually, she cried for her mother."

"And there goes your one line of defense—that a warm, loving father such as yourself would never harm his child's pet."

Jason didn't say anything.

D.D. moved two steps closer, jerking her head back toward the principal's office. "So what do you think of your competition? He might be young, but apparently Ethan Hastings spends more time with your wife than you do."

"You should talk to Mrs. Lizbet," Jason said.

"Oh yeah? She knows about Sandy and Ethan's relationship?"

"The true nature, yes."

"And what is that, Jason?"

"Student crushes are an occupational hazard. Ask any teacher."

"Sounds like more than a crush to me."

"Maybe for Ethan Hastings it is."

"You find out, Jason? Get jealous? Feel a need to put Sandy in her place?"

"I can honestly say I am not the jealous type."

D.D. arched a brow, openly skeptical. "Everyone's the jealous type. Even thirteen-year-old Ethan Hastings, to judge by the lump on your head."

"He had a textbook," Jason said automatically. "He caught me from behind."

D.D. smiled at him now, the very picture of friendliness. "Come on, Jason. This has gone on long enough. Tell us what happened Wednesday night. Couples fight, we all understand that. Especially a young couple, juggling work, parenthood. And of course Sandy, being young, beautiful, and very alone most nights...So you got mad. Maybe said some things you shouldn't have said. Maybe did some things you shouldn't have done. Sooner you tell us, sooner we can put an end to all this. Get some closure for you and your child. Imagine how scared Ree must be feeling right now. Imagine what it must be like, waking up each morning with her mother's last words running through her head...."

He didn't say anything.

D.D. stepped closer, until he could smell the scent of the soap she had used for her morning shower. She had blonde curly hair, not unlike Sandy's. Beautiful hair, Ree had said, no doubt already missing her mother.

"Tell me where she is," D.D. whispered next to his ear. "Just tell me where Sandy is, Jason, and I'll bring her home to Ree."

He leaned closer, so close his lips might have brushed the curve of her cheek, and he could feel the slight involuntary quiver of her body. "Ask Ethan Hastings," he whispered.

D.D. recoiled. "You're blaming a thirteen-year-old boy?" she asked incredulously.

"Never underestimate youth," he said, stony-faced. "Why, the things I did at that age..."

D.D.'s features had shuttered closed. "Jason," she said tersely, "for a smart man, you're being very stupid."

"Because I won't let you arrest me?"

"No, because you're not connecting the dots. Let me put it this way: By your own admission, you're not the one who harmed your wife—"

"True."

"Yet by your daughter's admission, someone entered your home Wednesday night and harmed Sandy."

His voice was rougher this time. "True."

"Your daughter knows something, Jason. More than she's willing to say. Marianne Jackson is convinced of it. So am I. And I'm telling you now, that girl gets so much as an unexplained freckle and I will pursue you to hell and back."

He didn't answer anymore. Mostly because he was too shocked to speak. "You mean...you mean..."

"We're watching you. Every minute of every hour of every day. You keep that girl safe."

He got it then, not just the threat, but more subtly, the detective's warning. Ree was the last person to see Sandy alive. Ree knew more than she was currently willing or able to say. Ree held the key to the puzzle.

Meaning whoever harmed Sandy had one helluva incentive....

Jason couldn't finish the thought. His chest had grown too tight. Fear or rage? It was too hard to tell. Maybe, for a man like him, those emotions were one and the same.

"No one will harm my child," he heard himself say. "I will keep my daughter safe."

D.D. just looked at him. "Yeah? And how many times did you think the same thing about your wife?"

Jason Jones stalked off. D.D. didn't follow. She returned to the principal's office, where she and Miller had another go at Ethan, with pretty much the same results. Ethan Hastings was convinced that Jason Jones was pure evil, yet could not offer a single compelling reason why Sandra Jones might claim her husband was dangerous. The boy had found his heroine, and in Jason Jones, the dragon guarding the keep.

His parents were distraught, the father going so far as to pull D.D. aside to mention his wife's brother, Ethan's uncle, worked for the state police....

D.D. didn't have the heart to tell the man that a family connection with the state police hardly bought you brownie points with the BPD.

She and Miller jotted down Ethan's statement, seized his cell phone to search for incriminating messages between him and his twenty-three-year-old teacher, then hunted down Elizabeth Reyes, aka Mrs. Lizbet, who had a more even-handed assessment of things.

By the time they finished up at the school, it was five o'clock and D.D. was in the mood for lasagna.

"You're awfully perky," Miller informed her.

"Good day," she agreed.

"We still haven't found Sandra Jones, and now we have a third suspect to consider—a thirteen-year-old Romeo."

"I don't think Sandra Jones was sleeping with Ethan Hastings. Though it'll be fun to search his cell phone."

Miller slanted her a look. "How can you be so sure? You been watching the same national news I have? Seems like all the pretty teachers have eighth grade boyfriends these days."

"True." D.D. wrinkled her nose. "And no, it doesn't make any sense to me. I mean, hell, it's not like a woman who looks like Sandra Jones would have a problem attracting male interest."

"It's a dominance thing," Miller assured her. "These women don't want an equal relationship. They want a relationship with a male who will do whatever they say. And since those of us with testosterone aren't known for our cooperation, they skew to the younger crowd."

"So the testosterone is to blame?" D.D. arched a brow. "Huh, maybe I should spend more time at the local middle school." She blew out a puff of air. "I still don't think Sandy was sleeping with Ethan Hastings. How could she? By all accounts, she always had her child with her."

Miller considered the matter. "Maybe it was one of those, what do they call it, 'emotional affairs.' Sandy basically seduced Ethan via cell phone, e-mail, etc. Then her husband stumbled across some of the messages, and killed her in a fit of jealous rage."

"Or she mentioned it to the local pervert, Aidan Brewster, and he killed her in a fit of jealous rage. You're right, we do have too many suspects. But look on the bright side."

"The bright side?"

"Sandra Jones's alleged relationship with a student gives us probable cause to seize her computer."

Miller perked up. "Good day," he agreed.

| CHAPTER TWENTY |

People go through their lives gearing up for the big moments. We plan blowout celebrations for key benchmarks—the twenty-first-birthday bash, the engagement party, the wedding celebration, the baby shower. We celebrate and hoot and holler and try to honor the big stuff, because, well, it's the big stuff.

Likewise, we steel ourselves for the major blows. The community that rallies behind the survivors of a deadly house fire. The family that comes together for the funeral of the cancer-stricken young father. The best friend who sticks around for your first weekend as a newly divorced mom. We see the big things coming and we prepare ourselves for the lead roles in our own personal dramas. It makes us feel better about things. Stronger. Look at me, I made it.

Of course, we're totally missing all the moments in between. The day-to-day life that is what it is. Nothing to celebrate. Nothing to mourn. Just tasks to perform.

I'm convinced these are the moments that ultimately make us or break us. Like a wave lapping against the same boulder day after day, eroding the stone, shaping the line of the shore, the ordinary minutia of our lives holds the real power, and thus all the hidden danger. The daily things we do, or don't do, without ever understanding the long-term ramification of such minor acts.

For example, I ended the world as I knew it on Saturday, August 30, the day I bought Jason an iPod for his birthday.

Ree and I were shopping together. She needed school clothes, I wanted some supplies to finish setting up my first classroom. We walked into Target, saw the iPods, and I thought immediately of Jason. He loved listening to music, and lately he'd taken up running. With an iPod he could combine two of his favorite activities.

We smuggled the credit card–sized musical masterpiece home by hiding it in my school supplies. Later, when he and Ree were wrestling together in the family room, I stashed the iPod in a kitchen drawer, beneath the stack of oven mitts, where it would be closer to the computer.

Ree and I had already plotted the whole thing out in the car. How we'd secretly set up the iPod for him, downloading tons of rock-n-roll, in lieu of Jason's beloved classical music. Thanks to the movie Flushed Away, Ree was familiar with the works of Billy Idol and Fatboy Slim. On Sunday mornings, when Jason's insomnia sometimes caught up with him and he slept past nine, Ree's new favorite way of waking her father was to blast Dancing with Myself throughout the entire house. Because nothing gets a George Winston lover out of bed faster than a British rock star.

We were very pleased with ourselves.

Saturday night was family night, so we held tight. Sunday, around five, Jason announced he needed to head for the office. He had to review some sources, get a first draft of a feature piece of Southie's Irish pub scene together, etc., etc. Ree and I practically ushered him out the door. His birthday was on Tuesday. We wanted to be prepared.

I started by booting up the family computer. Mr. Smith leapt up to supervise, taking a position next to the warm monitor, where he could watch me smugly through the golden slits of his eyes.

Like most things electronic, the iPod required special software that had to be installed. I hardly have Jason's skills with a computer, but most uploads are pretty idiot-proof even for me. Sure enough, the installation wizard appeared and I was off and running, clicking I Agree, Yes, and Next in every dialogue box that appeared.

"See, I'm smarter than you think," I informed Mr. Smith. He yawned at me.

Ree was already sorting through her CD collection. The more she thought about it, the more she was certain Jason needed some Disney music to accompany Billy Idol. Perhaps he'd run faster listening to Elton John from The Lion King. *Or, let's not forget Phil Collins's industrious work on* Tarzan.

The computer announced that the iTunes software was up and running. Ree scurried over with a fistful of CDs. I read a few instructions, then showed her how we could insert her CDs into the computer's drive, and all the music would be copied onto Daddy's iPod. She found this magical beyond words. Then of course we had to visit the online music store, and download some classics from Led Zepplin and the Rolling Stones. "Sympathy for the Devil" has always been a personal favorite of mine.

Next thing I knew, it was already eight o'clock and time to get Ree to bed. I returned the iPod to its hiding place beneath the oven mitts. Ree quickly gathered up her scattered CDs and stuck them back on the shelf. Then it was upstairs for a quick bath, teeth brushing, potty, two stories, one song, a parting scratch to the cat's ears, and at long last, quiet.

I returned to the kitchen, brewed a cup of tea. Tomorrow was Labor Day, essentially the last day of summer vacation for myself and Ree. After this would begin the weekly grind of shuttling Ree off to preschool, then getting myself to the middle school. Jason would pick her up by one P.M., *then I'd need to be home by five so he could get to work. Lots of hustle and bustle. My husband and me becoming two ships that passed in the night.*

I was nervous. I was excited. I was scared. I'd wanted a job. Something of my own. It had surprised me as much as anyone when I'd picked teaching, but I had enjoyed last year. The kids looked up to me, soaking in knowledge, but also kind words. I liked that moment when something I did made a roomful of tweens smile happily. I liked twenty-five kids calling, "Mrs. Jones, Mrs. Jones," probably because it wasn't my mother's name, therefore Mrs. Jones sounded like someone highly competent and respectable.

When I was in front of a classroom, I felt smart, in control. My own childhood fell away, and in the kids' eyes, I saw the adult I wanted to be.

Patient, knowledgeable, resourceful. My daughter loved me. My students liked me.

And my husband... I was never sure with Jason. He needed me. He respected my desire to get a job, though I knew he would've preferred it if I'd stayed home with Ree. He had encouraged me to return to school, even though that had been hard on the whole family. I had told him I needed something of my own, and he had immediately written a check to the online college of my choice.

He gave me space. He trusted my decisions. He showed me kindness.

He was a good man, I reminded myself yet again, as I often did on these nights when the shadows grew long and it felt once again like I was all alone.

So our marriage didn't involve sex. No marriage was perfect, right? This was adulthood. Understanding that the rosy dreams you had as a kid really weren't meant to come true. You made trade-offs. You sacrificed for your family.

You did what was right, even if it wasn't perfect, and you were grateful for all the nights you went to sleep without smelling the cloying scent of dying roses.

Thinking of Jason reminded me that Ree and I needed to bake his birthday cake in the morning. Perhaps I should wrap the iPod now, while he was still out. Then my gaze fell upon the computer and I realized the flaw in our plan.

Jason used the computer every night. Meaning tonight, when he returned from work and booted it up, the first thing he was bound to notice was the brand-new iTunes icon in the middle of the menu bar.

So much for our surprise.

I sat down at the computer, trying to figure out my options. I could uninstall the program. We'd already downloaded our favorite songs onto the actual iPod, so temporarily deleting the iTunes software shouldn't change anything. Or...

I had this vague memory that you could delete things on the desktop by moving them into the recycle bin. However, the item would remain tucked in the recycle bin until you gave the official command for the bin to empty. Given that, maybe I could drag the iTunes icon into the recycle bin, out of Jason's sight, and just leave it tucked there. Voila.

Before I got ahead of myself, I decided to test out my theory on an

*old teaching document. I found the file name, highlighted it, and
dragged it to the trash. Then, I double clicked on the recycle bin icon to
see what had happened.*

*The bin opened, and sure enough, there sat my teaching doc. As well
as one other item, labeled Photo 1.*

So I clicked on it.

The grainy black-and-white image filled the screen.

*And I stuffed my fist into my mouth so my sleeping daughter
wouldn't hear me scream.*

The distance from South Boston Middle School to Jason and Sandra's
home was approximately four and a half miles long, or an eight-
minute drive. The short commute was perfect for the daily scramble,
when Ree needed to be dropped off or picked up from location A
while Sandra or Jason were scrambling to reach location B.

Now Jason ticked off each block in his mind, while clutching the
steering wheel with both hands and thinking that eight minutes was
too short. He could not get composed in eight minutes. He could not
understand the impact of Ethan Hastings in eight minutes. He could
not recover from Sergeant D.D. Warren's grim warning about his
child in eight minutes. He couldn't prepare himself for what was
about to happen next, in only eight minutes.

Ree was the last person to see her mother alive on Wednesday
night. The cops knew it. He knew it. And by definition, one other person probably knew it.

The person who had harmed his wife. The person who might return to harm Ree.

"I'm tired, Daddy," Ree was whining in the back, rubbing her eyes.
"I want to go home."

Even Mr. Smith had abandoned his lounging to sit and stare at
Jason expectantly. The cat wanted dinner, no doubt, not to mention
fresh water and a litter box.

"Are we going home, Daddy? I want to go home, Daddy."

"I know, I know."

He didn't want to. He thought of taking them to a restaurant for
dinner, a cheap motel for nighttime. Or hell, filling up with gas and

heading to Canada. But in this day and age of Amber Alerts, running wasn't an impromptu act, especially with a four-year-old girl and an orange cat. Canada? he thought darkly. He'd be lucky if they made it to the Massachusetts border.

Ree wanted home, and home was probably still the safest bet. He had steel doors, reinforced windows. Forewarned was forearmed. Maybe he hadn't known everything going on in his wife's world, hadn't sensed the threat. Well, he was paying attention now. No way in hell anyone was touching his daughter.

Or so he told himself.

Of course, going home also meant facing an empty house without Sandy's cheerful welcome. Or worse yet, confronting the media that were no doubt camped out in his front yard.

"How'd you kill your wife, Jason? Knife, gun, garrote? Bet it was easy for you, given all your experience...."

He should have a spokesperson, he thought idly. Isn't that how it worked in this day and age? Become a victim of a crime, hire an entourage. A lawyer to represent your interests, a spokesperson to speak on behalf of your family, and, of course, an entertainment agent to handle the pending book and movie deals. Right to privacy? Solitude for shock and mourning?

No one gave a rat's ass anymore. Your pregnant daughter was kidnapped and killed. Your beloved wife was murdered on the subway. Your girlfriend's body had just been found cut up in a suitcase. Your life suddenly belonged to the cable news. Forget planning a funeral, you needed to appear on *Larry King*. Forget trying to explain to your child that Mommy wasn't coming home anymore, you needed to share a couch with Oprah.

Crime equaled celebrity, whether you liked it or not.

He was angry. Suddenly, viciously. His knuckles had whitened on the steering wheel, and he was driving too fast, way over the speed limit.

He didn't want this life. He didn't want to miss his wife. And he didn't want to be so terrified for his only daughter.

He forced himself to inhale deeply, then exhale slowly, easing off the gas pedal, working out his shoulders. Push it away. Lock it up tight. Let it go. Then smile, because you're on *Candid Camera*.

He turned onto his street. Sure enough, four news vans were stacked bumper to bumper on his block. The police were out, too. The cruiser parked right in front of his house, two uniformed officers standing on the sidewalk, hands on their hips as they surveyed the small huddle of smartly suited reporters and shabbily dressed cameramen. Local stations; story hadn't launched into national headlines yet.

Wait till they heard about Ethan Hastings. That would do it.

Ree's eyes had widened in the back seat. "Is there a party, Daddy?" she asked excitedly.

"Maybe they're happy we found Mr. Smith."

He slowed for the driveway, and the first surge of flashes exploded outside his window. He pulled into the driveway, parked the station wagon. The media couldn't trespass onto private property, so he had plenty of time to unfasten his seatbelt, tend to his child, figure out Mr. Smith.

Grieving husband, grieving husband. Cameras came with telephoto lenses.

He would carry Mr. Smith to the house, while holding Ree's hand. There was a photo op for you—bruised and bandaged husband clutching a pretty orange kitty with one hand and a beautiful little girl with the other. Yep, he'd get fan mail for sure.

He felt empty again. Not mad, not sad, not angry, not anything. He had found the zone.

Mr. Smith stood on Jason's lap, peering out the window at the commotion. The cat's ears were straight up, its tail twitching nervously. In the back, Ree already had the seatbelt unfastened and was staring at him expectantly.

"Can you get out of this side of the car, love?" he asked quietly.

She nodded, staring at the throng of strangers on the sidewalk. "Daddy?"

"It's okay, honey. Those are reporters. It's their job to ask questions, kind of like it's Daddy's job to ask questions. Except I write up stuff in the paper, while these reporters talk about it on TV."

She looked at him again, the anxiety building in her drawn features.

He twisted in the driver's seat, touching her hand. "They have to stay on the sidewalk, honey. It's the law. So, they can't come inside our home. However, when we get out of the car, it's gonna be loud. They're gonna start asking all sorts of crazy questions all at once, and get this—they don't raise their hands."

This caught her attention. "They don't raise their hands?"

"No. They talk right over the top of one another. No taking turns, no saying excuse me, nothing."

Ree blinked at him. "Mrs. Suzie would not like that," she said firmly.

"I totally agree. And when we get out of the car, you're going to see why it's so important to raise your hand in school, because when you don't..."

He gestured toward the noisy mob on the sidewalk, and Ree sighed in exasperation. The nervousness was gone. She was prepared to get out of the car now, if only to shake her head at a bunch of poorly mannered adults.

Jason felt better, too. Truth was, his four-year-old knew more than the jackals outside, and that was something to hold on to.

He tucked Mr. Smith beneath his left arm, and popped open the driver's-side door. The first question ripped across the yard, and the reporters were off and running:

"Jason, Jason, where is Sandy? Do you have any updates on her whereabouts?"

"Is it true that police interviewed your four-year-old daughter this morning? How is little Ree doing? Is she asking for her mother?"

"Are you the last person to have seen Sandy alive?"

"What do you have to say to reports that you are considered a person of interest in this case?"

Jason closed his door, opened Ree's door. Head down, cat tucked against his body, hand out for Ree. His daughter stepped boldly out the back. She stared at the reporters head-on, and Jason heard half a dozen cameras click and flash as one. The money shot, he realized in a distant sort of way. His little daughter, his beautiful, brave daughter, had just saved him from having his face aired on the five o'clock news.

"You're right, Daddy." Ree looked up at him. "They would *never* earn a good-manners medal."

He smiled then. And felt his chest swell with pride as he took his daughter's hand and turned away from the screaming press, toward the sanctuary of their front porch.

They made it across the yard, Mr. Smith squirming, Ree walking with steady feet. They made it up the stairs, Jason having to let go of Ree's hand now and focus on the panicking cat.

"Jason, Jason, you organized search parties for Sandy?"

"Will there be a candlelight vigil for your wife?"

"What about reports that Sandra's purse was found on the kitchen counter?"

"Is it true Alan Dershowitz is going to represent you, Jason?"

The keys dangled between his fingers. Jason juggled Mr. Smith awkwardly, searching for the right one. *Get inside, get inside.* Calm and controlled.

"What were Sandy's last words?"

Then, right beside him, the unexpected creak of a floorboard.

Jason jerked his head up. The man stepped out of the shadows at the end of the porch. Immediately, Jason stepped in front of his daughter, armed with a cat in one hand and a set of house keys in the other.

The man walked three steps toward them, wearing a rumpled mint green linen suit and clutching a battered tan hat. Shockingly white hair capped a deeply weathered face. The man grinned broadly, and Jason almost dropped the damn cat.

The white-haired man threw open his arms, beamed down at Ree, and exclaimed jovially, "Hello there, buttercup. Come to Papa!"

| CHAPTER TWENTY-ONE |

Jason swiftly unlocked the front door and thrust Mr. Smith inside.
He put his hand on Ree's shoulder. "Inside."

"But Daddy—"

"Inside. Now. The cat needs dinner."

Ree's eyes widened, but she recognized his tone, and did as she
was told. As she stepped into the house, Jason shut the door behind
her, locked it again, and turned to the white-haired man.

"Get off my property."

The newcomer tilted his head to the side, appearing puzzled.
Jason had met Sandy's father only once before, and he was struck
now, as he was struck then, by the man's crinkling blue eyes and
bright, flashing smile. "Now, Jason, is that any way to greet your father-in-law?"

Max extended a friendly hand. Jason ignored it, stating firmly:
"Get off my property, or I will have you arrested."

Max didn't move. His expression fell, however. He twisted his hat
in his hands, seeming to debate his options. "Where's your wife,
son?" the judge asked at last, his tone appropriately somber.

"I will count to five," Jason said. "One—"

"Heard she's been missing for over a day. Saw it on the news and skedaddled straight for the airport."

"Two."

"That my granddaughter? She's got her grandmother's eyes, she does. Beautiful little girl. Shame no one thought to call me about her birth. I know Sandra and I have had our differences, but I can't think of anything I did that deserves not knowing about such a sweet child."

"Three."

"I'm here to help, son. Truly. I may be an old man, but I have some fight in me left."

"Four."

Max's gaze grew narrower, more appraising. "You kill my only daughter, Jason *Jones*? Because if it turns out you harmed my Sandra, hurt one little hair on her head—"

"Five."

Jason stepped off the porch. Max didn't follow him right away. Jason was not surprised. According to Sandra, her father lived as the proverbial big fish in a little pond. He was a highly respected judge, an affable Southern gentleman. People instinctively trusted him, which is why no one had ever intervened to help his only daughter even as her mother poured bleach down her throat.

The reporters saw his approach, and optimistically stuck their microphones into the air, screaming louder.

"Where is Ree?"

"Who's the man on your porch?"

"Do you have any words for the person who may have abducted Sandy?"

Jason stopped next to the uniformed officer farthest from the press and gestured him over with his finger. The officer's nameplate read "Hawkes." Excellent, Jason could use a hawk.

The officer dutifully huddled close, having no more desire to share their conversation with the greater free world than Jason did.

"Old guy on the porch," Jason murmured. "He's not welcome on my property. I have asked him to leave. He has refused."

Officer arched a brow. Looked from Jason to the reporters to Jason again as a wordless question.

"If he wants to make a scene, that's his choice," Jason answered in a low undertone. "I consider him a threat to my daughter, and I want him gone."

The officer nodded, pulled out a spiral notebook. "What's his name?"

"Maxwell Black from Atlanta, Georgia."

"Relation?"

"Technically speaking, he's my wife's father."

The uniformed officer startled. Jason shrugged. "My wife did not wish for her father to be part of our daughter's life. Just because Sandy's...gone is no reason to disregard her instructions."

"He make a statement? Threaten you or your daughter in any way?"

"I consider his presence to be a threat."

"You mean you have a restraining order?" the officer asked in confusion.

"First thing tomorrow, I promise." Which was a lie, because Jason would need proof of threatening behavior, and the courts would probably require something stronger than Sandy's belief that Max had loved his psycho wife more than his battered daughter.

"I can't arrest him," the officer began.

Jason cut him off. "I consider him to be trespassing. Please remove him from my property lines. That's all I ask."

The uniformed officer didn't argue, just shrugged, as if to say, *It's your front-page funeral,* and prepared to stroll over to the front porch. Max, however, could see the writing on the wall. He descended the steps on his own, his jovial smile still firmly in place though his motions were jerky, a man doing what he had to do, not what he wanted to do.

"Guess I'll check into my hotel now," Max consented grandly, nodding once in Jason's direction.

The reporters had quieted. They appeared to be connecting the presence of the uniformed officer to the actions of the white-haired man and were now keenly watching the show.

" 'Course," Max said to Jason, "I look forward to visiting with my granddaughter first thing in the morning."

"Not gonna happen," Jason replied evenly, heading back toward the house, where Ree waited for him.

"Now, son, I wouldn't say that if I were you," Max called after him.

Despite his better intention, Jason found himself pausing, turning, regarding his father-in-law.

"I know something," the old man said quietly, soft enough that only Jason and the uniformed officer could hear. "For example: I know the date you first met my daughter, and I know the date my granddaughter was born."

"No you don't. Sandy never called you when she had Ree."

"Public record, Jason *Jones*. Public record. Now, don't you think it's time to let bygones be bygones?"

"Not gonna happen," Jason repeated firmly, though his heart was pounding hard. For the third time in one day, he was discovering danger where there hadn't been danger before.

He gave Maxwell his back, climbing the front steps, working the lock on the door. He got it open, to find Ree standing in the middle of the entryway, her lower lip trembling, her eyes glazed over with tears.

He shut the door and she threw herself into his arms.

"Daddy, I'm scared. Daddy, I'm scared!"

"Shhh, shhh, shhh." He held her close. He stroked his daughter's hair, inhaled the comforting scent of Johnson's No More Tears shampoo.

"I love you," he whispered against the top of Ree's head, even as he wondered if Max would take her from him.

Jason made waffles for dinner. Breakfast for supper was a time-honored treat, and the familiar ritual of beating water and waffle mix calmed him. Jason poured the batter over the steaming griddle. Ree sat on the edge of the counter, steadfastly watching the red griddle light. When it went off, it would be time to eat. She took her timer duties seriously.

Jason got out the syrup. Poured them glasses of orange juice, then scrambled the last two eggs in the fridge so his child would have something besides bread dipped in sugar as a meal. He could almost hear Sandy saying now, "Waffles with maple syrup are little better than doughnuts. Honestly, Jason, at least throw in a hard-boiled egg, something."

She had never complained too much, though. Her favorite meal was angel hair pasta with pink vodka sauce, which she ate anytime they went to the North End. Pinkalicious pasta, Ree called it, and the two of them would slurp away, sharing the same bowl with gastronomic glee.

Jason's hand shook slightly. He overshot stirring the egg, sending a yellow chunk onto the floor. He tapped by it with his toe, and Mr. Smith came over to investigate.

"The light's off," Ree singsonged.

"All righty, then. Let's eat!" He used his best Jim Carrey voice, and Ree giggled. The sound of her laugh soothed him. He did not have all the answers. He was deeply troubled about what had happened today, let alone what might happen next. But he had this moment. Ree had this moment.

Moments mattered. Other people didn't always get that. But Jason did.

They sat side by side at the counter. They ate their waffles. They drank their juice. Ree chased scrambled-egg bits around her plate, putting each bite through a maple-syrup obstacle course before finally popping it in her mouth.

Jason helped himself to another waffle. He wondered when the police would arrive to seize the family laptop. He cut his waffle into bite-sized pieces. He wondered how much Ethan Hastings had taught Sandy about computers, and why she'd never confronted Jason with her suspicions. He added half a dozen waffle bits onto Ree's daisy plate. He wondered which would be the hardest way to lose his daughter—to the police, sticking her in foster care when they came to arrest him for Sandy's murder, or to Sandy's father, stating in family court that Jason Jones was not Clarissa Jane Jones's biological father and thus should no longer be part of her life.

Ree put down her fork. "I'm full, Daddy."

He glanced at her plate. "Four more bites of waffle, as you're four years old."

"No." She hopped down from the bar stool. He caught her arm, frowning.

"Four bites, then you may be excused from the table."

"You're not the boss of me."

Jason blinked, set down his fork. "I'm your father, so yes, I am the boss of you."

"No, Mommy is."

"We both are."

"No, only Mommy."

"Clarissa Jane Jones, you may eat four bites of waffle, or you may sit on the timeout stair."

Ree thrust her chin out at him. "I want Mommy."

"Four bites."

"Why did you yell at her? Why did you make her mad?"

"Back to your chair, Ree."

She stomped her foot. "I want Mommy! She told me she'd come home. Mommy told me she wouldn't leave me."

"Ree..."

"Mommy goes to work, she comes home. She goes to the grocery store, she comes home. Mommy told me, she promised me, she'd always *come home!*"

Jason felt his chest tighten. Ree had gone through an attachment phase where she'd cried and carried on every time Sandy left. So Sandy had started a little game she'd read in some parenting book, always notifying Ree when she was leaving, and always hugging Ree first thing when she got home. *"See, look at me, Ree. I'm home. I always come home. I'd never leave you. Never."*

"Mommy's going to put me to bed," Ree said now, chin still sticking out obstinately. "It's her job. You go to work, she puts me to bed. Go to work, Daddy. Go on. Leave!"

"Ree..."

"I don't want you here anymore. You have to leave. If you leave, Mommy will come home. Go to work. You have to."

"Ree..."

"Get out, get out. I don't want to see you anymore. You're a big *meanie.*"

"Clarissa Jane Jones."

"Stop it, stop it!" She clapped her hands over her ears. "Stop yelling, I don't want to hear you yelling."

"I'm not yelling." But his voice was rising.

His daughter continued as if she'd never heard him. "Angry feet, angry feet. I hear your mean feet on the stairs. Get out, get out, get out. I want Mommy! It's not fair, it's not fair. *I want my mommy!*"

Then his daughter twisted away from him and ran sobbing up the stairs.

Jason let her go. He listened as Ree stormed down the hall. He caught the distant boom as she slammed her door shut. Then he was left alone at the kitchen counter, with a half-eaten waffle and a heart full of regrets.

Day two of his wife's disappearance and his daughter was falling to pieces.

He thought, in a spurt of ironic bitterness, that Sandy had better be dead or he'd kill her for this.

The police returned at exactly 8:45 P.M. Jason was standing in the middle of the kitchen, staring at the family computer, which was no longer the family computer, when they pounded up the front steps.

He opened the door. Sergeant Warren led the charge.

She thrust the search warrant in front of his face, rattling off in rapid legalese where they were allowed to go and what they were allowed to seize. As he'd suspected, they would be taking the computer, as well as miscellaneous electronic devices, including but not limited to gaming devices, iPods, BlackBerries, and Palm Pilots.

"What are gaming devices?" he asked her, as uniformed officers and forensic techs poured into his house. Across the street, klieg lights were firing up as reporters caught the action and geared up for a fresh round of photo ops.

"Xbox, Gameboys, PlayStation 2, Wii system, etc., etc."

"Ree has a Leapster," he offered. "If you want my advice, the Cars game is better than the Disney Princess cartridge, but, of course, the evidence techs can judge for themselves."

D.D. regarded him coolly. "The warrant gives us permission to seize all electronics we deem necessary, sir. So yes, we will judge for ourselves."

The "sir" rankled him, but he let it go. "Ree's asleep," he found himself saying. "She's had a very long day. If you could ask the officers to please keep things quiet..."

He strove for politeness, though maybe his voice hitched a little at the end. He'd had a long day, too, which was about to become a long night.

"We're professionals," the sergeant informed him stiffly. "We're not gonna ransack your house. We're going to take it apart piece by piece very politely."

D.D. motioned a uniformed officer over. Officer Anzaldi, it appeared, had drawn the short straw and would be serving as Jason's babysitter for the evening. The officer led him to the family room, where Jason took a seat on the love seat, much as he had done the day before. Except no Ree this time. No tiny warm body snuggled against him, needing him, grounding him, keeping him from screaming from the frustration of it all.

So Jason closed his eyes, put his hands behind his head, and went to sleep.

When he opened his eyes, forty-five minutes had passed and Sergeant D.D. Warren was staring down at him in quiet fury.

"What the hell are you doing?"

"Resting."

"Resting? Just like that? Your wife is missing, so you're taking a *nap?*"

"It's not like I'm going to find her while I'm being confined to a love seat, is it?"

D.D. appeared disgusted. "There is something seriously wrong with you."

He shrugged. "Ask a SWAT guy sometime. What do you do once you've been activated but not yet deployed? You sleep. So when the time comes, you're ready to go."

"That's how you view this? You're some elite warrior who's been activated, but not deployed?" She sounded dubious.

"My family is in crisis, and all I can do is stay with my daughter. Activated, but not deployed."

"You could leave her with Grandpa." The sergeant said the words neutrally, but there was a gleam in her eye. So she'd heard. Of course she'd heard. Apparently, all uniformed officers did these days was blab every detail of his life to Sergeant Warren.

"No thank you," he said.

"Why not?"

"I don't like linen suits."

But D.D. wasn't going to be put off that easily. She took a seat directly across from him, resting her elbows on her knees, all casual curiosity. While from the kitchen came the sound of cupboard doors being opened, closed, drawers being pulled out and pushed in. He suspected the computer was already gone. The iPod seized from his nightstand drawer. Maybe they'd taken his clock radio, too. Everything came with data chips these days, and any data chip could be rigged to store any kind of data. There'd been a major case just last year where a business exec had stored tons of incriminating financial docs on his son's Xbox.

Jason had understood the terms of the search warrant just fine. He'd simply liked making the pretty blonde sergeant work for it.

"You said Sandy and her father were estranged," D.D. stated now.

"True."

"Why?"

"That would be Sandy's story to tell."

"Well, she doesn't currently seem to be available, so perhaps you could help me out."

He had to think about it. "I think if you asked the old man, he'd say his daughter was young, headstrong, and reckless when she met me."

"Oh yeah?"

"And I think, as a seasoned investigator, you might wonder what had happened to make her so reckless and wild."

"He beat her?"

"I'm not sure."

"Call her bad names?" D.D. arched a brow.

"I think it's more like the mom beat the living shit out of her, and he never raised a hand to stop her. The mom died, so Sandy doesn't have to hate her anymore. The old man, on the other hand…"

"She's never forgiven him?"

He shrugged. "Again, you'd have to ask her."

"Why do you have jams in your windows, Jason?"

He looked at her. "Because the world is filled with monsters, and we don't want them getting our daughter."

"Seems extreme."

"Just because you're paranoid doesn't mean they're not out to get you."

She smiled a little. It added crinkles to the corners of her eyes, revealing her age, but also making her seem suddenly softer. More approachable. She was a skilled interrogator, he realized. And he was tired, making it seem like a better and better idea to tell her everything. Lay all his problems at the feet of smart, beautiful Sergeant Warren. Let her sort out the mess.

"When was the last time Sandy talked to her father?" D.D. asked.

"Day she left town with me."

"She never called him? Not once since moving to Boston?"

"Nope."

"Not your wedding, not the birth of your daughter."

"Nope."

D.D. narrowed her eyes. "So why is he here now?"

"Claims he saw word of Sandy's disappearance on the news and *skedaddled* for the airport."

"I see. His estranged daughter has gone missing, so *now* he pays a visit?"

"You'd have to ask him."

D.D. cocked her head to the side. "You're lying to me, Jason. And you know how I know?"

He refused to answer.

"You look down and to the left. When people are trying to remember something, they look *up* and to the left. When they're avoiding the truth, however, they look down and to the left. Interesting bit of trivia they teach us in detective school."

"And it took you how many weeks to graduate?"

Her lips curved in that little half-smile again. "The way Officer

Hawkes understood it," the sergeant continued, "Maxwell Black has some opinions regarding his granddaughter. Including that you're not her real father."

Jason didn't answer. He wanted to. He wanted to scream that of course Ree was his daughter, would always be his daughter, could never be anything but his daughter, but the good sergeant had not asked a question, and the first rule of interrogation was never answer questions you didn't have to.

"When was Ree born?" D.D. pressed.

"On the date listed on her birth certificate," he said crisply. "Which I'm sure you've already read."

She smiled at him again. "June twentieth, two thousand and four, I believe."

He said nothing.

"And the day you first met Sandy?"

"Spring two thousand and three." He made sure he looked her in the eye and absolutely, positively didn't look down.

D.D. arched that skeptical brow again. "Sandy would've been only seventeen."

"Never said the old man didn't have reason to hate me."

"So why does Maxwell believe you're not Ree's father?"

"You'd have to ask him."

"Humor me. Obviously you know him better than I do."

"Can't say that I know him at all. Sandy and I didn't exactly have a meet-the-parents courtship."

"You never met Sandy's father before today?"

"Only in passing."

She studied him. "What about your family?"

"Don't have any."

"You're the product of immaculate conception?"

"Miracles happen every day."

She rolled her eyes at him. "All right, Sandy's father, then. Grandpa Black. You took his daughter from him," she stated. "Moved to a godforsaken Yankee state and then never notified him when his granddaughter was born."

Jason shrugged.

"I think Judge Black has good reason to be angry with both you and Sandy. Maybe that's why he returned now. His daughter's gone, and his son-in-law is the prime suspect. One family's tragedy is another man's opportunity."

"I will not grant him access to Ree."

"Got a restraining order?"

"I will not grant him access to Ree."

"What if he demands a paternity test?"

"Can't. You read the birth certificate."

"You're listed as the father, ergo he has no probable cause. The Howard K. Stern defense."

Another shrug.

D.D. smiled at him. "As I recall, the other guy won that argument."

"Ask me who put the jams in the windows."

"What?"

"Ask me who put the jams in the windows. You keep circling around to it. You keep digging at it like it tells you something about me."

"All right. Who put the jams in your windows?"

"Sandy did. Day after we moved in. She was nine months pregnant, we had an entire house to set up, and first thing she did was secure all the windows."

D.D. thought about it. "All these years later, she's still locking Daddy out?"

"You said it, not me."

D.D. finally rose from the chair. "Well, it didn't work, because Daddy's back and he has more clout than you think."

"How so?"

"Turns out he went to law school with one of our district court judges." She flashed her paper. "Who do you think signed our warrant?"

Jason managed not to say a word, but it probably didn't matter, as the color draining from his face gave him away.

"Still don't know where your wife is?" D.D. asked from the doorway.

He shook his head.

"Too bad. Really would be best for everyone if we found her. Particularly considering her condition and all."

"Her condition?"

D.D. arched a brow yet again. This time, there was no mistaking the flash of triumph in her eyes. "It's another thing they teach you in detective school. How to seize a person's trash and how to read a pregnancy test strip."

"What? You mean…"

"That's right, Jason. Sandy's pregnant."

| CHAPTER TWENTY-TWO |

Fucking strangers isn't an easy proposition for a woman. Men have it easier. They pull out, wipe off, move along. For women, the entire process is different. By nature, we are receptacles, meant to take a man inside of us, to receive him, to accept him, to keep him. It's harder to wipe off. It's more difficult to move along.

I think this often on my spa nights, generally when I'm checking out of the hotel, making my way home, trying to transition from wanton floozy to respectable mom.

Have I given too much of myself away? Is that why I feel so trans- parent, as if a gust of wind will blow me away? I shower. I lather, scrub, rinse, repeat. I try to wipe the fingerprints of too many men from my body, just as I try to purge the imprint of their lust-filled faces from my mind.

I'm not bad at it. Honestly, the two kids from the first night... couldn't even pick them out of a lineup. And the episode after that and the episode after that. I can forget them easily enough. But I can't forgive them, and that doesn't even make sense.

I've started a new tradition on spa nights. After I return to my hotel room, I curl up in a ball and sob hysterically. I don't know who I'm crying for. Myself and the dreams of the future I once had? For my husband, and the hopes he probably had for us? For my child, who looks up at me so sweetly, without any idea what Mommy really does when she goes away?

Maybe I'm crying for my childhood, for the moments of tenderness and security I never had, so that some depraved part of me must continuously punish myself, as if picking up where my mother left off.

One day, standing in front of the hotel mirror, looking at the huge bruises slowly darkening my ribs, it occurs to me that I don't want to do this anymore. That somehow I have fallen in love with my husband. That by virtue of never touching me, he has in fact become the most special man in my life.

I want to stay home. I want to feel safe.

It's a good vow, don't you think?

Unfortunately, I'm no good at clean, healthy living. I have to hurt. I have to be punished.

If not by myself, then at least by someone else.

When I first saw the picture on the computer screen, that single black-and-white image of unspeakable violence being committed against such a small, vulnerable young boy, I should've packed up Ree and left. That would've been the smart, sensible thing to do.

No wasting time with denial. So Jason was kind, considerate, and, the best I could tell, a remarkable father. It wasn't like respectable family men couldn't have dirty little secrets, right? Of all people, I should know that.

Was it the cycle of violence? In my calculating attempt to run away from my family, to pick the one man I thought was the antithesis of everything my father had been, had I run right into the arms of another monster? Maybe darkness speaks to darkness. I didn't marry my husband because I thought he would save me; I married him to stay with the devil I knew.

I know the moment I saw that photo, I felt a stirring deep inside the ugly part of myself. A bitter sense of recognition. All of a sudden, my perfect husband was no better than me, and heaven help me, I liked that. I really, really liked that.

I told myself I needed more information. I told myself my husband *deserved the benefit of the doubt. One explicit photo in the trash bin did not a predator make. Maybe he'd received it by accident and immediately deleted it. Maybe it popped up on some website and he was getting rid of it. There could be a rational explanation. Right?*

Truth is, Jason came home that night, and I could still look him in the eye. Truth is, he asked me how my night was, and I told him "Just fine."

I am an expert on lying. I excel at pretend normal.

And some terrible, angry part of me was happy to once again be in charge.

I took Ree to school. I started teaching sixth grade social studies. I considered my options.

Four weeks later, I made my move. I'd been doing some research on the student population, and my dear friend, Mrs. Lizbet, was helpful as always.

I found Ethan Hastings in the computer lab. He looked up when I entered the room. Immediately, he flushed bright red, and I knew this was going to be even easier than I'd thought.

"Ethan," I said, the pretty, respectable Mrs. Jones. "Ethan, I have a project for you. I want you to teach me everything you know about the Internet."

D.D. was pissed off. She exited the Jones residence, slid into her car, and started punching buttons on her cell phone. It was nearly eleven P.M., well after the hour for polite conversation, but then again, she was dialing a state detective and he was used to such things.

"What?" Massachusetts State Detective Bobby Dodge answered the phone. He sounded sleepy and annoyed, which fit her mood nicely.

"Did I wake you, honey?"

"Yes." He hung up on her.

D.D. hit Redial; she and Bobby went way back, had even been lovers once upon a time. She liked calling him at odd hours of the night. He liked hanging up on her. The system worked for them.

"D.D.," he groaned this time, "I've been on call for the past four nights. Gimme a break."

"Married life is making you soft," she informed him.

"I believe the politically correct phrase is 'balanced lifestyle.'"

"Please, in a cop's world, balanced lifestyle is a beer in each hand."

He finally laughed. She could hear the rustle of sheets, him stretching out. She found herself straining her ears, listening for the low murmur of his wife's voice. It made her flush, feel like a voyeur, and she was grateful she wasn't on video conference.

She had a weakness for Bobby Dodge not even she could explain. She'd given him up, but couldn't let him go. Just went to show you that smart, ambitious women were their own worst enemies.

"All right, D.D., obviously you have something on your mind."

"When you were a sniper with the state's STOP team, did you sleep?"

"You mean more than I do now?"

"Nah, I mean, when you deployed, did you take a nap?"

"D.D., what the hell are you talking about?"

"You been watching the news? Missing woman in Southie?"

"Slept through the morning press conference, but Annabelle told me you had great hair."

D.D. felt mollified by that, which was just plain stupid. "Yeah, well, I'm at the house tonight, seizing the computer, yada, yada, yada, and get this, in the middle of the forensics foreplay, the husband took a nap on the love seat."

"Really?"

"Yep. Just closed his eyes, put his head back, and went to sleep. You tell me, when was the last time you saw a family member of a missing person take a nap in the middle of the investigation?"

"I'd consider that odd."

"Exactly. So I call him on it, and get this: He gives me some SWAT team song and dance that when you've been activated, but not deployed, the sensible thing is to sleep, so you're ready for action."

There was silence. Then, "What's this guy do for a living again?"

"He's a journalist. Works freelance for *Boston Daily*."

"Huh."

"Huh what? I didn't call you for grunting, I called you for expertise."

She could practically see him rolling his eyes in bed. "Well, here's the thing: For most tactical unit situations in policing, you are activated and deployed pretty much simultaneously. But I know what he means—couple of guys on my team were former military special forces. Navy SEALs, Marine Force Recon, that kind of thing. And yeah, I've watched those guys fall asleep in the middle of cow fields, school gymnasiums, and flatbed trucks. There does seem to be some kind of rule for military types—if you're not doing, you'd better be sleeping, so you can do later."

"Shit," D.D. said, and chewed her bottom lip.

"You think he's former military?"

"I think he could play poker with the devil himself. Son of a bitch."

A yawn now. "Want me to take a run at him?" Bobby offered.

"Hey, I don't need no state suit nosing into my investigation," D.D. bristled.

"Easy, blondie. You called me."

"Here's the kicker," she continued as if she hadn't heard him. "The wife is AWOL, and of course we suspect him, so we seized his trash. We found a pregnancy test. Marked positive."

"Really?"

"Really. So I decide to ambush him with it tonight. See how he responds. Because he's never mentioned this, and you'd think a husband would tell you if his missing wife was pregnant."

"Speaking of which . . ."

She paused. Blinked. Felt her stomach drop away. "Holey moley," she said at last. "I mean, when, how, where?"

He laughed. "How and where probably aren't necessary, but Annabelle's due August first. She's nervous, but doing well."

"Well, crap. I mean, congratulations. To both of you. That's . . . awesome." And it was. And she did mean it. Or would mean it. Goddamn, she needed to get laid.

"So okay," she cleared her throat, did her best to sound brisk. *This is Sergeant D.D. Warren, all business all the time.* "Regarding my person of interest. Tonight, I ambush him with the news—"

"You told him his wife was pregnant."

"Exactly."

"But how do you know that the test strip belonged to the wife?"

"I don't. But she's the only adult female in the house, and they don't entertain, I mean *never*, so it's a safe assumption. The lab geeks are gonna run DNA on the test strip to be definitive, but I gotta wait three months for those reports, and let's be honest, Sandra Jones doesn't have three months."

"Just asking," Bobby said.

"So, being *strategic*, I drop that little bomb into our conversation."

"And?"

"He doesn't react. Nothing. Nada. His face was so blank I could've told him it was raining outside."

"Huh."

"Yeah. You gotta figure if he's surprised, well then, he should choke up, because now both his wife and unborn child might be in danger. He should jump off the couch, start asking more questions, hell, start demanding more answers. Do anything but sit there like we're talking about the weather."

"In other words, he probably did know," Bobby filled in. "His wife got pregnant by another man, he kills her, now he's covering his tracks. That's not rocket science, D.D. Hell, that's a national trend."

"And if we were talking about a normal person, I'd agree with you."

"Define 'normal,' " Bobby said.

She sighed heavily. This is where things got murky. "Okay, so I've been dealing with this guy for two days now. And he's cool. Arctic cold. Miswired in some deep fundamental way that probably should involve a lifetime of therapy, six kinds of pharmaceuticals, and a total personality transplant. But he is who he is, and I've noticed a pattern to his deep freeze."

"Which is?" Bobby was starting to sound impatient. Okay, so it was almost midnight.

"The more personal something is, the more he shuts down. Like this morning. We're interrogating his four-year-old daughter in front of him. She's recounting her mother's last words, which don't sound promising, let me tell you. And this guy is leaning against the back wall as if a switch has been disconnected. He's there, but he's not there. That's what I thought tonight when I told him his wife was pregnant. He disappeared. Just like that. We were both in the room together, but he's gone."

"Sure I can't take a crack at him?"

"Fuck you," D.D. informed him.

"Love you, too, babe." She heard him yawn again, then rub his face on the other end of the phone. "Okay, so you have one really cool customer who seems to have some kind of tactical background and knows how to hold up under extreme duress. You think he's former special ops?"

"We ran his prints through the system, but didn't get any hits. I mean, even if he did top secret, deeply classified James Bond crap, the missions would be off the radar, but military service would put him in the system, right? We'd see that piece of the puzzle."

"True. What does he look like?"

D.D. shrugged. "Kind of like Patrick Dempsey. Thick wavy hair, deep dark eyes—"

"Oh for heaven's sake. I'm looking for a suspect, not a blind date."

She blushed. Definitely, definitely needed to get laid. "Five foot eleven, hundred and seventy pounds, early thirties, dark hair and eyes, no distinguishing marks or facial hair."

"Build?"

"Fit."

"Now, see, that does sound like special ops. Big guys can't make it through the endurance training, which is why you should always look out for the small guy in the room." Bobby sounded smug as he said this. A former sniper, he fit the small, dangerous model perfectly.

"But he'd have a record," she singsonged.

"Shit." Bobby was starting to sound tired. "All right, what kinds of things did light up?"

"Marriage certificate, driver's license, Social Security number, and bank accounts. Basic stuff."

"Birth certificate?"

"Still digging."

"Speeding tickets, traffic citations?"

"Nada."

"Credit cards?"

"One."

"When was it opened?"

"Ummm . . ." D.D. had to think about it, trying to recall what she'd read in the report. "Within the past five years."

"Let me guess, around the same time as the bank accounts," Bobby said.

"Now that you mention it, most of the financial activity fell around the same time Jason and his wife moved to Boston."

"Sure, but where'd the money come from?"

"Again, we're still digging."

Longer pause now. "In summary," Bobby said slowly, "you got a name, a driver's license, and a Social Security number, with no activity before the past five years."

D.D. jolted. She hadn't quite thought of it that way, but now that he mentioned it...."Yeah. Okay. Only activity is from the past five years."

"Come on, D.D., you tell me. What's wrong with that picture?"

"Crap," D.D. exclaimed. She whacked her steering wheel. " 'Jones' is an alias, isn't it? I knew it. I just knew it. I've been saying that all along. More we learn about the family, the more everything feels... just right. Not too busy, not too boring. Not too social, not too antisocial. Everything is just right. Goddammit, if they're with WitSec, I will slit my wrists."

"Can't be," Bobby assured her.

"Why not?" She really didn't want her case to be part of the witness protection program.

"Because if so, you'd have federal marshals already crawling all over your ass. It's been forty-eight hours, and the wife's disappearance is public info. No way they wouldn't have found you."

That made her feel better. Except: "What's left?"

"He did it. Or she did it. But one of them has a new identity. Figure out which one."

Coming from Bobby, D.D. took news of a probable alias as expert advice. After all, he'd married a woman who'd had at least twelve names, possibly more. Then it hit her. "*Mr. Smith.* Fuck. Mr. Smith!"

"Lucky Mr. Smith," Bobby drawled.

"He's a cat. Their cat. I never connected the dots. But think about it. The family is Mr. and Mrs. Jones, with their cat, Mr. Smith. It's an inside joke, dammit! You're right, they're mocking us."

"I vote for Mr. Arctic."

"Ah shit," D.D. moaned. "Just my luck. I got a prime suspect who by all appearances is a mild-mannered reporter, with a secret identity. You know who that sounds like, right?"

"I don't know. Who?"

"Fucking Superman."

| CHAPTER TWENTY-THREE |

When Jason was fourteen years old, his family had gone to the zoo. He'd been too old and cynical for these kinds of outings, but his little sister, Janie, had been madly in love with anything furry, so for Janie's sake, he'd agreed to the zoo.

He'd do most things for Janie's sake, a fact his mother exploited zealously.

They'd made the rounds. Eyed sleeping lions, sleeping polar bears, sleeping elephants. Really, Jason thought, how many sleeping animals did one guy need to see? They bypassed the insect exhibit without a word, but ducked into Reptile World. At ten years of age, Janie didn't really like snakes, but still liked to squeal while looking at snakes, so it made a crazy kind of sense.

Unfortunately, the key exhibit item—the albino Burmese python—was covered up, with a sign saying, *Out to Lunch. Deepest Apologies, Polly the Python.*

Janie had giggled, thinking that was pretty funny. Jason had shrugged, because it seemed to him that a python would be yet one more sleeping creature, so he fell into step behind his sister as their father led them toward the door. At the last moment, however, Jason had glanced over and realized the cardboard wasn't fully covering the glass. From this angle, he could peer right in, and Polly wasn't *out* to lunch, Polly was *eating* lunch, a very cute-looking lunch, too, quivering on the floor while the giant snake unhinged her jaws and began the slow, laborious process of drawing the jackrabbit into her massive yellow coils.

His legs had stopped moving on their own. He'd stood there frozen for a full minute, maybe two, unable to look away, as inch by fluffy brown inch, the freshly asphyxiated body disappeared into the snake's glistening gullet.

He thought at that moment, staring at the dead bunny: *I know exactly how you feel.*

Then his father had touched his arm, and he'd followed his dad out the exit into the white-hot blast of Georgia summer.

His father had watched him carefully for the rest of the day. Looking for signs of what? Psychosis? Impending nervous breakdown? Violent outbursts?

It didn't happen. It never happened. Jason got through each day as he got through the day before, step by painful step, moment by painful moment, a physically scrawny, painfully undersized boy, armed only with his thousand-yard stare.

Until the day he turned eighteen and came into Rita's inheritance. Had his parents planned him a party? Had Janie bought him a gift?

He'd never know. Because on the morning of Jason's eighteenth birthday, he'd gone straight to the bank, cashed out two-point-three million dollars, and vanished.

He'd returned from the dead once before. He never planned on hurting his family that badly again.

Sandy was pregnant.

He should do something.

As thoughts went, Sandy's pregnancy was a curious one. It floated right above him. Something he could state, something he could repeat, and yet the three words refused to sound like English.

Sandy was pregnant.

He should do something.

The police were gone. They had wrapped up their party a little after one A.M. The computer was gone. His iPod, Ree's Leapster. Some boxes had disappeared from the basement as well, probably cartons of old software. He didn't know. He didn't care. He'd signed the evidence logs where they had told him to sign, and none of it had made a bit of difference to him.

He wondered if the baby was his.

He would take Ree and run, he thought idly. There was a thin metal box up in the attic, tucked behind a thick piece of insulation, which contained two pieces of fake ID and approximately twenty-five thousand dollars in large bills. The pile of cash was surprisingly small, the metal lockbox no bigger than a hardcover novel. He knew the police couldn't have discovered it during their search, because it was the kind of find that would have immediately engendered conversation.

He would climb the stairs to the attic, retrieve the box, slip it into his computer case. He would rouse Ree from her bed, shear her long brown curls, and top them with a red baseball cap. Throw on a pair of denim overalls and a blue polo shirt and she would make an excellent Charlie, traveling alone with her freshly shaved father.

They'd have to sneak out the back to avoid the press. Climb over the fence. He'd find a car a few blocks away and hotwire a ride. The police would expect them to hit South Station, so instead he'd drive them to the Amtrak station on 128. There, he'd park the first stolen car, and help himself to a second. The police would eye all trains going south, because that's what people did, right? They headed south, maybe into New York, where it was easy for anyone to get lost.

Ergo, he'd drive the second stolen vehicle due north, all the way to Canada. He'd stick "Charlie" in the trunk and don a sports jacket and thick, black-rimmed glasses. Just another businessman crossing the border for Lasik. The border patrol was used to such things.

Then, once he and Ree hit Canada, they would disappear. It was a huge country, lots of land and deep green woods. They could find a small town and start over again. Far away from Max. Far away from the suspicions of the Boston police.

Ree could pick a new name. He'd get a job, maybe at the general store.

They could make it for years. As long as he never got back on a computer.

Sandy was pregnant.

He should do something.

He didn't know what.

Upon further contemplation, he couldn't run. Not yet. He needed to save Ree. It would always come down to Ree. But he wanted, he needed, to know what had happened to Sandy. And he wanted, he needed, to know about the baby. He felt that in the past forty-eight hours, fate had taken his legs right out from under him. And now, perversely, it was dangling a carrot.

He might be a father.

Or Sandy really did hate him after all.

If he couldn't run, then he needed a computer. Actually, he needed his computer and he needed to understand just what Sandy had done. How much had thirteen-year-old Ethan taught her?

Best he knew, the family computer was still safely stashed at the offices of the *Boston Daily*. But how to retrieve it? He could drag Ree with him over to the offices. Police would shadow him this time, and probably two or three reporters as well. His mere presence would make them suspicious. What kind of grieving husband woke his kid in the middle of the night to go to work two nights in a row?

If the police grew suspicious enough, they might check out the computers at the *Boston Daily*. Particularly if Ethan Hastings kept talking to them. How much had Sandy found? What pieces had she put together without ever confronting him on the subject? She should've been angry. Furious. Frightened.

But she had never said a word.

Had she taken a lover by then? Is that what this came down to? She'd found a lover, and then, once she'd stumbled upon the computer files, made her decision to leave Jason. Except then she'd discovered she was pregnant. His? The other man's? Maybe she'd tried to break it off with her lover. Maybe that had made the other man angry, and he'd taken steps.

Or maybe, on Wednesday night, armed with her newfound training from Ethan Hastings, Sandy had discovered Jason's computer files. At that moment, she'd realized she was carrying a monster's child. So she'd…what? Fled into the night without even her wallet or a change of clothes? Decided to save one child by abandoning the other?

It didn't make any sense.

Which brought him back to the only other new man he knew of in Sandy's life—Ethan Hastings. Perhaps the boy had assumed a more intimate relationship with Sandy. Perhaps she'd tried to tell him he was mistaken. Given all the hours he'd spent with her, trying to help her outwit her own husband, Ethan had taken this personally. So he'd come to the house in the middle of the night and…

The youngest killer in America had been sentenced for a double homicide at the tender age of twelve, so as far as Jason was concerned, Ethan Hastings met the age requirement for possible homicidal maniac. The logistics of murder, however, seemed complicated. How would a thirteen-year-old boy get to Jason's house? Ride his bike? Walk? And how would a kid as scrawny as Ethan Hastings dispose of a grown woman's body? Drag her out by her hair? Fling her over his handlebars?

Jason sat down at the kitchen counter, his head spinning. He was tired. Bone-deep weary. These were the moments he had to be careful. Because his thoughts might wander, and he'd suddenly find himself in a room that always smelled like fresh-turned earth and decaying fall leaves. He would feel the whisper of hundreds of spiderwebs brushing across his cheeks and hair. Then he would see the quick scrabble of one fat hairy body, or two or three, dashing across his tennis shoe, or down his pant leg, or across his shoulder, frantically looking for escape.

Because you had to escape. There were things in the dark much worse than shy, panic-stricken spiders.

He wanted to think of Janie. The way she and she alone had welcomed him home with a huge hug. He wanted to remember how it had been sitting on the floor beside her, dutifully drawing unicorns while she prattled away on the importance of the color purple, or why she wanted to live in a castle when she grew up.

He wanted to remember the look on her twelfth birthday, when he had saved all his money to take her horseback riding for the day, because they weren't the kind of family that could ever afford a pony.

And he wanted to believe that the morning of his eighteenth birthday, when she had woken up and discovered his room once again empty, that she hadn't cried, that she hadn't missed him. That he hadn't broken his little sister's heart all over again.

Because he was getting an education these days. He was learning that to be the family of the missing person was in its own way just as terrible as being the missing person. He was learning that living with so many questions was harder than being the person who had all the answers.

And he was learning that deep in his heart, he was terrified that the Burgerman was still alive and well. Somehow, some way, the monster from Jason's youth had returned to take his family from him.

Jason paced for another ten minutes. Or maybe it was twenty or thirty. Clock was ticking, each minute inching toward another morning without his wife.

Max would return.

The police as well.

And more press. Cable news shows now. The likes of Greta Van Susteren and Nancy Grace. They would apply their own kind of pressure. A beautiful wife missing for days. The dark mysterious husband with a shady past. They'd crack open his life for the world to see. And somewhere in Georgia, some people would connect some dots and place phone calls of their own....

Then both Max and the police would have real ammunition to take his daughter from him. How long did he have? Noon? Two o'clock? Maybe they'd break the story just in time to headline the five o'clock cycle. That would score them ratings. Some news anchorman would see his star soar.

And Jason... How in the world would he ever say goodbye to his daughter?

Worse, what would happen to her? Her mother gone, now dragged away from the only father she had ever known... *Daddy, Daddy, Daddy...*

He had to think. He had to move.

Sandy was pregnant.

He needed to do something.

Couldn't access his computer. Couldn't confront Ethan Hastings. Couldn't run. What to do? What to do?

It came to him, shortly after two A.M.: his last course of action.

It would involve leaving his daughter, sleeping alone upstairs. In four years, he'd never done such a thing. What if she woke up? Found the house once again empty and started screaming hysterically?

Or what if there was someone else out there, someone lurking in the shadows, waiting for Jason to make his first mistake so he could swoop in and grab Ree? She knew something more about Wednesday night. D.D. believed it; he did, too. If someone had abducted Sandy, and if that same someone knew Ree had been a witness...

D.D. had sworn the cops were watching his house. A promise or a threat. He had to hope it was a little of both.

Jason went upstairs, changing into black jeans and a black sweatshirt. He paused outside Ree's door, straining his ears for any sound of movement. Then, when the silence unnerved him, he had to crack the door open to reassure himself that his four-year-old daughter was still alive.

She slept in a rounded huddle, one arm thrown over her face, Mr. Smith tucked into the curve of her knees.

And Jason remembered clearly then, vividly, the moment he'd first watched her slide into the world. How wrinkly and small and blue. The flail of her fists. The tight, screwed-up pucker of her wailing mouth. The way he instantaneously, absolutely fell in love with every square inch of her. His daughter. His lone miracle.

"You're mine," he whispered.

Sandy was pregnant.
"I will keep you safe."
Sandy was pregnant.
"I will keep you all safe."
He left his daughter and jogged down the street.

| CHAPTER TWENTY-FOUR |

You know the thing that takes you the longest to get used to in prison? The sound. The sheer, unrelenting noise of men, 24/7. Men grunting, men farting, men snoring, men fucking, men screaming. Inmates muttering away in their own delusional world. Convicted felons, talking, talking, talking even as they're sitting on the john, as if shitting in plain sight is somehow easier if they talk through the entire freaking event.

First month in the system, I didn't sleep a wink. I was too overwhelmed by the smells, the sights, but mostly the unrelenting sound that never shuts up, never gives you even thirty seconds to escape to some far corner of your mind where you can pretend you aren't nineteen years old and this didn't just happen to you.

I got jumped week three. Knew that by the sound of soft-soled shoes suddenly rushing up behind me. Then came other time-honored prison sounds—the wet thump of one man's fist connecting against another man's kidney, the crack of a skull against the cinderblock wall, the excited cries of the other zoo animals as I lay in a stunned heap, my orange suit somewhere around my ankles as one, two, three—hell, maybe half a dozen guys went at it.

No one goes to prison and comes home a virgin. No sirree, Bob.

Jerry visited me week four. Only visitor I ever had. My stepdad sat across from me, took in my bruised face, shell-shocked eyes, and started to laugh.

"Toldya you wouldn't last a fucking month, you prissy little piece of shit."

Then my stepfather left.

He's the one who turned me in. He found my stash of letters, the ones I'd written to "Rachel." So he called the cops, but not before ambushing me the instant I walked in from school. He caught me above the eye with the metal locker I'd used to store my few personal possessions. Then he'd gone after me with his fists.

Jerry was six two and two hundred and twenty pounds. Used to be a star high school football player, back in the day, then worked the lobster boats before he lost two fingers and figured out he liked sponging off women instead. My mom had been act one. But after she died when I was seven, he'd found several replacements. I was just along for the ride after that, no more family, just the little blond-haired kid Jerry used to pick up chicks. Wasn't even his kid, I tried to tell them, but the women didn't care. Apparently, widowers are sexy, even ones with enormous beer guts and only eight remaining digits.

Jerry hit like a Mack truck, and I was done after the first blow. He landed twenty more, just to be thorough about things. Then, when I was curled up, coughing up blood, he called the cops to come take out the trash.

Cops didn't say boo when they walked through the door. Just nodded at Jerry, gazed down at my sorry ass.

"He's the one?"

"Yes suh. And she's only fourteen. I'm telling you, he's one sick sonuvabitch."

Cops dragged me to my feet. I was still coughing blood, swaying in the wind, eye swelling shut.

Then Rachel appeared. Came up the walkway, fresh off the bus from junior high, lost in her own thoughts. Then slowly but surely, she realized the front door was already open, that a whole cluster of blue suits were standing there. We all watched the comprehension wash over her face.

Then, gazing at my smashed-in nose and rapidly swelling eye, she started to scream and scream and scream.

I wanted to tell her I'd be okay.

I wanted to tell her I was sorry.

I wanted to tell her I loved her and it had been worth it. The pain, everything. I loved her that much.

But I never got to say anything. I blacked out. By the time I regained consciousness, I was in county lockup and I never saw Rachel again.

I pled guilty for her, spared her the trauma of the trial just like the DA asked me to. I gave up my freedom. I gave up my future.

But the courts will tell you it wasn't true love.

I know what I gotta do tonight, and it has me all pissed off. The pretty cop lady is gonna come back. She has that look about her. A dog with a bone. And the guys at the garage are gonna come over, too. Except they're gonna bring baseball bats, and rolls of quarters in their fists. They got that look about them, too—you know, the overexcited drool of muscle heads armed with pitchforks.

Even Wendell called me this afternoon, the fucking flasher from group therapy. None of us is supposed to have each other's personal info, but Wendell no doubt bribed some flunky just so he could grill me for the inside skinny. He'd watched the press conference on the missing woman and wanted to hear all about it. Not that he thought I was innocent, mind you. Not that he was calling to offer support. No, he wanted details. Exactly what Sandra Jones looked like, exactly what she sounded like, exactly what she felt like when I squeezed out her last breath. Wendell has no doubt that I killed her. And he doesn't care. He just wants me to share the glory so he has something fresh to fantasize about while whacking off.

Everyone's got an opinion about me, and I'm just plain fucking sick of it.

So I hit the liquor store. Screw my probation. I'm already gonna get arrested and I haven't done anything wrong. So following the time-honored tradition that I might as well commit the crime, since apparently I'm serving the time, I'm getting liquored up. No beer for me. I'm gonna do this the right away.

Maker's Mark whiskey. That's what my stepdad always bought. I used it the first night I seduced Rachel. Poured us giant shots mixed with lemonade. What are a couple bored kids gonna do after school but steal from the liquor cabinet?

I buy two bottles, practically jogging all the way home, because now that I've decided to be bad, I don't want to waste a moment of it. I crack open the first liter, drinking straight from the bottle. One sip down, I nearly cough up a lung. I've never been a big drinker, not even as a teenage slacker. I've forgotten just how badly whiskey can burn.

"Jesus Christ!" I gasp. But I keep at it. Oh, I keep at it.

Half a dozen swigs later, my belly is nice and warm and I already feel calmer, loose even. Perfect for what I gotta do next.

I go into my closet. Cast off all my clothes, and there it is. A giant metal locker. The object I'm pretty sure Officer Blondie found earlier and now wants to ask me lots of questions about. Let her. Just let her.

I pick up the locker, last piece of my old life, and stagger with it out to the back yard. Night's cold. I should put on a sweatshirt. Something other than my usual ugly white tee. I drink more Maker's Mark instead. That'll warm you to your toes, yes sirree, Bob.

I crack open the locker. It's filled with notes. I don't know why Jerry didn't toss them. My best guess is that Rachel grabbed the box, maybe that very afternoon. She carried it away. She saved it for me.

And somehow, some way, one afternoon while I was out working at Vito's garage, she left it on the front step of my apartment for me. I came home, and boom, there it was. No packaging. No note. Not even a follow-up phone call. I guess it had to be her, right, because who else would do such a thing? And it made me consider that she would be seventeen now, old enough to drive, fearless enough to brave the trip from Portland, Maine, into the big city of Boston.

Maybe she'd discovered my address on the checks I sent to Jerry. Maybe once she realized where I lived, she had to pay me a visit. See how I was doing.

Did she read the letters? Did it help her understand why I did what I did?

I went through the contents often the first few weeks. Best I could tell, every single letter I ever wrote was there, including the rough drafts of bad poetry, the get-well card I made when she had mono, the bits of verse I tried to write when really I oughtta stick to tuning engines. I searched for responses she might have scribbled in the margins, maybe hints of lipstick, a greasy print from the palm of her hand.

One night, in a fit of inspiration, I sprayed the letters with lemon juice, because I'd just watched a *MythBusters* episode where they used citric acid to uncover disappearing ink. Nothing.

So I waited for her to return, day after day after day. Because she knew where I lived, and God, I hoped, I prayed to see her again. Just to have five minutes to tell her something, to tell her everything. Just to…see her.

The waiting game has proved to be a lot like the searching-for-scribbles-in-the-margin game. All these months later, I got nothing to show for it.

And I wonder now, as I wondered every single fucking night in prison, did she ever love me at all?

I toss back another hit of Maker's Mark, and then, before the burn can leave my throat, I flick the match and watch the world's most expensive collection of love letters start to burn. I sprinkle them with whiskey for good measure, and the fire roars its approval.

Except, at the last moment, I can't do it. I just can't do it.

I'm reaching in with my bare hands. I'm grabbing whatever little scraps I can even as the fire licks my wrists and melts the hair on the back of my hands. The pieces of paper are curling up, disintegrating to the touch, floating away as burning embers.

"No," I cry stupidly. "No, no, come back. No."

Then I'm chasing floating pieces of fire around the back yard, as my forearms burn and my legs wobble unsteadily, and suddenly for the first time, it comes back to me: sound.

You never forget the sounds of prison.

And I hear prison sounds right now, coming from the other side of the yard.

———

My hair is on fire. I don't notice it at the time, and that's probably what saves my neighbor's life: me, tearing around to the front of the house, my arms waving wildly while my hair begins to spark bright orange flames.

I come careening around the corner and three guys look up at once.

"Aidan," the first one says stupidly. His name is Carlos; I recognize his voice immediately: he works at the garage.

Then they simultaneously glance down at the black heap on the sidewalk. "Oh shit," the second guy says.

"But if he's Aidan," the third guy starts, clearly not the sharpest tool in the box. He has his booted foot on the downed man's back, and he's bent over with his right arm drawn back, captured mid-punch.

I realize at that moment that I'm still holding the Maker's Mark bottle, so I do the sensible thing and smash the bottom on the corner of Mrs. H.'s vinyl-sided house. Then I hold the jagged remains above my head, and hyped up on cheap whiskey and unrequited love, I launch into the fray, screaming like a banshee.

Three black-clad figures scatter, Carlos leaping out to an early lead, his arms pumping. Bachelor number three proves once again to be slow and stupid. I catch him across the upper arm with my impromptu weapon, and he screeches like a cat as I draw blood.

"Shit, shit, shit," guy number two keeps saying. I jab him in the side. He jumps clear. I slash down and catch part of his thigh. "Carlos," he's screaming now. "Carlos, Carlos, what the fuck?"

I'm wild. I'm drunk and pissed off and tired of being a doormat in the game of life. I'm swinging at Stupid Slow Guy, I'm slashing at Screeching, Oh Shit Guy. I'm going nuts and the only thing that saves them is that I'm the world's worst brawler when I'm sober, let alone when I'm drunk. I'm all fire and no focus.

Soon enough, the two dudes manage to pull free from my windmilling madness and bolt down the darkened street in Carlos's long-gone wake. That just leaves me, lunging at shadows and roaring obscene death threats until finally I realize my skull is screaming in agony and I smell something terrible.

Next thing I know, I've dropped the shattered whiskey bottle and

I'm hopping up and down in the middle of the street, trying to suffocate the embers smoldering in my melted hair.

"Shit. Oh shit, shit, shit." My turn to be the doofus. I pat frantically at my head until it feels like the worst of the heat has subsided. Then, breathing ragged, as moment passes into moment, I realize the full extent of my crime spree. I'm drunk. I've singed off most of my hair. My arms are riddled with black soot and fresh burn blisters. My whole body hurts like hell.

The black heap on the sidewalk is finally groaning his way back to life.

I cross to the man, roll him over onto his back.

And meet my neighbor, Jason Jones.

"What the fuck are you doing out this time of night?" I demand to know ten minutes later. I've managed to drag Jones inside my apartment, where I got him propped up on Mrs. H.'s floral love seat with one ice pack on his head and another against his left ribs.

Guy's left eye is already half-swollen and there's a bandage that suggests tonight hasn't been his first beating of the day.

"Are you a fucking idiot?" I want to know. I'm coming down off my adrenaline high. I pace back and forth in front of the tiny kitchenette, snapping at the green elastic and wishing I could crawl out of my own skin.

"What the hell did you do to your hair?" Jones croaks out.

"Forget my fucking hair. What the hell are you doing skulking around the neighborhood dressed like a suburban ninja? Isn't the freak show at your house enough for you?"

"You mean the media?"

"Cannibals."

"Given that I'm one of them, and they're clearly feeding off me, an apt analogy."

I scowl harder. In my current mood, I don't give a rat's ass for *apt analogies*. "What the hell are you doing?" I try again.

"Looking for you."

"Why?"

"You said you saw something the night my wife disappeared. I want to know what you saw."

"Like you couldn't just pick up a damn phone and give me a call?"

"Like I couldn't read your face to see if you were lying while you answered."

"Please, you can stare me in the eye all you want; you still won't know if I'm lying."

"Try me," he says softly, and there is something in his half-swollen eye then that worries me more than the three bruisers who'd jumped him on the sidewalk.

"Oh yeah?" I try to sound macho. "If you're so big and tough, why was *I* the one chasing away the goon squad, then scraping *your* sorry ass off the pavement?"

"Jumped me from behind," he says ruefully, adjusting the ice packet. "Who were they, friends of yours?"

"Oh, just a couple of locals who found out there was a registered sex offender in the neighborhood. Come back tomorrow night. Same time, same place, you can probably catch the same show."

"Feeling sorry for yourself?" he asks quietly.

"Absolutely."

"That explains the whiskey."

"I got a whole 'nother bottle. Want some?"

"I don't drink."

For some reason, that pisses me off. *"Don't drink, don't smoke, what do you do? . . . Goody two, goody two, goody goody two shoes."*

Jones stares at me funny.

"Jesus," I explode, "it's Adam Ant. From the eighties? Where'd you grow up, under a rock?"

"In a basement, technically. And you're too young to remember the eighties."

Now I shrug uncomfortably, realizing too late how much I've given away. "I knew this girl," I mumble. "Big Adam Ant fan."

"This the one you raped?" he asks levelly.

"Oh shut up! Just shut the fuck up. I'm so sick and tired of every-one pretending to know all about me and my goddamn sex life. It wasn't like that. It. Was not. Like. *That.*"

"I looked you up," he continues, monotone man. "You had sex with a fourteen-year-old girl. That's statutory rape. So yes, it was like that."

"I loved her!" I explode.

He stares at me.

"We had something special. It wasn't all sex. I needed her. She needed me. We were the only two people who cared about each other. That's special, dammit. That's *love*."

He stares at me.

"Well, it is! You can't help who you fall in love with. Plain and simple."

He finally speaks. "Do you know that among hard-core pedophiles, the single largest common denominator is having had their first sexual experience be with an adult while they were under the age of fifteen?"

I close my eyes. "Oh fuck you, too!" I say tiredly. I find the surviving Maker's Mark on the counter and go to work on the cap, though I'm starting to feel so nauseous that my heart isn't in it.

"You shouldn't have touched her," he continues. "Restraint would've been love. Letting her grow up would've been love. Not taking advantage of a lonely and vulnerable junior high student would've been love. Being friends would've been love."

"You know, you're welcome to go lay back down on that sidewalk," I tell him. "I'm sure someone else will come along to rescue you shortly." But apparently, he isn't done yet.

"You seduced her. How'd you do it? Drugs, alcohol, pretty words? You thought about it, you planned it. Because you were older, you had maturity and patience on your side. Maybe you waited, picked the right moment. She was sad and lonely about something, and there you were. You offered to rub her back. Maybe you poured her a drink. 'Just a little drink,' you told her. 'It'll help you relax.' And maybe she was uncomfortable, maybe she tried to tell you to stop—"

"Shut up," I tell him, words hard, warning.

He merely nods. "Yep, she definitely asked you to stop. She absolutely asked you to stop, and you didn't listen. You kept touching and petting, pressing the advantage. What can she do? She's only fourteen, she doesn't understand everything she's feeling, that she wants you to stop, that she wants you to continue, that this isn't right, that she's awkward and embarrassed—"

I cross the room in three strides and backhand him across the face. The crack is surprisingly loud. His head snaps to the side. The ice pack falls on top of a doily. He turns back slowly, rubs his chin almost thoughtfully, then picks up the ice pack and returns it to his forehead.

He looks me right in the eye, and I shiver at what I see there. He doesn't move a muscle. Neither do I.

"Tell me what you saw Wednesday night," he states quietly.

"A car, driving down the street."

"What kind of car?"

"The kind with a lot of antennas. Maybe a limo service; it looked like a dark sedan."

"What did you tell the police?"

"That you're a homicidal motherfucker," I spit out. "Trying to offer me up on a serving platter to save your sorry hide."

He glances at my head, my hands, my forearms. "What did you burn this evening?"

"Anything I wanted to."

"Do you collect porn, Aidan Brewster?"

"None of your business!"

Jones sets down the ice pack. He stands up in front of me. I fall back. I can't help it. Those deep dark eyes, rimmed in blood and bruises and God knows what. I have a sense of déjà vu, that I have seen eyes like that before. Maybe in prison. Maybe the first guy who dropped me in a bloody heap and banged the hell out of me. I realize for the first time that something about my neighbor isn't quite human.

Jones steps forward.

"No," I hear myself gasp. "I burned love letters, dammit. My own personal notes. I'm telling you, I'm not a pervert!"

His gaze sweeps the room. "Got a computer, Aidan?"

"No, dammit. I'm not allowed. Terms of my parole!"

"Stay off the Internet," he says. "I'm telling you: One visit to one chat room to say one word to one teenage girl, and I will break you. You will swallow your own tongue just to get away from me."

"Who the fuck are you?"

He leans down over me. "I'm the one who knows you raped your own stepsister, Aidan. I'm the one who knows exactly why you pay your stepfather a hundred bucks a week. And I'm the one who knows just how much your *love* will cost your now anorexic victim, for the rest of her sorry life."

"But you can't know," I say stupidly. "Nobody knows. I passed the lie detector test. I tell you, I passed the lie detector test!"

He smiles now, but something about that look, combined with his flat eyes, sends shivers down my spine. He turns, walks down the hall.

"She loved me," I call out weakly behind him.

"If she loved you, she would've returned to you by now, don't you think?"

Jones shuts the door behind himself. I stand alone in my apartment, burned hands fisted by my sides, and think how much I hate his guts. Then I uncap the second bottle of Maker's Mark and get down to business.

| CHAPTER TWENTY-FIVE |

In the beginning, I worried about two things: how to ask my questions of Ethan Hastings without giving away too much and how to plot against my husband given my extremely limited free time. The solution to both problems turned out to be surprisingly simple.

I met with Ethan every day during my free period. I told him I was creating a sixth grade teaching module for Internet navigation. Under the guise of crafting a class project, Ethan answered all of my questions and more.

I started with online security. We couldn't have sixth-graders visiting porn sites, right? Ethan demonstrated for me how to manage account and browser permissions to limit where users could go.

That night after Ree went to bed, I booted up the family computer and went to work. I opened the security window in AOL and busily "per-missioned" away. Of course, after I went to bed, it occurred to me that Jason might not use AOL to surf the web. Maybe he used Internet Explorer or another browser.

I returned to Ethan the next day.

"Is there any way to see exactly which websites have been visited by each computer? You know, that way I can check and see if each student

is going where he or she is supposed to be going and that our network security protocols are working."

Ethan explained to me that each time a user clicks on a website, a cookie is created by that website and temporary copies of the web pages are saved in the computer's cache file. The computer also stores a browser history, so that by glancing at the right files, I could tell exactly where that computer had been on the World Wide Web.

I had to wait five more nights, until Ree was asleep and Jason was at work. Ethan had showed me how I could click on the pull-down menu of the Internet search bar, and it would show me the websites most recently visited by the computer. I selected the search bar, got the pull-down menu, and saw three options, *www.drudgereport.com*, *www.usatoday.com*, and *www.nytimes.com*.

Right away, this struck me as not enough options, because when Ethan had done it in the computer lab, we'd easily gotten twelve to fifteen sites. So I booted up Internet Explorer, and tried its browser history, which gave me the exact same results.

I was stumped.

I monitored the browser history for a bit after that. Every few days, random times, when I thought I could quickly call it up without Jason noticing. Always I found the same three sites, which didn't make any sense to me. Jason spent hours at a time hunched over the computer. No way he was simply reading the news.

Three weeks later, inspiration hit. I constructed a civics question to research for my social studies class regarding the five freedoms guaranteed under the First Amendment. Then I merrily Google-searched away. I found history sites, I found government sites, Wikipedia, all sorts of good stuff. I hit them all, and by the time I was done that evening, the pull-down menu showed a nice robust list of recently visited websites.

I went to school the next day and gave my class an impromptu lecture on freedom of speech, freedom of religion, freedom of the press, freedom to peacefully assemble, and freedom to petition.

Then I raced home, barely able to contain myself until Ree went to bed and I could check the browser history of Internet Explorer once more.

You know what I found? Three websites: Drudge Report, USA

Today, New York Times. *Every site I had visited just twenty-four hours before was gone. Wiped out.*

Somehow, some way, my husband was covering his online tracks.

The following day, I hit Ethan with my question the second he walked into the computer lab.

"I was talking to another teacher after school yesterday, and she implied that checking the computer's browser history isn't enough. That there are ways of tampering with the browser history, or something like that?"

I shrugged helplessly and Ethan immediately sat down at the nearest computer and fired it to life.

"Oh sure, Mrs. Jones. You can purge the cache file after going online. That will make it appear like that web visit never happened. Here, I'll show you."

Ethan logged on to the National Geographic website, then exited and showed me the options for clearing the cache on the computer. I was crestfallen.

"So I can't really track what the kids are doing at all, can I? I mean, if any of them figure out how to clear the cache—which is just a click away—then they can visit all sorts of places when I'm not looking and I'll never figure it out."

"Well, you have the basic security functions," Ethan tried to assure me.

"But they're not foolproof either. You demonstrated that the first time we set them up. It seems to me I can't really control where the students go or what they do. Maybe a teaching module on Internet navigation isn't such a good idea."

Ethan was thoughtful for a bit. He is a bright kid. Earnest, but lonely. I had the feeling his parents loved him but had no idea what to do with him. He is too smart, intimidating even for adults. The kind of kid who is meant to suffer for the first twenty years or so, but then would take his software company public at age twenty-one and wind up married to a supermodel and driving a Ferrari.

He wasn't there yet, however, and I felt bad for his painful shyness, the way he regarded the whole world through this highly analytical lens the rest of us could never see.

"You understand that when you delete something on a computer, it never actually goes away?" he said presently.

I shook my head. "No, I don't understand that at all."

He brightened. "Oh, absolutely. See, computers are inherently lazy."

"They are?"

"Sure. A computer's primary function is to store data. If you think about it, the hard drive is nothing but a giant library lined with empty shelves. Then you, the user, come along and start inputting documents, or downloading information, or surfing the Internet, whatever. You're creating 'books' of data, which the computer then stashes on the shelves."

"Okay."

"Like any library, the computer needs to be able to retrieve the books at a moment's notice. So it creates a directory, its own version of a card catalogue system, which it can use to find each particular piece of data on the bookshelves. Got it?"

"Got it," I assured him.

Ethan beamed at me. Apparently, in addition to being a good teacher, I was an excellent student. He continued his lecture: "Now this is where the computer gets lazy: When you delete a document, the computer doesn't take the time to track down the actual data on the bookshelf and trash it. That would be too much work. Instead, it simply deletes the reference to the document in the directory. The book's still there; the card catalogue, however, no longer shows its location."

I stared at my red-headed partner for a bit. "You mean to tell me, even if the cache is cleared, those particular Internet files are still on the computer somewhere?"

I got a second smile for that one. "Great job!"

I couldn't help it. I smiled back. This made Ethan blush, and reminded me I had to be careful. Just because I was using Ethan Hastings didn't mean I wanted to hurt him.

"So, if the card catalogue has been cleared," I asked, "how do I find the data?"

"If you really want to know what's in the computer's browser history, I recommend Pasco."

"Pasco?"

"It's a computer forensic software you can download from online. Here's the deal: When someone 'clears the cache,' the computer rarely clears all the cache. At least a few index.dat files get left behind. So you open the history files, run Pasco, and it'll spit out a CSV—"

"CSV?"

"Comma Separated Values, which opens an Excel spreadsheet that will show every URL that was visited by the computer with a date-time stamp. You can cut and paste one of the URLs straight into the computer's search engine and it'll take you to that website for inspection. Voila, you'll know everyplace the computer has visited."

"How do you know so much?" I had to ask.

Ethan blushed furiously. "My um...family."

"Your family?"

"My mother runs Pasco on my computer each week. Not that she doesn't trust me!" He flushed brighter. "It's just, um, 'due diligence,' she calls it. She knows I'm smarter than her, so she's gotta have something on her side."

"Your mother's right, Ethan. You are a genius, and I can't thank you enough for assisting me with this teaching module."

Ethan smiled, but he appeared more thoughtful this time.

At home that night, I got serious. Two stories, one song, and half a Broadway show later, Ree was down, Jason was out, and I was all alone with my newfound computer skills and a whole host of suspicions. First order of business: downloading and installing the Pasco forensic tool from Foundstone.

Next up, I started working the menu system, identifying possible history files and running Pasco on the contents. Shoulders hunched, head down, I pecked away at the computer with eyes glued to microscopic type on the screen and ears perked for the first sound of Jason's car in the driveway.

I didn't know what I was doing, and everything took longer than I thought. Next thing I knew, it was after midnight and Jason was due home any minute. I was still running reports and hadn't figured out yet how to uninstall Pasco, whose mere presence on the desktop would alert Jason that I knew something was going on.

I was hopped up and jumpy when I finally got the dialogue box asking if I wanted to open or save the CSV. I didn't know what I should do, but I was running out of time, so I hit Open and watched an Excel spreadsheet fill the screen before me.

I figured I would discover dozens of URLs. Porn sites? Chat rooms? More terrible photos of terrified little boys? Evidence that the man I'd chosen to raise my child was a hard-core pedophile, or one of those sick men who trolled MySpace, preying on twelve-year-olds? I wasn't sure yet what I hoped, or what I feared. My eyes were screwed shut. I could barely bring myself to look.

What, oh what, was my husband doing all those long nights?

Three values filled the screen. I already knew what they were before I ever entered the URLs into the web browser: Drudge Report, USA Today, and the New York Times.

My husband held his secrets well.

The next day during free period, Ethan was already waiting for me in the computer lab.

"Did it work?" he asked me.

I didn't know what to say.

"Well?" he said impatiently. "Did you find out what your husband is doing online or not?"

I stared at my star pupil.

He remained matter-of-fact. "Sixth-graders aren't that Internet savvy," he said. "I mean, I was, but you don't have a single me in your class, meaning you have nothing to worry about. That leaves your job, but I hack into the school's computer all the time, and there's nothing interesting going on here—"

"Ethan!"

He shrugged. "So the last possibility is that you're worried about something at home. Ree is only four, so it can't be her. That leaves your husband."

I sat down. It seemed better than standing.

"Is it porn?" Ethan asked with his guileless blue eyes. "Or is he gambling away your life savings?"

"I don't know," I said at last.

"You didn't run Pasco?"

"I did. It returned only three URLs, the same three I've seen before."

Ethan sat upright. "Really?"

"Really."

"Wow, gotta be a shredder. I've only ever heard about them. That's cool!"

"A shredder is a good thing?"

"It is if you're trying to cover your tracks. A shredder, or scrubber software, is like a rake, clearing all the cache file footprints left behind you."

"It's deleting things the lazy computer wouldn't otherwise delete?"

"Nope. Shredders are lazy, too. They're automatically clearing the cache file so you don't have to remember to do it manually. So a user can go all sorts of places, then 'shred' the evidence. But since a lack of browser history is also a red flag, your husband is attempting to be clever by rebuilding a fake Internet trail. Fortunately for us, he's not that good at faking it."

I didn't say a word.

"Here's the cool part, though—shredders aren't foolproof."

"Okay," I managed.

"Every time you click on an Internet page, a computer is creating so many temp files there's no way the shredder can get them all. Plus, the shredder is still only messing with the directory. So the files are still there, we just have to find them."

"How?"

"Better tool. Pasco is over-the-counter. Now you want prescription-strength meds."

"I don't know any pharmacists," I said blankly.

Ethan Hastings grinned at me. "I do."

| CHAPTER TWENTY-SIX |

D.D. was dreaming about roast beef again. She was at her favorite buffet, trying to decide between the eggplant Parmesan and a blood-red carving roast. She opted for both, sinking her right hand straight into the tray of eggplant Parm while plucking up thin, juicy slivers of beef with her left. She had strings of melted cheese trailing down one arm and dribbles of *au jus* on her chin.

No bother. She climbed straight onto the white-covered table, planting her ass between the green Jell-O fruit ring and the collection of cherry-topped puddings. She scooped up handfuls of squishy Jell-O, while licking creamy tapioca straight from the chilled parfait glass.

She was hungry. Starving even. Then the food was gone, and she was on top of a giant, satin-covered mattress. She was on her belly, face down, nude body stretched out in a cat-like purr while unknown hands worked magic down the curve of her spine, over her writhing hips, finding the inside of her thighs. She knew where she wanted those hands. Knew where she needed to be touched, needed to be taken. She raised her hips accommodatingly, and suddenly she was flipped over, legs spreading wide to receive urgent thrusts while she stared into Brian Miller's heavily mustached face.

D.D. jerked awake in her bedroom. Her hands were fisting her covers, her body covered in a light sheen of sweat as she worked to slow her breathing. For the longest time, she simply stared at her gray-washed walls, morning coming hard in the rainy gloom.

She released the sheets. Pushed back the covers. Stabilized her legs enough to walk to the bathroom, where she regarded herself in the mirror above the sink.

"That," she told her reflection firmly, "never happened."

Five-thirty A.M., she brushed her teeth and got ready for the day ahead.

D.D. was a realist. You didn't last twenty years in the biz without realizing some hard truths about human nature. First twenty-four hours of a missing persons case, she gave them even odds of finding the person alive. Adults did take off. Couples argued. Some individuals could stick it out, others needed to bolt for a day or two. So first twenty-four hours, maybe even the first thirty-six, she'd been willing to believe that Sandra Jones was alive and they, the fine detectives of the BPD, might bring her home again.

Fifty-two hours later, D.D. was not thinking of locating a missing mother. She was thinking of recovering a body, and even with that in mind, she understood that time remained of the essence.

Crime, and investigations, had a certain rhythm. First twenty-four hours, not only was there hope of the victim surviving, but also of the criminal screwing up. Abduction, assault, homicide, all involved high emotion. Individuals held in the sway of high emotion had a tendency to make mistakes. Flushed on adrenaline, overloaded by anxiety or even remorse, the perpetrator was in panic mode. *Did something bad. How to get away, get away, get away?*

Unfortunately, as each day went by without the cops closing in, the subject had time to calm down, settle in. Start thinking more rationally about next steps, form a more concrete plan for cover up. The criminal became entrenched, disposing of evidence, polishing his story, even perhaps swaying key witnesses, such as his four-year-old daughter. In other words, the perpetrator transitioned from bungling amateur to criminal mastermind.

D.D. didn't want to be dealing with any criminal masterminds. She wanted a body and an arrest, all in time for the five o'clock news. Close in, apply the thumb screws, and crack the case wide open. That was the kind of thing that made her day.

Unfortunately, she had a few too many people to pressure. Take Ethan Hastings. Thirteen years old, frighteningly brilliant, and hopelessly in love with his missing teacher. Budding Lothario? Or freaky teenmonster?

Then came Aidan Brewster. Bona fide felon with a history of choosing inappropriate sexual relationships. Claimed not to know Sandra Jones, but lived just down the street from the crime. Reformed sex offender or escalating perpetrator with a fresh appetite for violence?

Sandy's father, the honorable Maxwell Black, had to be included in the mix. Estranged father, who magically showed up when his daughter disappeared. According to Officer Hawkes, Black seemed to be threatening Jones, and clearly planned to see his granddaughter one way or the other. Grieving father, or opportunistic grandfather who'd do anything to get his hands on Ree?

Finally, she returned to Jason Jones, the cold-blooded husband who had yet to engage in a single activity to find his missing wife. The guy claimed not to be the jealous type. Then again, he had no paper trail prior to marrying Sandy five years ago. A definite assumed identity.

D.D. went round and round, and she still came back to Jones. His daughter's own assessment of Wednesday night, Jones's disengaged behavior since his wife vanished, the obvious use of an alias. Jones was hiding something—ergo, he was the most likely suspect in his pregnant wife's disappearance.

That was it. D.D. was bringing little Ree in for more questioning as soon as possible. She would arrange for two officers to track each of their other subjects, building history and establishing alibis. Better yet, she was assigning two of her best white-collar investigators to trace Jones's bank accounts. Follow the money, find Jones's real name, real history, real past.

Break the alias. Break the man.

Satisfied, D.D. pulled out her notepad and jotted down one major to-do for the day: *Squeeze Jason Jones.*

D.D.'s cell rang ten minutes later. It was barely seven, but she didn't lead one of those lives where people called during normal operating hours. She took another sip of coffee, flipped open her phone, and announced, "Talk to me."

"Sergeant D. D. Warren?"

"Last I checked."

The caller paused. She took another sip of cappuccino.

"This, uh, is Wayne Reynolds. I work for the Massachusetts State Police. I'm also Ethan Hastings's uncle."

D.D. thought about it. The number on her display screen looked familiar. Then it came to her: "Didn't you buzz me yesterday morning?"

"I tried your pager. I saw the press conference and figured we'd better talk."

"Because of Ethan?"

Another pause. "I think it would be best if we could meet in person. What do you say? I could buy you breakfast."

"You think we're gonna arrest Ethan?"

"I think if you did, it would be a huge mistake."

"So, you're gonna throw your state weight around, ask me to back off? 'Cause you should know up front, I don't take those kinds of conversations well, and buying me a bagel with cream cheese isn't gonna make a difference."

"How about we meet first, and you can be hostile and indifferent second?"

"It's your funeral," D.D. said. She rattled off the name of a coffee shop just around the corner, then went to fetch an umbrella.

Mario's was a locals' establishment. Tiny, with the original Formica countertop from 1949 and an enormous glass jar of fresh biscotti next to the ancient cash register. Mario II, the son, currently ran the joint. He served up eggs, toast, pancetta, and the best coffee you could buy outside of Italy.

D.D. had to wrestle for a tiny round corner table next to the front window. She got there early, mostly so she could enjoy a second cup of coffee in peace, while working her cell phone. She found the uncle's outreach to be fascinating. Here she was thinking she needed to push harder on the husband, and the family of the teenage wannabe lover entered the fray. Were they feeling overprotective, or guilt-stricken? Interesting.

D.D. hit speed dial, holding the tiny phone to her ear. Just because she had a sex dream last night was not the reason she was calling Bobby Dodge.

"Hello," a female voice answered.

"Morning, Annabelle," D.D. said, without a trace of the anxiety she immediately felt. Other women didn't intimidate her. It was a hard-and-fast rule she'd developed years ago when she'd realized she was prettier than ninety percent of the female population, and a hundred percent better with a loaded handgun. Annabelle, of course, would be the exception to that rule, and Annabelle had snagged Bobby Dodge. That made her D.D.'s personal nemesis, even if they were both properly civil to each other. "Is Bobby awake?"

"Didn't you call him in the middle of the night?" Annabelle asked.

"Yep. Hey, I understand congratulations are in order. Congratulations."

"Thanks."

"You, um, feeling okay?"

"Yes, thank you."

"When are you due?"

"August."

"Boy or girl?"

"Waiting to be surprised."

"Nice. So is Bobby around?"

"He's only going to hang up on you again."

"I know. It's part of my charm."

There was a distant shuffle as Annabelle handed the phone over to her husband, then some male grunting as Bobby was no doubt prodded awake.

"Tell me I'm dreaming," Bobby groaned into the phone.

"I don't know. Am I naked and covered in whipped cream?"

"D.D., I just talked to you eight hours ago."

"Well, that's the thing about crime. It never sleeps."

"But detectives do."

"Really? Must've missed that class at the Academy. So, I have a question for you about another statie. Name of Wayne Reynolds. Ring any bells?"

There was a long pause, which was better than the usual click of Bobby hanging up. "Wayne Reynolds?" he repeated at last. "No, can't think of any detectives by that name."

D.D. nodded, remaining quiet. Both the BPD and Massachusetts State Police were sizable organizations, but they still retained a family-enterprise sort of feel. Even if you didn't work directly with every officer, chances were you'd caught a name in the hall, read it on top of a report, even heard a juicy bit of gossip in the latest rumor mill.

"Wait a minute," Bobby said shortly. "I do know that name, but he's not with the detectives unit. He's at the Computer Lab. He handled the forensic analysis of some cell phones for last year's bank robbery."

"He's an electronics geek?"

"I think they prefer the term 'forensic specialist.' "

"Huh," D.D. said.

"You seize some computers and ask for state assistance?"

"I seized some computers and asked for BRIC assistance, thank you very much." BRIC was the Boston Regional Intelligence Center at BPD headquarters, basically BPD's geek squad, because like all good bureaucracies, the Boston police believed they needed to have all their own toys and specialists. It went without saying.

"Well, call someone in BRIC, then," Bobby grumbled. "They've probably worked with Wayne. I haven't."

"Okay. Good night, Bobby."

"Crap, it's already morning. Now I'll have to get up."

"Then good morning, Bobby." D.D. hung up before he could

swear at her again. She clipped her cell to her waist and contemplated her empty mug. Wayne Reynolds was a professional nerd with an amateur nerd nephew. She refilled her cup. Interesting.

Wayne Reynolds walked through the door of Mario's at precisely eight A.M. D.D. knew it was him by his burnished red hair, not so unlike his nephew's. All resemblance to a thirteen-year-old boy, however, began and ended with the coppertop.

Wayne Reynolds was tall, six one, six two. He moved easily and athletically. Definitely a guy who worked in a daily run, despite the pressing demands of ripping apart various hard drives. He wore a camel-colored light wool blazer that set off a forest green shirt and dark-colored slacks. More than one head turned when he walked in, and D.D. felt a slight bit of thrill when he headed for her, and only for her. If this is what Ethan Hastings was going to grow into one day, then maybe Sandy Jones had been onto something.

"Sergeant Warren," Wayne greeted her, extending his hand.

D.D. nodded, accepting the handshake. He had calloused palms. Short buffed nails. Positively beautiful fingers that didn't wear a wedding ring.

Honest to God, she was going to need some bacon.

"Want food?" she asked.

He blinked his eyes. "Okay."

"Great. I'll get enough for both of us."

D.D. used her time at the order counter to control her breathing and remind herself that she was a trained professional who absolutely, positively was *not* affected by having breakfast with a David Caruso look-alike. Unfortunately, she didn't believe herself; she'd always had a weakness for David Caruso.

She returned to the tiny table with napkins and silverware for both of them, as well as a cup of black coffee for him. Wayne accepted the oversized white ceramic mug with his beautiful fingers, and she bit the inside of her lips.

"So," she began tersely, "you work for the state?"

"Computer Forensic Unit in New Braintree. We handle the majority of the electronic analysis, as you can guess by the title."

"How long you been there?"

He shrugged, sipped his coffee black, eyes widening briefly at the dark roast. "Five or six years. I was a detective before that, but being a geek at heart, had a tendency to focus on the technology aspects of the cases. Given that everyone from a drug dealer to a crime lord is using computers, cell phones, or PDAs these days, demand for my technical skills grew. So I completed the eighty-hour course to become a CFCE—Certified Forensic Computer Examiner—and switched over to the Computer Lab."

"You like it?"

"I do. Hard drives are like piñatas. Every treasure you ever wanted is stored in there somewhere. You just gotta know how to break it open."

The food had arrived. Scrambled eggs with a side of grilled pancetta for both of them. The smells were rich and savory. D.D. dug in.

"How do you investigate hardware?" she asked, her mouth full.

Wayne had forked up a pile of eggs; he regarded her thoughtfully, as if trying to gauge the seriousness of her interest. He had deep hazel eyes with specks of green, so she made sure she looked interested.

"Take the rule of five-twelve. That's the magic number in forensic computer analysis. See, inside a hard drive are round platters that spin around to read and write data. These platters contain chunks of five hundred and twelve bytes of data, and they're constantly whirling under the seeker head. The seeker head, then, must divide all information into five hundred and twelve byte chunks in order to store the data onto the platters."

"Okay." D.D. went to work slicing up her pancetta.

"Now, say you're saving a file to your hard drive that doesn't divide neatly into five hundred and twelve byte chunks. It's not one thousand and twenty-four bytes of data, it's eight hundred bytes. The computer will fill one whole data chunk, then half of another available chunk. Then what? The computer doesn't pick up where it left off, mid-data chunk. Instead, a new file will start with a fresh five-twelve byte space, meaning the previous file has excess storage capacity, or what we call 'slack space,' in the existing data chunk. Often, old data gets left in that slack space. Say you called up that file, made some changes, then resaved it. The overwrite might not go exactly on top of the old data the way most people assume. Instead it might be tucked somewhere else inside the same data chunk. Then a guy like me can search that five-twelve chunk. In the slack space I might find the old document where you wrote the original letter asking your lover to murder your spouse, as well as the revised doc, where you deleted that particular paragraph. And voila, one guilty conviction is born."

"I don't have a spouse," D.D. volunteered, having another bite of eggs, "though I'm now deeply suspicious of my computer."

Wayne Reynolds grinned at her. "You probably should be. People have no idea how much information is retained unknowingly on their hard drives. I like to say a computer is like a guilty conscience. It remembers everything and you never know when it might start to speak."

"You been teaching your skills to Ethan?" D.D. asked.

"Haven't had to. Kid absorbs it on his own. If I can corral his skills for good versus evil, he'll be a hell of an investigator one day."

"What constitutes the dark side for computer technology?"

Wayne shrugged. "Hacking, code breaking, illicit data-mining. Ethan is a good kid, but he's also thirteen, so following in his uncle's footsteps doesn't sound as exciting as it once did. Join the state police or join the Internet underground. You be the judge."

"He seems to have valued Sandy Jones's opinions." D.D. had finished her food; she pushed back the white ceramic plate.

Wayne was thoughtful for a moment. "Ethan believes he is in love with his teacher," he conceded at last.

"Did he have sex with her?"

"I doubt it."

"Why?"

"She didn't view him that way."

"And how would you know?"

"Because I was seeing Sandra myself, every Thursday night. At the basketball games."

"Ethan contacted me regarding Sandra," Wayne explained a few moments later. They had paid the bill, left the coffee shop. Walking and talking seemed a better idea, given the subject matter. They headed aimlessly toward the waterfront, following the red line mapping the route once ridden by Paul Revere.

"My understanding," Wayne continued now, "was that Sandra had approached Ethan about developing a teaching module for the Internet. It didn't take Ethan long, however, to determine that her interest in online security ran deeper than mere classroom application. He believed her husband was up to something, perhaps involving child porn, and that Sandra was desperate to get to the bottom of it."

"You didn't open a case file?"

Wayne shook his head. "Couldn't. First time I met with Sandra, she made it clear that she would only accept my involvement as a personal favor. Until she learned exactly what was going on, she didn't want the police involved. She had to think of her daughter; Ree would be traumatized if her father was jailed unnecessarily."

D.D. arched a brow. "If Sandra suspected child porn, she should've been worried about her daughter being traumatized by a lot more than dear old Dad's arrest."

Wayne shrugged. "You know how families work. You can confront a mom with her seven-year-old daughter's semen-stained underwear, and she'll still insist there's a logical explanation."

D.D. sighed heavily. He was right and they both knew it. De Nile wasn't just a river when it came to child sexual assaults.

"Okay, so Ethan gives you a call. Then what?"

"As a favor to Ethan, who seemed very worried about his teacher, I agreed to attend one of the Thursday night basketball games and talk to Sandra myself. I confess, I figured I'd have a brief chat, give her a detective's contact information for follow up, that kind of thing. But..." His voice faded away.

"But?" D.D. prodded.

Wayne shrugged, looking almost chagrined. "Then I saw Sandra Jones."

"Not your typical social studies teacher," D.D. observed.

"No. Not at all. I figured out immediately why Ethan had taken a shine to her. I mean, she was younger than I expected. Prettier than I

expected. And sitting there on those wooden bleachers, this cute little girl tucked up against her knees...I don't know. I took one look
and I wanted to help her. It felt like I *had* to help her. That she
needed me."

"Oh yeah. Mary Kay Letourneau, Debra Lafave, Sandra Beth
Geisel. All beautiful women. Doesn't it seem strange to you that only
the pretty ones want to sleep with twelve-year-old boys? What's up
with that?"

"I'm telling you, she didn't have that kind of relationship with
Ethan."

"Did she have that kind of relationship with you?"

Wayne gazed at her flatly. "Look, do you want to hear what I have
to say or not?"

D.D. gestured with her hands. "Speak away. This is your party."

"That first night, Ethan sat with Ree while Sandra and I took a
short walk around the school to chat. She told me she had found a
disturbing photo in the recycle bin of the family computer. Only that
one image and only that one time; she hadn't discovered anything
since. However, she'd been learning about Internet browser histories
and data storage since then, and it was clear to her that her husband
was tampering with the computer, which made her wonder what
else he had to hide."

"Tampering with it in what way?"

"Ethan had taught Sandra how to track which websites are visited by a computer. That information is stored in the history file of
the computer's hard drive, and should be retrievable. She had made
a number of attempts at pulling up the family computer's Internet
browser, using various online tools Ethan had told her about. Every
time she did it, however, she could only retrieve the URLs for three
websites—the Drudge Report, *USA Today*, and *New York Times*."

D.D. was already lost. "Why is that suspicious?"

"Because Sandra herself had visited lots of different websites
preparing assignments for her class. All of those sites should have
shown up in the browser history, but none of them did. That meant
someone was clearing the cache file, then purposefully building a
false history by clicking on the same three websites when he was
done. That was sheer laziness," Wayne murmured now, probably

more to himself than her. "Like all criminals, even the techies sooner or later do something stupid to give themselves away."

"Wait a minute, back up: Why would someone create a false browser history?"

They'd reached the waterfront, walking along the docks toward the aquarium. It was still drizzling out, making the docks much less crowded than usual. Wayne made his way toward the railing, then turned to face her. "Exactly. Why *would* someone create a false browser history? That's the million-dollar question. Ethan had already recommended a downloadable forensic computer tool, but that hadn't been powerful enough. He suspected that Sandra's husband was employing something called a shredder, or scrubber software, to cover his tracks. So Ethan gave me a call, bringing in the big guns, so to speak."

D.D. blinked at him. "Could you help her?"

"I was trying to. This was December, mind you, so only a few months ago, and given that she suspected her husband, we had to proceed carefully. She and Ethan had already run Pasco on her computer, but Pasco can only find what you tell it to find. It's not nearly as powerful as, say, EnCase, the software we employ in the lab. EnCase can mine deep into a hard drive, inventorying the slack space, analyzing unallocated clusters, all sorts of good stuff. Better yet, given Sandra's concerns, EnCase has an image carver tool that will dig out any images on the hard drive, spitting out literally hundreds of thousands of photos. Finally, EnCase also has the ability to pull out Internet browser histories—"

"So you ran EnCase on Sandra's computer?"

"Don't I wish." He rolled his hazel eyes. "First off, you never work on the source. Bad forensic protocol. Secondly, Sandra needed to be discreet, and running EnCase on the family desktop for three to four days was bound to be noticed. Searching and seizing a computer is easy. Ripping one apart on the sly, however..."

"So what did you do?"

"I was working with Sandra to make a forensically sound copy of the family hard drive. I gave her instructions on what kind of blank hard drive to purchase, then how to attach it to the family computer and transfer over the data. Unfortunately, Jason had recently purchased a new five-hundred-gigabyte hard drive, and the copying time alone was over six hours. She'd made several attempts at it, but couldn't get the job done before he returned from work."

"Sandra Jones has spent the past three months basically plotting against her husband?" D.D. asked.

Wayne shrugged. "Sandra Jones has spent the past three months trying to outmaneuver her husband. As she has yet to get the hard drive copied, I have yet to run EnCase on it. So I can't tell you if she has genuine reason to be afraid of him."

D.D. smiled. "Wouldn't you know it, as of last night, BPD became proud owners of the Jones family computer."

Wayne's eyes widened. "I would love to—"

"Please, your nephew is connected to the case. You touch any piece of evidence and it'll be tossed out of court faster than you can say 'conflict of interest.' "

"Can I get a copy of the reports?"

"I'll have someone from BRIC get back to you."

"Assign Keith Morgan. You want to rip apart a hard drive, he's your boy."

"I'll take that under advisement." D.D. considered Wayne Reynolds for a minute. "Did Sandra believe her husband had figured out what was going on? She'd been at this for months. Long time to be living with someone she thought might be a closet pedophile. She had to be getting more and more nervous…"

Wayne hesitated, the first glimmer of discomfort crossing his features. "Last time I saw Sandra was two weeks ago, at the basketball game. She seemed withdrawn, didn't want to talk. She said she wasn't feeling well, then she and Ree left. I figured she really was sick. She had that look about her."

"You know Sandra was pregnant?"

"What?" Wayne seemed to pale slightly, genuinely startled. "I didn't… Well, no wonder she was nervous. Nothing like having a second child with a man you're already worried might be a pervert."

"She ever talk about her husband's past? Where he grew up, how they met?"

Wayne shook his head.

"Ever mention that 'Jones' might be an alias?"

"Are you kidding....? No, no, she never mentioned that."

D.D. considered the matter. "Sounds like Jason Jones is pretty computer savvy."

"Very."

"Savvy enough to use the computer to either hide a previous identity or build a new one?"

"All of the above," Wayne concurred. "You can open bank accounts, sign up for utilities, build credit histories, all online. A sophisticated computer user could both create and disguise multiple identities using the computer."

D.D. nodded, turning it over in her mind. "What would he need besides the computer?"

"Ummm, a mailing address, or P.O. box. Sooner or later, you have to provide a mailing address. Say, something he rented from a UPS store. And a phone number connected to that name, though in this day and age, he could buy a disposable cell phone for that. So he would need some tangible items to support the identity, but nothing too hard to manage."

Post office box. D.D. hadn't thought of that. Either in Jones's name or Sandy's maiden name. She'd do some digging....

"Sandy ever mention the name 'Aidan Brewster'?"

Wayne shook his head.

"And can you swear to me, as an investigator and law enforcement officer, that to the best of your knowledge, Sandra Jones was never alone with your nephew?"

"All Ethan ever talked about was meeting with Sandra in the computer lab during free period. Yeah, they were alone for a lot of those sessions, but we're talking in the middle of the day, in the middle of a public school."

"She ever talk to you about running away from her husband?"

"She would never leave her daughter."

"Not even for you, Wayne?"

He shot her that look again, but D.D. didn't withdraw her question. Wayne Reynolds was a handsome man, and Sandra Jones one very lonely young woman....

"I think Jason Jones killed her," Wayne said flatly. "He came home Wednesday night, discovered her trying to copy the hard drive, and blew his top. He was up to something, his wife figured it out, so he killed her. I've been thinking that since the second I saw the press conference yesterday, so if you're asking if I'm personally involved in this case, yeah, I'm personally invested in this case. I was trying to help a young, frightened mother, and in doing that, I may have gotten her murdered. I'm angry about that. Hell, I'm pissed off beyond belief."

"Okay." D.D. nodded. "You understand I'm going to need you to come in, give an official statement?"

"Absolutely."

"This afternoon, three o'clock? BPD headquarters?"

"I'll be there."

D.D. nodded, started to break away, then one last question came to her. "Hey, Wayne, how many times did you and Sandy meet?"

He shrugged. "I dunno. Eight, ten times maybe. Always at the basketball games."

D.D. nodded. She thought that was a lot of times to meet, given that Sandra had never had a copy of the computer's hard drive to share.

| CHAPTER TWENTY-SEVEN |

Jason woke up to a slow building hum, then a slash of bright lights across his eyes. He peered groggily at his watch, saw that it was five A.M., then peered at his backlit blinds with fresh confusion. Sun didn't rise at five A.M. in March.

Then he got it. Klieg lights. From across the street. The news vans had returned and were powering up for their morning visuals, everyone filming a fresh report from the crime scene, aka his front yard.

He let his head fall back against the pillow, wondering if there was any breaking news he should know about from the past three hours when he'd actually slept. He should turn on the TV. Watch an update of his life. He'd always had an overdeveloped sense of irony. He waited for it to kick in, appreciate this moment. But mostly, he felt tired, stretched in too many directions as he sought to protect his daughter, find his wife, and keep out of prison.

Jason extended his arms and legs, taking inventory after last night's pounding. He discovered that all four limbs appeared to be working, though some hurt more than others. He tucked his hands behind his head, peered up at the ceiling with his one working eye, and attempted to plan for the day ahead.

Max would return. Sandra's father hadn't come all the way to Massachusetts just to sit quietly in his hotel room. He would continue to demand access to Ree, threatening... legal action, exposure of Jason's past? Jason wasn't sure how much Max even knew of Jason's previous life. It wasn't like he and the old man had ever sat down. Jason had met Sandra in a bar, and she'd kept to that routine as much as possible. Only good girls take boys home to meet their fathers, she'd told him that first night, clearly wanting to establish that she wasn't a good girl. Jason would take her back to his little rental, where he would cook her dinner and they would watch movies together, or maybe play board games. They did everything but what she clearly expected them to do, and that kept her returning, night after night after night.

Until Jason began to notice her growing stomach. Until he started asking more questions. Until the night she broke down in tears and it became clear to him the solution to both of their problems. Sandy wanted away from her father for whatever reason. He just wanted away. So they'd taken off together. Fresh city, new last name, clean start. Right up until Wednesday night, Jason would've said neither one of them had ever harbored regrets.

Now Max was back in the picture. A man with money, brains, and local legal connections. Max could hurt Jason. Yet Jason still couldn't grant the man access to Ree. He'd promised Sandy that her father would never touch Ree. He wasn't going back on that now, not when his daughter needed him more than ever.

So Max would stir the pot, while the police continued to dog his heels. They were tearing apart his computer. Probably digging into his financial records. Interviewing his editor, perhaps even touring the *Boston Daily* offices. Would they spot the computer he'd left there, put two and two together?

How long could this game of high stakes poker go on?

Jason had taken basic steps when he'd become a family man. His "other" activities existed under a different identity, with a separate bank account, credit card, and P.O. box. Payment confirmations and the single credit card statement went to a suburban post office out in Lexington. He visited once a month, retrieving the paperwork, sorting through it, then shredding the evidence.

All good plans, however, had at least one central flaw. In this case, the family computer contained enough damning evidence to send him to prison for twenty to life. Sure, he employed a decent scrubber software, but any web visit generated far more temp files than one scrubber could cover. Three, four days tops, he decided. Then the forensic specialists would realize that something was wrong with the computer they had seized, and the police would return in earnest.

Assuming they hadn't already discovered Sandy's body and were even now standing on his front porch, waiting to arrest him.

Jason got out of bed, too keyed up to return to sleep. His ribs protested when he moved. He couldn't see out of his left eye. His injuries didn't matter to him, however. Nothing mattered, except one thing.

He needed to make sure Ree was still sleeping safely in her room, a tiny, curl-topped form with a bright orange cat at her feet.

He padded quietly down the hall, senses alert. The house smelled the same, felt the same. He cracked open the door to Ree's room, and discovered his daughter lying straight as an arrow in her bed, hands clutching the top of her comforter, big brown eyes staring up at him. She was awake, and, he realized belatedly, she had been crying. Damp lines of moisture smeared her cheeks.

"Hey, sweetheart," he said quietly, coming into the room. "You all right?"

Mr. Smith looked up at him, yawned, stretched out one long orange paw. Ree just stared at him.

He took a seat on the edge of the bed, where he could brush tangles of brown hair off her damp forehead.

"I want Mommy," she said in a small voice.

"I know."

"She's supposed to come home to me."

"I know."

"Why doesn't she come home, Daddy? Why doesn't she?"

He didn't have an answer. So he crawled in bed beside his daughter and pulled her into his arms. He smoothed her hair while she cried against his shoulder. He memorized the smell of her Johnson & Johnson skin, the feel of her head pressed against his shoulder, the sound of her tired little sobs.

Ree cried until she could cry no more. Then she spread her hand on top of his, aligning each of her short stubby fingers against his own larger, longer digits.

"We will get through this," Jason whispered to his daughter.

Slowly, she nodded against his shoulder.

"Would you like some breakfast?"

Another short nod.

"I love you, Ree."

Breakfast turned out to be more complicated than he'd planned. Eggs were gone. Same with the loaf of bread, the majority of fresh fruit. Milk was low, but he thought he could eke out two bowls of cereal. The Cheerios box was suspiciously light, so he went with Rice Crispies. Ree liked the talking cereal and he always made a big show of deciphering what the crackling crisps said:

"What, you want me to buy my daughter a pony? Oh no, you want me to buy myself a Corvette. Ooooh, that makes much more sense."

Jason got Ree to smile, then got her to giggle, and felt both of them relax.

He finished his bowl of cereal. Ree ate half of hers, then began creating floating patterns in the milk with the remaining rice puffs. It kept her amused and gave him time to think.

His body hurt. When he sat, when he walked, when he stood up. He wondered how the other guys looked. Then again, they'd jumped him from behind—he'd never seen them coming—so chances were, they looked pretty good.

He was getting sloppy in his old age, he decided. First getting taken out by a thirteen-year-old kid, then this. Hell, with these kinds of fighting skills, he wasn't gonna last a week in prison. A cheerful thought for the day.

"Daddy, what happened to your face?" Ree asked, as he pushed away from the countertop, standing up to clear dishes.

"I fell down."

"Ow, Daddy."

"No kidding." He set the dishes in the sink, then opened the refrigerator to eye their lunch options. No milk, leaving them with a six-pack of Sandy's prized Dr Pepper, four light yogurts, and some wilted lettuce. Second cheerful thought of the day: Just because you were public enemy number one didn't mean you got out of grocery shopping. If they planned on eating again today, they were going to have to hit the store.

He wondered if he should wear a bandana over his face. Or wear a T-shirt with the word "Innocent" scrawled on the front, and the word "Guilty" scrawled on the back. That could be fun.

"Hey, Ree," he asked casually, closing the refrigerator and eyeing his daughter. "What do you say to some quality time at the grocery store?"

Ree brightened immediately. She loved grocery shopping. It was an official Daddy-daughter chore, done at least one afternoon a week while they waited for Sandy to come home. He would strive to stick with the official wife-prepared grocery list. Ree would work to convince him to stray for such urgent purchases as Barbie Island Princess Pop-Tarts, or maple frosted doughnuts.

He generally shaved for the outing, while Ree preferred donning a full ball gown and a rhinestone tiara. There was no point in touring twenty aisles of food if you couldn't make a production out of it.

This morning, she bolted upstairs to brush her teeth, then returned to the kitchen wearing a blue-flowered dress with rainbow fairy wings and pink sequined shoes. She handed him some pink gauzy hair thing, and requested a ponytail. He did his best.

Jason wrote the grocery list, then made an attempt at general hygiene. Shaving his beard revealed an ugly bruise. Combing back his hair emphasized the shiner on his eye. No doubt about it, he looked like hell. Or more precisely, like an ax murderer. Third cheerful thought for the day.

He gave up on grooming and returned downstairs, where Ree was waiting eagerly by the front door, yellow daffodil purse in hand.

"You remember the reporters?" he asked her. "The people with cameras and microphones gathered across the street?"

Ree nodded solemnly.

"Well, they're still there, honey. And when we open that door, they're probably going to start shouting a ton of questions and taking pictures. They're just trying to do their job, okay? They're gonna be all crazy-like. And you and I are going to calmly walk to our car, and drive to the grocery store. Okay?"

"It's okay, Daddy. I saw them when I went upstairs. That's why I put on my fairy wings. So if they yell too much, I can fly right over them."

"You are a very smart girl," he told her, and then, because there was no time like the present, he opened the front door.

The screaming started with the first glimpse of his shoe.

"Jason, Jason, any news of Sandy?"

"Will you be talking to the police today?"

"When can we expect a formal briefing?"

He ushered Ree out, keeping her close to his side as he closed the door behind them, locking it. His hands were shaking. He tried to keep his movements slow and measured. No rush, no guilty sprints. Grieving husband, taking his little girl to purchase badly needed milk and bread.

"Will you be assisting with the search efforts, Jason? How many volunteers have turned out to find Sandy?"

"Love your wings, honey! Are you an angel?"

That comment caught his attention, made him look up sharply. He was resigned to them shouting at him, but he didn't want the pack of vultures going after Ree.

"Daddy?" his daughter whispered beside him, and he looked down to see the anxiety scribbled across her face.

"We're going to the car, we're driving to the grocery store," he repeated levelly. "We're okay, Ree. They're the ones behaving badly, not us."

She took his hand, keeping her body pressed tightly against his legs as they walked down the front steps, made their way across the lawn, headed toward the car parked on the driveway. He counted six vans today, up from four yesterday. From this distance, he couldn't make out the station call letters. He'd have to check it out later, see if they'd broken onto the national stage.

"What happened to your face, Jason?"
"Did the police give you a black eye?"
"Have you been in a fight?"

He kept himself and Ree moving, slow and steady, across the yard, homing in on the Volvo. Then he had the keys out, the doors clicking open.

Police brutality, he thought idly, as more questions followed about his face and his ribs protested as he swung open the heavy car door.

Then Ree was inside, the back passenger door closed. And he was inside, the driver's door closed. He started the engine, and immediately the reporters' shrill questions disappeared.

"Good job," he told Ree.

"I don't like reporters," she informed him.

"I know. Next time, I'm getting my own pair of fairy wings."

He cracked at the grocery store. Couldn't seem to find the parental fortitude to deny his traumatized daughter Oreos, Pop-Tarts, bags of bakery-fresh chocolate chip cookies. Ree figured out his weakness early on, and by the end of the trip they had a grocery cart half-filled with junk food. He thought he'd managed milk, bread, pasta, and fruit, but to tell the truth, his heart wasn't in it.

He was killing time with his daughter, desperate to give them a slice of normalcy in a world that had tilted crazily. Sandy was gone. Max was back. The police would continue asking questions, he'd been an idiot to have ever used the family computer....

Jason didn't want this life. He wanted to turn the clock back sixty hours, maybe seventy hours, and say whatever it was he should've said, do whatever it was he should've done, so this never would have happened. Hell, he'd even take back the February vacation.

The woman manning the cash register smiled down at Ree's glamorous getup. Then her gaze went to him and she did a double-take. He shrugged self-consciously, following the cashier's line of sight to the newsstand, where he saw his own black-and-white picture staring out from the front page of the *Boston Daily*.

"Mild-mannered reporter may have hidden dark side," the banner headline declared.

They had used the photo from his official press pass, a closely cropped image that was barely one step above a mug shot. He looked flat, even vaguely menacing, staring out above the fold.

"Daddy, that's you!" Ree declared loudly. She pranced over to the newspaper, staring at it more closely. Other shoppers had noticed now, were watching this cute little girl gaze upon a disturbing photo of a grown man. "Why are you in the paper?"

"That's the paper I work for," he said lightly, wishing they didn't have so many groceries, wishing they could just bolt out of the store.

"What does it say?"

"It says I'm mild-mannered."

The cashier lady went bug-eyed. He shot her a look, no longer caring if he appeared menacing or not. For God's sake, this was his daughter.

"We should take it home," Ree declared. "Mommy will want to see it." She fished the newspaper out of the rack, tossed it onto the conveyor belt. He noted the byline read "Greg Barr," his boss and the head news editor. He had no doubt now which quotes had been included in the story, basically anything Jason had said by phone yesterday.

He reached into his back pocket, working on his wallet before he grew so angry he could no longer function. *Buy the food, get in the car. Buy the food, get in the car.*

Drive to your house, where you can be harassed all over again.

He got out his credit card, handed it to the cashier. Her fingers were trembling so hard it took her three tries to take the plastic. Was she that afraid of him? Certain she was completing a transaction with a psycho killer who'd most likely strangled his wife, then dismembered her body and tossed it into the harbor?

He wanted to laugh at the absurdity of it, but the sound would come out all wrong. Too chilling, too disaffected. His life had gone cockeyed, and he didn't know how to get it back.

"Can I have Pop-Tarts in the car?" Ree was saying. "Can I, can I, can I?"

The woman finally had the card back to him, as well as his receipt. "Yes, yes, yes," he murmured, signing the slip, pocketing his credit card, desperate to make his getaway.

"I love you, Daddy!" Ree sang out in triumph.

He hoped the whole damn store heard that.

| CHAPTER TWENTY-EIGHT |

By the time Jason and Ree made it home and he'd run the major news gauntlet half a dozen times to bring in the groceries, Jason was beat. He stuck in a movie for Ree, ignoring the guilty twinge that so much TV couldn't be good for her, that he should be making more of an effort to engage his daughter during this challenging time, yada, yada, yada.

They had food to eat. The cat was back. He hadn't been arrested yet.

It was the most he could manage at the moment.

Jason was unloading the eggs when the phone rang. He picked it up absently, without checking caller ID.

"What happened to your face, son?" Maxwell Black's Southern drawl stretched out the sentence and sent Jason back to a place he didn't want to go.

"Think you're the boss, boy? I own you, boy. Lock, stock, and barrel. You belong to me."

"I fell down the stairs," Jason replied lightly, forcing the images back into a small box in the corner of his mind. He pictured himself shutting the lid, inserting the key in the lock, turning it just so.

Max laughed. It was a low, warm chuckle, the kind he probably used when making jokes from the bench, or holding court at neighborhood cocktail parties. Maybe he'd even used it the first time a schoolteacher had hesitantly approached him about Sandy. *You know, sir, I've been worried about how... accident prone... your daughter Sandy seems to be.* And Max had laughed that charming little laugh. *Oh, no need to worry about my little girl. Don't even bother your pretty self. My girl is just fine.*

Jason disliked Sandra's father all over again.

"Well, son, we seem to have gotten off on the wrong foot yesterday afternoon," Max drawled.

Jason didn't answer. The silence dragged on. After another moment, Max moved to fill the gap, adding lightly, "So I called to make amends."

"No need," Jason assured him. "Returning to Georgia is good enough for me."

"Now, Jason, seems to me if anyone should be bearing a grudge, I would have the right. You swept my only daughter off her feet, spirited her away to the God-awful North, then didn't even invite me to the wedding, let alone the birth of my grandbaby. That's no way to treat family, son."

"You're right. If I were you, I'd never speak to us again."

That warm molasses chuckle again. "Fortunately for you, son," Max continued expansively, "I have determined to take the high ground. This is my only daughter and grandchild we're talking about here. It would be foolish to let the past stand in the way of our future."

"I'll tell you what: When Sandra returns, I'll give her the message."

"*When?*" Max's voice sharpened. "Don't you mean *if?*"

"I mean *when,*" Jason said firmly.

"Your wife run off with another man, son?"

"That seems to be a popular theory."

"You couldn't keep her happy? I'm not pointing fingers, mind you. I raised the girl, single-handedly, after her dear mama passed away. I know how demanding she can be."

"Sandra is a wonderful wife and devoted mother."

"I have to say, I was surprised to hear that my daughter had become a teacher. But I was talking to that nice principal just this morning. What is his name... Phil, Phil Stewart? He raved about how wonderful Sandy is with her pupils. When all is said and done, it sounds as if you've done right by my daughter. I appreciate that, son, I truly do."

"I am not your son."

"All right, Jason *Jones*."

Jason caught the edge again, the implied threat. He fisted his hand at his side, refusing to say another word.

"You don't like me much, do you, Jason?"

Again Jason didn't answer. The judge, however, seemed to be talking mostly to himself. "What I can't understand is, why? We've never really spoken. You wanted my daughter, you got her. You wanted to get out of Georgia, you took my daughter and left. Seems to me, I have plenty of reason to be sore with you. Why, a father's list of grievances against the boy who runs away with his only daughter... But what have I ever done to you, son? What have I ever done to you?"

"You failed your daughter," Jason heard himself say. "She needed you, and you failed her."

"*What* in heaven's name are you talking about?"

"I'm talking about your wife! I'm talking about your crazed, boozed-up wife who beat Sandy each and every day while you did nothing to stop it. What kind of father abandons his child like that? What kind of father lets her be tortured on a daily basis and does nothing to stop it?"

There was a pause. "My wife beat Sandy? *That's* what Sandy told you?"

Jason didn't answer right away. The silence stretched out. This time, he broke first: "Yes."

"Now, see here." The judge sounded offended. "Sandy's mom was hardly a perfect parent. It's true she probably drank more than she should. I worked so many hours back in those days, leaving Missy alone with Sandra much too often. I'm sure that tried Missy's nerves, made her maybe more short-tempered than a mother should be. But beating... tormenting... I think that's a trifle melodramatic. I do."

"Your wife never harmed Sandy?"

"Spare the rod, spoil the child. I saw her whack Sandy's behind a time or two, but no more than any exasperated parent."

"Missy never drank to excess?"

"Well, it's true she had a weakness for gin. Maybe a couple of nights a week...But Missy wasn't a violent drunk. If she had a few too many, then she carried herself off to bed. She wouldn't have hurt a fly, let alone our daughter."

"What about chasing you around the house with knives?"

"Excuse me?" The judge sounded shocked.

"She hurt Sandy. Slammed her fingers into doorframes, forced her to drink bleach, fed her household objects just so she could take Sandy to the hospital. Your wife was a very, very sick woman."

The silence lasted longer this time. When the judge finally spoke, he sounded genuinely flummoxed. "This is what Sandy told you? This is what Sandra said about her own mother? Well then, no wonder you have been so curt with me. I take it back, I do. I can see your position entirely. Of all the crazy...Well. Well." The judge didn't seem to know what else to say.

Jason found himself shifting from foot to foot, no longer feeling so certain about things. The first trickle of unease crept up his spine.

"Am I allowed to speak in my defense?" the judge asked.

"I suppose."

"One, I swear to you, son, this is the first I have heard of such dreadful acts. It is possible, I suppose, that things transpired between Sandy and my poor wife that I never knew of. To be truthful, however, I don't believe that to be the case. I love my daughter, Jason. I always have. But I'm also one of the few men out there that can say I truly, completely head-over-heels loved my wife. Saw Missy the first time when I was nineteen years old, and knew at that moment I'd marry her, make her my own. It wasn't just that she was beautiful—though she was. And not because she was kind and well mannered—though she was. But she was Missy, and I loved her for that alone.

"Maybe you think I'm going on. This has nothing to do with anything. But by the time Sandy was twelve, I fear it had everything to do with everything. See, Sandy grew jealous. Of my deference to

Missy, or maybe the flowers I brought home for no good reason, or the pretty baubles I liked to bestow on my lovely bride. Girls get to a certain age, and they start, consciously or unconsciously, competing with their mamas. I think Sandy thought she couldn't win. It started to make her angry, hostile to her own mother.

"Except then her mama died, before Sandy and her had a chance to work things out. Sandy took it hard. My sweet little girl...She changed overnight. Developed a wild streak, started to run around. She wanted to do what she wanted to do and wouldn't take no for an answer. She had an abortion, Jason. You know that? Ree wasn't her first pregnancy, maybe not even her second. Bet she never told you that, did she? I'm not even supposed to know, except the clinic recognized her name and called me. I gave my permission. What else could I do? She was still just a child herself—she was far too young and unstable to be a mother. I prayed, Jason, I prayed for my girl like you wouldn't believe, right up until the moment you took her out of my life."

The judge sighed. "I guess what I'm trying to say is that I had always hoped Sandy would grow out of her recklessness. And talking to that principal this morning, I thought maybe she'd finally grown up, shown some maturity. But now, to hear what you are saying...I think my daughter may have some serious issues, Jason. First she ran away from me. Now maybe it's time to recognize that she's run away from you, too."

Jason opened his mouth to object, but the words wouldn't come out. Uncertainty took root in his gut. What did he really know of Sandy or her family? He'd always accepted what she said at face value. What reason would she have to lie to him?

Then again, what reason did he have to lie to her? About four million and one.

"Perhaps it's time to meet," Maxwell was saying now. "We can sit down, man to man, sort this all out. I have no ill will toward you, son. I just want what's best for my daughter and grandbaby."

"How did Missy die?" Jason asked abruptly.

"Excuse me?"

"Your wife. How did she die?"

"Heart attack," the judge replied promptly. "Dropped dead. Terrible tragedy in a woman so young. We were shattered."

Jason held the phone tighter. "Where did she die?"

"Ummm, at home. Why do you ask?"

"Was it in the garage? Behind the wheel of her car?"

"Why yes, now that you mention it. I suppose Sandy told you that, too."

"But it was a heart attack? You're certain it was a heart attack?"

"Absolutely. Terrible, terrible time. I don't think my little Sandy ever quite got over it."

"I read the autopsy report," Jason persisted. "My memory is that Mrs. Black was found with a cherry red face. That's a clear indicator of carbon monoxide poisoning."

There was a long silence on the other end of the line; it went on for thirty seconds, perhaps even a minute. Jason felt his stomach settle, his shoulders square. Sandy had been right—her father was a very, very good liar.

"Don't know what you're talking about, Mr. *Jones*," Max said at last. He didn't sound so congenial anymore. More like pissed off. A wealthy, powerful man who wasn't getting his way.

"Really? Because I'd think in this day and age of computerized records, you'd understand that all information is eventually accessible, especially for a guy who knows where to look."

"Cuts both ways, Jason. You dig around looking at me, I dig around looking at you."

"Knock yourself out. When'd you arrive in town?"

"What day did you first meet my daughter?" Max countered evenly.

"Rent a car, or use a car service?"

"Gonna volunteer a DNA sample for the paternity test, or wait for family court to order it?"

"Doesn't matter. This is Massachusetts, where gay marriages are legal and *in loco parentis* matters more than biology for determining who should have custody of a child."

"You think just because you know a little Latin, you understand the law better than I do, boy?"

"I think I recently wrote an article about a grandfather who tried to gain custody of his grandson because he disapproved of the child's lesbian parents. The court ruled that the child should stay with the only parents he had ever known, even if they were not his biological mothers."

"Interesting. Well, here's another bit of Latin for you. Maybe you heard of this phrase, too, working on your little story and all: *ex parte.*"

Jason froze in the middle of the kitchen, his gaze going belatedly out the window. He saw the uniformed officer approaching his walkway, heading for his front door.

"Means 'in an emergency,' " Max continued smoothly, low chuckle back in his throat. "As in, a grandfather can seek an *ex parte motion* in front of family court, and the court could grant an *ex parte order* regarding visitation, without you even being aware that such a hearing is going on. After all, you are the prime suspect in a missing person investigation. Surely staying with the prime suspect in her mother's disappearance is *not* in the best interest of the child?"

"Son of a—" Jason hissed.

Front doorbell rang.

"Might as well answer it," Max said. "I can see you, son. So can most of the free world."

That's when Jason spotted Max, too, standing over by the cluster of white news vans, cell phone held to his ear. The older man waved his hand, looking chipper in a fresh blue suit that set off his shock of silver hair. The phone call, why Max had chatted away so readily, keeping Jason in one place, all under the guise of making amends...

Jason's doorbell rang again.

"Got it, Daddy," Ree sang out.

It didn't matter. None of it mattered. Jason had died once, nearly twenty-five years ago. This was worse than that. This was his entire world shattering. As Ree stood on tiptoe to undo the first lock, then the second.

As she pulled the door fully open to reveal the uniformed officer.

The man carried a folded piece of white paper. His gaze went over Ree's head and found Jason standing in the entryway of the kitchen, still clutching the phone to his ear.

"Jason F. Jones."

Jason finally set down the receiver. He moved on autopilot, stepping forward, holding out his hand.

"Consider yourself served," the county officer said. Then, his mission complete, he pivoted sharply and returned back down the front steps. While across the street, the photographers began to snap away.

Jason unfolded the piece of paper. He read the official court order demanding that he produce his child tomorrow morning at eleven A.M. at the local playground, where she would have a one-hour visitation with her grandfather, the honorable Maxwell M. Black. A full hearing on visitation rights would follow in four weeks. Until then, Maxwell Black was permitted one hour every day with his granddaughter, Clarissa Jane Jones. So ordered the court.

Each day. Every single day. Max and Ree together. Max seeing Ree, talking to Ree, touching Ree. Jason, not allowed to supervise. Jason, forced to leave his daughter all alone with a man who'd participated in the abuse of *his* only child.

"What is it, Daddy?" Ree asked him anxiously. "Did you win something? What did that man bring you?"

Jason pulled himself together, folding up the paper, tucking it into his back pocket.

"It's nothing," he assured his daughter. "Nothing at all. Hey, let's play some Candy Land."

Ree won three times in a row. She kept producing the Princess Frostine card in four turns or less, a sure sign she was cheating. Jason was too distracted to call her on it, and she became even more disgruntled. She was looking for boundaries. The world had rules, those rules kept it safe.

Jason gave up on board games, and made them grilled cheese and tomato soup for lunch. Ree sulked at the kitchen counter, dipping her sandwich into the soup. He mostly stirred his soup around and around, watched the croutons turn bloodred.

Court order was still folded up, tucked in his back pocket. As if reducing it down to a small scrap of paper could reduce the power it held over his and his daughter's lives. He finally understood why

Sandra had walked away so easily from her home and her father, and why she'd never been tempted to call, not even once, for the past five years.

Maxwell Black played for keeps. And the judge knew how to twist the law to get exactly what he wanted. Son of a bitch.

"I want to look for Mommy," Ree announced.

"What?"

She stopped dipping her grilled cheese long enough to glare at him stubbornly. "You said police officers and friends were gonna meet at the school to help find Mommy. Well, I want to go to the school. I want to find Mommy."

Jason stared at his daughter. He wondered what parenting book might have a chapter on this.

The doorbell rang. Jason got up immediately to answer it.

Sergeant D.D. Warren and Detective Miller stood on his front porch. Instinctively Jason looked behind them for more officers. Seeing only the two investigators, he guessed he wasn't being arrested. He opened the door a little wider.

"Have you found my wife yet?" he inquired.

"Have you started looking for her yet?" D.D. replied evenly.

He still liked her better than Max.

He let the two detectives in, telling Ree that she could choose a second movie, as Daddy needed a moment to talk to the nice police officers. In response, she scowled at him, then bawled, "I'm gonna find Mommy and *you can't stop me!*"

She stormed into the front room, clicking on the TV and powering up a DVD now that she'd had the last word.

"It's been a long day," Jason informed D.D. and Miller.

"It's only eleven-thirty," D.D. pointed out.

"Oh goody, I have ten more hours to look forward to."

He moved BPD's finest into the kitchen, as his child finally settled down to watch her favorite dinosaurs in *The Land Before Time.*

"Water? Coffee? Cold tomato soup?" he offered halfheartedly.

D.D. and Miller shook their heads. They each took a seat at the kitchen counter. He leaned against the refrigerator, arms folded over his chest. *Grieving husband. Homicidal father. Grieving fucking husband.*

"What happened to you?" D.D. asked.

"Walked into a wall."

"With both sides of your face?"

"I hit it twice."

She arched a brow at him. He remained steadfast. What were they gonna do, throw him in jail for being bruised and battered?

"I want it on the record we didn't do that," Miller said.

"Define *we*."

"Boston PD. We haven't even called your sorry ass down to the station yet, so definitely, whatever wall smacked your face, it wasn't us."

"I believe your wall prefers Tasers, so no, it wasn't you."

That retort didn't win him any friendship with Miller, but then again, Jason was pretty sure Miller already thought he was the guilty party.

"*When* did it happen?" D.D. pressed, obviously the smarter of the two. "We saw you after Hastings's attack. No way Ethan did that kind of damage."

"Maybe I just take a while to bruise."

She arched a brow again. He remained steadfast. He could do this dance all day long. Come to think of it, she probably could, too. They were soul mates that way. Destined to piss each other off.

He missed Sandy. He wanted to ask his wife if she was really pregnant with his child. He wanted to tell her he'd do whatever she asked, if only she'd give him a second chance to make her happy. He wanted to tell her he was sorry, especially for February. He had a lot to be sorry about in February.

"Sandra knew what you were doing," D.D. stated.

He sighed, took the bait. "What was I doing?"

"You know, on the computer."

Jason wasn't impressed. He'd already guessed that much from Ethan Hastings. They were gonna have to hit him with something bigger to get his attention.

"I'm a reporter. Of course I work on the computer."

"Okay, let me rephrase that: Sandy found out what you were doing on the Internet."

Slightly more interesting. "And what exactly did Ethan tell you I was doing on the Internet?"

"Oh, it wasn't Ethan."

"Excuse me?"

"No, we haven't spent the morning with Ethan. We talked to him last night, and the boy told us a couple of interesting things, including that he introduced Sandra to his uncle, who is a certified forensic computer examiner with the Massachusetts State Police."

"We've been analyzing your bank records," Miller volunteered now, "so we know it wasn't gambling. That leaves kiddie porn and/or adult cybersex. Why don't you just do yourself a big favor and set the record straight? Maybe, if you cooperate with us, we can help you."

"I didn't do anything wrong." Jason said it automatically, his mind racing ahead, trying to see the angles. Sandra had somehow zeroed in on his middle-of-the-night activities. When? How much had she figured out? Not everything, or she wouldn't have needed Ethan Hastings. But a trained forensic computer examiner. Shit. A state police expert with access to a genuine computer crime lab…

"We have your computer," D.D. spoke up, continuing the full court press. "Being computer savvy yourself, you know we can find everything. And I mean everything."

He nodded vaguely, because she was right. With the forensic tools that existed these days, he should've run over the family hard drive with his truck, ground the components into smithereens, then tossed the plastic bits into a commercial-grade furnace, then blown up the entire furnace room. Only way to be safe.

He wanted to bolt to the *Boston Daily* offices. Grab his old computer and desperately run his own forensic diagnostics. How much had Sandra discovered? How many layers of his safeguards had she managed to unpeel? The chat room blogs? Financial transcripts? The MySpace page? Or maybe the photos? God, the photos.

He couldn't go back to the *Boston Daily* offices. He couldn't risk touching that computer ever again. It was over, done. Best bet, grab the lockbox from the attic and get himself and Ree over the border into Canada.

D.D. and Miller were staring at him. He forced himself to exhale loudly, to appear deeply disappointed.

"I wish my wife had mentioned this to me," he told them.

D.D. gave him a look, clearly skeptical.

"I mean it," he insisted, going with the role of injured party. "If she'd only mentioned her fears, her concerns, I would've been happy to explain everything to her."

"Define 'everything,' " Miller stated.

Jason went with another sigh. "All right. All right. I have an avatar."

"Say what?" Miller asked, glancing at his partner, stroking his mustache.

"An avatar. A computer-generated identity on a website called Second Life."

"Oh, give me a fucking break," D.D. muttered.

"Hey, four-year-olds have ears," Jason admonished, pointing toward the front room, where no doubt Ree remained in full TV coma.

"You don't have an avatar," D.D. said darkly.

"Sure I do. I, uh, logged on to the website as part of a story I was working on. Just wanted to check things out. But... I don't know. It's a cool place. Much more intricate than I ever imagined. Social. Has its own rules, customs, everything. For example, when you first log on, you begin with a basic body, basic wardrobe. Well, hell, I didn't know anything so I just started going into various bars and stores, checking things out. I noticed right away that none of the women would talk to me. Because I was still in the basic wardrobe. I had 'newbie' written all over me, like the transfer student in high school. Nobody likes the new kid, you know. You gotta earn your stripes."

D.D. gave him that skeptical look again. Miller, on the other hand, appeared interested. "You stay up all night pretending to be some other person on a computer-generated social site?"

Jason shrugged, stuck his hands in his pockets. "Well, it's not the kind of thing a grown man wants to admit, especially to his wife."

"What are you in this Second Life place?" Miller asked. "Rich, handsome, successful? Or maybe you're a busty blonde with a thing for bikers?"

"Actually, I'm a writer. Working on an adventure novel that may or may not be autobiographical. You know, a man of mystery. Women like that."

"Sounds like who you are here," D.D. said dryly. "Don't need to log on to the web for that."

"Which would be exactly why I didn't tell Sandra. Are you kidding? She works all day, then watches Ree every evening while I cover local events for *Boston Daily*. Last thing she wants to hear is that her husband returns home at night to mess around with a computer game. Trust me, not the kind of spousal conversation that's gonna go over well."

"So, you felt a need to keep it secret," D.D. stated.

"I didn't mention it," Jason hedged.

"Oh yeah? So secret you purged the browser history every time you went online?"

Damn, Ethan and the computer guy had taught Sandra well. "I do that as a reporter," Jason answered smoothly. It occurred to him that he lied just as easily as Maxwell Black. Is that why Sandra had married him? Because he reminded her of her father?

"Excuse me?"

"I purge the browser history to protect my sources," Jason said again. "It's something I learned in journalism school, class on ethics in the computer age. In theory, I'm supposed to work only on my laptop, but the family desktop is more comfortable. So I have a tendency to do my online research there, then transfer over the information. 'Course, my family computer isn't protected from search and seizure"—he gave them a look—"so I purge the history files as standard operating protocol."

"You're lying." D.D. was scowling, looking deeply frustrated and about five seconds away from hitting something. Probably him.

He shrugged, as if to say there was nothing else he could do for her.

"What journalism school?" she asked abruptly.

"What school?"

"Where'd you take this ethics class?" She made "ethics" sound like a dirty word.

"Oh, that was years ago. Online course."

"Give me the name," she pressed. "Even online colleges keep records."

"I'll look it up for you."

She was already shaking her head. "There was no course. Or maybe there was once, but you weren't Jason Jones back then, were you? From what we can tell, the Jones name only reaches back about five years. Who were you before then? Smith? Brown? And tell me, when you get a new name, does the cat get one, too?"

"Don't know," Jason said. "Cat's only three years old."

"You're lying to us, Jason." D.D. was out of the chair, walking closer, as if proximity would rattle him, make him blurt out answers he didn't have. "Avatar, my ass. Only second life you have is right here and now. You're running away from something. Someone. And you've gone to a lot of trouble to cover your tracks, haven't you? But Sandra started to figure it out. Something tipped her off. So she brought in Ethan, and Ethan brought in the big guns. Suddenly, you have the state police very interested in your online activities. How badly did that frighten you, Jason? What the hell is so terrible, it's worth killing your wife and unborn child?"

"Is she really pregnant?" Jason whispered. He didn't mean to ask that. But he waited for the answer anyway, because he wanted to hear it again. Wanted to feel it again. It was an exquisite pain, like someone filleting his skin with a boning knife.

"You really didn't know?"

"How long? I mean, she seemed a little under the weather. I thought she had the flu. . . . She never said anything."

D.D. seemed to be contemplating him. "Can't tell how long from a pregnancy test, Jason. Though you can be sure we'll be DNA testing it. I'm curious if you're the actual father."

He didn't answer. He couldn't. Because for the first time, he was connecting another dot. "The computer expert—" he began.

D.D. looked at him.

"—did he come to the school?"

"That's what he says."

"During school hours?"

"Nah, Thursday night basketball games."

And he could tell from the look in D.D.'s eye, she was thinking the very same thing—all along, he'd argued Sandra was too busy with Ree to have a lover. But Sandra had found a way to have a rendezvous after all. Thursday nights. Every Thursday night. His wife had gone to the school and met with another man.

"What's his name?" Jason's voice ticked up a notch. Another weakness he was helpless to call back.

D.D. shook her head.

Then, out of nowhere, his next random thought for the day: "What kind of car does the computer expert drive? Is it state-issued?"

"Tell me your name, Jason Jones. Your *real* name."

"Have you spoken with Aidan Brewster? Asked him what he saw Wednesday night? You need to talk to him about the car. Ask him for more details about the car."

"Tell us what you were doing on the computer, Jason. Tell us what you're so desperate to hide."

"I'm not!" he insisted, feeling anxious now, feeling trapped and frantic. He was down to a matter of days, maybe even hours. They needed to listen, they needed to consider. His daughter was at stake. "Look, according to you, a state computer expert has been working with Sandra to examine the family hard drive. Obviously, he didn't find anything, or you wouldn't be here pestering me. Ergo, I don't have anything to hide."

"What happened to your secret life as an avatar?"

"It's the state computer guy," he tried again. "You need to look at the state computer guy. Maybe his relationship with Sandra was more than professional. Maybe he wanted her, and he's the one who grew jealous when she wouldn't leave Ree."

"Don't you mean when she wouldn't leave you?"

"I didn't harm my wife! I wouldn't take Ree's mother from her. But this state guy, what would he care? Or Sandra's father, Maxwell Black. Did you know he just won an *ex parte motion* to have visitation with Ree? Basically, Max has come all the way up here *not* to assist with the search efforts for his own daughter, but to begin a custody battle for his granddaughter. He couldn't do that if Sandra was around. He wouldn't have grounds. But with Sandy missing, with me as the primary suspect... Don't you think that's pretty damn convenient for him? As in maybe too convenient to be purely coincidence?"

D.D. just stared at him. "This is your defense? The one-armed man did it? I thought you had your sights on the local pervert."

"I'm not sure Sandra knew him."

"I see. So her own father and the computer expert she enlisted to investigate your online activities make much more sense."

"And don't forget Ethan Hastings." He knew he was digging a hole, but couldn't seem to help himself. "Thirteen-year-old boys have done worse."

"Oh really? So which is it, Jason? Aidan Brewster, Ethan Hastings, Wayne Reynolds, Maxwell Black? Or maybe the Tooth Fairy's guilty."

"Wayne Reynolds?" he repeated.

D.D. flushed, realizing too late that she'd given away the state computer technician. She clipped out, "You're lying to us, Jason. You're lying about your identity, you're lying about your computer activities, you're lying about your whole damn life. Then you turn around and claim to love your wife and only want her back. Well, if you really love the woman so badly, start leveling with us. Tell us what's going on here, Jason. Tell us what the hell happened with your wife."

Jason gave the only answer he could. "Honestly, Sergeant, I have no idea."

| CHAPTER TWENTY-NINE |

It began with a single meeting at the basketball game. Ethan had an uncle who was a certified forensic computer examiner; Ethan brought him to the game to meet with me.

Wayne Reynolds was not what I expected. In my head, computer technicians looked more like Revenge of the Nerds and less like crime show TV stars. Wayne's burnished red hair was slightly untidy, his tie askew. The rumpledness only added to his appeal, gave him a disheveled charm that made you want to smooth his collar, brush away the loose strands of hair from his forehead. He was tall and athletic while at the same time touchable. Highly touchable.

I spent the entire forty-five minutes of our first conversation with my hands fisted by my sides so I didn't do anything that would embarrass me.

He talked about computers. How to copy hard drives. How to analyze unused data chunks for hidden content. The importance of using the proper forensic tool.

I watched his long legs eat up the school corridor. I wondered if beneath his tan slacks, his thighs and calves were as elegantly muscled as they appeared. Did he have light reddish hair all over his body, or only on the top of his head? Would it feel as silky as it looked?

By the time we returned to the gym for the end of the basketball game, I was slightly out of breath and Ethan regarded me suspiciously. I kept my gaze away from his uncle. Ethan was a frighteningly perceptive boy, as I'd already learned the hard way.

Wayne left me with the name of a hard drive to purchase. I tucked it, along with his business card, in my purse, then took Ree home.

Later that night, after putting Ree to bed, I memorized Wayne's e-mail address and phone number. Then I ripped his business card into tiny little pieces and flushed them down the toilet. I did the same with the hard-drive information. At this stage, I couldn't afford to be careless.

Jason came home after two A.M. I heard his footsteps in the family room, the creak of the old wooden chair as he pulled it out from the kitchen table and took his customary seat at the family desktop.

I woke again at four A.M., just as he was coming into the bedroom. He didn't turn on any lights, but undressed in a corner of darkness. I wondered about my own husband this time. What ripples of lean muscle might lurk beneath the long pants and plain, button-down shirts he always wore? Did he have waves of thick black hair on his chest? Did it form a silky line down to his groin?

After Brokeback Mountain, I used to pretend that Jason was gay, that's why he wouldn't touch me. It wasn't me, I told myself. He simply preferred men. But from time to time, I'd catch him watching me with a dark, hooded gleam in his eyes. Some part of him responded to me, I was certain of it. Unfortunately, it was only enough to keep me, not enough to love me.

I closed my eyes as my husband crawled into bed. I feigned sleep.

Later, four-thirty, five A.M., I rolled over and touched my husband's shoulder. I spread my fingers upon the warm T-shirt covering his back. I felt the muscles ripple at contact, and I thought he owed me at least that much.

Then his fingers closed around my wrist. He removed my hand from his shoulder.

"Don't," he said.

"Why not?"

"Go to sleep, Sandy."

"I want a second baby," I said. Which was partly true. I did yearn for another child, or at least someone else who would love me.

"We could adopt," he said.

"God, Jason. Do you hate me that much?"

He didn't answer. I stormed out of bed, stomped downstairs, sat at the computer. Then, just to be childish about things, I checked the empty recycle bin, and the three URLs left in the computer's web history: New York Times, USA Today, and the Drudge Report.

At that moment, I despised my husband. I hated him for taking me away, but for never really saving me. I hated him for showing me respect, but for never letting me feel wanted. I hated him for his silences and for his secrets and for a lone black-and-white image of a terrified little boy who still haunted me.

"Just what kind of monster are you?" I demanded out loud. But the computer had no answers for me.

So I logged on to my AOL account. Then, working from memory, I wrote: Dear Wayne, thanks for meeting with me. I am working on our project now. I hope to see you again, at the next Thursday basketball game....

| CHAPTER THIRTY |

"What do you mean you can't find the money? It's four million dollars, for God's sake. It takes a little more than a piggy bank to cart that much around." D.D. was ranting into her cell phone, held tight against her ear. They were exiting the Jones residence and half a dozen photographers were snapping away at them. The class they should have at detective school and don't: How to Always Have Photo-Ready Hair.

"No, I don't want the Feds involved. We've traced money before; we can do it again. . . . Okay, okay, so it's not a one-day project. I'll give you two more hours. . . .I know, so get cracking."

D.D. flipped the phone shut, scowling.

"Bad news?" Miller asked. He was stroking his mustache self-consciously, obviously not liking the glare of the media spotlight any more than she did. They paused at the base of the porch stairs, not wanting to have this conversation in earshot of the press, who were already banging out questions.

"Cooper hit a wall chasing Jones's assets," D.D. reported. "Something about the money was wired into Jones's current bank from an offshore account, and offshore banks are a little uptight about disclosing information. According to Cooper, we need to charge Jones with a crime first, then they might see things our way. Of course, we need to trace the money in order to expose Jones's real identity, so we can charge him with a crime. At this point, it's heads he wins, tails we lose."

"Bummer, dude," Miller said.

She rolled her eyes at him, chewed her lower lip. "I feel like we're stuck in a bad episode of *Law & Order*."

"How so?"

"Look at our pool of suspects: We have the mysterious husband who's probably engaged in online porn, the down-the-street neighbor who's a registered sex offender, a thirteen-year-old student who's in love with his missing teacher, a state computer technician who seems to have a very personal stake in the investigation, and, last but not least, the victim's estranged father who may or may not have known she was abused as a child and has lots of incentive to keep that quiet. It's all *'In a case that's been ripped from the headlines...'* Except I have no idea which fucking headline we ripped off."

"Maybe it's like that old movie. *Murder on the Orient Express.* They all did it. That would be cool."

She gave him a look. "You have a strange sense of humor, Miller."

"Hey, this job will do that to you."

When in doubt, keep everyone talking. D.D. wanted to question Ree again, but the expert, Marianne Jackson, waved her off. Three interviews in three consecutive days would not only be too much for the child, but would appear like badgering. Even if Ree did tell them something useful, a good defense attorney would argue they'd harassed her into disclosing. They needed to give the girl one more day; better yet, turn over some new piece of evidence that warranted a third interview. Then they'd be on safer ground.

So D.D. and Miller turned to their cast of suspects. In the past forty-eight hours, they'd hit Jason Jones, Ethan Hastings, Aidan Brewster, and Wayne Reynolds, which left the honorable Maxwell Black. Currently, the judge stood right across the street, working the crowd of reporters much the way a politician might work a room of high-net-worth donors.

Already, D.D. felt uneasy. Guy hasn't seen his daughter in five years, learns she's gone missing, so he catches a flight to Boston to smile for the cameras and press flesh with the local news personalities?

Judge seemed pretty relaxed about it, too. Wearing a dapper light blue suit with a pastel pink tie and coordinating pink silk kerchief, very Southern gentleman. Then, of course, there was that drawl that sounded so honey smooth in the land of dropped R's and guttural A's.

As they neared the news vans, Miller hung back, giving her the lead. D.D. waded into the fray.

"Detective, detective," the hordes began.

"Sergeant," D.D. snapped back, because they could at least grant her that much.

"Any news on Sandy's whereabouts?"

"Are you going to arrest Jason?"

"How is little Ree holding up? Her preschool teacher says she hasn't been to school since Wednesday."

"Is it true Jason wouldn't let Sandy talk to her own father?"

D.D. shot Maxwell Black a look. Clearly, they had the good judge to thank for that tidbit. She ignored the reporters, placing her hand firmly on Maxwell's shoulder and leading him away from the sudden forest of microphones and camera lenses.

"Sergeant D.D. Warren, with Detective Brian Miller. If you don't mind, sir, we'd like a word."

The judge didn't protest. Merely nodded his head elegantly while waving goodbye to his newfound media playmates. Man must be a lot of fun in his own courtroom, D.D. thought with irritation. Like the grand master of a three-ring circus.

She got him over to Miller and they walked him to their car, the reporters trailing behind greedily in a last-ditch attempt to catch a snippet of conversation, a juicy revelation. That Sandra was dead. That they were arresting the husband. Or perhaps the police wanted to question Sandy's father as a fresh person of interest. Either way, the reporters' wheels would be spinning for a bit, the attention ramping up exponentially.

Maxwell ducked into the back seat of D.D.'s car and they pulled away, D.D. laying on the horn and doing her best Britney Spears imitation as she aimed for the nearest photographer's foot. The cameramen immediately cleared, and she managed to drive down the street without incident. She felt vaguely disappointed.

"You're the detectives in charge of my daughter's case," Maxwell drawled from the back seat.

"Yes sir."

"Excellent. I've been looking forward to speaking with you. I have some information on my son-in-law. Starting with the fact that his name is *not* Jason Jones."

They took the judge down to the station. It was the kosher way of questioning someone, and Jason Jones had been giving them such a runaround on the matter, D.D. was pleased to get protocol right for at least one person. The detectives' interrogation room was small, and the coffee terrible, but Maxwell Black maintained his charming smile even as he sat down in the hard metal folding chair wedged between the table and bone white wall. They might as well have invited him back to their country estate.

The judge bothered D.D. He was too sure of himself, too easygoing. His daughter was missing. He was at a major police station in an airless room. He should sweat a little. That's what normal people did, even the innocent ones.

D.D. took her time sitting down, getting out a yellow legal pad, then setting up the mini-recorder in the middle of the table. Miller leaned back in his metal chair, arms folded over his chest. He looked bored. Always a nice strategy when dealing with a man who obviously liked attention as much as Judge Black did.

"So when did you get into town?" D.D. kept her voice neutral. Just making polite chitchat.

"Early yesterday afternoon. I always watch the news while taking my morning coffee. Imagine my surprise when I saw Sandy's picture flash across the screen. I knew right then her husband had gone and done something horrible. I bolted out of my office and headed straight for the airport. Left my coffee sitting on my desk and everything."

D.D. made a show of setting out her pens. "You mean that's the same suit you were in yesterday?" she asked, because that didn't jibe with what she remembered from the news clips.

"I grabbed a few items from my home," the judge amended. "I already anticipated this would not be a short trip."

"I see. So you saw your daughter's image on the screen, then returned home to pack, maybe tidy up a few things—"

"I have a housekeeper who tends to all that, ma'am. I called her from the road, she put everything together for me, and here I am."

"Where are you staying?"

"Ritz-Carlton, of course. I do so love their tea."

D.D. blinked. Maybe she wasn't Southern enough, because as criteria for picking a hotel, she'd never considered tea before. "What airline did you fly?"

"Delta."

"Flight number? When did it land?"

Maxwell gave her a look, but provided the specifics. "Why do you ask?"

"Basic protocol," she assured him. "Remember from that old TV show *Dragnet:* 'Just the facts, ma'am'?"

He beamed at her. "I loved that show."

"Well, there you go. Boston PD aims to please."

"Are we gonna talk about my son-in-law now? Because I'm telling you, there are some things you ought to know—"

"All in good time," D.D. assured him, polite, but remaining in control. Down the table from her, Miller started twirling his pen around his finger, drawing Maxwell's attention.

"When was the last time you spoke with your daughter, Sandra Jones?" D.D. asked.

Maxwell blinked at her, looking momentarily distracted. "Um, oh, years. Sandra wasn't the kind to pick up the phone."

"You didn't call her in all that time?"

"Well, if you must know, we had a falling-out right before she left town. My daughter was only eighteen years old, much too young for hanging out with the likes of Jason, and I told her so." Black sighed heavily. "Unfortunately, Sandy always was a headstrong girl. She ran out in the middle of the night. Eloped, I imagined. I've been waiting for a phone call or at least a postcard ever since."

"You file a missing persons report after your daughter left?"

"No ma'am. I didn't consider her missing. I knew she'd run off with that boy. That's the kind of thing Sandy would do."

"Really? She ran off before?"

Black flushed. "It is a parent's job to know his child's weaknesses," he stated primly. "My daughter—well, Sandy took the death of her mother hard. Went through a rebellious spell, and all that. Drinking, staying out all night. Being... well, an *active* teenage girl."

"You mean sexually active," D.D. clarified.

"Yes, ma'am."

"How'd you know?"

"Child made no bones about it. Would come in at the crack of dawn reeking of cigarettes and booze and sex. I was a teenager once myself, Sergeant. I know what kids do."

"How long did this go on?"

"Her mother died when she was fifteen."

"How'd she die?"

"Heart attack," Black said, then seemed to catch himself. He looked at her, then at Miller, who was still twirling his pen, then switched his attention back to D.D. again. "Actually, it was not a heart attack. That's a story we've been telling for so long it seems to have become the truth in the way lies sometimes do. But you might as well know: My wife, Sandra's mom, she committed suicide. Carbon monoxide poisoning. Sandra was the one who found the body in our garage."

"Your wife killed herself at home?"

"In her own Cadillac."

"Did your wife have a history of depression?"

That almost imperceptible hesitation again. "My wife probably drank more than what would be considered medicinal, Sergeant. I have a very demanding job, you understand. I guess the loneliness took its toll on her."

"Your wife have a good relationship with Sandra?"

"My wife may not have been a perfect mother, but she tried hard."

"And you?"

"As I said, I was probably gone more than I should have been, but I love my daughter, too."

"So much so that you never once tried to find her in the past five years?"

"Oh, I tried. I definitely tried."

"How so?"

"I hired a private investigator. One of the best in the county. Here's the kicker, though. The man Sandra introduced to me as her future husband was Jason Johnson, not Jason *Jones*."

D.D. excused herself to get a glass of water. While she was out, she swung by Detective Cooper's desk and gave him the heads-up—start running background checks on Jason Johnson as well as Jason Jones.

Cooper just gave her a look. He was the best in the unit at this kind of stuff, and without at least a middle initial or any other additional detail, sorting through the reams of Jason Johnsons in the world wasn't going to be any easier than sorting through the lists of Jason Jones.

"I know," she assured him. "You love your job and each day is more satisfying than the last. Have fun."

D.D. returned to the interrogation room, but rather than go inside, she opted to watch the show from the other side of the observation glass. Judge Black was entirely too comfortable with women. He would ooze Southern charm and spin easy tales until the cows came home. Given that, she thought it might be more productive to let Miller take a run at him.

So far, Miller had made no attempt to rouse himself from his slouch, and the detective's continued disinterest was already starting to make Maxwell fidget. The judge played with his tie, smoothed his pocket kerchief, then took several sips of coffee. His hand shook lightly when he raised his cup. From this angle, D.D. could see the dark age spots on the back of his hand. But his face was relatively unlined and attractive.

He was a nice-looking man. Wealthy, charming, powerful. It made her wonder why there wasn't a second Mrs. Black yet.

"Did you know Sandra had gotten knocked up?" Miller asked suddenly. "Before she eloped?"

The judge blinked several times, seemed to belatedly fix his attention on the detective. "Excuse me?"

"Did Sandy tell you that this Jason Johnson or Jones or whomever had gotten her pregnant?"

"I...I knew she was pregnant."

"That'd piss me off," Miller said conversationally. "Some thirty-year-old guy impregnating my eighteen-year-old daughter. I'd be rip-shit if that were me."

"I, um...well, as I said, you have to know your child. Sandra was on a reckless path. It was only a matter of time before she got pregnant—or worse. Besides, I don't believe Jason is the one who got her pregnant."

Miller stopped twirling his pen. "You don't?"

"No, sir. I remember how Sandy's mom was when she was expecting. First three months, Missy could barely crawl out of bed, she was so tired and nauseous. Same thing happened to Sandra. Suddenly, she was ill, sick enough to stay home and sleep all the time. I thought she'd come down with some bug, but then it went on long enough I began to suspect the truth. Shortly thereafter, she seemed to recover. She even started going out again. It was after that period that she first mentioned this new man she'd met, Jason Johnson."

"Wait a minute. You're saying Sandy got knocked up, then latched onto some wealthy older guy and got him to marry her?"

"I suppose that's one way of looking at it."

"Hey, pardon me, but wouldn't that be cause for celebration? Your daughter goes from unwed teen mom to wealthy trophy bride in six months or less. Can't hate Jason for that."

"Jason Johnson took my daughter from me."

"You told her she couldn't get married. Come on, know your child, right? Minute you told her no, 'course she was gonna run off."

"She was too young to be married!"

"Tell that to the guy who knocked her up. Seems to me she's lucky she got Jason to clean up some other guy's mess."

"Johnson took advantage of her vulnerable state. If she hadn't been so scared, she never would've left me for a stranger."

"Left you?"

"Left the security of her home," Maxwell amended. "Think about it, Detective. This thirty-year-old man appears out of nowhere, sweeps my vulnerable young daughter off her feet, and carries her away without so much as asking my permission."

"You're mad he didn't ask you for your daughter's hand in marriage?"

"Where we live, these things matter, Detective. It's protocol. More than that... it's good manners."

"You ever meet Jason?"

"Once. I was still awake when my daughter came home one night. I came out when I heard the vehicle in the drive. Jason got out of the car and walked her up the steps."

"Doesn't sound like such bad manners to me."

"He was gripping her arm, Detective, tightly, right above the elbow. It struck me at the time, the way he was touching her. Possessive. Like she belonged to him."

"What did you say?"

"I asked him if he was aware of the fact that my daughter was only eighteen."

"Was he?"

"He said, and I quote, 'Good evening, sir.' Never answered my question. Never even acknowledged it. He walked right past me, escorted my daughter to the front door, then walked calmly back down the steps and got in his car. Last moment, he nodded once, said, 'Night, sir,' and that was that. Arrogant son of a bitch drove off like he had every right to be parading around town with a high school girl." Maxwell shifted in his seat. "And I'll tell you something else, Detective. Back then, when Jason spoke, he sounded just as much like a good old boy as I do. Maybe he's gone Yankee now, but he used to be Southern, no doubt in my mind. You want to have some fun with him, take him out for some grits. Bet you he butters 'em up with the best of them."

On the other side of the glass, D.D. made a mental note. *Jason Johnson, perhaps born in Georgia or a neighboring state.* Interesting. Because now that the good judge mentioned it, she'd caught an inflection in Jason's voice from time to time. He always checked it, flattening his tone. But something lingered in the background. Apparently, their prime suspect could drawl.

"Wasn't but two weeks later Sandy disappeared," the judge was saying now. "Found her bed neatly made and half of her closet cleaned out. That was it, she was gone."

"She leave you a note?"

"Nothing," the judge stated emphatically, but he didn't look at Miller when he said this. Maxwell's first obvious lie.

"Now, you tell me, sir," the judge moved on quickly, "what kind of man spirits a young girl away to a completely new life under a completely new name? Who'd do such a thing? Why would he do that kind of thing?"

Miller shrugged. "You tell me. Why do you think Jason Johnson became Jason Jones?"

"To isolate my daughter!" Maxwell said immediately. "To cut her off from her home, her town, her family. To make sure there'd be no one Sandy could call for help, once he started doing what he really wanted to do."

"And what did Jason really want to do?"

"As you so eloquently put it, Detective, what possible reason would one man have to 'clean up' another man's mess? Unless he wanted the baby. Or rather, access to a child whose mother was too young, too overwhelmed, too troubled to attempt to protect it. I've served on the bench over twenty years, long enough to have seen this sorry story more times than I can count. Jason Johnson is nothing but a pervert. He targeted my daughter. No doubt, he's already grooming little Clarissa for what's gonna happen next. He just needed to get Sandy out of the way once and for all."

Holy crap, D.D. thought. She leaned closer to the glass. Was the good judge saying what she thought he was saying?

"Jason Jones is a pedophile?" Miller asked for the record.

"Absolutely. You know the profile as well as I do, Detective. The exhausted young wife, with a history of depression, sexual activity, drinking, drug abuse. Isolated by the older, dominant male, who slowly but surely makes her more and more dependent upon him. Jason and little Clarissa are alone together every single afternoon. That doesn't raise any hairs on the back of your neck?"

Miller appeared to be considering the matter, without commenting. D.D., in the meantime, felt like half a dozen lightbulbs were exploding inside her head. The profile the judge gave was dead-on. And it would fill in a lot of pieces of the puzzle—Jason's affinity for aliases, the tight rein on his daughter and wife's social circle, his clear panic that Sandy had started digging into the family computer.

D.D. needed to get Jason's picture faxed over to the National Center for Missing & Exploited Children immediately. They would run it through their database of images culled from various exploitive images recovered from the Internet and other sex abuse cases. If they found a match, she'd have her grounds for an arrest, let alone for a fresh interview of Clarissa Jones. Suddenly, they were getting somewhere.

Except then she felt uneasy again. She remembered the way Ree had flung herself into her father's arms following her interview, the naked tenderness on his face. At that moment, D.D. had believed their love was genuine, but maybe it was only because Ree hadn't given their secret away?

Sometimes, this job sucked a little, and sometimes, this job sucked a lot.

Miller was still grilling the honorable Maxwell Black. "You think your daughter is dead?"

Maxwell gave the detective a pitying glance. "Have they ever found one of these women alive? Please, Jason Jones murdered my daughter; there is no doubt in my mind. Now I want justice."

"That why you're moving for visitation rights with your granddaughter?"

"Absolutely! I've been doing the same asking around you've been doing, Detective, and the picture I get is not pretty. My granddaughter has no close friends, no extended family, no other primary caregiver. Chances are, her father has murdered her mother. If there was ever a time when a little girl needs her grandfather, this is it."

"You gonna push for custody?"

"I'm willing to fight."

"Jason Jones tells us Sandy wouldn't approve."

"Please, Detective... Jason Jones is a liar. Look up Jason Johnson. At least know who you are dealing with."

304

"You rent a car, Judge Black?"

"Excuse me?"

"From the airport. Did you rent a car, or maybe use a car service?"

"I, uh, rented a car, of course. I figured I'd need to move about the city."

"I'm gonna need the name of the rental agency. What time you picked the car up, when it's due to be returned."

"Fine, fine, fine. Why are you pestering me so? I'm not the suspect here. Jason Johnson is."

"Jason Jones, aka Jason Johnson. Got it. So why haven't you been out looking for your daughter?"

"I already told you: The only way we'll ever find Sandy is to expose her husband."

"Sad to lose your daughter and your wife, both so young."

"I'm focusing on my granddaughter. I can't pity myself for my own tragedies. My grandbaby's all who matters now."

"And obliterating Jason Jones."

"He took my daughter from me."

"Did it surprise you to find out that your daughter was doing well up here? Devoted mom, respected teacher, good neighbor. We certainly haven't found any stories involving depression, alcohol abuse, or general self-destructiveness. Maybe, since the birth of her daughter, Sandra finally pulled it all together."

Maxwell merely smiled. "Obviously, Detective, you don't know my Sandy at all."

| CHAPTER THIRTY-ONE |

Do you remember the moment you first fell in love? The way your body would tremble if you stood too close? Or how you would have to stare at a spot just beyond his shoulder, because if you actually looked him in the eyes, his beautiful, green-flecked hazel eyes, you would blush foolishly?

Thursday became my favorite night of the week. The culmination of a slow build of e-mail messages Wayne and I would exchange during the days in between. Nothing torrid. Nothing flagrant. I would relate stories of Ree, how she'd just mastered using a butter knife and now would only eat food she could cut in half, whether that was chicken fingers or green grapes. He would tell me of his latest assignment, maybe the cell phone he was analyzing from a bank robber, or an ongoing initiative to help the public secure their open wireless networks. I'd describe a funny episode that happened during the sixth grade's attempt to locate Bulgaria on a map. He'd tell me about dinner at his sister's house, where Ethan hijacked his father's BlackBerry and spent most of the meal hacking into a major bank's website.

By Wednesday, I'd find myself humming under my breath in anticipation. Only one more night. Twenty-four hours. Ree and I would put on fancy dresses, blast Loreena McKennitt, and prance around the house as two fairies attending a party at the Home Tree. Then we'd eat dinner served on bright flowered plates, with our milk poured into small crystal juice glasses, which we would toast with our pinkies in the air.

I felt younger, falling in love with Wayne Reynolds. I felt lighter, happier in my own skin. I wore more skirts and fewer pants. I painted my toenails bright pink. I bought all new underwear, including a leopard print WonderBra from Victoria's Secret.

I became a better mother. More patient with the endless routine of feeding, bathing, and tending a small child. More willing to laugh at Ree's precocious demands for exactly this fork positioned exactly this way on exactly this color plate.

Ironically enough, I even became a better wife. On the one hand, I managed to purchase a blank hard drive on which I was supposed to copy the contents of the family computer. On the other hand, I attempted the deed less and less, because once I had the "forensically sound" copy, I wouldn't have a reason to meet with Wayne again.

So I made excuses for my husband. One random photo over a few months' stretch of time did not a porn-addict make. Most likely, the image was downloaded to his computer by mistake. He'd stumbled upon the wrong website, copied the wrong file. My husband could not be a pedophile. Look at the way he smiled at his daughter or his endless patience for her attempts to braid his thick wavy hair or the way he spent the first snow day of the season pulling her around the neighborhood on her little purple sled. That photo was simply some odd, vaguely terrifying anomaly.

I fixed my husband's favorite meals. I praised his articles in the newspaper. And I shooed him out the door to work, because the sooner he left, the sooner I could go online and talk to Wayne.

Jason didn't question my new and improved mood. I knew he still remembered my middle-of-the-night request for a second child, and was grateful I'd let him off the hook.

I didn't try to touch my husband anymore, and he was happy.

Ree and I developed a new routine for Thursdays. I would pick her up at home and we would go to the little bistro around the corner for an early ladies' dinner. Afterward, it was back to the school for the basketball game, where Ree would take a seat next to Ethan, and, once the game got going, I would disappear with Wayne.

"We're just going for a little walk," I'd tell Ree, and she would nod placidly, already too engrossed in pestering Ethan to care.

We always started out talking about computers. Wayne would ask if I'd copied the hard drive yet. I'd report on my various failed attempts. Jason's schedule was highly unreliable, I'd explain. He would arrive home anytime after eleven P.M., and first I had to put Ree to bed and then grade papers, and by the time that was all done, I was already nervous Jason would return home at any second. I tried, I aborted. I had a hard time concentrating....

"It's all very nerve-wracking," I'd say.

Wayne would squeeze my hand in support and I'd feel the contact of his fingers as a tingle all the way up my arm.

We didn't hold hands. We didn't find dark corners. We didn't retreat to the back seat of his car and neck like teenagers. I was too aware that we were still in my place of work, where there were eyes and ears everywhere. And I was even more aware of my young daughter, never far away, who might need me at a moment's notice.

So we walked the halls. We talked—innocently really. And the more Wayne didn't touch me, the more his hands didn't graze across my breasts and his lips didn't brush along my collarbone, the more I wanted him. Crazily, insanely, until every time I looked at him I thought my body might spontaneously combust.

He wanted me, too. I could tell by the way his palm lingered on the small of my back as he helped me climb onto the bleachers. Or the way he paused at the end of an empty hallway, never saying a word, but his eyes burning into mine, before finally, reluctantly, we both turned around and headed back to more populated areas.

"Do you love him?" he asked me one night. No reason to define "him."

"He's my daughter's father," I said.

"That doesn't answer my question."

"I think it does."

I didn't tell him about my sex life, or the lack thereof. That felt too much like a violation of the family code. I could flirt with a stranger. I could tell him I suspected my husband was engaged in unlawful Internet activities. But I could not tell him my husband had never physically touched me. That would cross the line.

And I didn't want to hurt Jason. I just...I wanted Wayne. I wanted to feel the way I felt when I was around him. Young. Pretty. Desirable.

Powerful.

Wayne wanted me, and yet, he couldn't have me, and that made him want me more.

By the end of January, the e-mails were replaced by text messages. Only during school hours; Wayne was not stupid. He would send me a smiley face. Maybe a picture of a flower he'd taken with his cell phone at the grocery store. Then the questions began.

Maybe I could get a babysitter for Ree, or tell my husband I'd joined a book club. How long were my lunch breaks?

He never asked to have sex with me. Never commented on my body or made any overly suggestive comments. Instead, he began to actively campaign for a private rendezvous. It went without saying what we would be doing during this time.

I vetoed lunchtime. Too short, too unpredictable. What if Jason stopped by with Ree, or a student tried to find me? What if Ethan saw us leaving school grounds together? Ethan would definitely ask questions.

A babysitter was out of the question. All these years later, I didn't know anyone in the neighborhood. Furthermore, Ree was at the age where she would talk, and Jason would want to know immediately what I had to do that was more important than watching our child.

As for joining a book club... These things were easier said than done. Who would be hosting this book club? What contact information would I give Jason and what if he actually called during the appointed hours? He would do that, at least once, I predicted. He had a tendency to check up on me.

I could've arranged for a "spa" night. But again, I'd never told Wayne of my unusual marital arrangement, nor did I mention it now. Spa nights were for strangers. And this wouldn't be with a stranger. This would be different.

So we went round and round. E-mailing and texting, but mostly anticipating our chaste Thursday night walks around the South Boston Middle School, where this one man gazed at me with unrelenting hunger, wanting, needing, demanding...

And I let him.

The second week in February, Jason surprised me. School vacation week was coming up and he announced it was time for the family to go on vacation. I was standing at the stove at the time, browning hamburger. I was probably thinking about Wayne, because I had a smile on my face. Jason's announcement, however, jarred me back to reality.

"Yippee!" Ree squealed, sitting at the kitchen counter. "Family vacation!"

I shot Ree a dry look, because we'd never gone on family vacation, so how would she know it was such a good thing?

Jason wasn't looking at our daughter, however. He was regarding me, his expression contemplative, waiting. He was up to something.

"Where would we go?" I asked lightly, returning to the frying pan.

"Boston."

"We live in Boston."

"I know. I thought we'd start small. I got us a hotel room downtown. A swimming pool, atrium, all sorts of fun stuff. We can be tourists in our own town for a few days."

"You already booked it? Chose a hotel and everything?"

He nodded, still staring at me. "I thought we could use some time together," he said, his face inscrutable. "I thought it would be good for us."

I poured in the Hamburger Helper seasoning packet. A family vacation. What could I say?

I gave Wayne the news by e-mail. He didn't reply for two days. When he did, he wrote one line: Do you think it's safe?

That jarred me. Why wouldn't I be safe with Jason? Then I remembered the photo again, and the research I was supposed to be doing with the family computer, except I'd gotten so caught up in flirting with Ethan's uncle, I'd forgotten Wayne was supposed to be offering me expertise instead.

We have a four-year-old chaperone, I wrote back at last. What could go wrong?

But I could tell Wayne didn't approve, because the text messages dropped off. He was jealous, I realized, and was naive enough to be flattered.

Sunday night, I sent him a cell phone photo of Ree, dressed in a hot pink bathing suit with a purple snorkel, blue face mask, and two oversized blue flippers. Chaperone prepares for duty, *I wrote, and included a second photo of Ree's suitcase overflowing with the approximately five hundred things she believed she needed for a four-night hotel stay.*

Wayne didn't write back. So I cleared the inboxes of my cell phone, purged my AOL account, and prepared for four days of family vacation.

My husband will never hurt me, *I thought. I guess right up until that moment, I didn't realize how much both of us were living a lie.*

| CHAPTER THIRTY-TWO |

D.D. was on a roll. She could feel it. First the conversation with Wayne Reynolds, then the interview with Maxwell Black. The investigation was coming together, key pieces of the puzzle starting to fall into place.

The moment they were done talking to Sandy's father, D.D. had blasted Jason Jones's photo over to the National Center for Missing & Exploited Children, as well as the Georgia Bureau of Investigation. She was getting a solid profile in place now—known aliases, possible geographic connections, key financial information, and relevant dates. Jason had left a heavy paper trail from the past five years, after he disappeared from the radar screen. Now they were getting the sliver of insights necessary to crack his full identity wide open, including tracing his offshore funds.

At this point, D.D. was willing to bet that some other law enforcement agency in some other jurisdiction had the exact same file she did, except under a different alias. When she connected with that agency, Jason Jones/Johnson would finally be exposed, and she'd have her arrest. Preferably in time for the eleven o'clock news.

In the meantime, of course, they continued to work the basics. Currently, D.D. was reviewing several evidence reports, including preliminary findings of a trace amount of blood on the quilt they had removed from the Jones family washing machine. Unfortunately, "trace amounts of blood" hardly played well on a warrant. Trace amounts because the rest had been successfully washed away? Trace amounts because Sandra Jones had had a nosebleed sometime in the past few weeks? Blood type matched Sandra's, but not having the blood type of Jason and Clarissa on file meant that, theoretically, the blood could be theirs as well.

In other words, the evidence report alone didn't do much for their case, but perhaps later, when combined with other relevant data, it would become one more bar in the prison slowly but surely being constructed around Jason Jones.

D.D. touched base with the BRIC team in charge of analyzing the Jones family computer. Given the current level of urgency, the team was working round the clock. It had taken most of the night to create a forensically sound copy of the computer's hard drive. Now they were running report after report, focusing on e-mails and Internet activity. They expected to have their first update bright and early in the morning. Which made D.D. optimistic enough to assume that if she missed the eleven o'clock news, maybe she could make the morning cycle.

This was the type of momentum that made a homicide sergeant happy, and provided the whole team with enough incentive to work another long night after two previous midnight grinds. It didn't necessarily explain, however, D.D.'s sudden interest in the honorable Maxwell Black or her need to look up the death of Missy Black eight years prior. The local sheriff's office informed her that they'd never opened a case file on the matter, but gave her the contact information for the county ME, who would be available in the morning. The official ruling had been suicide, but the sheriff had hesitated just enough for D.D. to remain curious.

Maxwell Black bothered her. His drawl, his charm, his matter-of-fact assessment of his only child as a reckless young woman, capable of habitual lying and sexual promiscuity. It struck D.D. that Sandy spent the first two-thirds of her young life with an outgoing father who said too much, and the last third of her life with a highly compartmentalized husband who said too little. The father claimed the husband was a pedophile. The husband implied the father had been party to child abuse.

D.D. wondered if Sandy Jones had loved her husband. If she had viewed him as her white knight, her valiant savior, right up until Wednesday night when the last of her illusions had been violently, and sadly, stripped away.

Sandra Jones had now been missing three days.

D.D. didn't believe they'd find the young mother alive.

Mostly what she hoped for at this stage of the game was to save Ree.

Ethan Hastings was having a crisis of conscience. This had never happened to him before. Being smarter than any adult he'd ever met, the teenager was naturally disparaging of them. What they couldn't figure out, they didn't need to know.

But now, sitting on the floor with his mother's iPhone—yesterday's incident at school had resulted in a total loss of computer privileges for the next month, but technically speaking, no one had said he couldn't rifle his mother's purse—he was reviewing e-mail and trying to figure out if he should call the police.

Ethan was worried about Mrs. Sandra. He had been ever since November, when it became clear to him that her interest in online security extended way beyond what one might need to know to teach a sixth grade social studies class.

She'd never told him she suspected her husband, which meant, of course, that he was the most likely culprit. Likewise, she'd never used the words "Internet porn," but then again, what else would drive a pretty teacher to spend all of her free periods working with a kid like him?

Oh, she was kind about it. She knew that he worshipped her, because he wasn't so good about hiding these things. But he got the message, loud and clear, that she was not in love with him the way he was with her. She needed him, however. She respected his skills. She appreciated his help. That was good enough for him.

Mrs. Sandra talked to him, person to person. Not many adults did that. They either tried to talk over his head, or they were so terrified of his staggering genius they avoided engaging him in conversation altogether. Or maybe they were more like his parents. They both tried to talk to him, but sounded like they were grinding their teeth the entire time.

Not Mrs. Sandra. She spoke warmly, with this pretty lilt he could listen to again and again. And she smelled of oranges. He never told anyone, but he got her to mention the name of the lotion she used. Then he bought an entire case of it online, just so he could smell her when she wasn't around. He had the case of lotion stashed in his father's closet, behind all the suits his father never wore, because he'd long ago figured out that his mother searched his room on a daily basis.

She tried very hard, his mother. Having a kid as bright as him couldn't be easy. Then again, it wasn't his fault he was so smart. He'd been born this way.

In November, after deducing that Mrs. Sandra was worried about her husband's online activities, then determining that Mrs. Sandra's husband was surprisingly computer savvy, Ethan had decided he needed to take further action to protect his favorite teacher.

First, he'd thought of his uncle, the only adult Ethan considered intelligent. When it came to computers, Uncle Wayne was a pro. And, better yet, he worked for the state police, meaning that if Mrs. Sandra's husband was doing something illegal, Uncle Wayne could arrest him for it, and Sandra's husband would go away. This had been a very good idea, in Ethan's mind. One of his better plans.

Except Sandra's husband hadn't gone away. Neither, for that matter, had Uncle Wayne. Suddenly, his uncle had developed an enduring interest in JV basketball. Every Thursday night, Uncle Wayne would appear at the school, and off he and Mrs. Sandra would go, leaving Ethan all alone with pesky Ree.

Ethan had started to be annoyed by Thursday nights. It didn't take three months of weekly meetings to hack into someone's computer. Heck, he could've done it in five minutes or less.

Then it had occurred to him: Maybe he didn't need his uncle or state police involvement after all. Maybe all he needed to do was write some code. It was called a Trojan Horse. He could tuck it into an e-mail. He could send it to Mrs. Sandra. And the Trojan Horse would open up a gateway on her computer just for him.

He would have access.

He could see what Sandra's husband was really up to.

He could save the day.

Except that Ethan had never actually written the code before. So first he had to study it. Then he had to test it. Then he had to revise it.

Three weeks ago, he'd been ready to launch. He wrote an innocent little e-mail to Mrs. Sandra containing some links he thought she might find helpful for her social studies class. Then he'd embedded the code and sat back to wait.

It took her two days to open the e-mail, which annoyed him a little. Weren't teachers supposed to be more responsive than that?

But the Trojan Horse passed the gates, the computer virus embedding itself instantly into Mrs. Sandra's hard drive. Ethan tested it on day three, and yeah, he had access to the Jones family computer. Now he could sit back and catch Mr. Jones in the act—literally.

Ethan had been very excited. He was gonna be on *48 Hours Investigates.* A whole episode on the boy genius who nabbed a notorious child predator. Leslie Stahl would interview him, social websites would want to hire him. He'd become a one-man Internet security alpha team. A modern-day website Marine.

The first three nights, Ethan had definitely learned some things about Mr. Jones. He'd learned, in fact, quite a lot about Mr. Jones. More than he really wanted to know.

What Ethan hadn't counted on, however, was how much he'd also learn about Mrs. Sandra.

Now he was stuck. To rat out Mr. Jones, he'd have to also rat out Mrs. Sandra, and Uncle Wayne, too.

He knew too little, he knew too much.

And Ethan Hastings was a bright enough boy to know that was a very dangerous place to be.

He picked up his mother's iPhone, checked messages again. Told himself to call 911, set down the phone again. Maybe he could call that sergeant, the one with the blonde hair. She seemed nice enough. Then again, as his mother always told him, lies of omission were still lies, and he was pretty sure lying to the police would get him in even more trouble than school suspension and a four-week loss of computer privileges.

Ethan didn't want to go to jail.

But he was terribly worried about Mrs. Sandra.

He picked up the iPhone again, checked messages, sighed heavily. Finally, he did the only thing he could bring himself to do. He opened a fresh e-mail box and started, *Dear Uncle Wayne...*

Wayne Reynolds was not a patient man. Sandra Jones had been missing for multiple days, and as far as the forensics expert could tell, the lead detectives were taking a slow boat from China to find her. Hell, he'd practically had to hand them Jason Jones on a silver platter, and still, judging from the five o'clock news, no arrests had been made.

Instead, reporters had picked up the scent of a registered sex offender living just down the street from Sandra. Some pale, freaky-looking kid with a blistered scalp they'd caught walking down the street, then literally chased all the way to an old 1950s ranch. *"I didn't do it!"* the kid had cried over his shoulder. *"Talk to my PO. My girlfriend was underage, that's all, that's all, that's all."*

Pervert had bolted into the house, and the erstwhile reporters had documented half a dozen shots of a closed door and blinds-covered windows. Really scintillating stuff.

At least Sandra's father had entered the fray, deriding Jason Jones as a highly dangerous, manipulative man who'd isolated the beautiful young woman from her own family. The grandfather was demanding custody of Ree and had already won visitation rights to begin shortly. The old man wanted justice for his daughter and protection for his granddaughter.

The media were eating it up. And still no arrests had been made!

Wayne didn't get it. The husband was always the primary person of interest, and as suspects went, Jason Jones was perfect. Conspicuously lacking in credible background information. Suspected by his own wife of dubious online activities. Known to disappear for long periods of time after midnight, in a job that didn't really provide a concrete alibi. What the hell was Sergeant Warren waiting for, a pretty package with a bow on top?

Jason needed to be arrested. Because then Wayne Reynolds could finally sleep at night. God knows in the past few days he'd been frantically purging his personal computer as well as his Treo. Which was ironic, because he of all people knew he'd never get the electronic devices one hundred percent clear. He should buy a new hard drive for his computer, and "lose" his Treo, preferably while running over it with his lawn mower. Or maybe he could flatten it with his car? Toss it into the harbor?

It was funny, outsiders always assumed law enforcement officers had an advantage—they worked in the system, meaning they knew exactly what sort of misstep might trip a guy up. Except that was the problem. Wayne of all people knew how hard it was to cover one's electronic tracks, and, being fully aware of such things, he understood just how hard his own actions would be scrutinized under a microscope.

He'd spent three months going on walks with Sandra Jones, nothing less, nothing more, but if he wasn't careful, he'd find himself labeled as her lover and placed on administrative leave, a subject of internal investigation. Especially if the forensic computer expert "lost" his Treo, or "replaced" his home computer. That sort of thing simply wasn't going to play.

Which made him wonder why the BPD hadn't cracked open the Jones computer yet. They'd had it nearly twenty-four hours. Figure five to six hours to make a forensically sound copy, then getting EnCase up and running...

One to two more days, he figured, and sighed. He didn't think his nerves could take one to two more days.

Let alone what such a long period of time might mean for Sandy.

He tried not to think about it. The cases he'd worked on before, the crime-scene photos he often viewed in his line of work. Suffocation? Stabbing? Single gunshot wound to the head?

He had tried to warn Sandy: She never should have gone away on the February vacation.

Wayne sighed heavily. Consulted the clock again. Decided to stay a little later at the crime lab, do a bit more work. Except then his Treo buzzed. He looked down, to find a message from his sister's e-mail address.

He frowned, clicked open the message.

Five forty-five P.M. Wayne read his nephew's startling confession. And started to sweat in earnest.

Six P.M. Maxwell Black was sitting at a white linen–covered table in the corner of the dining room at the Ritz. His duck had just arrived, prepared with wild berry compote, and he was savoring a particularly fine Oregon Pinot Noir. Good food, fine wine, excellent service. He should be a happy camper.

Except he wasn't. After his conversation with the detectives, the judge had returned to his hotel and immediately called his law clerk to have him do some legal research on Max's behalf. Unfortunately, the case law unearthed by his clerk did not sound promising.

Most family courts—and Massachusetts was no exception—deferred to the birth parents as the primary caretakers in a child custody dispute. Naturally, grandparents did not start the process with any guaranteed rights, with the courts accepting the parents' decision in the matter.

Max had assumed, however, that Sandra's disappearance—and Jason's resulting position as a viable suspect in his wife's disappearance—might sway the court in his favor. Furthermore, Max was confident that Jason was not Clarissa's biological father. Hence, with Sandra gone, Max himself was now Clarissa's closest living relative. And surely that would count for something.

But no. Leave it to the state that had legalized gay marriage to accept *in loco parentis,* or the person that had served in the place of the parent, as the proper legal guardian. Which put Max back in the position of having to prove that Jason posed an immediate threat to

Clarissa in order to successfully challenge the current custodial arrangement. Take it from a judge, those standards were nearly impossible to prove.

Max needed Sandy's body to be found. He needed Jason to be arrested. Then the state would take Clarissa into custody, and he could argue that as her biological grandfather it would be in the child's best interest to live with him. That should work.

Except he had no idea how long it might take to find Sandra's body. Frankly, he'd driven by that harbor four times already, and as far as he could tell, Jason Jones could've dumped Sandy's body just about anywhere. It could take weeks, if not months, if not years.

It was enough to make him consider filing a case against Jason in civil court, where the burden of proof was lower. Except even in civil court, it was hard to proceed without a dead body. No corpse meant Sandra Jones might really have run off with the gardener, which meant she might really be alive and well in Mexico.

It all came back to dead bodies.

Max needed one.

Then it occurred to him. Yes, he needed a dead body. But did it necessarily have to be Sandra's?

Seven forty-five P.M. Aidan Brewster stood at the Laundromat, folding the last load of laundry. In front of him were four stacks of white T-shirts, two stacks of blue jeans, and half a dozen smaller piles of white briefs and blue-banded athletic socks. He'd started at six P.M., after his PO had graciously picked him up from his reporter-infested property and spirited him away. Colleen had offered to take him to a hotel for the night, to let things calm down. Instead, he'd asked her to drop him off at a suburban Laundromat, someplace far away from South Boston, where the reporters would have no reason to look for him and a man could bleach his tighty whities in peace.

He could tell Colleen had been uncomfortable with the request. Or maybe it had been the trash bag after trash bag of dirty laundry he'd loaded into the trunk of her car, while three cameramen had clicked away from across the street. At least when Colleen had pulled away, the photographers had abandoned their posts, as well. No use staking out a house when you knew the target wasn't there.

"What happened to your head?" Colleen had asked as she drove down the street.

"Kitchen fire. Left a paper plate too near a burner. Embers floated up and caught my hair on fire, but I was too busy dumping flour on the stove to notice."

She didn't look convinced. "You doing okay, Aidan?"

"I lost my job. I burned my head. I got my face on the evening news. No fucking way, but thanks for asking."

"Aidan..."

He stared at her, daring her to say it. She was sorry. What a shame. Things'll get better. Hold tight.

Pick a platitude, any platitude. The sayings were all bullshit. And he and Colleen both knew it.

She drove him the rest of the way in silence, biggest favor she ever did him.

Now he finished folding his towels, sheets, various coverlets, even three doilies. If it was a textile and it had been in his apartment, he'd washed it with Clorox color-safe bleach.

Let the police hash over that one. Let them hate him.

After this, he planned on returning to his apartment and packing up everything he owned. He was placing his entire collection of worldly possessions into four black trash bags, and he was bolting into the wind. That was it. Show over. He was done. Let his PO chase him. Let the police go apeshit looking for another registered sex offender.

He'd followed the rules, and look where it got him: The police were screwing him; his former coworkers had tried to jump him; and his neighbor, Jason Jones, just plain scared him. Then there were the reporters... Aidan wanted out. So long. See you. Bye-bye.

Which didn't explain why he remained here, sitting on the floor of a grungy Laundromat, snapping his green elastic band and clutching a blue ballpoint pen. He'd been staring at the blank piece of notebook paper for three minutes already. He finally wrote:

Dear Rachel:
I'm an ass. It's all my fault. You should hate me.

He paused. Chewed on the end of the pen again. Snapped the band.

> Thanks for sending me the letters. ~~Maybe you hate them. Maybe you couldn't stand to see them anymore. Guess I can't blame you.~~

He crossed out words. Tried again. Crossed out more.

> ~~I love you.~~
> I loved you. I was wrong. I'm sorry.
> I won't bother you again.

Unless, he thought. But he didn't write it. He forcefully kept himself from writing it. If she'd wanted to see him, she could've done it by now. So take the hint, Aidan, old boy. She didn't love you. She doesn't love you. You went to prison for nothing, you pathetic, stupid, miserable sack of shit....

He picked up the pen again.

> Please don't hurt yourself.

Then, almost as an afterthought:

> And don't let Jerry hurt you either. You deserve better. You really, really do.
> Sorry I fucked everything up. Have a nice life.
>
> Aidan

He set down the pen. Reread the letter. Debated tearing it to shreds and attempting another bonfire. Held it instead. He wouldn't send the letter. In group, the exercise was simply to write the note. Teach him empathy and remorse. Which he guess he felt, because his chest was tight, and it was hard to breathe, and he didn't want to be sitting in the middle of a seedy Laundromat anymore. He wanted to be back in his apartment, curled up with blankets over his head. Someplace he could get lost in the dark and not think about that winter and how good her skin had felt against his, or how much of both of their lives he had destroyed.

God help him, he still loved her. He did. She was the only good thing that had ever happened to him, and she had been his stepsister and he was the worst kind of monster in the world and maybe the guys at the shop should beat the snot out of him. Maybe that was the only solution for a jerkoff like him. He was a pervert. No better than Wendell the psychotic flasher. He should be destroyed.

Except, like any pervert, he didn't really want to die. He just wanted to get through the night and maybe the next day.

So he gathered up his laundry and hailed a cab.

"Home, James," he told the driver.

Then, sitting in the back seat of the taxi, he tore the letter into tiny, tiny bits, and flung them out the window, watching the night wind carry them away.

Nine-oh-five P.M., Jason finally had Ree down for the night. It hadn't been easy. The growing media camp had kept them housebound for most of the day, and Ree was punchy from lack of fresh air and exercise. Then, after dinner, the first of the klieg lights had powered on, their entire house now lit up bright enough to be viewed from outer space.

Ree had complained about the spotlights. She had whined about the noise. She had demanded that he make the reporters go away, and then, when that hadn't done the trick, she had stomped her foot and demanded that he take her to find her mother right *now*.

In response, he offered to color with her. Or maybe they could work on origami. Perhaps a stimulating game of checkers.

He didn't blame her for scowling at him and storming around the house. He wanted the reporters to go away, too. He'd like their old life to resume anytime now, thank you very much.

He'd read an entire fairy novel to his daughter, all one hundred pages from beginning to end. His throat hurt, he'd lost command of the English language, but his daughter was finally asleep.

Which left him alone in the family room, blinds and curtains tightly drawn, trying to figure out what to do next. Sandra remained missing. Maxwell had a court-ordered visit with Ree. And Jason was still the primary suspect in his pregnant wife's disappearance.

He had hoped, in his own way, that his wife had run off with a lover. He hadn't really believed it, but he had hoped, because given all the options, that one kept Sandy safe and sound. And maybe one day she'd change her mind and return to him. He'd take her back. For Ree's sake, for his own. He knew he was not a perfect husband, he knew he had made a terrible mistake during the family vacation. If she'd needed to punish him for that, he could take it.

But now, as day three closed and the hours dragged by, he was forced to contemplate other options. That his wife hadn't run off. That something terrible had happened, right here, in his own home, and by some miracle, Ree had survived it. Maybe Ethan Hastings had grown frustrated with his unrequited love. Maybe Maxwell had finally found them and abducted Sandy as a ploy to gain his grand-daughter. Or maybe Sandra had another lover, this mysterious computer expert, who'd grown tired of waiting for her to leave Jason.

She'd been pregnant. His baby? Someone else's? Had that been what triggered this whole thing? Maybe, with Ethan Hastings's help, she had figured out exactly who he was, and she had recoiled at the prospect of bearing a monster's child. He couldn't really blame her. He should be terrified at the thought of reproducing as well.

Except he wasn't. He had wanted...He had hoped...

If they had ever had that moment, the one where Sandy nervously confessed they were expecting a baby together, he would've been touched, awed, humbled. He would have been eternally grateful.

But they never got that moment. His wife was gone, and he was left with the ghost of what might have been.

As well as the specter of impending criminal arrest.

He would take his daughter and run. Only thing that could be done, because sooner or later, Sergeant Warren was going to appear on his front porch with an arrest warrant, and a family court officer. He'd go to prison. Worse, Ree would go to foster care.

He could not let that happen. Not for his sake and not for his daughter's.

He headed for the attic.

The access panel was in the closet of the master bedroom. He grabbed the handle in the ceiling, and pulled down the rickety folding stairs. Then he clicked on a flashlight and headed up into the pitch black gloom.

The attic space was only three feet tall, meant for storage, not comfort. He crawled along the plywood floor, shuffling around boxes of Christmas decorations until he reached the far corner. He counted two rafters over to the left, then shoved aside the exposed insulation and reached in for the flat metal box.

He pulled it out, thinking it felt lighter than he remembered. He set the flashlight down on the floor, raised the lid....

The metal box was empty. Cash, IDs, all gone. Cleared out.

Police? Sandy? Someone else? He couldn't understand it. He'd never told anyone about his emergency escape kit. It was his little secret, one that kept him from having to bolt awake screaming every night. He was not trapped. He had an escape plan. He always had an escape plan.

And then, while his mind was still frantically trying to process what had happened to him, how it could have possibly happened to him, he became aware of something else. A noise, not far below him.

The creak of a floorboard.

Coming from his daughter's room.

| CHAPTER THIRTY-THREE |

As family vacations go, Jason's choice of hotel shocked me. I had expected some moderately priced, kid-friendly establishment. Instead, we arrived at a five-star getaway resort, complete with a full-service spa and yawning indoor pool. A bellhop in a red coat with gold-braid trim led us up to the very top floor, which could only be accessed by inserting the room key into the elevator key pad. Then, he escorted us to a two-bedroom corner suite.

The first room contained a king-sized bed with sumptuous white bedding and enough richly brocaded pillows to furnish a harem. Our view overlooked Boston Harbor. The bathroom featured wall-to-wall rose-colored marble.

In the adjacent sitting area, we discovered a sleeper sofa, two low-slung camel-colored chairs, and the world's largest flat-screen TV. When Jason announced that this would be Ree's room, her eyes nearly bugged out of her head. So did mine.

"I love it!" Ree squealed, and immediately went to work disgorging her overstuffed suitcase into her deluxe chamber. In five seconds or less, the room was covered in bright pink princess blankets, half a dozen Barbies, and, of course, Lil' Bunny, given the perch of honor in the middle of the sofa. "Can we watch a movie?"

"Later. First, I thought we'd put on fancy clothes and I would escort my two favorite ladies to dinner."

Ree's scream of delight threatened to shatter the bank of windows. I continued to regard my husband with shell-shocked surprise. "But I didn't bring anything fancy...I wasn't expecting..."

"I took the liberty of throwing in a dress and your boots."

My eyes went wider, but Jason maintained his inscrutable features. He was up to something. I just knew it. And for a moment, Wayne's warning came back to me. Maybe Jason knew what I'd been doing. He'd guessed that I'd been tracking his online activities and he was...wining and dining me to death? Spa-ing me into submission at a sumptuous resort?

I retreated to our half of the suite, where I put on the shimmering blue dress Jason had packed for me, as well as knee-high black leather boots. I hadn't worn this dress for Wayne yet. I wondered if Jason had known that, and I felt uneasy all over again.

Then Ree came barreling into the room, spinning around in a cranberry-colored dress sprinkled with embroidered flowers and finished with a giant looping bow in the back. "Mommy, do my hair. Hair time, Mommy. I want to look fabulous!"

So I fashioned Ree's hair into a bun on top of her head, with curly wisps springing around her face. And I spritzed and styled my own golden curls, even finding some makeup packed away by my clever husband for our family getaway. I did eyes, cheeks, and lip gloss for me. Lip gloss only for Ree, who then pouted because she personally believed the more makeup you wore, the more "fabulous" you were bound to be.

Jason appeared in the doorway of the bathroom. He was wearing dark slacks I'd never seen before, with a deep plum-colored shirt and a dark flecked sports jacket. No tie. The top two buttons of his sharply pressed shirt were undone, showing off the strong column of his throat. And I felt a stirring then, low in my belly, that I had not felt in the past four months.

My husband is a handsome man. A very, very handsome man.

My gaze came up. Our eyes met, and I felt it then, genuine, spine-tingling, bone deep.

I was afraid of him.

Jason wanted to walk. While the evening held a bracing, February chill, it was not raining and the sidewalks were clear. Ree loved this idea, as she loved everything about family vacation thus far. She walked between us, her left hand tucked in Jason's, her right hand tucked in mine. She would count to ten, then it would be our job to hoist her into the air so she could squeal at passing pedestrians.

They would smile at us, a well-dressed family out and about in the big city.

We followed the red line tracing Paul Revere's ride toward the Old State House, then took a left and continued past Boston Commons, toward the theater district. I recognized the Four Seasons, where I passed my spa nights, and walking toward it, holding my daughter's hand, I couldn't bear to glance at the glass doors. It was too much like looking at a crime scene.

Fortunately, Jason veered away, and soon we arrived at a charming bistro, where the air smelled like fresh-pressed olive oil and ruby red Chianti. A tuxedoed maitre d' led us to a table, and another black-vested young man wanted to know if we wanted still or sparkling water. I was about to say tap, when Jason replied smoothly that we would like a bottle of Perrier, and of course, the wine list.

I blinked at my husband of five years, struck speechless yet again, while Ree squirmed around in her wooden seat, then discovered the bread basket. She stuck her hand beneath the linen covering, producing a long thin breadstick. She snapped it in half, obviously liking the noise it made, and proceeded to munch away.

"You should put your napkin in your lap," Jason told her, "like this."

He demonstrated with his napkin and Ree was impressed enough to follow suit. Then Jason helped scoot her chair closer to the table, and explained the various pieces of silverware.

The waiter appeared. He poured elegant pools of olive oil onto our bread plates, a routine Ree recognized from our usual North End haunts. She fell to work soaking each piece of bread from the bread basket, while Jason turned to the waiter and very calmly ordered a bottle of Dom Pérignon.

"But you don't drink," I protested, as the waiter nodded efficiently and once more disappeared.

"Would you like a glass of champagne, Sandra?"

328

"Maybe."

"Then I would like to share some with you."

"Why?"

He merely smiled and returned to studying his menu. Finally, I did the same, though my mind was racing. Maybe he was going to get me drunk. Then, when Ree wasn't looking, he'd push me into the harbor. No walking near the water on the way back to the hotel, I thought with a vague sense of rising hysteria. Must stick to the opposite side of the street.

Ree decided she would like angel hair pasta with butter and cheese. She did her parents proud by ordering in a nice clear voice and remembering to say both please and thank you. I, on the other hand, stuttered like an idiot, but managed to order scallops with wild mushroom risotto.

Jason had the veal.

The champagne arrived. The waiter made a discreet show of uncorking it with a delicate little burp. He poured two glasses in paper-thin flutes that showed off the sparkling bubbles. Ree declared it the prettiest drink she'd ever seen and wanted some.

Jason told her she could when she turned twenty-one.

She pouted at him, then returned to drowning bread in olive oil.

Jason lifted the first flute. I took the second.

"To us," he said, "and our future happiness."

I nodded and took an obedient sip. The bubbles tickled my nose and I thought, quite absurdly, that I was going to cry.

How well do you know the person you have married? You exchange vows, gold rings, build a home, raise a family. You sleep side by side every night, gazing upon your spouse's naked body so often it becomes as mundane as your own. Maybe you have sex. Maybe you have felt your husband's fingers digging into your ass, urging you closer, guiding you faster, asking you in a low guttural tone, "How do you like that? Is it good for you?" Yet this is the same man who will slip out of bed six hours from now and prepare waffles with your daughter's favorite ruffled apron tied around his waist and perhaps even a butterfly barrette, graciously supplied by the four-year-old, clipped into his hair.

If you can marvel at his sweetness, your husband's ability to be both your carnal lover and your daughter's indulgent father, is it not so much of a stretch then to wonder what other roles he could play? What other parts of his personality are just waiting to be dialed into place?

All through dinner, Ree giggled and Jason smiled and I sipped champagne. I thought of my husband and his lack of family and friends. And I sipped more champagne. I remembered how easily he'd convinced me to adopt a new name when we'd moved to Boston—all to help protect me from my father, he'd claimed at the time. And I sipped more champagne. I recalled his late nights hunched over the computer. The websites he frequented that he had gone to great lengths to hide. And I thought of that photo. I finally, six months later, fixated on that lone black-and-white photo of a terrified young boy, the hairy black spider clearly visible as it crawled across the boy's naked chest.

And I sipped more champagne.

My husband was going to kill me.

It was so clear to me now I didn't know why I hadn't realized it sooner. Jason was a monster. Maybe not a pedophile, maybe something worse. A predator of such miswired proportions that he remained indifferent to his beautiful young wife, while lasciviously cultivating terrible images of frightened young children.

I should've listened to Wayne. I should've told him where we were going, except I had never thought to ask. No, I trusted my husband, let him lead me straight to slaughter without pressing for a single detail. Me, the very person who spent her entire childhood learning you can't trust anyone.

I sipped more champagne, moved the seared scallops around on my plate. I wondered what he would tell Ree when it was all over. There had been an accident, Mommy won't be coming home anymore. So sorry, baby, so sorry.

I poured Jason a second glass of champagne. He wasn't a big drinker. Maybe if I could get him drunk enough, he'd miss me and fall into the harbor himself. Wouldn't that be fitting justice?

Jason finished eating. Ree, too. The black-vested waiter appeared, ready to whisk our plates away. He gazed down at me with great consternation.

"Was it not to your satisfaction? May I present you with another choice?"

I waved him off with vague excuses of having eaten a big lunch. Jason was watching me, but he didn't comment on the lie. His dark hair had fallen across his forehead. He looked rakish, the open collar of his dress shirt, the rumpled waves of his thick hair, the deep impenetrable pools of his eyes. Other women were probably admiring him when they thought I wasn't looking. Perhaps everyone was admiring us. Look at that beautiful family with that gorgeous little girl who is so well behaved.

Didn't we make a pretty picture? A perfect little family, if only we survived the night.

Ree wanted ice cream for dessert. The waiter took her to the gelato case to pick out a flavor. I topped off Jason's glass with the last of the champagne. He had barely touched his second glass. I thought that was grossly unfair of him.

"I propose a toast," I declared, definitely tipsy now and feeling reckless.

He nodded, picked up his glass.

"To us," I said. "For better or for worse, for richer or for poorer, in sickness and in health."

I tossed back a quick hit. Watched my husband take a more conservative sip.

"So what else are we going to do on family vacation?" I wanted to know.

"I thought we'd visit the aquarium, maybe take the trolleys around town, check out Newbury Street. Or, if you'd prefer, we could do the museums, book a spa appointment or two."

"Why are you doing this?"

"What do you mean?"

"Why are you doing this?" I waved my hand around the restaurant, sloshing champagne. "The extravagant hotel, the fancy restaurant. Family vacation. We've never done anything like this before."

He didn't answer right away, but twirled his own champagne flute between his fingers.

"Maybe we should've been doing this before," he said at last. "Maybe you and I spend too much time surviving life, and not enough time enjoying it."

Ree returned, clutching the waiter's arm with one hand and the world's largest bowl of gelato with the other. Apparently, picking one flavor had been too hard, so she had settled on three. The waiter gave us a wink, distributed three spoons, and quietly disappeared.

Jason and Ree went at it. I just watched them, my stomach churning, feeling like a condemned woman stepping up to the chopping block and waiting for the ax to fall.

Jason called for a cab to take us back to the hotel. Ree had hit the point where the gelato sugar rush was colliding with the late hour to form one hypercranky child. I wasn't moving so steadily on my feet by then. The three glasses of champagne had gone straight to my head.

I thought Jason seemed less than razor-sharp as he opened the cab door and attempted to load Ree in, but I couldn't be sure. He was the most self-possessed man I'd ever met, and even two glasses of alcohol barely seemed to affect him.

We made it to the hotel, managed to find our room. I got Ree out of her fancy dress and into her Ariel nightie. A maid had magically transformed the sofa into a bed, topping it with thick blankets, four pillows, and two gold-foiled chocolates. Ree ate the chocolates when I went in search of her toothbrush, then tried to hide the wrappers by sticking them under the pillow. Her deception would've worked better if not for the smear of chocolate ringing her lips.

I herded her to the bathroom for face washing, tooth brushing, and hair combing. She squealed, whined, and complained for most of it. Then I corralled her back to her sleeping quarters, tucking her into the bed with Lil' Bunny snug in her arms. Ree had packed twelve books. I read two of them, and her eyes were already heavy-lidded before I finished the last sentence.

I dimmed the desk lamp, then crept out of the room, closing the door to a small crack behind me. She didn't complain, a sure sign of success.

In the master bedroom, I found Jason lounging on the bed. His shoes were off, his jacket tossed over a chair. He had been watching TV, but turned it off when I came in.

"How is she?" he asked.

"Tired."

"She did very well tonight."

"She did. Thank you."

"Did you have a nice night?" he asked.

"Yes. I did." I moved closer to the bed, feeling awkward, unsure of what to do, of what was expected of me. The champagne had made me tired. But then I looked at my husband, his long, lean body sprawled out on the expansive white comforter, and the emotion I felt wasn't exhaustion at all. I didn't know what to do with myself, so mostly I stood there, twisting my hands over and over again.

"Sit," he said presently. "I'll help you with your boots."

I sat on the edge of the bed. He got up, kneeling before me and taking the first boot between his hands. His fingers worked the zipper, sliding it down the inside of my calf slowly, careful not to snag the skin. He eased the right boot off, went to work on the left.

I found myself leaning back, feeling his fingers whisper down my calves, cup the heel of my naked foot as he stripped off my sheer stockings. Had he ever touched my legs? Maybe when I was nine months pregnant and couldn't see my own feet. I swore it hadn't felt like this back then, however. I would've remembered this.

My stockings were off, and yet his fingers remained on my skin. His thumb brushed down the inside arch of my foot. I almost jerked away, but his other hand held my foot in place. Then, both his thumbs were moving, doing positively delicious things and I found my back arching, my breath expelling in a little groan at the decadence of a foot massage after a long night in tight leather boots.

He moved from my right foot to my left foot, then his fingers were working their way up my calves, finding small knots, kneading. I felt his breath behind my knee cap, the whisper of his mouth brushing the inside of my thigh. The sensations kept me transfixed, unable to move, reluctant to break the spell.

If I opened my eyes, he would disappear and I would once again be alone. If I said his name, it would bring him back to consciousness and he would bolt downstairs to the goddamn computer. I mustn't move, I mustn't react.

Yet, my hips were beginning to writhe on their own and I was keenly aware of each touch of his rough-padded fingers, the tickling sensation of his wavy hair, the silky smoothness of his fresh-shaved cheeks. The champagne warmed my belly. His hands warmed my skin.

Then he got up and walked away.

I bit my cheeks to stop the moan. Tears pricked the corners of my eyes, and in that moment, I felt my loneliness more acutely than I had during all of those nights he'd left our bed. It isn't fair, I wanted to scream. How could you?

Except then I heard the click of the door shutting between our room and Ree's sleeping area. Another rasp as he tended the chain lock on the main door.

Then the bed sagged as he returned to me, stretching out beside me. I opened my eyes to discover my husband of five years looking down at me. His dark eyes were no longer so calm, no longer inscrutable. He appeared nervous, maybe even shy.

But he said, in that calm voice I knew so well, "May I kiss you, Sandra?"

I nodded yes.

My husband kissed me, slowly, carefully, sweetly.

I finally figured out that my husband had heard me the other night. He wasn't trying to kill me. He was granting me a second child instead.

There are things you always wished you had known sooner versus later. If you had spoken up earlier, before the lie grew too big. Or if you had braved the conversation in the beginning, before by its very omission it became too much to handle.

I had sex with my husband. Or rather, we had sex with each other. And it was slow, delicate, careful. Five years later, we still had to learn the feel of each other's bodies, the way one gasp meant I had done something well, and another gasp meant it was time to ease back.

I had the impression that of the two of us, I was the one with more experience. Yet it was important for him to take the lead. If I pushed too hard, moved too fast, it would be over. A switch would be thrown and we'd be right back where we had started, strangers who shared a bed.

So I let his fingers dance across my skin, while discovering the lean outline of his ribs beneath my fingers, the ripple of muscle on his sides, the taut feel of his butt. There were indentations across his back, markings of some kind. But if I tried to touch them, he drew back, so I contented myself with threading my fingers through the light whorls of hair on his chest, the broad, solid feel of his shoulders.

I reveled in the feel of his body, and hoped he found some kind of satisfaction in mine. Then he loomed between my legs and I parted them gratefully, arching my hips, taking him into me. At the first moment of penetration, maybe I cried out, maybe I had wanted him that much.

Then he was moving, and I was moving, and we didn't have to be careful anymore and we didn't have to be awkward anymore. Everything was as it should be and it all felt right.

I held him afterward. Pressed his head against my shoulder and stroked his hair. He didn't speak, and there was moisture on his cheeks which could've been sweat or maybe something else. I liked lying with him like this, our legs entwined, our breaths co-mingled.

I may have had sex with a lot of men, but I have slept with very few of them, and it felt like I should grant my husband that much.

I fell asleep thinking that family vacation was a positively brilliant idea.

And woke up to the sound of a guttural cry.

My husband was rocking beside me. In the dark, I could feel his movements more than I could see them. He seemed to be rolled into a tight ball, caught in the throes of a nightmare. I reached out a hand to his shoulder. He jerked back.

"Jason?" I whispered.

He moaned lower, rolling away from me.

"Jason?" I tried again, voice louder now, but not too loud, as I didn't want to wake Ree. "Jason, wake up."

He rocked and rocked and rocked.

I placed two hands on his back and shook him hard. He went shooting out of bed, scrambling across the room, crashing against a wingback chair, tripping over a standing light.

"Don't you fucking touch me!" he screamed, careening into a corner. "I fucking killed you! You're dead, you're dead, you're dead."

I was up out of the bed, hands out as if to brace myself. "Shhh, shhh, shhh. Jason, it's only a dream. Wake up, sweetheart, please. It's only a dream."

I reached for the bedside lamp, clicking it on, hoping the sudden infusion of light would snap him back to his senses.

He turned his face away, grabbing the curtain and holding it across his body as if to shield his nakedness.

"Go away," he whimpered. "Please, please, please just go away."

But I didn't. I took one step closer to him. Then another. Willing my husband to wake up, even as I willed my daughter to remain asleep.

Finally, very slowly, he turned his face toward mine.

I sucked in my breath as I gazed at his oversized dark eyes, still dilated by fear, wild with terror. Something clicked in the back of my mind and all the pieces of the puzzle finally fell into place.

"Oh Jason," I whispered.

And I realized at that moment that I had made a terrible, terrible mistake.

| CHAPTER THIRTY-FOUR |

The taxi pulled up in front of Aidan's house slightly after ten P.M. Aidan didn't step out right away. He took his time counting out a wad of wrinkled bills, while covertly studying the surrounding bushes for signs of trouble. Was that hulking shadow Mrs. H.'s rhododendron or another goon from Vito's garage? What about that dark spot over to the right? More photogs hidden in the trees? What about the entire darkened block, yawning behind him. Maybe somewhere, out there, Jason Jones was ready to finish him off.

Screw it. Just move.

Aidan tossed twelve bucks at the driver, grabbed his laundry, and scrambled from the cab, house keys clutched in hand. He made it up the walkway while the taxi was still idling in place. Aidan dropped the trash bags, jammed the key in the lock, and managed to twist the door open the first time, though his hands were trembling now, and he was so overloaded on adrenaline and fear he could barely function.

He could hear the taxicab revving up, pulling away. *Gotta move, gotta move, gotta move.*

He forced the door open, swinging the laundry bags inside, then using his leg to kick the door shut behind him, leaning against it for good measure while he struggled to work the lock, finally firing it home.

He sagged then, sliding down the door, overcome with relief. He was still alive. No goons had jumped him, no neighbors were picketing his front door, and no photogs were peeking into his windows. The lynch mob had yet to arrive.

He started to laugh, hoarsely, maybe a tad hysterically, because, honest to God, he hadn't felt this strung out since prison. Except he was a free man now—meaning, what was there to look forward to? When would he ever complete this time served?

He forced himself to stand, picking up his laundry, schlepping the bags down the hall. He needed to pack. He needed to sleep. He needed to get away from here. Become a new person. Preferably a better person. The kind of stand-up guy who could actually sleep at night.

He made it to the family room, dropping the trash bags on the floral love seat. He was just turning toward the bathroom, when he became aware of the wind on his face. He could feel a draft, floating into the tiny sitting area.

The sliding glass door was open.

Aidan realized for the first time that he was not alone.

D.D. was finishing up paperwork when her cell chimed at her waist. She recognized Wayne Reynolds's mobile number, placing the phone to her ear.

"Sergeant Warren."

"You have the wrong computer," Wayne said. He sounded slightly breathless, as if he were running.

"Excuse me?"

"Got an e-mail from Ethan. Kid's smarter than we thought. He sent Sandy an e-mail infected with a Trojan Horse—"

"What?"

"It's a kind of virus that allows you access to someone else's hard drive. You know, a friendly little e-mail that allows the sender to be accepted inside the gates..."

"Holy crap," D.D. said.

"That's my nephew. Apparently, he didn't think I was moving fast enough to protect Sandy from her husband, so he took steps to expose Jason's online activities himself."

D.D. heard the rat-a-tat of feet on a stairwell. "Where the hell are you, Wayne?"

"At the lab. Just got off the phone with Ethan, however, and am bolting out to the car. Told him I'd pick him up, we'd meet you there."

"Where?" she asked in bewilderment.

"Here's the thing: Ethan still has access to Sandy's computer, and according to him, in the past forty-eight hours, over a dozen users have utilized the computer to conduct various online searches."

"Is that part of the forensic evaluation? The computer techs tracing Jason's online tracks?"

"Absolutely not. You never work on the source. If your guys had Jason's computer, we should be seeing no activity at all."

"I don't get it."

"You don't have his hard drive. He switched it on you. Replaced either the guts of the computer, or maybe the whole damn thing. Don't know; have to see it to believe it. In the meantime, he hid the real computer in a flipping brilliant location."

"Where? Dammit, I'll have a warrant in the next twenty minutes!"

"*Boston Daily.* Ethan can read the e-mail addies of the users, all of whom are *Boston Daily* accounts. Best guess: Jason stuck his computer in the newsroom offices, probably at some random desk. I'll grant him this much—the son of a bitch is clever." From the background came the groan of a steel fire door being forced open, then the corresponding slam as Wayne exited the building.

D.D. heard the jangle of keys, the longer thump of Wayne's stride hitting the parking lot. She closed her eyes, trying to process this news, foresee the legal implications. "Crap," she said at last. "I can't think of a single judge who'd let me seize every single computer at a major media outlet."

"Don't have to."

"Don't have to?"

"Ethan's currently tracking the computer's activity on his mother's iPhone. Minute a user logs on, he can see the e-mail address. Meaning, all we have to do is be at the office, locate the user with that e-mail address, and wherever that person is sitting, there's your computer." There was another muffled sound, then a curt, "Hold on a sec, getting the door."

From the background came the creak of a car door opening, then slamming shut. D.D. was out of her chair, grabbing her jacket. She'd need to prep a quick warrant, find a succinct way of defining such avant-garde search perimeters, then decide which judge to call this time of night. . . .

"So," Wayne's voice returned. "I'll grab Ethan. You grab the warrant. We'll meet you there."

"I'll grab Ethan," she corrected him, exiting her office. "Miller will get the warrant. *You* can't be there."

"But—"

"You can't be alone with a witness, or at a scene with the suspect's computer. Conflict of interest, tampering with evidence, witness coercion. Need I go on?"

"Goddammit," Wayne exploded. "I did not hurt Sandra! I'm the one who called you, remember? Furthermore, this is my nephew we're talking about. The kid's scared out of his mind!"

"Tell me you never slept with Sandra Jones," D.D. replied evenly.

"Come on, I'm in my car already. At the very least let me be at Ethan's side. He's only thirteen, for Christ's sake. He's just a kid."

"Can't."

"Won't."

"Can't."

"Tough. My sister's house is still fair game."

"Don't you dare!" D.D. started. Except she never got to finish. She heard the roar of the car engine firing to life as Wayne turned the key. Then she heard a curious little click.

He heard it, too.

"Dammit, no!" the forensic tech screamed.

Then his car exploded in the middle of the crime lab parking lot.

D.D. dropped her phone to the ground. She remained rooted in place, clutching her ringing ear and screaming for Wayne to get out, get out, though of course it was much too late.

Detectives were running. Someone told her to take a seat. Then the first of their pagers started to sound. *Officer down, officer down.*

Ethan, she thought.

They had to get to Ethan. Before Jason Jones did.

Aidan Brewster did not beg.

Maybe once, he would have. He would've fought to live, he would've argued he still had value, he was a young guy with plenty of potential. Hell, if he could just get beneath the hood of a car, his hands on the engine...

But he was tired. Tired of being afraid, tired of feeling hunted. But mostly tired of missing a girl he never should've fallen in love with in the first place.

So he stood in the middle of the family room. Right next to the floral love seat, his hand on Mrs. H.'s favorite crocheted doily.

As the gun appeared in front of him, took aim at his gut.

No more worries, Aidan figured.

He thought of Rachel. She was smiling in his mind. She was holding out her arms to him, and this time, when he took her hands, she didn't cry.

The gun fired.

Aidan fell to the floor.

Dying took longer than he thought. That made him mad, so at the last moment, he flipped onto his belly, tried to crawl to the phone.

Second shot took him in the back, between the shoulder blades.

Well, fuck me, Aidan thought. He didn't move again.

Jason turned off his flashlight. He clutched the heavy metal object as a weapon and eased himself carefully toward the rickety attic stairs. The lit hallway provided a pool of illumination spilling across the bedroom floor. He used it as his target, placing his left foot on the top rung of the ladder, then his right. The top step creaked, the attic ladder trembling unsteadily beneath his weight.

Screw it. He slid down in a rush, landing with a solid thud and rolling low into the darkened master bedroom. Then he was up on his feet, preparing to dash into his daughter's bedroom and fight for her life.

He discovered his wife standing in front of him instead.

| CHAPTER THIRTY-FIVE |

"I don't understand," he faltered.

"I know."

"Are you alive? Is this for real? Where have you been?"

She took the flashlight from him. Belatedly, Jason realized that he'd been brandishing it before him, threatening his wife, who, apparently, had just returned from the dead.

She wore all black. Black trousers, black shirt. It wasn't an outfit he recognized, cheap, ill-fitting. He saw now that there was also a dark baseball cap on the bed. The perfect outfit for stealth. Was she stealing in, or stealing away? Why couldn't he understand what was going on?

"I saw the news," she said quietly.

Jason stared at her.

"My father made the five o'clock broadcast, claiming he deserves custody of Ree. I realized then that I had to come back."

"He claims you're a liar," Jason murmured. "Your mother was a fine, upstanding woman, and your father's only sin was loving his wife more than his daughter."

"He said *what*?" Sandy asked sharply.

"You're troubled, have a history of drinking, promiscuity, perhaps multiple abortions."

She colored, didn't say a word.

"But your parents were solid. You were just jealous of your mother, then furious about her untimely death. So you ran away from your father, and then...you ran away from me. You left us." He was surprised, now that he was saying the words out loud, how much they hurt him. "You left me, and you left Ree."

"I didn't want to go," Sandy said immediately. "You have to believe me. Something bad happened. And maybe he didn't kill me Wednesday night, but it was only a matter of time. If I stayed, if he could find me. I...I didn't know what to do. It seemed better if I disappeared for a bit. If I was gone, he couldn't want me anymore. It would make things all right."

"Who? How? What the hell are you talking about?"

"Shhh." She took his hands, and the first touch jolted him. He didn't know if the feel of her fingers against his skin was the best or the worst thing that had ever happened to him. He had wanted her. Prayed for her to come home. Despaired over her return. And now, heaven help him, he wanted to wrap his fingers around the white column of her throat and hurt her as badly as her leaving had hurt him....

She must have seen some of it in his eyes, because her grip on his hands tightened, becoming painful. She urged him closer to the bed, and after a moment, he followed her. They sat on the edge of the mattress, a couple returning to their marriage bed, and still none of it made sense to him.

"Jason, I screwed up."

"Are you pregnant?" he asked.

"Yes."

"Is it mine?"

"Yes."

"From...from family vacation?"

"Yes."

The breath finally left him. His shoulders sagged. He felt bewildered, but less pained. He shrugged off her hands because he had to touch her. This is what he had dreamed of doing, what he had wanted to do, since he'd first heard the news.

He splayed his fingers across the slender expanse of her stomach, seeking some sign of growth. That a little miracle existed here. A real life. One they had made together and—at least on his part—with love.

"You're still flat," he murmured.

"Honey, it's only been four weeks."

His gaze finally came up. He stared at her, taking in her shadowed blue eyes, gaunt cheekbones. He could see the remains of a bruise above her right temple. A swollen cut on her upper lip. His hands moved on their own, across her stomach to her waist, her shoulders, her arms, her legs. He had to feel each piece of her, to assure himself she was all here, whole, intact, okay. That she was safe.

"I had to learn that you were pregnant from the police. From some sergeant who's one step away from hanging me."

"I'm sorry."

He turned the screws a little tighter. "If they'd arrested me, Ree would've become a ward of the state. They would've placed her in foster care."

"I never would've let that happen. Jason, please believe me. I knew when I disappeared it might be risky. But I also knew you'd take good care of Ree. You're the strongest person I know. I never would've done this otherwise."

"Let me be accused of killing my pregnant wife?"

She smiled wanly. "Something like that."

"Do you hate me?" he whispered.

"No."

"Is our little family that intolerable?"

"No."

"Do you love the other man more?"

She hesitated, and he felt that, too, another bruise to nurse in the days and nights to come.

"I thought I did," she said at last. "But then, I thought my husband was Jason Jones. So I guess we're both very good at wanting what we can't have."

He winced, then forced himself to nod. This is what it came down to in the end. He had started their marriage with a lie, so if she chose to end it with a lie, well, who was he to judge?

He removed his hands from her body. Sat upright, squared his shoulders, steeled himself for what had to come next. "You came back for Ree," he stated. "So your father can't have her."

But Sandra shook her head. She lifted her hand, brushing the moisture from his cheek.

"No, Jason. You still don't understand. I came back for both of you. I love you, Joshua Ferris."

D.D. made it out of Roxbury in record time. She had sirens blasting, lights twirling, the whole nine yards. She was simultaneously working her radio, demanding that officers be immediately deployed to the Hastings residence. She wanted Ethan Hastings safely in police custody and she wanted it *right now.*

In addition, she wanted BPD detectives dispatched to the state police crime lab crime scene, even if that pissed the state off. Wayne Reynolds might be their man, but he was BPD's witness and whatever he'd known about Sandra Jones had no doubt gotten him killed.

Furthermore, she wanted officers dispatched to the *Boston Daily* offices. Not a single computer was to be touched until they had further word from Ethan Hastings.

Finally, she had explicit instructions for the two officers watching the Jones residence. If Jason Jones so much as cracked open his front door, he was to be arrested. Pick him up for loitering, late parking tickets, she didn't care. But he was not to leave the confines of his house unless he was wearing a pair of BPD bracelets.

They had just lost a man, and she was furious.

So it definitely didn't help when Dispatch returned to tell her that two officers had arrived at the Hastings residence. Unfortunately, the thirteen-year-old boy was not in his room and his parents had no idea where he might have gone.

Three minutes past eleven, Ethan Hastings had vanished.

"How did you finally figure it out?" Jason was asking his wife.

"Your birthday. I was installing the iPod software on the computer and I found a photograph in the recycle bin."

"Which one?"

"You were naked, badly beaten. There was a tarantula crawling across your chest."

Jason nodded. His gaze was on the floor. "That's the hardest part," he said, softly. "On the one hand, it's been over twenty years. I got away. The past is the past. On the other hand, the man took so many photos...and movies. He sold them. That's how he earned money. Selling child porn to other pedophiles, who of course are still reselling the pictures, over and over again. There are so many images out there, hundreds of countries, ten of thousands of servers. I don't know how to get them back. I can never get them all back."

"You were abducted," she said quietly.

"Nineteen eighty-five. Not a good year to be me."

"When did you get away?"

"Three or four years later. I made friends with an elderly neighbor woman, Rita. She let me stay at her place."

"And the man just let you go?"

"Oh no. He came looking for me. Tied Rita up, handed me the gun, and ordered me to kill her. That was my punishment for disobeying him."

"But you didn't."

"No." He finally looked at her. "I shot him. Then, when he went down, I kept plugging him with bullets, just for good measure."

"I'm sorry."

He shrugged. "It's been a long time. I killed the man. The police returned me to my family. The case records were sealed, and I was told to get on with my life."

"Was your family mean to you? Did they resent what had happened, what you'd been forced to do?"

"No. But they were normal. And I...wasn't." He regarded her thoughtfully. Inside, the bedroom was dark and gloomy. Outside, the media mob blasted the front of their home with a thousand watts of klieg lights. To him, it seemed somehow fitting. They were like two kids, hunkered under the blankets, exchanging scary ghost stories long after the adults had gone to bed. They should have done this the first night, he realized now. Other couples went on honeymoons. They should have done exactly this.

He could feel Sandy's leg against his leg, her fingers intertwined with his fingers. His wife, sitting beside him. He wanted to keep her here.

He said, "You once told me, what's done can't be undone. What's known can't be unknown. You were right. We're marked, you and I. Even in the middle of a crowded room, we will always feel alone. Because we know things other people don't know, because once we did things, or had to do things, that other people have never had to do.

"The police sent me home, but not even for my parents could I magically become a real boy. It distressed them. So on the morning of my eighteenth birthday, when I came into the stock Rita had left for me, I took off. Being Joshua Ferris didn't feel right. So I took another name. Then another, and another. I became something of an expert on inventing new identities. It soothed me."

Sandra rubbed the back of his hand. "Joshua—"

"Jason, please. If I had wanted to be Joshua, I would've stayed in Georgia. I moved here, we both moved here, for a reason."

"But that's what I don't understand," she blurted out. "By your own words, you and I have so much in common. So why didn't you tell me these things before? Especially once you knew about my mother. Surely you could've shared then."

He hesitated. "Because I don't just retrieve pornographic photos off the web. I, uh... Well, let's just say I tried therapy, but it didn't work for me. Then, one night, I got onto my parents' computer and I started visiting the chat rooms. I... made the rounds, found the kind of guys who liked to prey on a kid like me. And I developed a system: I entice them to hand over their credit card numbers and other personal information in return for my old pornographic photos. Then I nail them to the wall. I liquidate their accounts, max out their credit cards, open home equity lines of credit in their names, transferring all of their assets to the National Center for Missing & Exploited Children. I wrap them up and drain them.

Like a spider. I have become, I suppose, just as good a predator as the one who once trapped me.

"It's all highly illegal," he finished. "And it's the only thing that keeps me sane."

"That's what you're doing at night? Why you spend all your time on the Internet?"

Jason shrugged. "I don't sleep well. Probably never will. Might as well do something useful with the time."

"What about your family?"

"My family wanted Joshua, and Joshua doesn't exist anymore. On the other hand, Jason Jones has a beautiful wife and a gorgeous little girl. He couldn't ask for a better family."

"I don't understand," she said. "Why did you marry me? If you just wanted a child, surely there are easier ways than saddling your-self with a wife—"

He placed two fingers over her lips, silencing her. "It's you, Sandy," he whispered softly. "It's always been about you. Since the first mo-ment I saw you, you were the woman I wanted. I'm a terrible hus-band. I can't...do...everything a husband should do. I can't say everything a husband should say. I'm sorry for that. If I could turn back time, so maybe I wasn't out on my bike that day, heading down the road, when this guy turned right in front of me and my bike went down and I fell to the ground and then there he was, looming above me..."

He shook his head. "I know I'm not perfect. But when I'm with you, when I'm with Ree, I want to try. Maybe I can never be Joshua Ferris again. But I've worked real hard at being Jason Jones."

She was crying now. He could feel her tears on his fingers. He lifted his other hand to her face, using his thumbs to brush the mois-ture from her cheeks. He was gentle, unbearably conscious of the cut on her lip, the bruise on her temple, the rest of the story he had yet to hear but would no doubt break his heart.

His wife had been beaten, and he hadn't been there for her. His wife had been hurt and he had not protected her.

"I love you," she whispered against his fingertips. "I fell in love with you the day Ree was born, and I've been waiting for you to love me ever since."

He studied her in bewilderment. "Then why did you leave me? Was it because of Aidan Brewster?"

Her turn to look confused. "Aidan Brewster? Who's that?"

D.D. was just hitting Southie when Dispatch returned. *Reports of gunfire, nearest units please respond.* Dispatch rattled off the address, and D.D. immediately connected the dots.

She was on her radio in an instant. "Does that address belong to a Mrs. Margaret Houlihan? Please confirm."

A moment's delay, then the muffled reply.

"Dammit!" D.D. hit the wheel. "That's Brewster's address. Who the hell is on the scene?"

"Officers Davis and Jezakawicz are at the residence. There has been no response to their repeated knocks on the door."

"Break it down. I'll be right there."

Then D.D. pulled a hard left and was racing for Aidan Brewster's apartment. An explosion. A missing teenager. Shots fired. What the hell was going on tonight?

"Ever since September," Sandra was saying, "I've been worried that you were some kind of predator, doing terrible things online. So I started learning more about computers, and in the course of doing that, I met Wayne Reynolds."

"You fell in love with the state computer guy," Jason stated. He withdrew his hands, fisted them on his lap. Maybe that wasn't fair of him, but he could only give as much as he could give.

"I became infatuated."

"You slept with him."

She immediately shook her head, then hesitated. "But sometimes, on the spa nights..."

"I know about the spa nights," Jason said curtly.

"Then why did you let me go?"

He inhaled, exhaled. "I didn't think it was fair to punish you for my failings."

"You can't have sex."

"We did have sex."

"Did you like it?" she asked curiously.

He managed a crooked grin. "I'd be willing to try it again."

That made her smile, eased some of the tension. But then her expression grew somber again, and he leaned closer, so he could study her eyes in the dark.

"After our family vacation," she said, "when I realized that the photo I saw wasn't something you'd done, but something that had been done to you, I tried to break it off with Wayne. Except he didn't take it so well. He thought you were coercing me, that I didn't know what I was doing. He threatened to turn you in to the police if I didn't keep seeing him."

"He wanted you for himself."

"I found out I was pregnant," Sandra whispered. "I took the test last Friday. And I realized then that I really did need to end things with Wayne. I'd been stupid, reckless. But...I wanted you, Jason. I swear, I just wanted to be with you and Ree and whatever little life we've made together. So I e-mailed Wayne again, told him that I'd made a mistake, and that I was sorry, but I'd decided to save my marriage.

"He called me immediately. Agitated, angry. He kept trying to tell me that I wasn't thinking straight. He seemed to think that you had some kind of hold over me, maybe you were beating me into submission, I don't know. But the more I tried to tell him everything was okay, the more he became convinced he had to save me.

"I broke off all contact. Stopped answering his calls, his text messages, his e-mails. I purged accounts. I did everything I could think of. I just wanted him to go away. And then, Wednesday night..."

She looked away. Jason caught her chin in his hand and brought her gaze back to him. "Just tell me, Sandy. Let's just get it all out, then we can determine where to go from here."

"Wayne appeared. Right here. In our bedroom. Apparently, he'd made an impression of my house key the last time I'd met with him. His face was red, angry. He was holding a baseball bat."

She broke off. Her gaze was out of focus, seeing something only she could see. Jason didn't interrupt. Just waited.

"I tried to stop him," she whispered. "Tried to calm him down, tell him everything would be okay. I'd resume talking to him, go to the basketball games, whatever. Just, he needed to leave. He needed to go home.

"He hit me. With his hand. He struck me, here. Here." Her fingers idly brushed the bruises on her face. "I fell on the bed and he came after me. I stopped fighting. There didn't seem to be any point, and I thought, maybe if I just submitted, he wouldn't be so angry. He'd finish and go away, before something worse happened. I was terrified about the baby, and Ree, of course. And you, too. What if you came home and found us, and he grabbed the bat....

"So many terrible things were going around in my head. Then... Ree appeared. She'd heard the noise and come to our bedroom. She was standing in the doorway, half-asleep. She said, 'Mommy.'

"The second he heard her voice, he stilled. I thought that was it. He'd kill her, kill me. It was over. So I pushed him off. Told him not to move. Then I pulled my nightgown down, walked over to our daughter, and escorted her back to her room. I told her that Mommy and Daddy had been wrestling. Everything was okay. I'd see her in the morning.

"She didn't want to let go of my hand at first. I got anxious. I thought if I didn't get out of the room fast enough, maybe he'd come in. Bring the Louisville Slugger. So I swore to her that I had to go away for a moment, but that I'd be back. Everything was okay. I wouldn't be gone long."

"She let you go."

Sandra nodded. "And when I returned to the room, Wayne was gone. I think Ree scared him. Maybe she shamed him back to his senses; I'm not sure. I went downstairs, redid the locks, not that they would do much good against a man with a key. Then I started to clean up. The bloody comforter, the broken lamp. Except..."

He rubbed the back of her hand. "Except..."

She looked at him, "Except I started to realize that nothing I did would be enough. Wayne works for the state police. He has a key to our house. Maybe he didn't kill me that night, but what about the next, or the next? It's not like a guy shows up with a baseball bat

352

when all he wants to do is talk. He might press charges against you for the computer image, putting my husband in jail. Or heaven help us, he might go after Ree. She thinks he's a friend. She'd get in a car with him. I started to realize…I started to realize that I'd made a huge mess of things."

"So you ran away."

She smiled thinly, catching the edge in his voice even as he tried to flatten it out. "I thought the only way to be safe from a man like Wayne was to have public knowledge of our relationship. If it was known that he was involved with me, then he couldn't hurt me or my family, right? He'd be an automatic person of interest."

Jason couldn't follow her train of thought. "I guess."

"So, I decided to disappear. Because if I disappeared, then the police would investigate, right? They'd learn about Wayne, then when I reappeared, I'd be safe. He wouldn't dare do anything; it would cost him his career. So I retrieved your lockbox from that attic—"

"I never told you about the lockbox."

"Ree did. She saw you after Christmas, when you were putting away the ornaments. She spent most of January chattering away that you had a treasure chest in the attic and now constantly demands to go 'treasure hunting.' I thought she meant that you had a box of mementos or something, but then, in the past few months, given everything that's been going on, I've been reconsidering you. How easily you changed your name from Johnson to Jones. Our considerable cash reserves, which you never talk about, but I know are there from reading the bank statements. I decided to do a little digging around in the attic. It took me a couple of tries, but I finally discovered the metal box. The cash was very useful, the fake IDs…troubling."

"Escape plans are important to me," he said.

"There's only ID for you. Not for a family."

"I can change that."

She smiled, more warmly now, and he found himself taking her hand again, tucking her fingers inside his.

"I threw on your old clothes, all in black," she said. "I stuck the cash and IDs in my pocket—cash for me to use, IDs for me to hold so you didn't disappear while I was gone. I used one of our spare keys to

lock the door behind me, then I hid behind the bushes until you returned."

"You hid in the bushes?"

"I couldn't leave Ree alone," she said earnestly. "In case Wayne returned. I couldn't just leave her. It was hard—" Her voice broke.
"It was very hard to walk away. You have no idea. Leaving the two of
you...I kept telling myself it would only be for a few days. I'd lay low,
stay at some cheap hotel, paying cash. Then, when the police started
questioning Wayne, I'd reappear, say I'd gotten overwhelmed, some
sort of Mom excuse, and after a few embarrassing days, the dust
would settle and we'd continue on with our lives.

"I never expected my father would show up. Or they'd put Ethan
through the wringer. Or...I don't know. Everything grew bigger than
I expected. The media attention, the police scrutiny. It's all gotten
out of hand."

"You have no idea."

"I had to cut through four back yards just to sneak into my own
home tonight. It's crazy out there."

"So how are you going to do this?"

She shrugged. "Throw open the front door and declare, 'I'm
back....' Let the photographers click away."

"The reporters will eat you alive."

"I have to pay for my mistakes sooner or later."

He didn't like it. And pieces of the story nagged at him. Sandy's
lover hadn't taken no for an answer, so she'd thought to expose the
relationship by disappearing? Why not just go public with the affair?
Tell him, notify the state police. Her vanishing act seemed extreme
to him. Then again, she'd just been assaulted, had been terrified for
Ree. Her level of physical duress, mental exhaustion...

He wished again he had been home Wednesday night. He
wished he had kept his family safe.

"Fine," he said. "We'll do this together. Walk out together, hand in
hand. I'm already the menacing husband. You can be the ditzy wife.
Tomorrow they'll crucify us; by end of week, we'll have our own reality TV show and be sharing a couch with Oprah."

"Can we do it in the morning?" Sandy asked. "I want to wake

up with Ree. I want her to know I'm all right. Everything's good again."

"Can't argue with that."

They stood together. They had just taken the first step, when they heard a sudden dull roar from outside. Curious, Jason crossed to the bedroom window, cracking the blind and peering out.

One by one, all the news vans with their enormous klieg lights, camera crews, and news reporters were suddenly packing up and pulling away. He watched the first one do a U-turn, then another, then another.

"What the hell?" he murmured. Sandra had come up behind him.

"Something bigger must've happened."

"Bigger than your return from the dead?"

"They don't know about that yet."

"True," he said. But the sudden darkness outside discomfited him after two nights of blazing lights. Then, suddenly, he was aware of something else. A high-pitched scrape, like tree branches against a bare window, except their property didn't have any trees that close to the house. From the back yard, he realized, and it was already moving away from the window, toward the hall.

"Stay here," he ordered.

But he was too late. They both heard it at the same time: the tinkling of shattering glass, someone breaking through a back window.

| CHAPTER THIRTY-SIX |

"Shot twice," D.D. was reporting to Miller, who'd just arrived at the Brewster scene after being called out of bed. D.D. had been at the house for nearly twenty minutes already, so she was bringing him up to speed. "First time in the stomach, second time in the back, between the shoulder blades, apparently as he tried to crawl away."

"Messy," Miller observed.

"Certainly not professional. This was personal business, through and through."

Miller straightened, wiping at the Vicks he'd smeared on his mustache. Gut shots weren't just messy, they were smelly. Feces and blood and bile, all churned up and soaked into the carpet.

"But Wayne Reynolds was taken out with a car bomb," Miller countered. "That's a professional-grade hit."

D.D. shrugged. "Guy can't be in two places at once. So he rigs a bomb for bachelor number one, and pays a visit to bachelor number two. Either way, in one night, his competition is eliminated."

"You think Jason Jones did it."

"Who else had links to both men?"

"So Jones kills his wife first, in a fit of jealousy, then sets out to get revenge against the men he believes were her lovers."

"Hey, crazier things have happened."

Miller arched his brows, just to show his doubt. "Ethan Hastings?"

"Bolted. Maybe he heard what happened to his uncle and is scared it might be him next. Hell, maybe it could be him next."

Miller sighed. "Crap, I hate this case. Okay, so where's Jason Jones?"

"Sitting in his house, contained by two of Boston's finest and most of the major news outlets."

"Not the news outlets," Miller corrected. "This made the airwaves. By the time I pulled up, they were already lining the street. Might want to fix your hair before you exit, because we're tomorrow's news lead."

"Ah shit. Can't anything stay quiet anymore?" D.D. self-consciously touched her hair. It'd been nearly twenty hours since she'd last showered or tended to personal hygiene. Not the look any woman wanted to present to the world. She shook her head. "One last thing," she informed Miller. "Out here."

He obediently followed her to the glass sliders leading outside. The back yard was dark compared to the lights blazing around front. But Southie had small yards, mostly fenced in, which kept the media at bay.

D.D. led Miller over to the tree she had checked out during their first visit. The one with limbs perfect for climbing up to see into the Jones residence. It occurred to Miller now that those same tree branches made a nice ladder over the neighbor's fence. And sure enough, he saw exactly what D.D. had meant.

Up on the second branch, a smudge of black, which upon closer inspection with their flashlights turned out to be a dark brown leather glove.

"Think that glove fits Jason Jones?" D.D. asked.

"I think there's only one way to find out."

"Hide," Jason whispered urgently. "In the closet. Now. You're missing, remember? No one will think to look for you."

Sandy remained rooted in place, so he pushed her toward the open closet, getting her inside and partially closing the door.

The footsteps were on the stairs now. Slow, stealthy. Jason grabbed two pillows and shoved them under the sheets, a poor attempt at fashioning a sleeping body. Next, he pressed his back against the wall next to the door and waited. He was very aware of his four-year-old daughter, sleeping just twenty feet away. He was very aware of his pregnant wife, standing in a closet only ten feet away. It made him feel icy, preternaturally calm. Deep inside a zone, where if he had a gun, he'd be emptying a clip into the intruder by now.

The footsteps paused in the hallway, probably outside Ree's closed door. Jason found himself holding his breath, because if the intruder opened that door, woke up Ree, tried to grab her...

A soft shuffling sound as the intruder eased forward one step, then another.

Another pause. Jason could see a shadow in the doorway, hear the sound of low, even breathing.

"Might as well come out now, son," Maxwell Black drawled. "I heard you moving when I was coming up the stairs, so I know you're awake. Keep this simple, and your daughter won't get hurt."

Jason didn't move. He held the heavy metal flashlight by his hip, debating his options. Maxwell hadn't stepped far enough into the room for Jason to ambush him. The crafty old man stayed a foot back from the open doorway, enough in the hallway so he could see into the room while keeping his sides protected.

The hall floor creaked slightly, a man moving backward, one step, then two, then three.

"I'm at her door now, son. All I gotta do is turn the knob, flick on her light. She'll wake up. Ask for Daddy. What do you want me to tell her? How much do you want your little girl to know about you?"

Jason finally eased away from the wall. He moved out just slightly, enough that Maxwell could see his profile, without exposing all of his body to the hallway. He kept the flashlight behind his back.

"Little late for a social call," Jason said evenly.

The old man chuckled. He stood in the middle of the lit hallway, outside of Ree's room. He hadn't been bluffing; the man had one gloved hand on Ree's doorknob. In the other black-gloved hand, he held a gun.

"You've had a busy night," Maxwell said, gun coming up, aiming somewhere around Jason's left shoulder. "Shame you had to kill young Brewster like that. Then again, most people think death is too good for those perverts."

"I don't know what you're talking about."

"That's not what the police are thinking. Bet they're tossing his place right now. Finding some old love letters Sandy wrote years and years ago stuffed under his mattress. Then there's the discarded glove here, broken branch there. I give them twenty, thirty minutes, and they'll be here to arrest you. Means we'd better keep this quick."

"Keep what quick?"

"Your suicide, boy. Christ almighty, you killed your wife, shot her lover. You're wracked with guilt, consumed with remorse. No way a man like you can be a fitting father. So, of course, you came home and shot yourself. The fine detectives will find your body, read your note. They can dot the *i*'s and cross the *t*'s. Then I'll take Ree away from all this sadness to a whole new life in Georgia. Don't worry: I'll do right by her."

Jason heard a sharp hiss of indrawn breath from the closet. He took a step closer to the doorway, trying to keep Max's focus on him.

"I see. Well, it sounds like quite a plan, Max. But I see one flaw in it already."

"What's that?"

"You can't shoot me from the hallway. Surely, you've learned from enough criminal cases by now. First thing that gives away a fake suicide is the lack of gunshot residue. No GSR on the contact wound means the gunshot was not self-inflicted. I'm afraid if you want this to be suicide, you're gonna have to be up close and personal."

Maxwell contemplated him from the hallway. "The thought had occurred to me," the old man said. "All right, step into the light."

"Or what, you'll shoot me? I don't think so."

"No. I'll shoot Ree."

Jason shivered. But he forced himself to call the bluff. "No dice. According to you, this whole game is precisely so you can have Ree. Killing her would be like cutting off your nose to spite your face."

"Then I'll wake her up."

"No you won't. Come on, Maxwell. You want me. Well, here you go. I'm armed only with my wits and charming disposition. Come and get me."

Jason dissipated into a dark corner of the room. He was grateful now for the tightly drawn blinds, the lack of revealing shadows. The room was not large, and he could not outrun a speeding bullet, but this was his bedroom, one he'd wandered at all hours of the night. Plus, he had a secret: He had Sandra, tucked safely inside the closet.

There was a moment's pause, then Jason knew Maxwell was coming because the hall light winked out. Another half a dozen beats of time, the old man letting his vision adjust to the gloom, then came the first cautious footsteps into the bedroom.

Banging, directly below. *"Police. Open up. Police!"*

Max cursed under his breath. He turned toward the sound and Jason pounced. He crossed the room in three strides, catching the older man around the waist and sending them both crashing to the floor. Jason hoped for the skittering sound of Maxwell's gun sliding across the hardwood floor. No dice.

Jason had half his weight on the man's legs, trying to pin Maxwell to the floor while he grappled for possession of the handgun. Maxwell surprised him with his wiry strength. The old man twisted around, nearly breaking free.

The gun, the gun. Dammit, where was the gun?

"Police. Open up! Jason Jones, we have a warrant for your arrest."

He was grunting. Trying not to make too much noise but aware now that youth was no match for a bullet and if he didn't get his hands on that damn weapon... He felt the barrel dig into his thigh. Jerked his hips left, trying to roll his lower body clear while his hands followed the line of Maxwell's arms. The gun, now between them, both of them heaving on the floor. Maxwell, getting his arms half up...

The closet door, flying open, Sandra standing there. "Stop, Daddy, stop! What are you doing? For heaven's sake, let him go."

Maxwell spotting his daughter. His stunned expression as the gun exploded.

Jason felt the first searing pain in his side, lightly at first. A scratch, he thought vaguely. Just a scratch. Then his rib cage exploding with agony. *Holy Mother of God . . .*

And somewhere in his mind, he was seeing the Burgerman again, the man's shocked expression as Jason's first bullet caught him in the shoulder. The man's legs starting to crumple, his body sliding to the floor. As Jason lined up the heavy Colt .45 for the next shot, and the next . . .

So this is what dying feels like.

"Daddy, oh my God, what have you done?"

"Sandy? Sandy, you're all right? Oh baby. Baby, it's so good to see you."

"You get away from him, Daddy. You hear me? You get away from him."

Jason was rolling away. Had to. Hurt, hurt, hurt. Trying so hard to escape from the agony. His side was on fire. He could feel his insides burn, which was funny, given the wet, wet blood.

Crashing, downstairs. The police trying to break into his home through a steel reinforced door.

Oops, he wanted to tell them. *Too late.*

He stumbled onto his knees, raised his head.

Maxwell was still on his ass. He was looking up at his daughter, who now had the handgun and was staring down at her father. Sandra's arms were trembling violently. She had both hands wrapped around the pistol grip.

"Baby, it was self-defense. We'll explain it to the police. He hurt you. I can see the bruises on your face. So you had to get away and I was trying to help you. We came back . . . for Ree. Yes, for Ree, except this time he had a gun and he went crazy on us and I shot him. I saved you."

"Tell me why you killed her."

"We'll go home, baby. You, me, and little Clarissa. Back to the big white house with the wraparound porch. You always loved that porch. Clarissa will, too. We can set up a porch swing. She'll be so happy there."

"You murdered her, Daddy. You killed my mother and I watched you do it. Getting her drunk. Dragging her passed-out body to the car. Attaching the hose to the exhaust pipe, curling it around to the cracked window. Then starting the engine, before bolting out and locking the car doors behind you. I watched her wake up, Daddy. I stood in the doorway of the garage, seeing the look on her face when she realized that you were still standing right there, but that you had no intention of helping her.

"I remember her screams. For so long, I fell asleep smelling dying roses, and woke up hearing her goddamn pitiful wails. But you never broke. Never lifted a hand. Not as she tore off her own fingernails on the door latch or bloodied her knuckles against the front windshield. She screamed your name, Daddy. She screamed for you, and you stood there and watched her die."

"Baby, listen to me. Put down the gun. Sandy, sugar plum, everything's gonna be all right."

But Sandy only tightened her grip on the weapon. "I want answers, Daddy. After all these years, I deserve the truth. Tell me. Look me in the eye and tell me: Did you kill Mama because she hurt me? Or did you kill her because I was finally old enough to serve as her replacement?"

Maxwell didn't reply. But through the haze of pain, Jason could read the expression on the man's face. So could Sandy. The steel doors and reinforced windows; all these years later, she was still trying to lock Daddy out. Except now she had something better than bolt locks. Now she had a gun.

Jason reached out his hand for his wife. *Don't,* he wanted to tell her. *What's done can't be undone. What's known can't be unknown.*

But she had already done and known too much. So Sandra leaned forward, pressed the barrel of the gun to her father's sternum, and pulled the trigger.

Downstairs, the front window finally crashed in.

While in the room next door, Ree started to scream.

"Jason—" Sandy started.

"Go to her. Get our daughter. Go to Ree."

Sandy dropped the gun. She raced out of the room as Jason picked up the pistol, rubbed the grip clean against his pant leg, then wrapped his own fingers around it.

Best he could do, he thought, and watched the ceiling fade to black.

| CHAPTER THIRTY-SEVEN |

"You're telling us you caught a taxi to the *Boston Daily* offices. All by yourself? Entered the offices with no ID and nobody tried to stop you?"

"Asked and answered," Ethan Hastings's lawyer interjected, before his thirteen-year-old client could speak up. "Move along, Sergeant."

D.D. sat in BPD's conference room. She had Miller on her right-hand side, and the deputy superintendent of homicide on her left. Across from them sat Ethan Hastings, his parents, and a top Boston shark, Sarah Joss. Two weeks after Wayne Reynolds's untimely murder in the parking lot of the state police crime lab, the Hastingses had finally allowed the BPD access to their son. Given their choice of lawyers, however, they weren't taking any chances.

"Come on, Ethan," D.D. persisted. "Your uncle told me by phone that you had located the Joneses' computer at the *Boston Daily* offices. Then, all of a sudden, after wandering the offices for three hours, you changed your mind?"

"Someone changed the security protocols," Ethan declared flatly. "I already told you that. I'd sent a virus. A newer virus-protection software eradicated it. At least that's my best guess."

"But the computer is still there. Has to be one of them."

The boy shrugged. "That's your problem, not mine. Maybe you should hire better people."

D.D. fisted her hands under the table. Better people, her ass. They had security cameras showing Ethan entering the *Boston Daily* offices shortly before eleven-thirty, apparently driven there by a taxi he'd called using his mother's iPhone. While D.D. and the rest of the BPD had been running to the state crime lab, the Aidan Brewster shooting, and then, ultimately, the discovery of both Sandra Jones and her wounded father and husband at the Jones residence, Ethan had been working in the *Boston Daily* offices. Several late-night reporters remembered seeing him there. But all had been too busy with deadlines to pay attention to a kid.

They assumed he belonged to someone else who was working late, and that had been that. They'd tended to their stories and Ethan Hastings had...

Definitely done something to the Jones computer, which by all accounts no longer existed.

"We know your uncle was pursuing a relationship with Mrs. Sandra," D.D. tried now. "There's nothing illegal about two adults having a relationship, Ethan. You don't need to protect him."

Ethan said nothing.

"On the other hand, your uncle implied that Jason Jones might have been using the computer to engage in various illegal activities. That, we're very concerned about. So we need to find the computer. And I'm pretty sure you can help us."

Ethan stared at her.

"Remember what you said, Ethan," D.D. tried again. "Jason's not a good husband. He made Mrs. Sandra unhappy. Let us do our jobs, and maybe we can help with that."

It was an underhanded ploy, but then, D.D. was feeling desperate these days. Two weeks after one of the bloodiest nights in BPD's history, she had three corpses and nobody to arrest. It went against her DNA.

Sandra Jones was claiming she'd disappeared to get away from an affair gone bad with Wayne Reynolds. Unfortunately, the publicity had drawn her estranged father back into the picture. He had killed her mother eight years ago, then sexually abused Sandra until she became pregnant at the age of sixteen. She'd terminated that pregnancy with an abortion. After that, she'd stopped staying home at night.

The police had found evidence in Maxwell Black's hotel room that tied him to Aidan Brewster's shooting, plus bomb-making materials consistent with what was used in Wayne's car. According to Sandra, her father had confessed to killing both men in an attempt to frame Jason. Maxwell had hoped this would finally motivate the police to arrest Jason, paving the way for him to seize sole custody of his granddaughter, who would no doubt have become his next target.

Instead, when he broke into the Jones residence to frame his son-in-law, he'd discovered his daughter alive and well. He'd attacked Jason before Sandra had managed to wrestle the gun from him and, according to Sandra, shoot her own father in self-defense.

Maxwell Black was dead. Jason Jones had recently been upgraded to serious condition at Boston Medical.

According to Sandra Jones, she deeply regretted the damage caused by her impulsive disappearing act. She had returned, however; her husband had never harmed a hair on her head; and they could all move on with their lives now.

The whole thing rubbed D.D. the wrong way. Sandra was sorry? Tell that to Aidan Brewster, who'd basically been executed as a convenient fall guy. Tell that to Wayne Reynolds, who may have shown bad personal judgment, but up until the moment of his death, remained professionally adamant that Jason Jones was engaged in improper online activities.

Then there was Ethan Hastings, who'd disappeared for nearly four hours on the night in question, but claimed he had no idea what had happened to the Jones family computer.

For the record, D.D. had managed to get a warrant to search every computer in the *Boston Daily* offices to identify whether it belonged to the newspaper or to a private individual. They had used serial numbers retained by the newspaper and they had been very thorough. The Jones family computer was not in the offices. It had vanished. Just like that.

Ethan Hastings had done something. No doubt in her mind.

Unfortunately, the teenage whiz kid was proving a tough nut to crack.

"Are we done?" his father was asking now. "Because we're here in good faith, and it seems to me that there's nothing more my son can tell you. If you can't find the computer you need for your investigation, that's your problem, not ours."

"Not if your son tampered with evidence—" D.D. started to growl.

Her superintendent held up a quieting hand. He looked at her, and she knew that expression. It was the investigative equivalent of "Time to piss or get off the pot." She had no evidence to piss. Dammit.

"We're done," she announced in clipped tones. "Thank you for your cooperation. We'll be in touch if we need anything more."

Subtext being, it'll be a cold day in hell....

The Hastings entourage exited, Ethan staring at her balefully as he walked out the door.

"He did something," she muttered to her boss.

"Most likely. But he's also still in love with his teacher. As long as he feels like he's protecting poor Mrs. Sandra..."

"Who got his uncle killed."

"Who was attacked by said uncle, at least according to what she says."

D.D. sighed. They had seized Wayne's computer, with the forensic techs recovering a fair number of e-mails between the state geek and the beautiful social studies teacher. No smoking gun, per se, but more e-mail volume than one would expect in a strictly platonic relationship. And true to Sandra's assertion, all e-mails from her ceased five days before her disappearance, while Wayne's computer showed dozens and dozens of IMs sent by him to her, trying to get her attention.

"I want to arrest someone," D.D. muttered. "Preferably Jason Jones."

"Why?"

"I don't know. But a guy that cool and collected has skeletons buried somewhere."

"You thought the same thing of Aidan Brewster," her supervisor reminded her mildly, "and in the end, he had nothing to do with anything."

D.D. expelled her breath. "I know. Just makes you wonder how the hell we're supposed to know who the real monsters are anymore."

My husband came home from the hospital today.

Ree prepared a huge banner for him. It took her three days to make it, covering the white butcher paper with pictures of rainbows and butterflies and three smiling stick figures. She'd even included an orange cat with six gigantic whiskers. Welcum Home Daddy! *the banner read.*

We hung it in the living room, above the green love seat, where Jason would get to recuperate for the next few weeks.

Ree positioned her sleeping bag next to the sofa. I set up my own nest of pillows and blankets. We camped out the first four days, a haggard little trio needing to wake up each morning and see one another's faces. Day five, Ree declared she'd had enough of camping and returned to her bedroom.

Just like that, we moved on with our lives. Ree returned to preschool. I finished out the school year. Jason picked up several freelance gigs for various magazines, while his ribs finished knitting together and his insides healed.

The press had to get in its digs. I was cast as Boston's very own Helen of Troy, a woman whose beauty led to great tragedy. I don't agree. Helen started a war. I ended one.

The police continued to sniff around. The loss of our computer bothered them and I could tell from the look on the sergeant's face that she didn't consider the matter closed.

I got to take a polygraph where I told the absolute truth: I had no idea what had happened to our hard drive. The Boston Daily *offices? Ethan's possible involvement? It was a mystery to me. I hadn't moved the computer and I certainly hadn't coached Ethan in the matter.*

I could tell that Jason expected to be arrested the moment he re-

turned home. The doorbell would ring and he would tense on the love seat, steeling himself for what he thought would happen next. It took him weeks before he finally seemed to relax. Then I would catch him regarding me thoughtfully instead.

He didn't ask the obvious questions. I didn't volunteer the answers. Even with our newfound closeness, we are a couple who can appreciate the value of silence.

My husband is a very smart man. I'm sure he has connected the dots by now. For example, I had fled on Wednesday night from Wayne Reynolds, who was rather conveniently blown to smithereens the same night I returned to my family. Or that my father confessed to killing Aidan Brewster, but never mentioned Wayne. Interesting, if you consider that all the bomb-making materials were discovered in my father's hotel room.

Of course, anyone can figure out how to make a car bomb in this day and age. All you have to do is search the Internet.

No doubt, this led my husband to connect a few more dots. For example, what would lead Ethan to suddenly track down our computer? Furthermore, why would he risk tampering with said computer in a public area? He certainly wouldn't care that the hard drive contained enough damning evidence to send Jason to prison for life.

On the other hand, the true significance of several online visits probably became clear in the moments after Ethan learned that his uncle's car had exploded. His Trojan Horse had shadowed my activities as much as Jason's, and let's just say that the full scope of my Wednesday night Internet activities are best not to mention.

I have never spoken to Ethan on the subject. Nor will I. His parents have banned all contact between us, transferring Ethan to a private school. Out of respect for Ethan, I have honored their wishes. He gave me my family back, and for that, I will owe him always.

I know Jason worries about me. I wonder if he gets the irony—that my father murdered bachelor number one to frame my husband, even as I murdered bachelor number two to frame my father. Like father, like daughter? Great minds think alike?

Maybe I have simply learned a valuable lesson from my husband: You can be the hunted or you can be the hunter. Wayne Reynolds threatened my family. After that, his fate was sealed.

I will tell you the truth:

I don't dream anymore of blood or decaying roses or my mother's high-pitched giggle. I don't wake up with the sound of my father's last words in my ears, or the image of my almost lover disintegrating in a giant fireball. I don't dream of my parents, or Wayne, or faceless men pounding into my body.

It is summer. My daughter is running through sprinklers in her favorite pink swimsuit. My husband is smiling as he watches her. And I laze in the back hammock, my hand on the gentle curve of my rounded stomach, feeling our newest family member grow.

Once, I was my mother's daughter. Now, I am my daughter's mother.

So I sleep well at night, tucked inside my husband's solid embrace, sound in the knowledge that my daughter is safe in the room next door, with Mr. Smith curled up at her feet. I dream of Ree's first day of kindergarten. I dream of my newborn baby's first smile. I dream of dancing with my husband at our fiftieth wedding anniversary.

I am a wife and a mother.

I dream of my family.

| ACKNOWLEDGMENTS AND DEDICATION |

As always, I'm indebted to the countless experts who patiently answered my pestering questions, as well as numerous family and friends who patiently tolerated my writer-like (cranky) ways. These are kind and brilliant people. I just type very fast for a living. Oh yeah, and they are very smart. I, on the other hand, have been known to make mistakes with the information they have tried so hard to drill into me.

First up, Rob Joss, Forensic Evaluator, who educated me on the ways and means of assessing risk factors for sexual predators. He also added the interesting insight that he'd rather evaluate sex offenders for criminal courts than evaluate parents for family court. After all, sex offenders are bad people on their best behavior, while divorcing parents are good people on their worst behavior.

Also, Katie Watkins, Executive Director, and Liz Kelley, Forensic Interviewer, of the Child Advocacy Center of Carroll County. These two women spend 24/7 working the kind of child sexual assault cases that would break mere mortals. The rest of us would like the world to be a better place. They are actively making it so.

To Carolyn Lucet, a licensed independent clinical social worker who specializes in the treatment of sex offenders. Thank you for opening my eyes to both sides of the story. As a parent, I started this novel echoing Sergeant D.D. Warren's sentiments regarding sex offenders (not enough room in hell for all of them). I'll confess, Carolyn helped me appreciate the value of rehabilitation, and that complex problems probably deserve a more complex answer than, Hang them all and let God sort it out.

To Theresa Meyers, Probation Officer, for offering insight into the role of one of the least understood law enforcement officers. A PO for more than eighteen years, who now has second-generation parolees, Theresa astutely observed that if we spent more on kids in the beginning, perhaps we wouldn't have to spend so much on law enforcement later on. I couldn't agree more.

To Wayne Rock, of the Boston Police Department, who previously assisted me with *Alone*, and kindly consented to another round of questions so I could be current for this latest D.D. Warren adventure. I appreciated the overview of proper search-and-seizure, rules for questioning suspects, and, of course, the nice tidbit on strategic use of trash night in the neighborhood. Thanks, Wayne!

To Keith Morgan, Computer Forensic Technician, whose insights into a hard drive's lazy nature and guilty conscience were fascinating, if a bit troubling, to a non-techie such as myself. Keith wins the patience award, as it took me a few tries to get all of the material right. At least I hope I got it all right. Hey, all mistakes are mine, remember? That's the joy of being a writer.

Rounding out the pros are: Jack McCabe, Principal; Jennifer Sawyer Norvell, Esquire, of Moss Shapiro; Liz Boardman, Laura Kelly, Tara Apperson, Mark Schieldrop, and Betty Cotter with the *South County Independent*; and finally, the Divas, who approved all Barbies, games, books, and movies enjoyed by four-year-old Ree in this novel. Never have I received so much advice from such adorable consultants, who were compensated entirely in Cheddar Bunnies.

In the fun but dangerous category: Congratulations to Alicia Accardi, winner of the fifth annual Kill a Friend, Maim a Buddy. Alicia Accardi nominated Brenda J. Jones, "Brennie," as the Lucky Stiff. According to Alicia, "Brenda's had to fight for what she's got, has overcome a lot, and still struggles every day, but has a heart as big as the whole outdoors, and would give you the shirt off her back.... She deserves to be immortalized."

Also, Kelly Firth was our first-time winner of the Kill a Friend, Maim a Mate Sweepstakes, the international competition for literary immortality. Kelly nominated Joyce Daley, her mother, who just turned sixty-eight and loves reading crime thrillers. "She's my mum and I wanted to show her how much I love her.... I have told her, I couldn't contain myself, and she was absolutely thrilled."

For those of you still hoping to get in on the action, never fear. Both contests run every year at www.LisaGardner.com. Check it out, and maybe you can nominate someone you love to die in my next novel.

In closing, my deepest appreciation to my husband, whose skills with his new ice cream maker made revisions to this book much more fun and fattening than they otherwise would've been; to my adorable daughter, who, yes, helped inspire Ree, while always being a True Original; to Sarah, for your constant care; to Mimi, who we still miss and wish the best; to my brilliant editor, Kate Miciak, who definitely improved this novel, even if I was *very* writer-like (cranky) about it at the time; and finally to my fabulous agent, Meg Ruley, and the rest of the team of the Jane Rotrosen Agency, for having just the right way with writer-like (cranky) authors.

ABOUT THE AUTHOR

A self-described research junkie, LISA GARDNER has par-
layed her interest in police procedures, twisted plots, and
compelling characters into a streak of *New York Times*
bestselling suspense novels, including *Say Goodbye*, *Hide*,
Gone, *Alone*, *The Killing Hour*, *The Survivors Club*, *The Next
Accident*, *The Other Daughter*, *The Third Victim*, and *The
Perfect Husband*. Lisa lives with her family in New England,
where she is writing her next novel, *Live to Tell*.

www.LisaGardner.com